HONOR

KILLING

Also by Kenneth R. Timmerman

§Nonfiction §

SHADOW WARRIORS:
Traitors, Saboteurs, and the Party of Surrender

COUNTDOWN TO CRISIS:
The Coming Nuclear Showdown with Iran

THE FRENCH BETRAYAL OF AMERICA

PREACHERS OF HATE:
Islam and the War on America

SHAKEDOWN:
Exposing the Real Jesse Jackson

SELLING OUT AMERICA:
The American Spectator Investigations

THE DEATH LOBBY:
How the West Armed Iraq

§Fiction §

THE WREN HUNT

www.kentimmerman.com

HONOR

KILLING

A NOVEL

KENNETH R.

TIMMERMAN

ISBN 978-0-9797229-0-5

Order online at www.kentimmerman.com

Cover photo: Department of Energy, Ivy Mike nuclear test. Author photo: Rich Gibson/Newsmax.

Disclaimer:

The scenes recorded in *Honor Killing* are fictional and a work of the imagination. Any resemblance between the characters in this book and real persons would be, to quote a famous passage from the 9/11 Commission report, "a remarkable coincidence."

Published by Middle East Data Project, Inc., Bethesda, Maryland - 20814
1.0

For Roozbeh and Elham

"Americans should not expect one battle, but a lengthy campaign, unlike any other we have ever seen. It may include dramatic strikes, visible on TV, and covert operations, secret even in success."

- President George W. Bush, addressing a joint session of Congress, September 20, 2001

PROLOGUE

2130 hours, June 6 – Ramadi, Iraq

Her ears were still ringing from the explosion, which blew out the front wall of sandbags leading into their bunker in what used to be a neighborhood Baath party headquarters in the Sunni triangle. She could see people moving rapidly in the smoke, their lips twisted in screams, but no sound was coming out of their mouths. The smell of cordite and phosphorus burned her nostrils as she ran to the front of the blown-out bunker. And that's when she saw him, slumped against the sandbags, his helmet dangling by a strap, the blasted arm of his jacket covered in blood. His eyes were closed, caked with dirt and sand and blood. Inwardly, something in her burst. My love, she said to herself as she cradled his head. Speak to me, my love….

"I thought you were dead," she said when he opened his eyes.

"No, baby. Not dead yet."

"You were dead," she said. "You're alive!"

He tried to laugh, until the shattered bones beneath his flak jacket cut into him with incredible fingers of pain. "Oh no. Not dead yet. Not as long as you."

"Danny," she murmured. She saw his lips move, but she couldn't tell if any words came out.

"Aryana...."

She cradled the head of the man she loved, and thought of the prisoners inside the bunker who had come from her own country, Iran. They were safe, they were alive, but they should have been here on the outside when the suicide bomber following their orders came. They were the ones who should have died, not Danny. They had commanded the killing, and yet they lived. She vowed she would never rest until they and their sort were defeated. She would pursue them until the ends of the earth.

"Aryana," Danny murmured again, grasping a strand of her long dark hair as it fell across his chest. Then he closed his eyes and said nothing more.

"Don't die on me, my love," she whispered. "Don't die."

If Danny lived, she vowed to God on high that she would never rest until she saw his murderers roast in Hell, where they belonged. She would pursue them, and the mullahs who sent them to die in their name, until her dying breath.

Three years later...

1

CARGO

2300 hours, Thursday, May 10 – Bandar Lengeh, Iran

The night was sticky and hot with the gun-metal saltiness that made the Persian Gulf so unbearable in the summer months. Even in the darkness, the dust kicked up by the Nissan Patrols as they slammed to a halt in front of the chain-link fence was thick with flies. The security men jumped out and pushed past the startled guards, sipping their small glasses of hot, sweet tea. "Where's Rahimi," the one in the lead shouted, tapping the guard on the chest with the back of his hand. "He's expecting us." He spoke Farsi with a distinct Arabic accent.

Behind them, still in shadow, a flat-bed tractor-trailer with military markings rocked to a halt under its heavy load. On the other side of the perimeter fence, beneath bright sodium lights, was the small naval repair facility with its cranes and dry docks. Rahimi emerged from a low building and joined them in the guard house. "All is ready, *hajji*," he said quietly.

He gave the order to open the gates and the small procession roared into life, the security men shouting as they jumped back into their SUVs. Rahimi knew the short, clean-shaven man well. They had shared many meals together with their families. This *hajji* was famous not for the piety the pilgrimage to Mecca was supposed to induce, but for his cruelty.

At the pier, two Swedish-built Boghammars patrol boats were tied up on either side of a grimy cargo ship, their rocket launchers covered with grey tarps. The crew had swung open the long doors to the hold and waited on deck, silhouetted in the sodium lights against the inky backdrop of the Gulf. The water was still and glassy, a pool of oil.

Once the truck came to a halt in the swirling dust, Colonel Rahimi gave a hand signal to the crane operator and the gantry jerked noisily into position. He was careful to keep his distance from the *hajji* and the security men from Tehran. Everyone knew you could disappear if you crossed the thugs from the *etelaat* with their expensive shoes and scruffy civilian clothes. And these men were particularly dangerous, Rahimi knew. The first time they had come to inspect his base they had shown him the special ID cards that gave them immunity from prosecution "for any crime." They took over now, shouting orders to men in the truck to strip off the tarpaulin, waving to the crane operator to lower the hook. Rahimi could now make out a dark, squat metallic object, perhaps twelve meters long. It looked like a gigantic bomb, but it was just too big. He had never seen anything quite like it.

As the object swung up into the air on the crane, Rahimi's cell phone rang noisily. He flipped it open, holding it in front of him like a talkie-walkie, *Yes, sir, they have arrived*, he said. *All is in order.*

Phone in hand, he whistled to the crew of the Boghammars boats to tighten their mooring ropes, as the small patrol boats had begun to knock against the pier with the waves caused from the loading. Before snapping the phone shut, he saw the name of the cargo ship in freshly-painted black letters on the bow: *East Wind III.*

1300 hours, Friday, May 11 – Bandar Abbas, Iran.

Harbor-master Hossein Sadeghi had survived nearly thirty years of the revolutionary government by keeping his head down. He began life as a junior Customs clerk under the old regime, but shifted his allegiances as the Revolution gathered steam. At age 22, he joined the mob that stormed Bandar Abbas seaport in the name of Imam Khomeini and the provisional revolutionary government.

Because he was the only member of the mob who had the slightest clue how the freight business worked, the local *Komiteh* put him in charge of day to day operations at the sprawling commercial port, although the local mullah retained ultimate control. Sadeghi learned early never to question the wisdom of his political masters, no matter how unusual their decisions might be. If mullah Rastegari wanted him to transform the loading cranes into a gallows to hang officers from the old regime, he shut down the port and allowed the *Komiteh* to do their worst. Many years later, when they wanted to expand trade with Dubai, he waived Customs formalities for the coastal freighters favored by the oil and opium smugglers whose names were handed to him by Rastegari himself during an unannounced visit to his dusty office. Hossein Sadeghi was like a father to the large family of Customs officers and stevedores and foremen and shipping clerks who made Bandar Abbas thrive. He made sure they all benefited from the trafficking, consistent with their risk. It was an equitable system, and it kept everyone happy. And quiet.

Sadeghi parked his jeep along the quai side and, pulling his clipboard from between the seats, climbed down onto the oily loading docks to begin his rounds. The *East Wind III* had arrived that morning from Capetown and was scheduled to pick up pistachios, carpets, and scrap metal. But as he looked through the shipping manifest and compared it to the Customs seals on the doors of the containers, something didn't add up. He frowned. Two deck hands were arguing in Arabic around the loading crane on deck, but fell silent when they caught his steady gaze. Sadeghi didn't like Arabs. It was something in the blood. When he heard Arabic, he thought: *Saddam.* No Persian could forget the eight-year war with the Arab, Saddam Hussein. And when they remembered, it was never pleasant. "Mahmoud!" one of the deckhands yelled to someone behind him. "*Y'allah! Shouf!*" Come, look.

Sadeghi had climbed the ribbed gangplank by now, and surprised Mahmoud as he emerged from below-decks, wiping his hands on a rag. The captain collected himself rapidly, masking his astonishment. "How can I be of service?" he asked in heavily-accented English.

The Harbor master leafed through the cargo manifest on his clipboard, clicking off items with his pencil. "You are supposed to be taking on six containers of carpets, 12 containers of scrap metal, and 2 containers of pistachios. "

"The papers are in order," the captain said.

"Almost," he said. "I can see the pistachios." He pointed to two twenty-foot containers on deck. "But you are missing the Customs stamp for one container of scrap iron."

"I think you should check again," the captain said. "It has already been loaded.

"I will need to see it to collect the stamp."

The deck hands exchanged angry, suspicious glances with the captain. "It is below decks. I will get you the receipt."

He went to the wheelhouse and returned with a large ledger, which he handed to the harbormaster. "Please inspect it yourself."

The harbormaster flipped through the ledger to the last page, extracted five crisp $100 bills, pocketed them, then shut the ledger. "Everything seems to be in order," he said pleasantly. "You are returning to Capetown?"

The captain grunted. "Is there anything else that you require?"

"No. No, that's all. Have a safe journey."

Arabs, he thought. God must have invented them to torment us, like mosquitos and flies.

That evening, after he had finished his second inspection round and the stevedores had gone home, the harbor-master sat at his small desk to compose his report. He wrote laboriously, by hand, in block letters.

```
EAST  WIND  THREE  STOP  CAPTAIN
ALI   HASSAN   MAHMOUD   STOP
CAPETOWN  ETA  THIRTY  MAY  STOP
ELEVEN  CONTAINERS  SCRAP  STOP
ONE UNKNOWN STOP
```

Beneath, he transformed the words into numbers, using a variant of a simple numerical value code. Each word group was shifted using the numerical value of the first letter of the corresponding word in Section II, Rule 13 of the 4th edition of Strunk & White's Elements of Style, which reads thus:

```
Make   the   paragraph   the   unit   of
composition; one paragraph to each
topic
```

Applying the coded grid, the numerical value for the word "East" used an alphabet beginning with the number 13. It became:

```
17-13-5-6
```

The word "Wind" used an alphabet beginning with the number 20, taken from the word "the" in the control text. It became:

```
16-2-7-23
```

When Sadeghi was satisfied with the result, he went into the communications room and sat at the Morse key they used to communicate with some of the older ships. He dialed the proper frequency, tapped out the number groups twice, then took a match to the paper and burned it in the ashtray.

It was another little sideline he practiced. No one could live on a bureaucrat's salary anymore.

2200 hours, Sunday, May 13 – Bandar Abbas

Colonel Rahimi had traded his Revolutionary Guards uniform for slacks and an open shirt, as he often did when strolling downtown. He left the tea house near the commercial harbor and headed along the wide boulevard with its palm trees into the secret back alleys of the souk. Beyond the carpet sellers, who sat clicking prayer beads inside their cramped shops, he found an Internet café and went in. From time to time, Iran's political leaders decided to close them down, claiming they were drenching the country's young people with pornography and foreign notions such as blue jeans, rock-n-roll, and freedom. For now, however, they were in a period of remission, and Rahimi made a point of going onto the Net at least once a week to check the news and to email his grown daughter in Tehran. You never knew how long it would last.

Rahimi was a child of the revolution. Just thirteen when the shah was chased out of Iran, he had been swept into the student *Komiteh* by his social studies teacher, who was a secret supporter of Ayatollah Khomeini. Less than two years later, war erupted with Iraq. Like most young men of his generation, Rahimi enlisted in the people's militia, the *bassij,* and was sent to the front. By the age of sixteen he had been wounded twice. Shortly after he turned eighteen, he nearly died in an Iraqi poison gas attack. After many months in hospital, he was reassigned to a logistics depot well behind the front lines and promoted to 2nd Lieutenant. It was the first real rank he'd ever earned. The Revolutionary Guards Corps leaders had abolished the old system of ranks years earlier. It took six years of a badly executed war for them to realize their error.

He would never forget the final campaigns in the war. He'd been redeployed to the front near Marivan, in an Action Intelligence unit *(vahed etelaat va ameliat)* that operated behind enemy lines. They'd gone out one evening, crawling like rats behind the Iraqi trenches, until they stumbled across an enormous field kitchen, its canvas walls glowing from within like a gigantic lightning bug. He counted as fourteen canvas-sided trucks unloaded fresh food and dry ice. He was stunned.

In the dark of night, the Iraqis were reinforcing their defenses. Clearly the enemy had discovered the Iranian plans to attack in this area, where very little had happened for years. When Rahimi reported back early the next morning, his battalion commander urged the high command to postpone the long-planned offensive so he could shift his forces to the north, but they were thrown into battle none the less. Of more than 650 men, only ten came back. Most of them, like Rahimi, were severely wounded.

Later he learned that the mullahs running the war were planning to meet the Chinese prime minister the night of the Kerbala 5 offensive, and wanted the meeting to coincide with the "historic occasion" of a major victory against Saddam. They disregarded the intelligence and sent his men into a trap, and he never forgave them. Rahimi was not the only war veteran who bore a grudge – a highly-personal grudge – against every robed cleric wearing a turban. When the day of reckoning came – and it would – he would make it a personal badge of honor to slit the throats of four of them, at least: one for each of the four young men under his command in the recon squad who learned the truth and died for it during that final wasted offensive of the war.

Rahimi's daughter had two email accounts, one with a local Iranian server and another one with Yahoo! First he sent a message from his own local account to her Yahoo! account, and when that didn't get kicked back he logged onto her Yahoo! account using the special username and password he had set up. It was virtually impossible for the watchers to track back messages sent from U.S.-based servers, which is why they often blocked them.

The message was long, and read like gibberish, Here is what he sent:

Attn: Ali Kourosh Mohammad-Ahmadi

Have you been in need of date palm oil of the best quality? If so, meeting representatives of Fars Oil will be soonest opportunity to riches. We would like to propose that you consider trying a single sample, just one. I guarantee you will be back in just a week. From already today, enjoy wonderful Dubai every day in early morning. Promotion begins this evening. You feel like wearing a crown. Come stay in your very own palace. Enjoy several bottles of our oil, and room for friends and family. If you prefer, buy in quantity for steep discount. I guarantee you will like my mother's own name brand. You have all the best elements to choose from. Think of what you need for the proof. Can anything be better? Be sure your order is complete before you praise the country living pride. Faithful as the date nut falling is in this life, so date palm oil is in next. By land, sea, or to end of earth. My message to you is the same: take Fars Oil opportunity now.

Rahimi reviewed the text, counting carefully, then clicked on the "send" button. Looking casually around him to see if he was being watched, he reached into his pocket for the memory stick which contained the Trojan horse program Kourosh had sent him by courrier. It went into action with the next log-on, and was disguised to look like an e-mail bug. Once it did its work, the hard drive could never be used again.

Suddenly, the owner of the café jumped up and headed toward him. Rahimi palmed the memory stick and pecked angrily at the keyboard with thick, clumsy fingers, as if the computer had frozen. But the owner wasn't interested in him. He rushed right past Rahimi, as did several other Internet users, drawn by the commotion out in the street. *Etelaat!* One of them shouted from the door.

Outside, people were shouting, and Rahimi heard the rapid scuffling of military boots on the pavement, echoing through the narrow alleyway. If the intelligence people came in now they would immediately find his message and the memory stick, and there was no way they would fail to make the connection, even if they couldn't decipher the code. Steeling his nerves, Rahimi inserted the device into the computer's USB port, and waited for it to be recognized. Once it mounted, he knew he needed another two seconds to open it and click on the Trojan horse. Ten more seconds and the program would install itself as a hidden file in the root directory. Then he could simply reboot the computer and log-on, triggering it to trash the hard-drive directory.

Outside, the intelligence men were pounding on the metal shutters, so hard he could see the thin panels of the wall shake. They were shouting for someone to open. What if the man they were searching for escaped into the alley behind the Internet café and they stormed in here before he had finished?

Finally the log-in dialog appeared on the screen. If he retyped his temporary user code, the machine would fry and the Internet café owner would be furious. But something made him wait. Concealing the memory stick in his palm, he joined the others at the door to catch a glimpse of the commotion outside. When he saw what was happening, he froze.

They had come for the harbor master. Rahimi knew him well. Everybody in Bandar Abbas knew him. Now he stood like a crumpled flower in the doorway to his house, his white undershirt marked with sprays of blood as the intelligence man beat his cheeks and nose with the butt end of his revolver.

A chill came over him as he recognized the *hajji,* his eyes blazing in ecstasy, his nostrils flaring. He had come for the kill.

Rahimi hurried back to the computer, hoping he hadn't been seen. He logged-on and let the computer fry, then joined the crowd at the door, out of sight.

He knew he wouldn't be using this place again for awhile. But at least he was safe. For now.

0945 hours, Sunday, May 13 – Woodland Hills, CA

Manoucher Amir stared hard at his computer screen in the small office off the strip mall in Woodland Hills, in the Persian quarter just north of Los Angeles, trying to remember which code he used with the young woman from Tehran with the Yahoo! account. He remembered that her father was a Rev. Guards Colonel from Bandar Abbas, who worked for the Protection and Intelligence Department, the dreaded commissars whose job was to watch their fellow Pasdaran officers. Many times, he had suspected that the father was using his daughter's account, but he could never be quite sure. Hopefully, the regime had never figured out the truth either. With the twelve and a half hour time difference, the message had been sent just fifteen minutes ago.

They used to receive reports from her on a regular basis – something like once or twice a month. Then, clearly, her father had been transferred to a new position. Either he had less access to intelligence of interest to the opposition, or it had become harder for him to find a safe transmission point. Manoucher Amir couldn't remember the last time they had received one of his reports. That's why he was having trouble with the code.

They used a variety of simple codes when communicating with sources inside Iran. Most involved transforming ordinary Persian-language text that was sent in clear, since the regime immediately tagged encrypted transmissions as suspicious. That's what Rahimi – or his daughter – had done this time. The letter was in clear text, but pure gibberish.

There was no doubt that the message was urgent, however. That is why it was sent directly to the attention of Kourosh, the chief of the Iranian opposition secret intelligence organization. Some of the words leapt out at him. "To end of earth. My message" – clearly that meant "end of message." The first two words were right next to each other, whereas the word "message" was three steps after the word "of." If he was using a one-three transformation, the text would read:

```
Attn: Ali Ahmadi. Have in need palm
oil best quality...
```

Clearly, that wasn't it.

Perhaps it was a three-step transformation. To decipher the real message, he took the first word, then the second word from there, the third word after the second, then the first word after that, and so on repeating the sequence. That looked promising until he got to:

```
Have you in date palm of best so...
```

He continued extending the steps to four, five, six, and gradually a coherent message began to emerge.

After an hour, he realized that Rahimi had used a full ten-step transformation. Decoded, the message read as follows:

> Attn: Kourosh. Have need of meeting soonest. Propose one week from today, Dubai, early evening. Crown Palace. Room in my mother's name. Have elements of proof. Your country is next. By sea. End message.

Because of the danger, he knew that Kourosh would insist on going alone. They had lost operatives before when meeting sources in Dubai, Istanbul and other cities neighboring Iran, where Iranians now could travel freely. Once, in Dubai – not far from the Crown Palace, in fact – their courier was gunned down in his hotel room only minutes after he had arrived from the airport. The place was crawling with regime agents.

As a matter of tradecraft, Manoucher had his couriers avoid Dubai. Besides, the Ruler's own chief of intelligence was a fluent Farsi-speaker, who entertained the head of the mullahs' *etelaat* twice a month in his own Officers Club! While the Ruler did not like regime killers operating on his turf, at the same time he was terrified of getting in their way. His family was soaking up tens of billions of dollars of loose money from neighboring sheikhdoms by building Disneyworld plantations on artificial islands off Dubai's desert shores. For just over a million dollars, you could buy a luxury villa in "Great Britain," one of many island nations in "The World." For two million, you could have your own yacht pier and a six bedroom blockhouse on stilts at "The Palm," a huge development built on a causeway four kilometers out at sea in the form of a gigantic palm tree, with houses and private docks radiating out from the trunk. All of that fabulous wealth was possible because the Ruler had bought off the beast – he even admitted it once to Manoucher Amir, over a late dinner at the Officer's Club. If the price was a few Iranian opposition leaders, it was a small one to pay.

Kourosh had set up a small office in the Djebel Ali free trade zone, down the coast from the city-state, using a computer software company they ran out of a mailbox in Beverly Hills. It gave them a good reason to travel frequently to the Emirates. At least, until someone started seriously checking out their cover.

He couldn't possibly allow Kourosh to go there alone. It was simply too dangerous. So he phoned his partner at his construction company, and told him he would be taking off for a few days. You can't make a revolution as a part-time job, he often joked. But it was the only option available.

He sent Rahimi a one word reply. *Yes.*

0900 hours, Monday, May 14 – Tel Aviv, Israel

Israel Tan's office bespoke his importance. On the top floor of a spectacular new glass and stone building, he was just down the hall from the minister. Known as the "Kirya," the defense ministry was a sprawling campus, closely-guarded, with dozens of buildings connected by open walkways, sheltered from the searing Mediterranean sun by rare trees. Covering the entire wall behind Tan's desk was a gigantic map of Iran and the Persian Gulf, with a half dozen high resolution satellite photographs that zoomed in on areas marked with thick red circles. Tan sat in his shirt sleeves, sweating slightly as he sipped the unsweetened Arabic coffee one of many stunning female conscripts who ran the outer office brought to him regularly. An old floor fan whirred by the long conference table. The building designers forgot to calculate the heating effect of so much glass when they designed the air conditioning system.

An old veteran, Tan knew the Persians well. He had been Israel's last "ambassador" to Iran under the Shah, and the only foreign diplomat to have accurately predicted the monarch's imminent downfall. It had come to him in a flash six months before the disturbances began in earnest, nearly a full year before the shah's final departure in January 1979. One weekend in early spring, the shah and his family flew down to the private vacation resort they had constructed for their personal use on the Persian Gulf island of Kish. Tan remained in Tehran, as did the prime minister and most of the shah's cabinet. At a dinner over the weekend at the prime minister's house, Tan was stunned to hear him mock the monarch, and especially his wife, whom he accused of being in league with "communists" and "mullahs" – pronounced to sound like a curse. The shah had lost the respect of his closest associates, Tan cabled back to Jerusalem. They felt free enough to mock him, virtually in public. It was a clear sign that he had lost the will to rule. If the opposition can mount an organized challenge, he will be gone in six months, not more, Tan wrote. History had proven him right, almost to the day.

"So what do you have for me?" he asked, as his deputy burst into the room, a red portfolio under his arm.

Zvi Reuben was twenty years younger than Tan, but had gone prematurely bald. He spoke fluent Persian, Arabic, English, French and German – and a few other languages no one could ever quite remember.

"The *East Wind III* used to be called the *German Emperor*," he began, "but it changed hands a few weeks ago. We got lucky when they reflagged her."

"Liberia?"

"No, Tonga. A tiny island kingdom in the Pacific. When the new Liberian government tried to get the shipping registry from Chucky Taylor after his exile to Nigeria, a whole bunch of Liberia wannabes tried to become the new flag of convenience. Hence, Tonga. Their data base identifies the new owners as Traventus Ltd., a holding company registered in the British Virgin Islands. That was the easy part."

"And so the hard part is what?"

"The BVI. We don't have a clue who Mr. Traventus is when he goes to the bank or takes a plane. We don't even know if he really exists. The BVI keeps corporate ownership confidential – I mean, *really* confidential. This is not Switzerland. They are really serious about protecting the identity of the bad guys."

"Well, it's not as if the Swiss have discovered virtue. They had quite a lot of help. So is the *Memuneh* willing to help?"

Tan still referred to the Mossad director by his secret title, "the Anointed One," although the Israelis had given up years ago on keeping his identity secret.

Major General Motta Singer was an old friend from a lifetime ago, when as young men they had been parachutists together.

"He grumbled."

Tan chuckled quietly. "So what does he want?"

"First crack."

Tan quickly nodded his assent. "*If* we get anything. You can't expect him to give us something for nothing. What about the crew?"

"No trace of them anywhere. Not known terrorists. More like ghosts. They don't show up on any crew listing for the past twelve months, which is as far back as our friends at Lloyds could access for us quickly. We're looking at Filipinos, a few Malaysians, a Libyan, two Egyptians, and an Indian from South Africa."

"All potential al Qaeda recruits. And the captain?"

"Name is Ali Hassan Mahmoud. He's wearing a Filipino passport, believe it or not. Got his captain's license in 1998. But hasn't had a command we can trace for the past five years."

"Borrowed identity?"

"We don't know that as a fact."

"Family? Children? Last known place of abode?"

"Like I said, he's a ghost just like all the others."

Israel Tan knew there was a 98% chance that this threat was aimed at America, not Israel. But after so many wars and so many deaths, he was unwilling to take that 2% chance. He knew the *Memuneh* agreed.

Motta Singer and Israel Tan were survivors. They lived near each other in Gush Etzion, a community built and rebuilt on the ashes of dead Jews, just 12 miles south of Jerusalem. On a clear day, you could see the Mediterranean town of Hadera from the ravine. Three generations of Jews had settled Gush Etzion since 1927, when the Jewish Agency bought the barren hillside from Arab landowners. And three generations of Jews had been slaughtered there by those same Arab landowners and their descendants. Israel Tan and his wife had been among the first families who returned to rebuild Gush Etzion after the 1967 war. When the Oslo peace agreement was signed in 1993, they believed – like so many others! – that peace truly was at hand. Just four years later, driving home from Bethlehem, his wife Zippora was shot dead by a gang of Arabs. Not long after that, Israel Tan and Motta Singer and the Gush Etzion elders built a 10-foot high fence along the road. They called it "the Oslo fence."

Israel Tan was tired of war. Tired of wide-eyed fanatics screaming for blood. Tired of the constant vigilance survival required. But he knew the alternative all too well. They had to find out who these people were, and what murder they intended. "Do we have visuals yet?" he said, rubbing his eyes.

"No," Zvi said. "But they put out to sea a few hours ago. An Air India flight from Dubai to Delhi is scheduled to fly over them in the Indian Ocean later today. We've logged our request."

"Good. I want to know everything about these bastards and what they've got on board."

1930 hours, Sunday, May 20 – Dubai

Colonel Rahimi looked very small in the fisheye of the hotel room door. He was wearing a cheap grey business suit and a starched but collarless white shirt, buttoned up to his neck in the style approved by the Islamic Republic, which banned neckties and shirt collars as signs of *ghobzadeh* – corrupt Western influence. He was clearly nervous, constantly flicking the ash off his cigarette with his thumbnail, although he had allowed no ash to accumulate. His skin was sticky with sweat.

Manoucher Amir opened the door and waved him into the suite. But Rahimi stopped in the doorway when he saw the big dark hair of the woman's head, seated with her back to him in the sofa in the next room. "I am here just to see you," he whispered hurriedly. "I am not here for other things. Please."

The woman stood up and approached them as Manoucher closed the door. Pointedly, without a word, she extended her hand, shaking the hair from her face with a quick movement. Rahimi didn't move. Her large dark eyes, set deep in high cheekbones, held him like the two deliberate ends of a see-saw, appraising him. "You will not shake a woman's hand?" she said.

"It is forbidden, *haram*."

"Then take off your jacket. I want to see your weapons," she said.

He raised his hands in innocence, palms facing her, smiling indulgently to Manoucher, his friend. "I have no weapons. I am here – "

"– I know why you say you are here," she said icily, cutting him off. "*I* am Kourosh. Manoucher, search him."

Rahimi looked stunned, clearly not expecting the head of the National Freedom Party intelligence outfit to be a woman, especially not one like this. A classic Persian beauty, but somehow too thin, too hard, too intense. Instead of mystery and invitation, her eyes were hard and penetrating, full of contempt. He submitted without another word as Manoucher had him lift his hands higher, then carefully patted down his sleeves, the lining of his jacket, the breast pockets, his shirt, trousers and both sides of his legs. He found nothing.

"Empty your pockets," the woman said. "I want to see everything."

When Rahimi had placed his wallet, passport and other papers on the coffee table, she picked up his Pasdaran ID card and handed it to Manoucher. "Is this him?"

Manoucher put on reading glasses and examined it slowly, opening the document, examining the seal, the way the photograph was attached. He knew these documents well, and knew also that if the regime wanted to fake one, they simply had to issue a real one in a fake name to their own agent.

"It's a real ID," Manoucher said finally. "But it proves nothing."

"What is your full name," the woman asked.

"Abd al-Rahman Rahimi Golpour," he replied.

"Why did the regime send you here?"

"I came here with information," he said quietly, nodding to the CD-ROM on the coffee table that Manoucher had taken from his pocket. "I want to come out."

"If there is anything of importance on that CD, why did you bring it with you? How do you know the regime did not intercept your message to us?"

The questions came in a quick staccato burst.

"They would have gotten to me by now," he said. "They always do."

"Not if they wanted to use you as bait."

Rahimi was burning with shame. She couldn't know – and he would never tell her! – just how close he had come to arrest. He avoided looking at her as he mumbled replies to her questions. As all Pasdars had been taught, he believed it was *haram* – forbidden – to look at a woman who was not your wife or a member of your own immediate family. The eyes were the portals of the Devil, and the Devil was everywhere, tempting. Somewhere inside of him, a steel door slammed shut.

"Why don't you sit over there," she said finally, indicating a deep sofa. She went into the bedroom and brought out a laptop computer, which she placed on the coffee table across from him. "Let's see about your information."

Rahimi submitted, looking down at his hands. He kneaded them together as she clicked on the keyboard, scrolling through the directory on the CD.

"What's this?" she said, squinting instinctively when the dark pictures Rahimi had taken with his cell phone appeared on the screen.

"I don't know," he said simply. "But they came to load it in the middle of the night. Men from Tehran. From VEVAK, Section 12."

"How do you know they were Section 12? Surely, they didn't tell you that."

Section 12 was the counter-intelligence and security department of the *Vezarat-e Ettelaat va Amniyat-e Keshvar*, generally known in the West as the Ministry of Information and Security, MOIS. They interrogated suspected spies, and provided security for top officials, and were among the most dreaded of the regime's many killers.

"No. But they were giving orders to the Pasdar officers who brought the object. I believe it is a weapon of some sort."

"Why is that?"

"The truck. It came from the Self Sufficiency department of the Sepah navy. That is where we experiment on new weapons systems."

Kourosh didn't believe him, and she let it show. She had seen dozens of fake "defectors" before, whose real goal was to lure opposition leaders into private meetings where they could be killed.

"If it was a weapon, why so little security?"

"So not to attract attention," Rahimi said. "Whatever they are doing, they wanted it done as quietly as possible. That's why I have brought you the pictures. Surely your friends in America will know what it's about."

She let his comment ride, pushing back the memory his words called up to her.

"One of them was an Arab. We call him *hajji*. It is said that at the end of Ramadan, he personally slaughters the lamb for the *aid al-fitr* feast, and smears blood from the knife on his own children's necks."

Kourosh raised an eyebrow at this, letting her skepticism show. But behind the mask, her mind rapidly calculated the possibilities. If this were the *hajji*, Rahimi's information could be worth gold. The *hajji* was the regime's top operations officer. Born in Lebanon, exfiltrated to Iran after blowing up the U.S. Marine barracks in October 1983, he was deadly, efficient, and – until now – completely untraceable. He used seventeen different identities, and had undergone extensive plastic surgery. The last known sighting of him outside of Iran occurred ten months before the September 11 attacks, when he escorted a group of future al Qaeda hijackers onto an Iran Air flight from Damascus to Tehran. And even then, only one of his aliases showed up, no passport photos. She copied the pictures from the CD onto her hard drive, then closed the computer. She knew exactly who she needed to see in Washington, and just the thought of him made a faint smile come to her lips. She could still trace the muscles along his spine, burned like a map into her fingertips. How many years had it been?

"I want to come out," Rahimi said again, staring down at his hands. "My daughter – "

"Then you should leave," Kourosh said simply. "We don't run a welfare program. It's a hard life out there, once you're free. Nobody's going to catch you when you fall."

"But will you help?"

"That depends on this," she said, tapping the CD. "But if I know the Americans, they're going to want you to stay in place, to see what you can pick up."

Rahimi looked panicky. "If I have contact with the Americans, the *etelaat* will find me."

"I know," she said. "But you won't."

1020 hours, Tuesday, May 22 – Bolling Air Force Base, Washington, DC

"Gentlemen... lady," said Richard Stapleton, turning to acknowledge the single woman seated across from him in the soft artificial light of the underground conference room. "Now that we have finished with ongoing business, Mr. Wilkens has brought something new for us to look at. Danny, you may proceed. And please, there's no need to be nervous."

He gave a patronizing little wave, like a teacher encouraging a reluctant pupil to the blackboard, indicating that Wilkens should join him in the privileged zone across the oval conference table from the muckety-mucks. Then he collapsed into his seat, the new leather cushion wheezing as it adjusted to his bulk, and turned to watch the metal protective shields slide back from the panoramic screen covering the curved wall behind them. Contented. In charge. The Man.

Wilkens got up and clicked on a small laser pointer to begin his presentation, clearly uncomfortable in civilian clothes. He was not a big man, like Stapleton, but every inch of him seemed to be strung on wires. Even the thin snake-like muscle that flexed involuntarily along his cheekbone betrayed the low opinion he had of Richard Stapleton – and it wasn't because Stapleton had been called back from retirement to head the new Joint Threat Integration Center. For four years, Stapleton had been the U.S. delegate to the International Atomic Energy Agency in Vienna. As evidence of Iran's nuclear cheating became so overwhelming that even the IAEA secretary general denounced them, Stapleton continued to counsel Washington to greater patience. Diplomacy. Process. Consensus. In this very room, he had heard Stapleton call it, "Vienna rules." If Danny's informant was right, the Vienna rules were about to get them all killed.

Major Danny Wilkens was the DIA's point man for all things Iran. In the four months since he had returned to Bolling from Fort Huachuca in Arizona, where he had been training tactical intelligence officers in lessons learned from Iraq ("When intelligence is actionable, you *act* on it"). Wilkens had been summoned by his division chief to sit in the back row at the weekly sherpas meetings in case he was needed for some detail. Until now, he had never been called upon to make a major presentation, and this explained the solicitude Stapleton, his ultimate superior, was showing him. Today, it was show time. His case. His joe. His turn to talk to the suit. He knew it was going to be a tough sell.

Iran had become increasingly aggressive since it had tossed out the IAEA inspectors. With no one on the ground, America's intelligence was scanty. They had satellites of several flavors patrolling the skies over much of Iran, and flew a new, high-altitude version of the Predator unmanned drone that could loiter over targets up to three hundred kilometers from launch point. But they didn't have a clue what was going on inside the buried nuclear plants, or in the counsels of power in

Tehran. They had no one on the inside, no one who could give them a glimpse into the thinking of the boy zealot who had been elected president and who seemed intent on taking his country – and the world – to the brink of nuclear war. And without that, the best tactical intelligence they could gather was useless.

Wilkens had cut his teeth tracking terrorist suspects in Bosnia with Army J-2. They were a grab-bag of Chechens, Pakistanis, Saudis, Egyptians and Moroccans, with a smattering of European Muslims who could have passed themselves off as locals. At the time – March 1995 – these bin Laden protégés, all trained in Afghanistan, were known simply as Afghan-Arabs.

But when Wilkens and his men raided a local safe house in Sarajevo, they found video-tapes and training manuals that bore the markings of the Iranian intelligence service, MOIS. Iranian assistance for a mainly Arab terrorist group should have been a wake-up call. He certainly hadn't been prepared for anything like it, but the evidence was simply stunning: the Iranians were teaching the Afghan-Arab terror-recruits how to conduct video-taped surveillance and how to make bombs. Among the targets the Iranians had designated was the residence of a junior diplomat at the U.S. embassy.

Wilkens was given the job of briefing the deputy chief of mission, a wheezing blowhard of a man, whose chief worry was making sure that Wilkens didn't create a diplomatic stir. As it happened, the MOIS trainers were in Sarajevo at the personal invitation of the Bosnian Interior minister, but the DCM had no intention of raising that information with the host government or even with Washington. They'd send dependents and non-essential U.S. personnel home, and shift the remaining diplomats into more secure quarters, he said. But if word ever got out that the government of the United States had hard proof that the Bosnian Interior Minister was working for Iranian intelligence, he promised he would break Wilkens' career.

That deputy chief of mission was Richard Stapleton. Today, Danny was glad he had saluted, swallowed his indignation, and washed it down with generous portions of *slivovice* at the local post bar with his men. For the suits, there was always a good reason to do nothing.

As the newly-appointed Principal Assistant Deputy National Director of Intelligence, Stapleton ran a so-called "fusion" center where analysts from the Pentagon, State, FBI, the Department of Homeland Security and the National Security Council came together with the CIA. These were the sherpas Danny now had to convince that incomplete intelligence obtained from an unknown man who was betraying his country justified mobilizing all the assets of the United States government.

"We have two pictures, and we had to enhance them significantly," Wilkens began, rolling his titanium shoulder slightly to fit better into the confines of his off-the-rack suit. "They were taken by a source who had access only to a picture phone – albeit, a very good quality one. Initial resolution was 1.2 mega pixels. Both pictures were taken at night under sodium light, probably within seconds of each other. Our photo analysts created this enhancement of the object being loaded into the hold of the ship. We believe it is an Irani-made mini-submarine."

Wilkens showed a blow-up of the object being loaded into the *East Wind III* as a handful of Iranian Revolutionary Guards officers and plainclothesmen stood watching.

"What's your estimate of how many men it could hold?" asked Haas, the CIA man. "Did your source give you any clue as to the crew of the minisub? Or the mission?"

Sure, Wilkens thought. *Here are photocopies of their passports, and the ports of call they filed with the insurer.*

"Negative, sir. Last we heard they were holed up in Al Mukalla, Yemen. Ostensibly with engine trouble."

"Ducking for cover?"

"That's what I was hoping you could tell us," Wilkens said. "After all, you're the HUMINT guys."

Under the new rules, crafted as Director of National Intelligence, Vice Adm. Mike McConnell, re-centralized U.S. intelligence-gathering capabilities under his personal control, the Pentagon no longer ran human agents, or at least, they weren't supposed to do so. Danny's old unit – the 4th Psyops group out of Fort Bragg, NC – had been rolled into special operations. And if by any chance a walk-in came their way out in the sandbox, the CIA had a veto – that is, if they ever found out about him.

"Hold on a second," said Victoria Brandt. "Who is this "source" anyway? The one who provided you with the photos? Why do we have any confidence that these photographs are real? I mean, good

Photoshop artists aren't so hard to find these days. Wouldn't the Iranians just *love* to send us on a wild goose chase?"

Wilkens had been waiting for this, and so, apparently, had the others. Victoria Brandt was the State Department rep on the sherpas committee, from the Bureau of Intelligence and Research (IN/R). Even Agency types joked that when IN/R actually had intelligence of its own it was RUM/INT – planted stories and official leaks gathered by diplomats on the embassy cocktail circuit. In her late thirties, single, and highly ambitious, Victoria Brandt went out of her way to hide her good looks. She would come down on him like a ton of bricks if he treated her with anything less than the utmost seriousness, Danny knew. He chastened himself for imagining the curves beneath her lawyer-class suit, for unwinding the frugal bun at the back of her head so her long brown hair spilled out. *Lord, forgive me the sin of thought.*

"That might have been the Soviet model," Wilkens said. "But we're not seeing the Iranis play that sort of game."

"Victoria's got a point, Danny," said Jason Steinberg, the National Security Council rep. "Imagine the embarrassment if we boarded a ship on the high seas and found nothing but pistachios and carpets? Everyone would be calling the president a gun-slinger."

"Tell us about the source," Stapleton said gently.

"Rev. Guards Colonel. Early 40s, married, grown daughter. A child of the revolution who hates the mullahs because he was a victim of their stupidity during the war with Iraq. He's scared out of his wits and won't talk to us."

Charles Haas waved the air past an ear. "Yeah yeah yeah. So you're running him through a cut-out. It's no secret we have no spies in Iran. So is this another one of Aryana's gold-plated blow-jobs?"

Stapleton shot him a glance of reproach.

"Who's Aryana?" Victoria Brandt said quickly.

"Go ahead, Danny. Tell her," said Haas, not about to apologize for his language.

Wilkens took a deep breath. He was prepared as he would ever be for this, but Haas's sarcasm unnerved him. What did Haas know about her, anyway? What did he know about *them?*

"Aryana is an Irani-American we hired as a translator during my second tour in Iraq, to help with the Iranian Revolutionary Guards officers we were capturing with the insurgents. She got their real stories long after the rest of us had given up. Absolutely first class."

"Yeah, I bet," said Haas.

"After my last tour in Iraq, we kept contact. She now runs a small computer software outfit in L.A. And handles Intel operations for the National Freedom Party. She goes by the code name Kourosh. That's Persian for Cyrus – as in, Cyrus the Great."

"So let me get this right. This is Iranian *exile* intelligence?" said Victoria Brandt, rolling her eyes. "We've been down that road before. I see red flags all over this."

"Our people have tested the pictures every way from Sunday and we believe they are absolutely authentic," said Wilkens.

"Why don't we just turn it over to the Israelis?" said Steinberg. "On the surface, if it *is* real, it looks like another *Karine-A*."

The Israelis had intercepted the *Karine-A* in January 2002 as it entered the Red Sea. The Palestinian crew had rigged the Iranian weapons she was carrying onto 82 specially-built submersibles and planned to release them off the coast of Gaza, where they could be picked up later on by Palestinian fishing boats. All of them were familiar with the *Karine-A*. For Danny, it proved once again the utter mastery of the Israelis when they knew their security was at risk. *We could learn a few,* Danny thought.

"So the Iranians are moving guns to the Palestinians," said Haas. "Why is this our problem?"

"It's our problem if they're not," said a quiet voice.

Nathaniel Charles wore two hats, as Director of the FBI's Washington Field Office and as Assistant Director for Counter-Terrorism. Although he was the highest-ranking black Special Agent in a Bureau known for its sliced bread clubbiness, Nate Charles had won his chops because of an ability to bring focus to back-stabbing bureaucrats, and they admired him and feared him for it. The back and forth bickering reminded him of the morning of September 11th, when fingers were pointing madly in every direction. Thanks to Nate Charles, the hunt for the al Qaeda terrorists went from zero to light speed in about thirty minutes.

"Our job is to think the unthinkable," he went on. "That's why we're paid those high salaries. We don't want the goalie to be our first line of defense."

The man seated next to Charles shifted uncomfortably in the high-backed leather desk chair, as the attention of everyone in the room shifted momentarily in his direction. Roger Kaminski was director of Customs and Border Protection within the Department of Homeland Security. His men and women were responsible for securing the nation's borders and seaports from terrorists, illegal immigrants, and drug dealers. They were the goalies and everyone knew they were fighting a losing battle. There was simply no way any government could defend every port of entry into the United States without shutting down commerce. All you could hope for was to raise the price sufficiently so the terrorists would think twice before trying.

"If there's even the remotest possibility that this weapon could be coming to the United States, I want to know about it," Charles said.

"F--k if I'm going to talk to the Israelis," said Haas. "They wouldn't give me jack, anyway. Nothing to tell mother. Ever since Pollard—"

"—Forget Pollard," Charles said. The U.S. Navy analyst had been arrested in 1987 for spying for the Israelis, and had been serving a life sentence ever since. "*I'll* talk to the Israelis and report back. And if you're not happy about that, Mr. Haas, I suggest you take a couple of aspirin. This ain't your mama's world no mo'."

Danny Wilkens nodded inwardly, taking note. At least one of the sherpas didn't think he was totally nuts.

1930 hours, Tuesday, May 22 – Burtonsville, Maryland

> *"Now I lay me down to sleep,*
> *"I pray the Lord my soul to keep.*
> *"And if I die before I wake,*
> *"I pray the Lord my soul to take."*

On his knees by the single bed, Danny Wilkens led his three-year old son, Paul, in his evening prayers.

"God bless Mommy and Daddy. God bless Grandma. God bless Papa. God bless Mrs. Miller." The boy glanced sideways at his father, who was smiling, his eyes open. "God bless Truman?"

"God will bless Truman, even though he's just a dog," his father said. "You forgot somebody, Paul."

"God bless me!" the boy said.

"God bless you, my son. And God bless tantie Aryana and nuncle Manoo."

"Amen," said Paul, jumping into bed. He emerged from beneath the covers a moment later. "Where's Ratty Raccoon?"

"He must be sleeping already," Danny said. He reached beneath his son's pillow and found the slip-on puppet he had saved years ago, when his father had been shot down in a U.S. Army Chinook helicopter in the first Gulf War and he moved his mom into a smaller house. She had cried when he found it, and cried again when he received his commission just weeks later and told her he was shipping out to Fort Carson to join the 77ᵗʰ Armor.

"Where's Paulie?" he made the puppet say, twisting left and right in front of his son's head. "A kiss for Ratty Raccoon?"

"No kiss."

"No kiss for Ratty Raccoon?" the puppet hung its head.

"Yes, kiss!" the boy said, and they pecked at each other, the puppet jerking back and forth.

As he was miming their bedtime ritual, Danny warmed, sensing the presence of his wife at the door. She watched them for a full minute, unseen, then came into the room and bent over Danny's back to give their son a goodnight kiss. He could feel the Goosebumps shoot from his neck down to his sides as she brushed across him with the fine silk of her Victoria's Secret nightgown. "Goodnight, sweetheart," she said.

She pulled her husband after her and gently closed the door, leaving the room dark except for a constellation of fluorescent stars the boy had stuck onto the wall over his head.

"It's still early," Danny said, stopping her at the dining room table to sip from a half-empty glass of wine. "It's not even dark."

"I'm learning to plan ahead if I want to have the man of my dreams," she said.

"I like that kind of planning." He offered her the wineglass, then pulled her down onto his lap into the sofa and gave her a long kiss.

They had met in Iraq, just two weeks after the fall of Baghdad in April 2003. Danny had won a billet as chief operations officer for the 313th Military Intelligence Battalion. Their job was to scour suspected WMD sites for evidence that Saddam Hussein had hidden weapons stockpiles, as the pre-war intelligence had indicated. They had been all through the south with the first wave of the invasion, blowing up bunkers where they found leaky barrels labeled "agricultural chemicals" which Danny's bio-chem experts believed were precursors for a binary nerve agent similar to sarin gas. They had been hoping that captured officers would tell them during interrogation whether Saddam had given the orders to use the weapons when coalition troops approached Baghdad, but they encountered only dazed looks of shock and confusion. The truth was, Saddam's field commanders didn't have a clue. They knew the *rais* had large stockpiles of chemically-filled rockets and artillery shells, but no one seemed to know where they had been stored or which unit was supposed to use them. Each commander thought someone else had received the order and was stunned when the weapons were never used.

By mid-April, Danny reached Baghdad, and took his team to Thuwaitha, the site of Iraq's bombed-out nuclear reactor and a series of secret uranium enrichment labs. One of his men had uncovered a buried cache of oil-drums his DoE weenie believed could be filled with uranium yellowcake. Dr. Martin was telling him everything he didn't want to know about uranium enrichment when he saw her.

"Who's that?" Danny asked.

"Oh that's Dr. Romera," the older man said. "Our rising star. Keeps us grey beards on our toes."

She was dressed in cammo trousers, a tight-fitting tan tee-shirt, metal sunglasses, and was swinging a daypack by a strap as she headed over to one of the bombed-out laboratories. He jogged over to her and found her in a crouch, just shaking her head as she picked through the wreckage of millions of dollars of scientific instruments, turned into charred spaghetti by the allied bombing.

"I've heard so much about you, Dr. Romera," Danny said. "I hear that if it weren't for you, the Department of Energy would be running on empty."

"And who told you this?" she said, amused, but wary.

"That's my job, ma'am. They actually pay me over here to know everything about you."

It was a pick-up line, and they both knew it, but he delivered it with such utter innocence that she just laughed, shaking her head.

"Somehow I have a feeling that won't be as easy as you think –uh – Major."

"Danny Wilkens, J-2," he said, extending a hand.

Danny was smitten; but later, whenever they joked about that first encounter, Eva swore up and down that she had been unimpressed. He was just another guy with no hair and a uniform.

That was nearly four years ago, when he was still whole.

"I've got something to show you," he said finally.

"I know," Eva said, stretching her head back and nibbling at his ear.

"I meant something else. I really need you to take a look at something. It's important."

She sighed. "You know how to choose your moments, don't you, baby?"

"Sorry."

Eva straightened herself out as he went to get his briefcase. Married to Danny, moving from post to post, she had learned to take these moments with him as a gift. She was always careful to keep their passion private and mentally shed her negligee for a business suit, as if by changing clothes she could keep the dangers of their professional lives from penetrating that secret private place they shared.

Trained as a physicist, Dr. Eva Romera-Wilkens had worked a half dozen years at Lawrence Livermore National Laboratory in northern California designing a new generation of earth penetrating nuclear weapons, aimed at destroying deep-buried underground bunkers in countries such as North Korea and Iran. Because Congress never fully authorized their work, they did feasibility studies and computer analyses to prepare for the day they could test the weapon.

Shortly after returning from Iraq and a tumultuous courtship, she and Danny were married. He had returned to DIA Headquarters at Bolling AF base to continue processing the data gathered on Saddam's WMD programs for the Iraq Survey Group, while she managed to get herself detailed to a special unit of the Department of Energy in Washington, DC that developed new technology to detect radiation emissions from non-fissile nuclear material − a dirty bomb. (So much for the fiction that she wasn't really interested in the guy with no hair and a uniform!) The Nuclear

Emergency Search Team (NEST) was one of the most secret elements of the United States government, and prowled overhead the nation's capitol in military helicopters and on the streets in unmarked vans at times of crisis. If ordinary citizens understood what NEST actually did, they would be truly frightened. The websites that sold potassium iodide and Geiger counters would crash from frenzied visitors, hoping to buy protection from nuclear attack.

Unlocking the briefcase, Danny took a document from a black folder. It had red borders, and the word "Top Secret" inscribed across the front. Eva scowled.

"Did you sign for this?" she said. She was well aware of the procedures for checking out numbered copies of classified documents, and didn't like to see them show up in her home.

"No, I generated it," he grinned. "Remember Aryana?"

"How could I *forget* Aryana?" she said archly. "You obviously haven't."

Danny didn't take the bait. They'd been through this one many times and he hoped that by now the sting had gone. It hadn't helped that Eva then had been six months pregnant. "The pictures come from one of her sources in Iran. I need your professional opinion, because none of our guys have a clue."

"And you're surprised *because*?"

Danny snorted, and handed her the first picture of the minisub being loaded onto the *East Wind III,* then a series of blow-ups that revealed a set of hollow bolts along the hull. "Our people think these are hard points for attaching external torpedoes or a sidecar," he said. "The problem is here."

The second photograph showed what appeared to be a cigar-shaped tube, smaller than the mini-sub, swaying in mid-air over the hold of the *East Wind III*.

"We thought it might just be a bad picture, taken from a different angle or from farther away. But when the photo-analysts mapped it out, they concluded that it was about half the length of the sub and had some distinct features. That's when they thought it might be a torpedo, or possibly a sidecar crammed with weapons."

Eva knew when not to ask questions, and Danny loved her for it. Instead, she scrutinized the pictures, shifting from one to another, comparing, thinking, drawing on that computer brain of hers for anything remotely similar.

"We don't know for sure where it's headed," he said. "The last info we had, it ducked into Al Mukalla. Maybe engine trouble. Maybe just lying low. That's about half-way down the east coast of Yemen, just inside the Gulf of Aden."

"So it could be headed for Israel."

"Or somewhere else."

"Haven't the Iranians done this before, shipping weapons to Gaza through the Suez Canal?"

"They tried," Danny said. "The *Karine-A*. The Israelis boarded her in the Red Sea."

"So this time, they decide to launch the weapons from a mini-sub, before the Israelis can board them."

Danny did a double-take. "Who said anything about launch?"

"You don't mean that your guys think they're going to go to all this trouble just to bring in a bunch of rocket launchers and AK-47s to commit retail mayhem? They've got to have something much more valuable. Something they know they can get through the net."

She scrutinized the cigar-shaped tube again, comparing it to the mini-sub, and shook her head. "Let me do a bit of research tomorrow. I need to take another look at the Pakistan-Iran file. Can you get me precise dimensions? I want to run them against the designs of dear old Dr. Khan."

"You mean A.Q. Khan, the nuclear black market guy?"

"The one and only."

Jesus Christ, son of God, have mercy on me, a sinner. It was a short prayer he had learned years ago from a brigade chaplain, who recommended repeating it during those long forced marches with 80 pound packs you never thought you would survive.

"Eva, you know what's going on here?" he said. "After the fiasco in Iraq, nobody wants to tell the president the Iranians have WMDs—until the mushroom clouds go off."

Danny shook his head, numb. He felt like those Iraqi officers they had interrogated near Nassiriyah, who simply couldn't believe what was happening to them because it went beyond everything they were drilled to expect. He could picture the *East Wind III*, slowly approaching America's shores with all the inevitability of a bad dream. Was it really going to take a mushroom cloud to wake them up? He could see Stapleton and the sherpas arguing around the conference table, pointing fingers, blaming each other for missing the signs, for not connecting the dots. But before you could connect the dots, you had to collect them. And they had no spies in Iran. That was their refrain. No spies.

He wrapped Eva in his arms, burrowing his head into her silky hair, and a great sinking feeling came over him. If he was wrong he would be reassigned to drive a desk at some Pentagon annex in Reston, Virginia (commonly known as Siberia), but they would all live to fight another day. But if he was right... He shuddered as he realized that Eva could be the one called by the NEST in the dead of night to defuse a nuclear weapon whose design nobody had ever authenticated before.

1100 hours, Wednesday, May 23 – Tel Aviv

The satellite operations center, buried deep beneath the Kyria, already felt crowded with its six person crew. There was no visitor's gallery or conference room, so Israel Tan and Zvi Reuben fell in behind the operators who were tracking the orbit of the Safir-7 radar satellite as it began making its regular pass over Iran. Images of Iran's Busheir nuclear power plant, dazzling in the midday sun, shifted slightly every three seconds or so as the satellite progressed across the sky.

"We got lucky," said Major Almog, as he swiveled toward his visitors from twin computer screens. "I thought you might like to see."

"Yes, indeed," said Tan. "You were absolutely right to call us down here. The minister can wait."

Almog pulled up a directory of the past week's saved imagery on the left-hand screen and scrolled down until he found the folder he wanted.

"This first set of images is from Saturday, the 19th. You can see the time stamp on the screen."

"Which port is that?" Tan asked.

"Al Mukalla, Yemen. Not the type of place you'd like to stop for an oil change."

Tan grunted. The image on the screen was so sharp he could read the name of the ship on the bow – *East Wind III* – and see four members of the crew up on deck, apparently securing the ropes as the ship cast off from dock. "How long were they there?"

"Close to three full days, from what we can make out. Here, she goes out."

Almog clicked on a command that sped up the footage, so the images ran like a slow-motion movie. He grinned, clearly enjoying himself.

"Major, you don't have to impress me," said Tan. "I have no budget authority. Just tell me which way she's headed."

"That's just it," he said. "She appeared to be headed for the Indian Ocean when we finished our fly by, but then we lost her – until this morning. We picked her up here about an hour ago. It was just by accident. She happened to cross our flight path. But there you have it."

He called up an image of a tiny speck in the ocean, then zoomed in so they could see the bright red flag of Tonga flying on the mast. "That places her roughly mid-way down the coast of Somalia, headed south."

"How long would it take her to make Capetown, assuming for a moment that she's headed there and not here?"

"I'm on it, sir," the soldier at the next screen said. Tan and Zvi Rueben shifted over to watch the young man pull up a map of Africa, criss-crossed with Mercator lines, and type in a series of coordinates into the computer.

"At their current speed, which has been averaging 12 knots, it should take them around 14 days to reach Capetown from Al Mukalla. They're four days out, so ten days from now."

"June second," Tan said. "And just assuming, for the sake of argument, that they decide to sail from Capetown to Alexandria, Egypt? Let's say, somewhere within missile range. What are we looking at here?"

The young officer shifted the map to the west, then plugged in new coordinates. "Around 19 days sir, give or take a day. They could probably make more than 12 knots without breaking a bolt. It'd slice off a day or two, if they had a plane to catch."

"So if they laid over for a day to take on food and fuel, they could be within striking distance by June 20," Tan concluded.

Straightening up, he thanked the young officer and waved Almog back into his chair, not to accompany them out. "Gentlemen, that doesn't give us much time."

A young female conscript was standing by the secure elevator, waiting to accompany them back upstairs.

"I almost forgot to ask," Tan said, turning to Zvi Reuben. "How are things going down in the Caribbean?"

"What do you expect?" the younger man smiled. "The weather is fine – no hurricanes yet. And our friend is very found of the girls."

Tan grunted, but said nothing. When they got out of the elevator, he turned to Zvi. "Remind me when this is over that it's about time for me to retire."

"Remind you, I can do. Convince you? I doubt very much."

1930 hours, Thursday, May 31 – Jost Van Dyke, British Virgin Islands

Trevor Pettigrew was nursing his second Painkiller when the group of young Americans fell into the bamboo lounge chairs at the far end of the bar overlooking the beach. There were so many of them who came down to Tortola to charter sailboats, and they all seemed to look the same: sloppy clothes, hair matted from too much sun-drenched exercise, and a bubbly brunette or two brought along as beach chum. If they made it over to Jost this late in the afternoon, it usually meant they were rolling in cash. The regular ferries to Road Harbor stopped at 6 PM.

Pettigrew didn't go over to the main island more than once a week any longer. His run-down office by the Customs Dock handled most of its business through referrals, and Goodwill knew how to prepare the paperwork so Pettigrew could submit it to Corporations House once a week. That was what the agencies in London and Hong Kong expected him to do, besides cashing their checks. It was a racket that could handsomely support a middle-aged British lawyer with few ambitions other than rum and the occasional stray brunette. His little secrets.

Eleanor hardly came down to the islands any more, thank God. Once she had inherited Bainesbridge Stables along with her sisters, she had her work cut out, she liked to say. She hardly ever made it back to their London *pied à terre* off the Brompton Road, just south of Harrods. It was a lovely place, really, quiet, clean, respectable. So middle class, she called it. *Just like you, my dear.*

Pettigrew had no interest in horses, but he understood enough about horse farms to know he wanted nothing to do with Bainesbridge Stables. He wouldn't spend a pound on upkeep, and wanted not a penny of income. When they died, Eleanor's share would go to their grown daughter and her children, when she had them. He wanted out of the loop, totally. It might look like millions on paper, but it was old gentry stuff, land poor. There wasn't much income to speak of, so Eleanor kept using the credit cards. And he kept getting stuck with the bills.

He'd thought of divorce. That usually swept over him after the fifth Painkiller, like lust for the charterer's castaways. Most of the time, it was just too much effort. Besides, as an ageing divorcee, he'd be just another dirty old man in the eyes of the kiddies. This way, at least he had the allure of sin, with his white linen trousers and starched white shirts, which he left open rakishly to show the deep tan of his arms and chest.

The Yank's question woke him from his daydream, even though he couldn't make out all he was saying.

"We're looking for Trevor Pettigrew. Is he the owner?" the young American inquired of the bartender.

The huge black man with the saucer-shaped eyes gave a belly laugh that made the entire bamboo-stalk bar shake. "Him, de owner? No, man. He just one old English drunk. Epoxy Foxy, *him* de owner. Over dare."

He pointed to a life-size effigy of himself, open tropical shirt, bead necklaces reaching down to his navel, knee bent to hold a guitar, and laughed until even the very serious young American with his short hair and fair skin reddened with sun had to join in. "You become one big lobster, man. And you call me colored! Trevor, you got one customer, ma'man."

Pettigrew sized up the young American over the edge of his Painkiller, while giving a friendly little wave. He was older and more serious than the others of his tribe. *Tribe.* Why did that word immediately come to mind?

"Mr. Pettigrew, may I offer you a drink?" the younger man said.

"There's no refusing, now is there?" he said, taking the fresh Painkiller, chilled to the touch, that the American thrust into his hand. "And to whom might I have the honor of drinking?"

The young American laughed, tipping his own glass so the frosted edge just barely touched his. "I can think of many. How about, big-spending women with horse farms?"

Pettigrew had already launched into the new glass, and caught himself from swallowing just before he sputtered in astonishment. "Well, that might be a bit premature." He wiped his lips and frowned, trying to gather his thoughts. "Now that I think of it, didn't I see you last week in Road Harbor?"

"My name is Scott Harper, Mr. Pettigrew," the young American said, without seeming to acknowledge Pettigrew's question. "And I'm going to get straight to the point. Me and my friends here would like to make you a business proposition. Straight-forward. Clean. No strings attached. And utmost discretion guaranteed."

The British lawyer took a long sip of the sweet rum drink and gazed at the twists of fishing tackle and sea shells that formed a tapestry along the back of the bar. He sighed. "And what if I'm not in business, Mr. Harper? What then, eh? You'll have to kill me?"

The American burst into a smile that exposed a huge set of perfectly-white Hollywood teeth. His laugh almost appeared good-natured, although Pettigrew knew that it concealed a far more sinister meaning. "No, no, Mr. Pettigrew. You've got me all wrong. We want to help you, not hurt you. You can trust me on that."

I'll remember that when you start extracting my teeth, he thought. Was it the younger ones who did the dirty work, and this slightly older man who was the ringleader who – he was a Jew, that was it!

"Mr. Harper, I am not sure if you understand the full reach of the law. I know that it might appear to you to be quite distant here. Everyone is quite relaxed.

We're all having a good time. But my profession, sir, is placed under high surveillance. Steady surveillance, I might say."

The American moved his bar stool closer, so Pettigrew could feel the bristles of the reddish-blonde hair of his forearms against his own. It was an uncomfortable sensation, and he shrank from it instinctively. Harper seemed to grow larger the closer he came to him.

"We're not asking you to break the *law*, Mr. Pettigrew," he said quietly. "We just want some information. And we're prepared to reward you handsomely for it."

"You don't understand. I don't sell information, Mr. Harper. That's why I am still in business."

"That's truly a shame," the American said, reaching into a pocket of his reporter's half-vest. He pulled out an envelope, and began leafing through its contents. A name and an address were written on front, and Pettigrew shifted on his barstool ever so slightly so he could get a glimpse of it.

"I wonder what Mrs. Eleanor at Bainsbridge Stables would think of these," Harper said, as he started to extract 4X6 glossy photographs from the batch in the envelope. "Monica, Michelle, Marise. Is it all the emms this month, Mr. Pettigrew?"

He stretched out one hand, then another, to cover the photographs the American started to lay out on the bar counter like cards in a game of solitaire. Casting quick glances over his shoulder, Pettigrew tried to cover them with a bar napkin, panicking at the broad smile of Foxy Callahan, who was rocking back and forth, enjoying it.

"That's — That's illegal, that's what it is," he gasped.

"That's true," Harper admitted. "But we didn't break anything."

Shuffling the photographs together, he looked the British lawyer square in the eyes. "What you've done, Mr. Pettigrew, is quite different. You've become an accessory to mass murder."

"That's quite enough, Mr. Harper. I get your point."

"My favorite, actually, is Marise. Like her behind, don't we?"

"I said, that's enough, Mr. Harper."

"We're not interested in your infidelities, Mr. Pettigrew," the American said. "In fact, my guys just do this as a hobby, something to keep 'em busy on Saturday nights." Leaning closely now, conspiratorially: "Just a peak, that's all we want. No more than a peak. We're quite modest, Mr. Pettigrew. Really."

"What do you want?"

"Traventus. We want to know who he is when he's at home. Where are the checks drawn that pay your fees? And we're quite willing to defray your expenses, Mr. Pettigrew. We thought something in the neighborhood of ten thousand U.S. ought to be sufficient. Cash, of course."

Ten thousand U.S. dollars was more cash than Trevor Pettigrew had seen in many years, and he must have let it show.

"We might ask to take a few pictures for that amount. I'll admit, Mr. Pettigrew. It's a tad more than just a peak. But we'll throw in this little envelope as well. Icing on the cake, so to speak."

He waved the envelope of photographs back and forth, fanning the damp rum-soaked air from his face. "What do you say, Mr. Pettigrew? Tomorrow morning, 9 AM sharp, at your office? Just the two of us? And don't worry. I'm planning to knock."

0845 hours, Friday, May 25 – Tortola, British Virgin Islands

At 8:45 AM, the Customs house in Tortola looked like an all-night bar that had not quite woken up, rather than a place where business was conducted. All along the government dock, beer cans and papers had been swept into small, tidy piles awaiting pick-up. The concrete was still damp from its morning hosing. A small Coast Guard patrol boat rocked gently against its moorings. The only noise came from swarms of flies, busily sucking nourishment from the garbage.

Pettigrew picked his way across a pair of kids spread motionless in their sleeping bags in the patch of grass in front of his building, indignant as he always was to find disorder trouble his world, especially so early in the morning. He had a good mind to ring up Constable D'Estres. But somehow, this morning it didn't seem like a good idea.

Goodwill was already in the office, brewing tea as he sorted through the morning mail. Pettigrew greeted him curtly, as always; inquired whether the mail had brought anything of interest; then sent him downstairs for boiled eggs. He drew hot water from the samovar and plumped himself down behind the broad, empty desk in the next room. He stared out at the harbor, wondering which of the many chartered boats belonged to the American and his friends.

It was the laughter that stirred him from his dread. Goodwill's strong, good-natured laugh, echoing off the empty stairwell, ringing against the frosted glass panel of his front office door. He heard the lock click, but remained motionless. The American's voice came next. "I bet you've seen it a thousand times."

"Epoxy Foxy never miss a newcomer. In high season, he makes that plastic guitar *sing*."

He knocked twice on the thick wood of the inner door as he opened it. "Mr. Scott here to see you, sir."

Pettigrew assented, prepared for the worst. At least he was punctual. Not a minute early, not ten seconds late. Right on the dot of nine.

"Good morning, Mr. Harper. I hope you will excuse me if I peck at my eggs while we talk. Can I get you something? Coffee? Bacon and eggs? Something more serious, perhaps?"

"I'll pass, thank you," the American smiled.

"Thank-you, Goodwill. That will be all," Pettigrew said.

Once the door closed behind him, Pettigrew withdrew a thin black leather folder from a drawer and placed it on the desk, protectively. Harper didn't move to take it.

"I'm afraid that's all I can do for you, Mr. Harper. It's not much, but it's the entire file. It's not unusual, you know."

Opening the file, he withdrew a single sheet of paper and slid it across to his guest.

Harper looked perplexed for a moment. He turned the registration certificate sideways. He flipped it over and examined the watermark.

"It's the same," he said finally. "No doubt about that."

"What do you mean, the same," Pettigrew said.

"Come on, Mr. Pettigrew. I am not going to pay $10,000 to look at a duplicate of the registration certificate, which I can see for myself down at Corporations House. No games, please. We are very serious people."

The British lawyer lost several shades of the deep tan poking out between the buttons of his starched white shirt.

"I told you yesterday, Mr. Harper," he said finally. "My profession is under serious surveillance. The government takes privacy concerns very seriously."

"Listen carefully, Mr. Pettigrew," Harper said quietly. "I am going to count to ten. By the time I reach ten, I would like you to be standing in front of the open door of that safe over there – yeah, yeah, the safe that's behind the picture, over there – and I want you to be withdrawing the beneficiary letter. No gentleman of means is going to go to the trouble of contracting with a Hong Kong law firm, who then contracts with you, to set up a company that owns assets he can't control. Let's start with the count of one...."

"Mr. Harper, please. I beg of you to consider the sensitivity of what you are asking. If word of this ever gets out, I will lose my entire business."

By the count of four, he had flipped the portrait back on its hinges and, trembling, dialed the combination to the safe. Inside were more black leather folders, similar to the one on his desk. He took out a stack and flipped through them until he found the one that he wanted.

"I really don't know how this is going to help you," he said, withdrawing a large envelope. Instead of an address, it bore the heading: "Beneficiary Agreement, Traventus, Ltd." He held it up, not offering it. "As you can see, it is sealed. I am forbidden by law to break that seal."

Harper took a quick look at the green wax seal on the envelope then extracted a Nextel phone from his pocket. It beeped like a walkie-talkie. "Avi?" he said, his voice changing as he pronounced the Hebrew name. "Avi, meet me for drinks at five. Usual place. Do you copy?"

"Roger that, boss. See you at five."

Five minutes later, the young man Pettigrew had seen in the sleeping bag with last night's squeeze appeared at the door, carrying a small backpack. Once Goodwill showed him in and closed the door, Harper explained. "Avi is an artist. He really is one of the best. If Avi can't duplicate it, it can't be done. If you don't mind?"

He extracted the envelope from Pettigrew's hands and handed it to Avi, who scrutinized the green seal. He held the envelope up at eye level, to gauge the thickness of the wax. Then he placed it on the desk and went to work, extracting the tools of his trade from his backpack.

"First," he said as he started to work, "we'll take a putty imprint. Wax has been around for so long, these are really very old techniques. When we're ready, we will transfer the imprint to a rapid-set mold. Next, we simply liberate the envelope from the seal, using just the slightest amount of heat and a razor blade."

Pettigrew blanched as Avi pulled out a portable hair dryer and began to insert a flat razor blade beneath the green wax, rocking it ever so gently back and forth.

"The only real tricky part," he said, is steaming open the envelope. If it's too old, you risk leaving water stains. So we generally apply hot air to dry the moisture that is released at the same time we use the steam."

Within minutes, he had extracted a single sheet of expensive-looking paper, written on the letterhead of a Hong Kong law firm. He smoothed the fold carefully and placed it out flat on Pettigrew's desk, then brought out a small, digital camera from his backpack and climbed up on the desk, kneeling just above the letter to shoot it.

"See, Mr. Pettigrew?" Harper said, extracting an envelope from the hip pocket of his trousers. "That wasn't all that difficult. As promised, your payment."

Pettigrew trembled as Avi started heating the wax he had scraped from the letter. He just held onto the envelope full of money, shaking, unable to open it. "Wh-what about the negatives, Mr. Harper?" he said finally.

The American laughed. "This is the 21st century, Mr. Pettigrew. No one does negatives any more. It's all digital. I could give you the chip that's in the camera. But how do you know I haven't already sent it somewhere else electronically?"

Pettigrew shook his head back and forth, betrayed.

"I'm afraid you're just going to have to trust us. Just as we trust you. Don't you see, Mr. Pettigrew? Isn't that the proper foundation for a sound business relationship? Trust?"

Avi signaled that he was ready to go. As Harper gripped the doorknob, he turned back to face Pettigrew, who was stuffing the envelope full of cash into a drawer. "But if it amuses you, I can always give you these," he said, reaching into Avi's backpack and withdrawing the manila envelope with the pictures he had shown Pettigrew the night before on Jost.

He wagged a finger, as he tossed the envelope onto the desk. "Really, Mr. Pettigrew. At your age!"

2300 hours, Saturday, June 2 – Capetown, South Africa

Crystals of frost were spreading across the bare metal of the gunwales as the *East Wind III* steamed slowly into Capetown harbor. The crewmen on the deck prepared the thick, oily ropes, rubbing their hands to keep warm. It was dark, and the dock was scantly lit at the late hour.

Two black longshoremen were sitting on rusting oil barrels. "Ho! Wake up! Look sharp," one of the crew called down to them. When they didn't move, he threw the leader directly at them. The fellow on the left caught the balled twine with a grin, then the two of them slowly got up and began pulling the heavy rope the sailors heaved over the side, slipping the looped end over the huge iron mooring. Another pair of longshoremen repeated the same procedure at the stern of the ship as the Captain cut the engines and barked orders to the deckhands manning the winches to pull them in.

A pair of crewmen lowered the gangplank and came down to check the ropes. Suddenly, one of them nodded to the other and walked off, ducking between the rows of containers stacked up on the quai side. A moment later, Captain Mahmoud saw the figure – dressed only in a dark blue jogging suit – darting between the containers and the huge loading cranes, heading toward a well-lit area deep inside the port.

"Selim!" he roared, opening the wheelhouse door. "You son of a whore, Selim! Get back here!"

Hearing the Captain's voice, Selim broke into a run. The Captain called down to the deckhands working the bow winches. "Ahmad! Behnam! Go after him!"

The first mate, an Indian Muslim from Capetown, came out of the wheelhouse and put a hand on the Captain's arm. "He'll be back," he said quietly. "He's just cold."

The Captain spun around, his eyes red with anger. "You mean, he told you? And you said nothing?"

"All the Malays are cold," he said. "They are not used to it, and all they have are those jogging suits."

The Captain grunted. "They are forgetting our mission, Ibrahim."

"No, they are not. But the cold spooks them. I sent him to a bar."

The Captain snorted again, this time in contempt. "I am not surprised. You have lived too long among these sons of monkeys and pigs."

"Listen, my brother. We are here to kill Jews," Ibrahim said. "This is our honor, as Muslims. Did not the Prophet, Peace Be Upon Him, say that in the End Days a Jew would hide behind a stone or a tree, and the stone or the tree would say to the Muslim, 'O Muslim, Servant of Allah. A Jew is hiding behind me. Approach and kill him?'"

"Indeed, he did."

"We are all ready to die to accomplish our great task, just as the tree or the stone. But you need also to reward, not just punish."

The Captain pondered this a moment. "So what is it that they want?"

Ibrahim laughed. "Long underwear and heavy sweaters, my friend."

"That's it?"

"Praise Allah."

The two men broke out into raucous laughter, loud and as out of place in the empty night as plastic chairs tossed onto the shore by a flood tide.

"The Americans, they are all Jews," Ibrahim said.

"That they are," the Captain replied. "And soon we will destroy them, God willing."

He rubbed his hands together and slammed shut the metal bulkhead door. "Like Khomeini said, the Americans, they can do nothing."

11

MURDER

2345 hours, Saturday, June 2 – Burtonsville, Maryland

The flashing lights of the police cars sliced through the dark like lasers for some Saturday night party. There was water in the distance; thick foliage; a narrow path along the water, not yet invaded by kudzu and Virginia creeper. By the time Special Agent Michael Brannigan arrived on the scene, it was clear that it was no party – at least, not he kind he would want his kids to attend. Yellow crime scene tape had been stretched everywhere. The paramedics had already arrived and were working on what appeared to be a body.

"Hey, Rex," he said to the ageing Montgomery County police detective, who was jotting down information on a clipboard.

"Brannigan! There you are at last."

The two men had bonded over the past two years during the crack down on the MS-13 gang that was ravaging the Salvadorian community in the

Washington, DC suburbs. They needed no introductions.

"FBI?" said a female officer, visibly sizing him up. Like Brannigan she was around 35, but more compact, and with a full head of reddish-blond hair beneath the police hat. "Rex, you didn't file a 163, did you?"

Form 163 was a formal request from local police to the FBI, seeking their assistance in a capital crime case.

"Filed, no. At least, not yet," he grinned. "But the phones work. I think Special Agent Brannigan can sign the form while we show him the body. Don't you think?"

"Let's play by the rules, Rex. You never know when some freakin' ACLU lawyer is going to mess with us."

Visibly amused, Montgomery County police detective Morgan snorted and turned to Brannigan. "You heard the lady. Got a pen?"

"Sure."

Brannigan worked out of the FBI field office in Calverton, Maryland, just off Interstate 95 and the Washington, DC Capitol Beltway. Officially, he was the Senior Supervisory Resident Agent – SSRA – if anyone his age could be senior at anything. Headquarters had posted him to what traditionally had been a dead-ender of a job after the September 11 attacks, as the FBI beefed up its Joint Terrorism Task Forces in high risk areas around the country. Nothing the FBI wanted him to do was too small or too insignificant, ever since his father had been killed those many years ago. He wanted to be on the ground, to give back. With the nation at war, now was the time.

"What do we have, Rex?"

"I'm going to let Detective Slotnik bring you up to speed."

"Brannigan," the slightly heavy-set woman said, sticking out her hand. It was a statement, introduction, and question all at once. He liked the way her service revolver jutted outwards with the thrust of her hips. There was a hidden sensuality to the way she flicked the reddish-blond hair off her shoulders that he couldn't possibly ignore. The rough sensuality of a wrestler – a *female* wrestler. He covered that thought with a self-deprecating laugh.

"Michael," he replied. "In fact, just Mike."

She gripped his hand hard. "I know. I've heard quite a bit about you, Brannigan."

Before the MS-13 investigation, Brannigan had volunteered to join the forensics team that sifted through the rubble of al Qaeda safe houses in Afghanistan, for evidence relating to the September 11 plot. The FBI involvement in Afghanistan wasn't widely known to the public, but it was legendary within the law enforcement community. Although Brannigan didn't think that way about himself, he was something of a star, and Maryjo Slotnik was going to make him pay for it. He was one of the elite few who had been given the opportunity to take the war on terror into enemy territory.

"OK, this isn't a pretty sight. Are you ready?" She pulled out a surgical mask, fixing it over her nose and mouth. "If you don't have one of these, I suggest you get one."

Brannigan pulled a mask from the pocket of his sports coat, and joined her in pushing through the high grass toward the river.

"A dog-walker phoned it in, after her dog got to the body," Slotnik said.

Brannigan caught his breath involuntarily when she pulled the rubber sheet back from the face, or what was left of it. In the mountains outside Kunduz, well after the first snows turned the dirt roads to mud, he almost had tripped over the decomposing body of an al Qaeda fighter. Half the face had been blown off by a smart bomb. Undisturbed for several weeks after the attack, the maggots had eaten out his eyes and begun to expose the brain. He'd had to instruct the army Major from intelligence how to search the body, then they went over the evidence together, at a distance. At least the girl hadn't yet begun to smell, he thought. The smell was always the worst of it.

Detective Slotnik opened the jaw of the bloated corpse, revealing a perfect set of teeth. "You see our problem? How do we identify the DI? Dental records? Nada. Scars? Tattoos? Believe me, we've looked."

"What was the cause of death?"

"As far as we can tell, broken neck. Maybe a fall – maybe a push. There's a dam not too far upriver from here."

"Off New Hampshire? Brighton dam?" Brannigan said.

He knew the area. It was at the narrow end of the Triadelphia Reservoir, in the upper reaches of Montgomery county, and fed into the sluggish Patuxent River. Brannigan made a note of the black plastic cable ties that bound the girl's wrists. They had used them in

Afghanistan on prisoners. Whoever used them here had applied them expertly. Whether they'd tossed her off the dam or dumped her into the river below, the poor girl never had a chance.

"What do you make of the coat?" he said, pulling the thin black hood back from the girl's hair and neck.

"I guess you haven't been around high schools lately," Slotnik said. "That's the regulation hijab worn by observant Muslim girls. Covers the hair, forehead and ears."

He knew all about hijab, and had to admit that it was beyond his comprehension. He just couldn't figure why any woman in her right mind would willingly cover herself.

"Maybe if you lived around Muslim men, you'd get it," Slotnik said. "Some of the women say they like it. Feel protected."

"She sure looks like she could have used a bit more protection," he said, drawing the hood back over the remains of the girl's face. They stood for a moment in silence, an involuntary prayer.

Suddenly, Brannigan grabbed Detective Slotnik's arm and put a finger to his lips. "Did you hear that?" he whispered.

Slotnik nodded, quietly unfastening the clasp that held her sidearm and drawing it out.

Brannigan pulled the 9 mm Beretta M9 from the shoulder holster beneath his sports jacket, and pointed off into the woods. He mimed to her to head off into the darkness, while he pursued whoever had made the noise closer to the water.

Another sharp *craaack!* deeper in the woods made them change plans, and the two of them ran forward into the darkness, crashing through saplings and knee-high grasses and stumbling over exposed roots, as someone or something ran noisily away from them. The lights the Montgomery County police had set up around the crime scene grew fainter behind them, but they pressed on.

After a few minutes, out of breath, Brannigan touched her arm and signaled her to stop. "Do you hear them?" he whispered.

Instead of answering, she whirled around. Instinctively, Brannigan turned in the opposite direction, the back of his trousers bumping up against the bulky regulation trousers and heavy belt that Slotnik wore. They turned in a circle, guns drawn, facing the darkness, until the unmistakable sound of a car starting brought them to an abrupt halt. Before he could localize where the noise was coming from, Slotnik caught his arm and pointed and the two of them broke into a run, trying to catch up to the car headlights before they disappeared.

"Damn!" he said when they crashed through the last thick wall of undergrowth and stumbled out onto the road. A pair of red tail lights receded quickly ahead of them. "Did you catch the license plate?"

Out of breath, Slotnik shook her head and replaced her firearm. "Only thing I can tell you," she got out. "They were Maryland plates."

Whoever had just fled was no woodsman, Brannigan knew. But why were they watching? What did they want?

1330 hours, Monday, June 4 –
Baltimore, Maryland

Dr. Rajiv Kumar, deputy medical examiner for the State of Maryland, slipped on a fresh pair of green latex gloves and a surgical mask, and pulled the corpse out of the freezer. The wheels on the tray squealed, and he apologized. But it was just a small inconvenience compared to the frequent breakdowns of the freezer system itself, which at times made the morgue unbearable. The entire facility should have been replaced a decade earlier, but it never made it into the Governor's budget until just recently, he explained. Before he pulled the rubber sheet off the corpse, he offered green gloves and masks to Special Agent Brannigan and Lt. Slotnik.

"I think I'll just watch," Brannigan said.

"You'll want the masks, I'm afraid," Dr. Kumar said.

They stepped back instinctively when he pulled back the sheet and hurriedly pulled down the surgical masks.

"The victim is a young female, age 18. 5 foot six, roughly 115 pounds – hard to tell because of the water damage, but that's a reasonable estimate based on bone size and body fat. Cause of death was a traumatic fracture of the cervical vertebrae – a broken neck. The trauma was so severe that it appears to have instantly snapped her spinal cord. We found virtually no water in the lungs."

"So that means she was dead by the time she hit the water," Slotnik said.

"Oh, undoubtedly," said Dr. Kumar. "And she was not in the water for more than two days. With all the heat, the body bloats quickly."

"So the time of death was sometime Thursday?"

"Thursday evening." Dr. Kumar said. "At the earliest, 9 PM. We found heavy contusions on the back of her scalp, on her arms near the elbows, and on her knees." He walked over to a light panel, and put up an x-ray. "If you look here, at the back of her head, it looks as if she hit a rock – "

"– Or someone hit her with a rock," Brannigan said.

"Possibly," said Dr. Kumar. "But she didn't die from those blows. She died from this." He put up another slide, showing a huge dent in the top of her head and the beginnings of what once had been her spine. "The force of the blow to her skull was so intense that it compressed her vertebrae by more than 70% and snapped the spinal cord. The only thing consistent with this type of injury is someone falling on their head from a significant height."

"Tossed off a bridge," Brannigan said, turning to Slotnik. "Sounds like you were right."

Slotnik nodded curtly, acknowledging the compliment. She was used to dealing with macho male law enforcement officers, generally many years older than she was, who thought all a woman was good for was rearing children and shedding tears. That was why she always wore her service revolver and uniform. But Brannigan wasn't the typical g-man. She could see the wheels turning as he listened, calculated, dissected, compared. *Who are you, Michael Brannigan?* she wondered.

"We found a few other things as well," Dr. Kumar said.

Covering up the girl's head, he leaned over her body to them. "There were traces of the sedative Ambien in her stomach. Certainly not enough to kill her; but enough to put her to sleep. We also found traces of pistachio nuts."

"Pistachio nuts?' Slotnik said.

"That was the last thing she ate, still undigested."

"So maybe she was at a party."

"I doubt that, Agent Brannigan. You know, Muslim girls would not likely go out by themselves. Except – she was no ordinary Muslim girl."

"What do you mean?"

"We also ran gynecological tests. It's standard procedure, to determine if the victim was raped."

"And?" Slotnik said.

"No rape. But she was three months pregnant."

Dr. Kumar sighed. "You know, detective, in parts of my country we tolerate certain practices by the Muslims that any normal person would find – well, frankly inhuman. They call it honor killing. When a girl, such as this one, dishonors her family before marriage, the family elders can condemn her to death. The authorities know all about it, but in most cases they are helpless because no witnesses ever come forward. I hope that's not what we're seeing here. I would have thought Muslims in this country would be coming here precisely to get away from that kind of – barbarity!"

Brannigan just nodded, seeming to take in this information with the same studied objectivity he had absorbed the other details of the case. But this was truly momentous, Slotnik knew. If Dr. Kumar was right, this was no ordinary murder. And that meant she'd be spending a lot more time with Agent Brannigan.

Maryjo Slotnik allowed herself to indulge that thought just an instant too long, and noticed that Brannigan was expecting her to say something. After all, it was her case.

"Well, duh," she said, shaking her head good-naturedly. "Doctor, can you put those x-rays of the skull onto a CD for me?" Turning to Brannigan: "Let's go on over to your shop. I want you to show me that fancy software Rex has been telling me about."

He had caught her hesitation. He knew she was interested. *Damn!*

1500 hours, Monday, June 4 – FBI regional office, Calverton, MD

The FBI office in Calverton, Maryland was not much to look at. At full staffing, Brannigan had three junior Special Agents working under him. But with Homeland Security focusing on Washington, DC, and the port of Baltimore, they had temporarily downsized, and one of the grey government issue metal desks was littered with soda cans, newspapers, and a pair of jogging shoes.

"Paige, we need your help," Brannigan said as they went over to the large computer screen in a corner of the main office. "This is Montgomery County Police detective Lt. Maryjo Slotnik. She needs you to run a facial on a victim."

"Whatever," replied a young, blond-headed man, tossing down the computer magazine he had been reading. His boredom was feigned, Slotnik saw. His entire existence was pegged to Brannigan's commands. That was one thing about him: without any ostentation or self-importance, he commanded respect, drawing others into the vital world of Michael Brannigan.

"This is the latest whiz-bang production from the geniuses down at Quantico," Paige said, scuttling over to the computer in his wheeled desk chair. "Digital Facial Ageing Simulation – Dee-FAS, for government types. It was brand new around 25-years ago. We got it this year. So what do you got for me?" He clicked on the eject key to open the CD drive and held out the other hand. Slotnik handed him the first CD.

"These are the crime scene photos. The victim was bloated from prolonged exposure to water. And part of the face is missing."

"Ouch!" said Paige, when the picture of the girl came onto his screen. "Who did that?"

"We think it was the dog. The lady who found the body was all upset. Some kind of scientist at the Department of Energy. Said she had to tear the dog away from it."

She cringed slightly as she heard the words come out. There she went, telling the emotional side. Had he noticed? But no, she was over-reacting. *Be professional. Stick to the facts.*

"That's got to be Danny's wife," Brannigan said.

"Who's Danny?" Slotnik said.

"Long story. Buddy of mine from the dark side," he said.

Paige selected the best of the pictures, giving a straight frontal view of what remained of the face, then entered it into the DFAS program. "Anything else?"

"Yes," Slotnik said. "We got these today from the morgue. Head X-rays."

"That'll help," Paige said. "The software will compare the flesh to the bone structure and then let you play with the portrait. You plug in height, weight, age, whatever – and it does the rest."

As they watched, he superimposed the bloated crime scene photo onto the x-ray, and began plugging in the figures Slotnik read off to him. In less than a minute, the face lost its bloating, the missing cheek reappeared, and matted hair took on a more normal appearance. Out of death, a living face began to emerge, stunningly vivid. Slotnik let out an involuntary gasp. "You'd think she could talk," she said.

"Let's hope she does," Brannigan said. "Paige, why don't you give us a few versions of the girl. Bring her weight down to, say, 105 pounds; and then up to around 130. Let's see what happens." Paige made the manipulations and they watched as the girl's face shrank around the bone structure, and then filled out. Although the differences were significant, there could be no doubt they were looking at the same girl.

Clearly, Brannigan had already made up his mind, but he was waiting on her. Slotnik set her wonder aside. She knew her instincts were right.

"I say we stick with the one in the middle," she said. "If anything, at three months pregnant, she'll be losing weight, not gaining it."

"Good point," Brannigan said.

The printer slowly inked the pictures, line by line. In five minutes, they had three slightly different views. "Thanks, Paige," Brannigan said, handing the last of them to Slotnik to wave dry. "That gives us something to work with."

Honor killings. She had read about that somewhere. Wasn't it in Sweden, some family from the Middle East, sending the girl back home to a cave to marry an old goat? When the girl refused, the father and the uncles held some kind of tribal council and then murdered her. Just the thought of it made her angry. *Barbaric!*

"I'll check the Teenage Pregnancy Hotline centers in Rockville and Olney," Slotnik said. "I'm sure Rex will give me backup so we can send teams to all the local high schools tomorrow morning. What with graduation, there's not going to be a lot of folks hanging around. Maybe we'll get the principals or the guidance counselors."

"I'll check central records to see if we've got any ongoing cases involving American Muslims in this area," Brannigan said. "Let's call each other in the morning."

"Roger that."

1600 hours, Tuesday, June 5 – James Hubert Blake HS, Silver Spring, MD

There were twenty-four public high schools in Montgomery county, and most of them had two thousand students each. It was a gigantic school system stretched across a suburban area that covered more than 500 square miles. Each year, the graduating class averaged 11,000 students. Even with the photographs, they were betting on a prayer and a chance that someone, somewhere remembered the girl.

Brannigan and Slotnik had been running down the schools in the northeastern quadrant of the county since morning, and by 4 PM they were ready to call it quits. It was early summer in Maryland and so hot the air conditioner in the Crown Victoria police cruiser struggled to keep up.

"My kids ought to be home from school by now," Brannigan said. "I told my wife last night that I'd take them to the pool."

Here comes the stiff arm, she thought. *Keep it casual. Don't react.* It was always that way when someone interesting came along. Either they were gay, or they were married.

"So where do you live?"

"Just outside of Laurel, in Anne Arundel county."

"Saves you Prince George's county schools."

"Amen to that."

They were sitting in the parking lot of Springbrook high school, just off of New Hampshire avenue. Brannigan seemed far away, lost in thought. Was it the children, or something else?

"We've got one more to go," Slotnik said. "Hey, it's almost on your way home. Just a straight pop up New Hampshire."

"If you say so."

Detective Slotnik hit 70 mph in her police cruiser up the four-lane divided highway, then popped on her siren at the intersection of Norwood road and spun expertly left on the red light. It took them just three and a half-minutes to reach the turnoff to James Hubert Blake High school. She slowed to 15 mph and they glided down the long driveway into the woods.

Blake was one of the most recent schools the county had built to accommodate the huge influx of high-tech workers and the immigrants who served them in recent years. The sprawling low buildings stretched tastefully across a clearing with views onto the fields beyond. As they walked across the parking lot to the main entry, she pointed out the brand new science lab with its black countertops, and the computer lab with huge 22 inch graphics terminals.

"Not bad if you were brought up in a village with no running water, don't you think?"

"No kidding," Brannigan agreed.

They found the principal standing in the glass-walled office, talking to a member of his staff. Slotnik and Brannigan showed their badges and introduced themselves.

"Alton Jones," he said. "Is there something I can help you with?"

"We're hoping so. Do you recognize this girl as one of your students?" Slotnik said, handing over the photograph.

Jones gave the photograph a quick glance, then scrutinized his two visitors skeptically. "Does this have something to do with her family? Are they trying to get her in trouble?"

"Why? Has that happened before?" Brannigan said.

"Look," Jones said. "Salima is a good girl and she's going to do just fine at College Park this fall. Her parents are trying to send her back to Pakistan."

"I don't think you have to worry about that any more, Mr. Jones," Slotnik said. "We found her body over the weekend. She's dead."

Jones shook his head and sighed. "Why am I not surprised?"

"What do you mean?" Brannigan asked.

"Look, let me get you her file and you can see for yourself. It's the family profile."

1700 hours, Tuesday, June 5 – Khan residence, Silver Spring, MD

The Khan's home on Bryant's Nursery Road was a modest brick rambler, overlooking a broad field that sloped down to a wooded stream in the distance. The multi-acre plot was unusual for the suburbs, but had once been the norm in this pocket of the county. For Sale signs were up all over the place as home-owners sought to cash in on the skyrocketing land prices now that the long-delayed Inter-county connector was finally being built just beyond the stream.

Mrs. Mahnaz Khan was only 44 years old, according to the information the school principal had given them, but Slotnik thought she looked at least fifteen years older. She was barefoot, and wore a dingy beige head scarf over a baggy black dress. Her dark face was heavily wrinkled and her feet were gnarled. She looked like a gnome, some kind of throw-back to a more primitive era, long before electricity and flush toilets. When they showed her their badges she waved her hand rapidly back and forth. "No Ingleesh! No Ingleesh!" she shouted. When that didn't make them go away, she called out to someone behind her, "Hani!" careful that her bulk blocked entry to the house.

A teenage boy appeared from the shadows, taking his place next to his mother in the open doorway. He was tall and lanky, but with soft brown eyes and a delicate nose. Slotnik exchanged a glance with Brannigan and could see he was thinking exactly the same thing. The resemblance was striking. There was no doubt that this boy was the dead girl's brother.

"I'm Hanif," the boy said. "Mom can't speak English very well. What can we do for you? You can call me Hank."

"We need to come inside for a moment, Hani," said Brannigan. "It's about your sister."

When the boy translated, the mother let out a cry and brought her two hands up to her head, saying "Allah! Allah!" Whether it was a prayer or a curse was hard to tell. They followed her into a small breakfast alcove, overlooking the huge grassy field below the house. A bowl of pistachios was in the center of the table. An open, American-style kitchen was just behind them, smelling strongly of dead meat, and they could see deeper into the house to a living room area beyond.

"When was the last time you saw Salima, Mrs. Khan?" Slotnik asked, once they were all seated.

Hani didn't even bother to translate. "A few days after graduation."

"So why didn't anybody report her missing?" Brannigan asked.

Hani lowered his head. "We were ashamed," he said. His mother tugged as his arm, and he hastily said a few words in Pashto.

"Mom thinks Salima went with the Devil. She thinks he brought evil to this house."

"Is that what you think, Hank?" said Slotnik, leaning toward him across the table, seeking him out with her eyes.

The young man lowered his gaze a second time. But was it shame, fear, or secret guilt? There was something soft about the young man that she liked. Curious thing was, he showed no grief. None of them showed any grief.

"I figured she went down to Ocean City for beach week with Scooter and his friends," he said quietly.

The mother grabbed his arm again, clearly upset to hear the name.

"Who's Scooter," Brannigan asked.

"Mom doesn't like him," Hani said.

"Yeah, we kind of figured that," said Slotnik.

Brannigan shot her a glance that told her to back off. Did he have a better understanding than she had thought of these people? It was clear they were hiding something, yet Brannigan was treating them with kid gloves.

"Scooter was dating Salima, but nobody wanted to admit it. Mom said he was sent by the Devil."

"But you don't think that," said Slotnik.

"Hey, I was born in this country, okay?" said Hani. "I'm a good Muslim, I pray, but I don't believe in all this bullshit. Mom comes from a village near the

Afghan border in Pakistan. They won't let you do anything there. You wouldn't believe it."

Brannigan nodded as if he had no trouble at all in believing it.

"So," she pressed on. "The person Salima was dating. His real name is – "

"Scott. Scott Glazer. He lives off Georgia Avenue near Leisure World."

"Do you have an address?"

"No... But he was in her high school class," he added quickly. "They ought to have it."

"Did you know him well?"

"Are you kidding? I'm just a freshman. They wouldn't hang out with me."

"What is this?" said a voice behind them. "What are the police – "

"Dad!" said Hani.

Brannigan got up and nodded to acknowledge him. When Slotnik started to extend her hand, he caught it before it left her side and moved forward slightly. But it wasn't a macho thing, she realized. It was something else.

"Mr. Khan?" Brannigan said, showing his badge.

"Yes… Is something the matter?"

He put down a heavy, old-fashioned briefcase on the breakfast room table. It was the kind that was made before laptop computers were invented, to carry everything from a cheap novel, lunch, to the occasional work paper. It was Faizul Khan's badge of belonging, his ticket to the workaday world of middle-class America. He wore a loosened tie over his sweat-stained white shirt, but no suit jacket. He screwed his head to one side, scrutinizing his visitors without saying a word, as if he could divine their thoughts. Then he said something quickly in Pashto to his son.

"Baba, they don't want anything to drink. They are here on business."

"But you must be polite."

"Mr. Khan," said Brannigan. "Please sit down. We appreciate your offer of hospitality, but we have something serious and urgent to tell you."

Without further protest, Faizul Khan slumped into a chair, grabbed his head in his hands, and began to sob quietly. His wife knocked his elbows off the table with an angry chop and a few muttered words in Pashto that needed no interpreting. She was angry at his show of emotion.

"We've found your daughter," Detective Slotnik said gently. "She's been murdered. In fact, we found her body not too far from here, in the Patuxent River. We are going to need your help, Mr. Khan, if we are going to find the people who did this."

"Had she been – violated?" Faizul Khan asked finally, looking up at them with red eyes.

"Not that the medical examiner could find."

"The mercy of Allah is great," he said quietly. Then he hid his face in his hands again, shuddering imperceptibly, trying to get a grip on himself.

"You know, Detective, why I brought my family to this country?" he said finally. "It was so we could get away from this kind of thing."

Brannigan nodded sympathetically, but Slotnik wanted to hear him explain more thoroughly. Did he know about the honor killings? Was this something that really happened in our day and age? Was it possible for it to happen here, in America? "What kind of thing?" she asked.

Faizul Khan shrugged. "You know, the clans. They have some very bigoted ideas. I wanted everything for Salima. She was going to go to College in September here in Maryland. We brought her up as a good Muslim. She prayed. She observed Ramadan. She gave money to the mosque. They wanted her to go back to Pakistan to marry."

His wife kicked him under the table, clearly unhappy to hear him talking to the police. Slotnik was less certain than she had been earlier of the woman's lack of English. She seemed to be following what her husband was saying quite well.

"Mr. Khan, would you mind showing me Salima's room?" Slotnik asked. "Maybe Hank – Hani - can stay down here with your wife, while Special Agent Brannigan asks her a few more questions." Brannigan shot her another warning glance, but this time she ignored him. No man, not even a Muslim, wanted a strange man to see his daughter's room, so it had to be her. And there was no way she was going upstairs with the gnome in the black bag. She got up, and Mr. Khan led her upstairs without protest.

The girl's room was extraordinarily neat, but otherwise looked like any teenager's room, with a bookcase, a desk, posed pictures of her smiling with her girlfriends on the wall, and CD-s with American rap music by a small stereo. Only one thing stood out: a large, color poster of a mosque with a golden dome, set in what looked like an immense, peaceful park up on a hill.

"What's the mosque?" Slotnik asked.

"That's al Aqsa in Jerusalem," Faizul Khan said. "It was a present from one of her uncles."

"On your side, or your wife's?"

"Oh, hers. My only brother lives in California and couldn't care less about Islam."

"We're going to need names and addresses for your wife's brothers here in the States. Are there any other relatives?"

"Not here, no. Just Sayeed, and Fayez. They ought to be home any minute."

"Your other sons?"

"That's right."

They had arrived by the time Slotnik came down with Faizul Khan, and seemed as Americanized as their young brother. Sayeed, the oldest, wore a dark business suit, well-cut, and carried a slim attaché case. He was an accountant, like his father, but was broader in the chest, as if he lifted weights. Fayez, 22, was two years his junior and had just picked Sayeed up from the bus that brought him home from his job in downtown Washington, DC. Fayez had just graduated from the University of Maryland - College Park and was looking for a job as a mechanical engineer. Unlike Sayeed, who was clean-shaven and could have passed for a Hispanic, he wore a pencil thin moustache and had finer traits that belied his South Asian origin.

"So who is the sailor?" Brannigan asked, seeing a sailing magazine on the kitchen counter.

"That's Sam," said Fayez. "He's down in southern Maryland almost every weekend, now that the weather has turned nice."

He was obviously proud of his older brother, but Sayeed did not appear pleased. "Don't exaggerate," he said.

"No way! You won the St. Mary's regatta last weekend down at Solomon's with uncle Manny!"

Brannigan was about to ask something when Slotnik stood up. "I think that's all for now, thank-you," she said. "We'll certainly be back in touch with you in a few days, if not sooner. In the meantime, if you think of anything that might help, please give me or Special Agent Brannigan a call."

Out in the car, Brannigan asked her why she had cut him off from asking about the uncle. "Gee, I guess you didn't get that, Agent Brannigan," she dead-panned.

"I guess I didn't. I was more worried about you humping into the bedroom with Dad."

She flushed slightly, not quite sure whether it was a compliment or just a guy thing. "The uncle's our next stop. Owns Manny's Gas and Oil, right out on New Hampshire avenue by the Korean church. His real name is Manijeh."

"My wife's going to be thrilled that I'm missing the swimming pool," Brannigan said, pulling out his cell phone. "But hey – that's why I took this job," he grinned.

Clearly, Brannigan liked the hunt. And the hunt was on.

1800 hours, Tuesday, June 5 – Manny's Gas and Oil, New Hampshire Avenue

Manijeh Dal owned a Crown station by a strip mall, and emerged from beneath a car on the lift in tan-colored overalls with hardly a speck of grease on them. The garage had three bays in front, facing New Hampshire avenue and the far end of Bryant's Nursery Road, and a drive-through bay around the back that he used for oil changes. All three front bays were occupied when Slotnik and Brannigan got there at 6 PM. It was over 95 degrees and the garage was not air-conditioned.

When she caught sight of him, Detective Slotnik closed her eyes for just a half second, trying to blink away the recollection that had never dimmed despite all the years that had passed. How old had she been? Eight years old? Ten? It was well before Tito's death and the former Yugoslavia was still a central, Serb-dominated state, but the Muslims were already on the rise. And attempting to assassinate their Serb masters. Manijeh looked just like the man who had broken into their house and tried to kill her father, before the bodyguards shot him dead before her terrified young eyes.

"Looks like you've got a thriving business, Mr. Dal," said Brannigan, dabbing at the sweat on his forehead with a handkerchief. "Mind if we ask you a few questions?"

"What's this about?" the short mechanic asked.

"Your niece, Salima."

"The one that just graduated? Has she gotten in trouble with that idiot football player she was seeing?"

"That's what we're trying to find out. She was found dead over the weekend."

He looked them over, wiping his hands carefully on a paper towel, and asked them to come into his office. Slotnik repressed the feeling of repulsion that had overcome her. *Be professional. Use the uniform.* Once again, she was struck by the lack of shock, sorrow, or remorse. *Salima's dead? Oh, okay. Pass the sugar, won't you?* It all seemed about the same.

The back office was little more than two battered steel desk chairs, half a desk, a telephone, a coffeemaker and a hotplate. But a window air conditioner provided some relief from the damp heat outside. Slotnik chose to stand against the wall, while the two men sat down.

"I warned Faizul about that boy," Manijeh said, shaking his head. "I told him, no good can come of this. But he wouldn't listen to me. He said, we're in America now, so we have to behave like Americans. But tell me, Detective: who is American here these days? I am just as much an American as you are! So why shouldn't I behave like myself?"

"I see your point," Brannigan said, noncommittally. "So how did you tell Faizul he should behave?"

"I told Faizul, look. You cannot allow your daughter to go out alone with this young man. At the very least, she should have another girl with her. Preferably a man from her own family."

"And he ignored you?"

"That's right."

"What about her getting married in Pakistan?"

Slotnik thought that Manijeh shook his head ever so slightly, but then covered his surprise. She felt like she could read him already.

"Oh that. That was my sister's idea. She sometimes has crazy ideas, you know. She'd found a boy near Peshawar from a good family we have known since we were children. I never thought anything would come of it."

Brannigan placed a card on the desk and got up. "Give us a call if you hear anything we might need."

"Have you talked to that idiot boy?"

"Scooter?"

"That's where you need to start!"

"I'll remember that. Thank-you," Brannigan said.

Out in the car, she suggested they make the three-hour drive down to Ocean City the next morning at 7 AM. They had to get a break in this case. So far, they didn't even have a solid lead.

"These kids are partying. Make it 9," he said. "No one's going to be up before noon."

Brannigan looked pensive. Something was bothering him. Too much white bread, the Serb in her thought. She repressed a laugh at the thought of it: Michael Brannigan, Irish Catholic, brought up on PBJs, communion wafers, boiled oatmeal and skim milk. Not the tough dry sausages and red wines of her childhood, wine so thick a fork would stand up in your glass, her father said.

"Come on, Brannigan. Get over it," she said, chucking him on the shoulder.

"Over what?"

"Hanif, Sayeed, Manijeh. You know. We're no longer a nation of Donahues and Wilsons and George Washingtons. We're a real melting pot now. Hell, my Dad was killing Muslims back in Bosnia just twenty years ago. Today, they are good next door neighbors."

He gave her a skeptical look. "You betray yourself, Slotnik."

"Maryjo, remember?"

"Sure. Maryjo."

"I was brought up on this crap. Dad, the baby-killer and all that. But the world has changed. We've moved on."

"Has it really?" said Brannigan.

"I'm sure they're just fine upstanding citizens. Aren't you?"

Brannigan sank back against the head rest and closed his eyes for a long moment, traveling off to some distant world. When he opened his eyes and stared at her, she felt her stomach tighten with the sudden intensity of his gaze.

"Do you have any idea what the medical examiner was talking about back there?" he said. "Honor killings?"

She shrugged. "I think I've read something about it."

"Well let me paint you a picture."

And that's when he told her about Afghanistan. He told her about the tribes, their willingness to die for a friend, the ease with which they took blood and accepted death. He told her of the ferocity with which they defended their honor, willing to wait fifty years to exact revenge for a slight carried out by someone long dead, as if it had just happened yesterday. It was a crude, brutal world, hard to imagine back home in America, a world he never would have thought still existed.

After they had found the body and the laptop computer at the safe house, a woman in a stunningly beautiful indigo-blue hijab tried to approach them, bearing a plastic bag, motioning to them to eat. When the sentries approached, she blew herself up. Just like that. One minute alive, beckoning to eat, then nothing but a flash of light and a ear-numbing blast. It was her kinsman they had found, and she had come to reclaim him. An eye for an eye.

Brannigan never actually saw her blow up, because just a split second before she reached beneath her hijab to push the button the Army Major who accompanied him blew out his legs in a football tackle, throwing him hard against a rock and covering him with his own body. When he picked himself up, he quickly realized that the bits of white, bloodied flesh that covered his jacket were not his own. If it hadn't been for Danny Wilkens, he would have been dead.

The two of them might think that Montgomery County, Maryland was still in America, Brannigan said. But to Manijeh Dal and his family, they could just as well be in the no-man's land controlled by the tribes.

"Peshawar, where they come from, is in the North-west Frontier Province," he said. "We always knew it as the wild, wild East."

After a pause, he gave her a look that almost scared her. "That's what we're dealing with here."

1200 hours, Wednesday, June 6 – Ocean City, Maryland

It was beach week in Ocean City, when graduating seniors from virtually every high school in Maryland took over the town for a week-long orgy of liberation. The parties began in late afternoon and lasted into early morning, with stragglers singing beneath the boardwalk at sunrise. By the time Brannigan and Slotnik arrived, the streets were virtually empty. The bars were just opening to serve coffee and scrambled eggs.

They found the small beach house on a sand-strewn street that dead-ended into the boardwalk. The front door was shaded by a screened-in porch directly above. All of the houses had second-floor party rooms, and dark shapes in sleeping bags began moving up and down the street when they saw Maryjo Slotnik in her tan police uniform and stiff-rimmed hat get out of the unmarked FBI Mercury Grand Marquis. They could hear bare feet scurrying overhead as they waited for someone to come to the door.

They knocked a second time, and a sun-burned teenager in boxer shorts and tousled blonde hair finally opened the screen door, rubbing his eyes in the sun. They were beginning to work well as a team, Slotnik thought.

"Are you Scooter?" Brannigan said. "Scott Glazier?"

"Yah, that's me," he said. He stepped outside the screen door and let it fall shut behind him. "What's up?"

"Where's your girlfriend, Scooter? Where's Salima?" Maryjo said icily.

"Hey," he stage-whispered, glancing behind him. "She's not my girlfriend, okay? She and I broke up weeks ago."

"Anybody tell you she was pregnant, Scooter?"

"Huh?"

"You heard me," Slotnik said. "You want me to say it louder?"

"No no, okay, I get it," he said.

"Well?"

"I guess not. Look, Salima was having a hard time at home. She couldn't handle it, okay? She just wasn't cool."

"She's cool now, Scooter," said Brannigan.

"She's dead," Slotnik added.

The boy's astonishment seemed real to both of them, so they backed off a bit. "We'd like to talk to you about Salima, Scooter," Brannigan said quietly.

"Look. Can't we go someplace else? I mean, you can't come in here, can you?"

"Calm down," Brannigan said. "Go inside, put on some clothes, and we'll take you out for breakfast. How's that?"

"Okay, thanks."

He turned to Slotnik after the boy went inside and shrugged. "No point in freaking him out. Not yet, at least."

Brannigan parked in front of the Ocean Spot café, across the main street from one of the bars that was beginning to come back to life. He buttoned his sports jacket as he got out of the car so it covered the 9mm Beretta he carried in the shoulder holster. "Your choice," he said, pointing in either direction.

"Here is fine," Scooter said, still nervous.

The Ocean Spot was a family dinner and was virtually empty at the noon hour. They squeezed into a booth in the back. Scooter ordered scrambled eggs and bacon and orange juice. Brannigan and Slotnik got roast beef sandwiches.

"So when was the last time you saw Salima?" Brannigan asked, once the food arrived.

"Last Tuesday. Graduation," Scooter said. "But we weren't seeing each other by that point. It was just, hello, how are you. Her brothers hated me."

"So did the mom, from what I gather," said Slotnik.

"I never met the mom," Scooter said. "From what Salima said, she sounded like a real witch."

"You'd better eat some," Brannigan said. "It's getting cold."

"Yeah, okay."

They ate for a minute in silence, then Brannigan wiped his mouth on his napkin.

"So where were you last Thursday, Scooter?" he asked.

"Thursday? That's when we drove down here. In the morning."

Slotnik moved closer. "You say Salima never told you she was pregnant. But did you know?"

"No!" he said, alarmed.

"You didn't guess?" She'd known boys like this when she was younger, and didn't even try to hide her scorn.

"How do you want me to guess? She's a girl," Scooter said. "I mean, she didn't talk about it, that's all."

"How did it happen?" Brannigan asked.

"At a friend's house, in the basement," the boy said, avoiding their eyes. "We were at a party. They had a separate bedroom around the corner from the main room. We kind of went in there in turns. But she wanted it! Look, I didn't rape her, if that's what you mean."

"How long ago was that?"

"A month ago? Maybe six weeks?"

"Was she a virgin?"

"How should I know?" said Scooter.

Slotnik started to roll her eyes, but caught herself before the boy could catch her contempt. "So when did you break up?" she asked.

"About two weeks ago," Scooter said. "Before finals. She said she had to study to keep up her grades."

Brannigan wanted to try another tack. "Did Salima ever sound afraid to you, Scooter?" he asked.

"Yah, actually. Now that you mention it. She said her uncles would kill her if they ever found out about us."

1145 hours, Saturday, June 9 –
Burbank, CA

Danny loved to fly into Burbank. It was a small airport, north of Los Angeles, just beyond the Hollywood hills, and the approach through the valley hugging the ridgeline was spectacular. In the distance, as they came down, the sun made the Pacific sparkle. Beneath them, rows of palm trees quivered in the ocean breeze. And all without the traffic jams of LAX.

It was hot and muggy when he saw Manoo waiting for him by the baggage carousel. They hugged each other briefly, in Persian fashion, and Danny clapped him on the back. "You didn't have to come pick me up," he said. "But hey – it's great to see you again so soon."

"Anything for you, my friend," Manoo said.

Manoucher Amir was in his early forties and had a slight paunch and a great bald spot at the crown of his head, which he normally covered with a yachting cap. But today, in the heat, he went bare-headed. Was it just California, or was everyone here just trying to look like a movie star? Danny wondered. Manoo was wearing ridiculous sun-glasses that covered half his face. They were so polished that Danny could count the bricks in the parking garage mirrored in them. He could also see the dark Mercedes 320 Kompressor sports sedan with dark-tinted windows, parked halfway up on the sidewalk.

Manoo's ice-grey Lincoln Aviator SUV beeped and flashed its lights, and Manoo pointed for him to get in. It was an easy 30-minute drive out to Woodland Hills along the 101.

They had just crossed the 405 when Manoo hit the gas and abruptly cut across two lanes of traffic into the HOV lane. Even with his eyes invisible behind the sunglasses, Danny saw the muscles in his cheek contract as he gave a quick look into the rear-view mirror.

"What do we got?" Danny asked.

"Looks like that Mercedes from back at the parking garage."

Danny adjusted his side view mirror so he could see what was going on behind them, just as Manoo squeezed in between a truck and a delivery van. He saw his opening and cut abruptly into the right hand lane and hit the gas. Danny watched the speedometer jerk back and forth as Manoo braked and lurched forward. They peaked well over 85 mph.

"Do you mind if I readjust the mirror?" Manoo said calmly.

Danny laughed nervously. "Sorry."

"This is going to take a bit longer than planned."

Danny turned around and watched openly now as the black Mercedes tried to nudge its way out from between cars to follow them. Manoo slalomed around cars, shifting lanes liberally, and the black Mercedes fell behind, flashing its lights at a car that refused to move out of the way. Then Manoo pulled in front of white, slow-moving Volvo 18-wheeler and parked himself just to the right of it and slowed down, until the traffic caught up and blocked the lane behind him. In another moment, he nodded up ahead as the black Mercedes sped past them, swerving wildly between lanes in pursuit of the phantom Lincoln.

"And now we double-back," Manoo said. "We should have gotten off two exits back. We'll take the surface streets from here to the office."

When they pulled up at the strip mall where Manoo had his office ten minutes later, the Mercedes was long gone.

"This happen often?" Danny asked.

Manoo shrugged. "Regime agents. It's never the same ones. We phone in the license plates to the FBI all the time, but nothing ever comes of it. Just their way of letting us know they're watching."

Danny surveyed the parking lot warily.

"Don't worry, they won't come here," Manoo laughed. "We're too much out in the open. It's the best place to hide."

They went up an outside staircase made of weathered cedar wood and black glass, and Danny marveled at the airiness of the structure. East coast born and bred, from the armpit of northern New Jersey, he loved coming to California. La-la-Land the folks at Newsmax called it. The Left Coast. Nevertheless, it was home to nearly one million Iranians, most of whom fled Iran for their lives in the frantic weeks and months after the Shah fell so many years ago.

And home to Aryana.

He tried to steel himself as Manoo opened the door ahead of him. This was all business, after all. But the smell of her perfume blasted his resolve and her presence swept over him like salt water. It had been years since he had seen her. It had been days. *No, minutes,* he thought. There she was, leaning down over him as he drifted in and out of consciousness, his arm half-torn off, her dark hair falling over him, her full lips moving and tears streaming from those dark eyes.

"You met the watchers, I gather," a voice said from behind him.

He turned abruptly, angry with himself that she had managed to sneak up on him unobserved. But when he saw her, his jaw hung open and he just stared at her, stupid and speechless.

"Nice to see you, too," she smiled mockingly, thrusting out her hip and striking a pose. She pecked him on both cheeks. "Come on, Danny boy. We have work to do."

She took him into the computer room, and for an instant Danny thought he was back at Bolling. A plasma TV covered the far wall, which she commanded from a remote. Danny and Manoo took seats in comfortable leather swivel chairs, as Aryana stood before them, running the show.

His mind told him it was all vital information. She had done her own analysis of the photos from her source in Iran, and had tracked the mini-sub to a Rev. Guards naval production facility hundreds of miles in the interior, fronting a large lake, where the Iranian regime believed no one would suspect them of making submarines. One of her agents had a brother-in-law who worked at the facility and had provided the National Freedom Party with complete drawings of the main buildings, and schematics of major projects. The mini-sub that had been loaded onto the *East Wind III* was based on a North Korean design, she said, itself copied from an Italian company that had gone bankrupt years ago.

Danny heard the words, but he found himself drifting off. The white silk shirt she wore was stunning, unbuttoned just enough to reveal the beginning of her cleavage, but not enough to be more than suggestive. She must have followed his eyes because at one point she coughed, and tapped the remote against the back of his chair.

"Sorry. The jetlag," he said lamely.

She arched her back and continued, but it only made things worse. He found himself focusing on the contours of her breasts beneath the silk until he actually had to shake himself awake. *What's the matter with me,* he wondered. But he knew exactly what was the matter. Good thing Manoo was there, he thought. He was a happily-married man.

"We think the mystery man is Hajj Imad," she was saying. "Danny?"

Then it hit him. "Hajj Imad?"

"The one and only. And our sources tell us he is the Rev. Guards' chief liaison to the al Qaeda networks."

That opened up a whole new universe. Egyptians, Lebanese, Saudis, Pakistanis – hell, even Palestinians. Not just Persians, who would be easier to trace. How many Arabs, Pakistanis, even Indian Muslims were in the United States who had been through the al Qaeda camps? He shuddered just to think of it. Thousands, at least. And no one had a clue who they were. They could have set up shop years ago, running legitimate businesses, blending into the community. Sleeper cells, just waiting for the call.

"No one is going to believe that," he said. "I'm going to need more."

"As much as you want," she said. "Just say when."

Danny groaned inwardly and wanted to shout, *When!* Instead, he just shook his head. "It's going to be a tough sell. You know that."

"So. Are you going to invite me to Washington, if I make myself presentable?"

If you only knew, he thought.

But of course, she did.

1000 hours, Sunday, June 10 – Tel Aviv, Israel

Nathaniel Charles and Brian Porter left their driver on the street at David's Gate rather than take the car through the laborious security procedures at the official entrance to the Kirya around the corner. Although Porter was the Legal Attaché at the U.S. embassy in Tel Aviv, the local FBI liaison, Charles had set up the meeting with Israel Tan directly.

When Porter opened his jacket to reveal his service revolver, the young woman at the security desk waved them around the metal detector with a smile. "I've never figured out how you do this, Mr. Charles. But I am impressed," he said.

"You've got to actually like people, Brian. Not just *deal* with them."

Nate Charles had grown up with the gospel that for generations had formed the soul cement between American blacks and a mythical nation of Israel, yearning to escape from bondage. But he had never visited Israel itself or even been curious about the country until after the September 11 attacks when he was contacted by the Jewish Institute for National Security and Economic Concerns, JINSEC, to learn how the Israelis were fighting the war on terrorism. At one of those briefings, he met Israel Tan. When the older Israeli invited him to his home in Herzliya, just outside of Tel Aviv, Nate Charles accepted, astonished and pleased by the honor. The two became fast friends and had visited each other's homes several times a year ever since. Through their friendship, they also established a secret backchannel for information neither government was usually willing to share with the other.

Israel Tan and Zvi Reuben were waiting for them upstairs, along with a young man Nate Charles did not know.

"Well, well, my old friend," Israel Tan began, his arms outstretched to welcome the American with a hug. "I cannot let you come to Israel without offering you some of our good Turkish coffee. It's good for your blood pressure."

"I wouldn't miss it for the world."

"I've asked a colleague to join us today, Jacob Ginzburg. I think he will be able to answer many of your questions."

'Jacob Ginzburg' turned out to be Scott Harper, although Nate Charles wouldn't have recognized either name. There were a lot of other names Ginzburg had used as a Mossad case officer, or *katsa,* that Nate wouldn't have recognized, either.

"We've been tracking a ship by the name of *East Wind III.* I'm sure you must know about it by now," Charles said.

Tan nodded, his lips pursed in scarcely concealed amusement. "It has a dozen Irani containers on board," he said. "The contents of one of them has been dissimulated, kept off the cargo manifest."

"I figured you'd already be on it," Charles said. Every time he came to meet with Israel Tan, he found yet more reasons to be impressed with his new friend. He was always one step ahead of him, smiling, patient, waiting for the dull-witted American to catch up. "We believe that container is carrying a mini-submarine," Charles said. "We don't know what their plan is. We don't know where it's going. And as long as it's not armed, it's not illegal. So even if we stopped the ship, we can't seize it unless they try to enter a U.S. port."

"So why didn't you come to us earlier?"

"Our guys figured that if the ship turned into the Red Sea you'd pick it up."

"That's true," said Tan.

"And some of our guys didn't like the source of the intelligence."

"I am guessing that these are the same people who didn't like the intelligence on Saddam Hussein either, even though 99% of it was right."

Charles snorted. He had never had a dog in that fight, and was glad he didn't. "Our latest information is that the *East Wind III* left Capetown last Monday, June 4. At this point, it's steaming up the west coast of Africa. If it's headed your way –"

"I know," said Tan. "It'll be within range in about ten days. Please tell our friends it was kind of them to give us the heads up."

He shot Nate Charles his Old Warrior glance: the arched eyebrows and thin smile that knew of many betrayals, and expected more. Charles wondered sometimes why the Israelis still cooperated with the United States at all, given the overwhelming hostility of the U.S. intelligence establishment to Jews. And yet, they did.

"I have something I think you will find of interest," Tan said. "Jacob? Tell us what you know."

Ginzburg/Harper wore round gold-framed glasses that gave him almost a studious look. He opened a laptop at the head of the conference table to start his PowerPoint presentation, methodical, neutral, professional. But his muscular frame and blond good looks piqued Nate's interest. Beneath it all, was a potential for sudden violence – the same quality that had so intimidated the British lawyer in Tortola.

"We thought it would be useful to trace the ownership of the *East Wind III*," he began, showing a high resolution photograph of the ship that was better than anything Nate Charles had seen with the sherpas.

"As you know, it is registered in Tonga" – his next slide zoomed in on the red flag with the small white cross in the corner – "a Pacific island kingdom noteworthy for white beaches, cannibalism, and a shipping registry favored by pirates of all stripes.

"We discover that the *East Wind III* has been purchased shortly before its current voyage by a company in the British Virgin Islands named Traventus, Ltd." Ginzburg clicked to show a copy of the registration certificate from Tonga, and then the corporate registry of Traventus. "Then we run up against a brick wall."

"I understand," Charles said. "I used to do white collar crime before I switched over to Counter-terrorism. I know how hard it is to get anything out of the BVI. That place is *sealed*."

"Anyone can form a company in the British Virgin Islands," Ginzburg went on. "All you do is send money to a law firm in Hong Kong or London, choose your name, and you're in business. They handle all the details. File all the papers through local agents. No names of principals appear anywhere. So we wonder. Maybe we are looking at a corrupt Rev. Guards general? Maybe he has a lucrative fiddle on the side? Carpet smuggling? Oil? Or maybe we are looking at something more dangerous. So we set about acquiring more information."

His next slide caused Nate Charles to whistle. It was the Beneficiary Letter Ginzburg had photographed in the office of Trevor Pettigrew in Road Harbor, Tortola, This was the type of document Nate would have killed for when he was trying to crack the money-laundering networks of the Cali cartel years ago.

"Saleh Abd al-Rahman Ibrahim. I'll be damned," Charles said. "I'm not even going to *ask* how you got that."

"Yes, Saleh Abd al-Rahman Ibrahim. Saudi billionaire, based in London. Banks, trading companies. Aluminum smelters in Dubai, steel company in Germany. Huge stock portfolio. Owns ten percent of Disney, which owns ABC News, which shows millions of Americans every day what heartless bastards those Israelis are for oppressing the poor Palestinians. Gives $25 million to Harvard to endow a Middle East Studies chair filled by a notorious anti-Semite. Highly-respected gentleman."

The next slide showed a portrait of the smiling Ibrahim dressed in a well-cut Western suit, sitting at the head of a polished conference table. Above his head was the corporate logo, SARI Group.

"He uses his own initials as his trademark. So you've got SARI Investments, SARI Steel, SARI Trading. You name it."

"So why Traventus?" Charles asked.

"So why Traventus," Ginzburg repeated. But from his lips, it wasn't a question. It was the next clue in a detective story that would lead ineluctably to the ultimate surprise he was going to unmask. "Clearly, Saleh Ibrahim doesn't want to broadcast his ownership of the *East Wind III*. Because this is not a purely commercial venture."

Something didn't add up. Charles scratched a spot above his ear as he weighed the information he had just heard.

"Look, this guy is one of the biggest financial backers of al Qaeda," he said finally. "We busted his charity in Virginia six months after 9/11. Froze their accounts, put Saleh on the watch list. He can't come anywhere near the U.S. Is he in bed with terrorists? You bet. But he's a Saudi, a Wahhabi. So why is he doing business in Iran?"

"That's what we'd like to know," said Israel Tan.

Nate Charles gave them a skeptical look. "I'm going to have a hard time selling this back in Washington," he said. "Sunnis and Shias, al Qaeda and Iran: they're like oil and water. They don't mix. I mean, we *know* that."

"Wahhabis eat Shia for breakfast. Right?" said Israel Tan.

"That's right."

"Like fascists and Communists?"

"Sure."

"1939. Ribbentrof-Molotov, remember? The alliance between Hitler and Stalin that everyone said could never happen?"

Nate Charles chuckled openly. He had always admired Israel Tan, but now he thought he was an absolute genius.

"When it comes to killing Americans and killing Jews, Wahhabi Islamists and Shia Irani Islamists get along just fine," Tan concluded.

All of a sudden he could see it, and it made infinite good sense. Why wouldn't a Wahhabi Saudi financier who backed al Qaeda help the Iranian regime bring a terror weapon into the United States? Both of them openly proclaimed their desire to destroy America. Both of them wanted to see Islam triumph over the *Dar al Harb*, the House of War – the Muslim miscreants and the non-Muslim infidels who comprised 80% of the world's population. But Nate was less certain of his own persuasive powers in making the case to the sherpas. After all, Israel Tan had been present at the creation.

"It would help if I could have a copy of that document," he said.

But Israel Tan was one step ahead of him, as always. He slid an unmarked white envelope across the conference table to the FBI man with a smile.

"For you, anything, my friend," he said.

1100 hours, Tuesday, June 12 – Calverton, MD

Nothing would be the same in the Salima Khan investigation after Special Agent Joanna Greary stormed into the FBI regional office in Calverton, Maryland. Later, as he looked back over these events, Brannigan always found himself drawing a line down the page in his mind, separating things into Before Joanna, and After. And it was only *after* she came onto the scene, he realized then, that he began to get it. That was the effect she had on people. No one could remain indifferent.

After flashing her badge into the security camera, the steel door popped open and in she came, dominating the small office in her bright green tank top, her long blond hair, the white linen pants suit that showed the tiny cut of her underwear, and the huge, old-fashioned .357 magnum strapped beneath her left breast. "Alright. Which one of you is Brannigan?" she said to the three pair of male eyes whose attention she commanded instantly and utterly.

Paige smirked, and quickly covered his mouth with a hand to keep from laughing. Brannigan raised his hand sheepishly, turning red. For an instant, he contemplated taking a bow. "That would be me. To whom do I have the pleasure—"

"Special Agent Greary," she said, cutting him off. "Baltimore field office. I need you to get your flat feet out of my case before you f--k it up any further."

"Can I get you some coffee?" said Brannigan.

"No," she said, sizing him up. "If I want you for coffee I'll take you down to Starbucks. But that's a big if."

"What case are you talking about?" he asked coolly. "I wasn't aware we had a Baltimore—"

"Let's cut the crap, Brannigan. You are endangering equities. I'm very sorry that a girl gets murdered, but the older brother is my CI and I want you to lay off of him."

"Sayeed Khan is a Confidential Informant?" he said, surprised. That changed everything. There were rules covering the treatment of Confidential Informants, and rule number one was that you kept them confidential. "What for?"

"I can't tell you that," Greary said. "It's CT. National Security. And it's being handled by Assistant Director Nathanial Charles – in person. So if you have any problems with that, Brannigan, talk to him. Do I make myself clear?"

"Actually, no," he said. "This is a murder investigation. A capital crime. If I need to pull Sayeed Khan in for questioning, that's what I'm going to do."

"If you do that, Brannigan, I'll have your ass hanging from the Washington monument. Sayeed wasn't anywhere near the girl when she disappeared."

"How do you know that?" Brannigan asked.

"Because he was with me. Debriefing."

That got everyone's attention. Paige and Kevin Jackson exchanged a lewd glance. Brannigan got off the corner of the desk where he'd been sitting and came right up to her, where he could see the sweat glistening above her upper lip. He stood a full head higher than she did, but she didn't back off.

"Do you mind telling me why he's got a prescription for Ambien, and why we found traces of Ambien in the girl's stomach?"

"I got him the prescription. He's under a lot of stress. This kid's life is on the line, Brannigan. That's all I am able to tell you, and that's all I'm going to tell you."

"So she stole his meds, is that it?"

"Yeah. Probably. And so what? That wasn't what killed her."

"No, it sure wasn't," he agreed.

"You've been warned, Brannigan."

And with that, Special Agent Joanna Greary left. No goodbyes, no card, no phone number. Brannigan slumped down onto the empty desk, shaking his head, half in amusement, half in shock.

"What are you going to do?" Paige asked.

"I don't know," Brannigan said slowly, a smile gradually forming on his lips. "But it sure makes me want to know more about Sayeed Khan. What do you say, Paige? Are you with me?"

"You bet, boss."

"Kevin?"

Kevin Jackson answered with a huge grin. "You mean, I'm finally going to get out of this sh—uh, office? Let's go have us some *fun*."

III

SATAN

IN THE FLAMES

0530 hours, Wednesday, June 13 – Parchin, Iran

Shortly after dawn a pair of white Nissan Patrols, their windows clouded over with mud, screeched to a halt outside the gate of the cemetery. In the distance, the call to prayer from a dozen muezzins was dying down. The city of Parchin lay beyond the range of hills; ten kilometers to the north, the shantytown suburbs of Tehran began. In between the two was a no-man's land of rocky desert and plastic bags, broken only by the main highway.

Hajj Imad hopped out of the passenger seat of the first car before the dust had settled. He was a short man – no more than 5 foot six – around forty-five years old, his dark brown hair died to hide the grey at the temples and around the ears. Although slight of build, his stomach was beginning to paunch and he wore his suit jacket open over a white shirt. A pair of bodyguards jumped out of the back seat and accompanied him on either side as he approached the second car. They were rough men, bearded, wearing army trousers and t-shirts. The clean-shaven Hajj Imad, with his long thin fingers and scrubbed, white neck, appeared almost delicate by contrast. He waited as the bodyguards opened the passenger door of the second car and got the Arab onto his feet. Although his hands were not tied, he was wearing a blindfold.

"Y'allah," said Hajj Imad. "Let's go."

The Arab wore a thick beard and the long loose shirt and baggy trousers of the *shalwar khamiz* that his men had adopted during the many years in Afghanistan. His skin was rough and dark from extended exposure to the sun. If he weren't a terrorist with a price on his head, he could easily pass for a farm laborer back in his native Egypt.

Hajj Imad led the way along a narrow path across from the cemetery, the bodyguards following closely behind, guiding the Arab by the arms. Around twenty meters from the dirt road, they came to the remains of a one-story bathhouse, built so worshippers could perform their ablutions before attending to the dead. Hajj Imad pushed open the broken door, then folded back a dusty carpet in the entryway. Beneath the carpet were two handles, set into a trapdoor. He lifted the door until it caught over his head. Reaching up, he took the Arab's hand.

"Ten steps down," he said. "Then you can take off the blindfold."

At the landing beneath the bathhouse floor, Hajj Imad flipped a switch, and lights appeared below them. The guards eased the trapdoor shut, and they went through a long corridor until they reached a large steel door with an electronic lock. Hajj Imad entered the code in a keypad set in the cement wall, and the door folded back.

Inside was a large living room, with sofas set around the walls and a half-dozen armed guards sitting around drinking tea. At the far wall, was another door. "Is 2500 here yet?" he asked one of the guards. The man nodded, and motioned toward the far door.

Beyond the well-lit corridor were a set of French doors, the windowpanes obscured by bright yellow curtains hung from the inside. Hajj Imad knocked and a guard appeared almost instantly to let them in.

The man at the far end of the long conference table stood as they entered and welcomed them. He too was in his mid forties, with a rough, pock-marked face, a graying beard, and almost emaciated features. Ali Akbar Parvaresh headed Section 43, and answered directly to the Supreme Leader of the Islamic Republic of Iran. Hajj Imad reported to him. Only a few hundred people around the world – some of them, his victims – knew who Parvaresh was. Even fewer of them would recognize his face.

"There are many developments," said Hajj Imad. "The news is good."

"God willing," said Parvaresh. "There must be no mistakes. Not one. Our enemy is clever, and he is watching. He has greatly improved his defenses since the glorious operations of September 11. Our task is much more complicated than before."

Sometimes he wondered about the unbounded self-assurance of Hajj Imad. The man had nothing but contempt for the enemy. Had he been blinded by his own success? Was he becoming sloppy? Hajj Imad had executed some of the regime's most daring operations against the Americans in Lebanon, Argentina, Saudi Arabia, and Iraq, and so far he had made no mistakes. That unbroken track record made him a prized possession – *his* prized possession, Parvaresh thought. But still.

"You, al-Masri," he said, turning to the Egyptian. "Your men can no longer just fly in and fly out of the United States. You need greater preparation. More testing. Dry runs."

"This we have done, my brother," the Egyptian said. "Most of my men have been in place for years already. Ask Hajji. Only the Engineer needs to fly in for the operation."

"No Persians," Parvaresh said. "Not one. Is that clear?"

"Of course. My networks are everywhere. No one suspects them. One of our men can get into the White House whenever he wants! Another one works for their Department of Security. He tells us in advance when they plan to step up their terror alert. We throw these Jews bones and watch them chew. There is no part of the Zionist government of America whose secrets we cannot access. We have people who work for their FBI, feeding them false information! We know how they think, how they move. Then we set upon them as upon a virgin in the night."

"This is good," said Parvaresh quietly. While he shared the Egyptian's zealotry, it was his job to ensure that this operation was a success. If they failed... But he didn't want to think about failure. He had twin twelve-year old daughters, and he knew what his own men did to innocent girls before they executed them in front of their parents. He had worked hard to ensure zero contingencies for this operation. There was no room for failure. He closed his eyes for moment, gathering his composure.

"Tell me about the Engineer," he said.

"Al-Libi? He was trained in Libya, then in Pakistan."

"No Libyan passport."

"Not to worry, my brother. Through our contacts in Pakistan, he obtained a new birth certificate, then moved to Britain. Today, he uses a real British passport. No visas. No stamps. No questions."

"This is good. I prefer that to some of the identities you've been using," he said to Hajj Imad. "Our document section is the best in the world. Still, nothing compares to a real British passport."

"Al-Libi has made the run several times," the Arab went on. "He flies into the United States on business. He has bought phones and other supplies, always with cash. Even if those Jew bastards wanted to trace him, they would never find him."

"That is good. Hajji, what do our Sepah experts say of his training? Is he ready? Can he work under pressure? Has he memorized the codes? Does he know how to handle the special material? Does he understand the importance of the shielding? So much depends on this one man. I have never been happy with this aspect of the operation."

"The Sepah is never happy. You know that. They were not happy with the weapon. They want to use it here. They want to test openly, declare our new capability to the world."

Parvaresh stroked the five-day stubble on his chin as he mulled the deep rivalry between his own service and the heavy-handed goons of the Revolutionary Guards, the Sepah Pasdaran. "Sometimes the Sepah are idiots," he said. "They don't realize that if we test, even the Russians and the Chinese will come down on us. Our best friends will be forced to turn against us. Still, I would feel better with a backup. What happens if the Engineer gets compromised? If the Americans arrest him?"

"He will not be compromised, God willing," al-Masri said. "Only one of my men knows his identity, and his purpose. And the others, on the ground, they know only this one."

"But his training?" Parvaresh insisted.

"The Sepah has trained him as if he were one of them," Hajj Imad said. "He can dismantle the initiator and reassemble it with his eyes closed. He is professional."

Parvaresh looked from one to the other, then closed his eyes. He had asked these questions dozens of times before, but he needed to hear the answers again. There was too much at risk to allow any room for mistakes. Everything had to go exactly as planned, or else they aborted the operation.

"Agha will be pleased with our work," he said, relaxing for the first time. "For five years, we have been planning for this day. God's fire on the infidels. *Shaitan der artash.* This time, we will not just damage them. We will destroy them utterly!"

Shaitan der artash. It was the codeword he had devised for the operation. These were the words that would be spoken at Friday prayers as the final signal, the final go-ahead.

Shaitan der artash. Satan in the flames.

0900 hours, Wednesday, June 13 – Livermore, Ca

Eva had chosen a motel just off the freeway in Livermore, California so she could avoid the morning rush hour. Although many of the scientists who worked at Lawrence Livermore National Laboratory prided themselves on biking to work, traffic frequently backed up for several miles in the morning as more and more businesses moved beyond the Bay Area in search of cheaper real estate. She showed her purple Q clearance pass to the armed guard at the main gate. After passing a mirror beneath the engine and searching the trunk, he waved her through. The dry heat of her native California hit her with a welcome blast as she left the cheap rental car in the parking lot and headed into the lab. Her first stop was a courtesy call to lab director Martin Osborne.

The instant she saw him, all the reasons why she hated him flooded over her. Now she knew why her stomach had been in such an uproar during breakfast. She pressed her lips together, fighting back her emotions.

"It's such a pleasure to see you, Dr. Romera," Osborne said, oozing conviviality. "Whatever ill fortune has caused your visit is a good day for us. Welcome. Welcome, my dear."

She tensed involuntarily as he moved to embrace her on both cheeks. How she hated the overly-long white hair, the thick blond moustache as it brushed against her cheek, the stale pipe smoke on his breath, the blackened teeth, the bulging Hawaiian shirt, the rugged sandals, the round gold-framed glasses. Dr. Osborne was something left over from the 1960s. And yet, here was the man in charge of America's newly-revived nuclear weapons programs, a man who mastered awesome powers of destruction; her former boss. She required his blessing to get the information she needed, and so she smiled and let him hover over her just slightly too long.

"And so, my dear," he said, looking her up and down, noting the flat stomach beneath her black stretch top. "Still waiting on the next baby, are we? Time's a-wasting, if you ask me!"

I didn't ask you, you old fool, she thought. Just because she was a Latina didn't mean she had to drop babies like a rabbit. "Time is friendly to some of us, Dr. Osborne," she replied, feigning innocence.

"Well. Hmm. Yes. So what can I do to make your visit more—er, productive?"

"I need to sit down with the folks at Z Division who pulled together the analysis on the A.Q. Khan network," she said. "I also need someone to make a database run for me. The 1998 Pakistani tests."

"The evil Dr. Khan is not on the loose, I hope?"

"Let's hope not," she said.

Two hours later, she was seated in a small, air-conditioned conference room with Zachary Miller and Rick Randell, the lead analysts at Z Division.

Zach Miller was one of those California sunshine boys who biked to work and went hiking in the mountains in the afternoons. In his early forties, he looked ten years younger, with a full head of reddish-blond hair and a rugged tan. He had the easy manner of someone who had another, full life outside of work.

But Miller was the lab's foremost specialist on Iran. He had been posted to the International Atomic Energy Agency's technical lab in Seibersdorf, Austria for two years during the confrontation with Iran over its nuclear programs. Whenever the IAEA inspectors brought back samples from suspect sites, Zach Miller ran the particle analysis. This required him to irradiate the swipes to determine which particles were of interest, then select them one by one under an electron microscope for detailed spectroanalysis. Miller's work allowed the Agency to assert that the Iranians were conducting experiments with highly-enriched uranium, despite their most heated denials, because he had found the evidence. He was a pro, and Eva knew it.

Randell, on the other hand, was a cyber creature. His high, bald forehead, big glasses, and slight build made it unlikely that he engaged in vigorous exercise beyond what he could accomplish with a keyboard and a mouse. But he knew every trip Dr. Khan had made outside of his native Pakistan, every company he had ever done business with, every front man he had ever used. Rick Randell redefined the meaning of institutional memory. Together, he and Zach Miller made a pair.

"I want to show the two of you some pictures," Eva said. "But before that, bring me up to speed on the Iranian nuclear program, in particular, their cooperation with A.Q. Khan."

"A vast program," said Randell. "Where would you like to start?"

"Perhaps not at the beginning," Eva said. "I've read all the IAEA reports. I know what they say about the uranium processing facility at Isfahan and the enrichment plant at Natanz. My question is: have they already done it? Was the whole showdown with the inspections and the IAEA just a circus they put on for us, while they continued in secret to enrich material for the bomb?"

"That's a judgment call," Randell said. He could scarcely hide his eagerness. Clearly, it wasn't a question he was asked often enough. "Let Zach fill you in first with the facts on the ground. Then perhaps I can give you my informed opinion of what it all means."

Zach Miller brought out a series of satellite photographs, which he passed to her one by one across the conference table as he spoke.

"Here's what we know," he began. "1987: the Atomic Energy Organization of Iran signs a consulting contract with Dr. A.Q. Khan. 1989: the Islamic Republic announces vast discoveries of natural uranium ore in the east, and begins work on milling plants. 1995: Tehran signs a secret agreement with the Khan network to import two thousand uranium enrichment centrifuges. This only comes to light in 2003, once the nuclear showdown with the IAEA begins.

"In public, the regime signs a vast nuclear protocol in January 1995 with the Russian Federation that includes a full-scale industrial centrifuge plant. That finally begins to turn some heads. Under U.S. pressure, Russian president Boris Yeltsin says he will cancel "all military aspects" of the contract, including the centrifuge plant, but offers no explanation of what he means by 'military'."

"Bomb designs? Delivery systems?" asked Eva.

"Mystery," said Zach. "Although we do know that Russian firms began helping Iran to design long-range ballistic missiles at this point. Today, those missiles are capable of launching a small satellite into orbit. He who can launch an object into orbit can generally manage to have that object fall on his enemies."

He passed her another photograph. "1996," Zach went on. "Western intelligence agencies discover that Iran is negotiating to buy an industrial-scale uranium conversion facility from China, to transform yellowcake into uranium hexafluoride gas, the feedstock used in a centrifuge cascade."

"Why did they need a hex plant if they didn't have a working enrichment plant?" Eva asked.

"Bingo! Today, we think we know the answer: the 2,000 centrifuges of Dr Khan—"

"Which the Iranians say they kept in some warehouse," Eva said.

"Precisely... So we tell the Chinese we won't sell them nuclear goodies if they go through with the deal. They make a big fuss; the Iranians have paid money up front. But because it's us, they'll make the sacrifice."

"The only thing is," Randell cut in, "the Chinese were lying."

"They pulled a fast one," Zach went on. "While we closed our eyes and thought the worst was over, the Chinese simply sold the Iranians the blueprints for the entire facility — right down to production schematics for individual pieces of equipment. By the time the IAEA finally gets wind of what's going on it's February 2003, and the place is ready to go operational. In the meantime, the Chinese were delivering hex to them on the sly."

Eva summarized by ticking off items on her fingers. "So they've got uranium. They've got hex. And they've got the centrifuges from Dr. Khan. Is there some reason I've missed why they wouldn't put all of it together?"

Randell leaned forward, placing his two hands on the conference table as if he were about to play a concert piano. "Now we come to the fun part. Let's say, just for the sake of argument, that they behaved like any rationale proliferator would have behaved who was willing to spend over a billion dollars importing equipment through the black market to build all these facilities in secret. Let's assume for an instant that they had the bad intentions that their actions suggest. Now I know this is not what we are supposed to assume. Innocent until proven guilty. But when you're talking nuclear weapons, you can't really afford that kind of legal nicety. After all, if a nuclear weapon ever went off in one of our cities, you wouldn't be calling in lawyers to bury the dead."

"I'm with you," Eva said. "So what does it give them?"

"Let's say it took them two years to get Dr. Khan's centrifuges up and running. Let's say they shut them down once they saw that the IAEA was serious about coming in to inspect. That gives them a six year window – six full years of enrichment."

Zach picked up the thread. "By our calculations, using those two thousand centrifuges, Iran could have made enough weapons grade material during that time for at least ten bombs. Double that, if the Chinese hex was lightly enriched."

Eva let the numbers sink in. It was a significant arsenal, not just onesies and twosies. If true, the world's most dedicated terrorist regime today possessed the world's most dangerous weapons – or at least, the material to produce them. And no one seemed to be the wiser.

"Do you recognize these pictures," she said finally, sliding across the table the enlargements Danny had made for her of the fat, torpedo-shaped object being loaded onto the East Wind III.

Randell took one quick look, then passed the photo to Zach. "Any doubt?" he said.

Zach shrugged. "It could just be an engineering dummy, or an overly-large protective casing. We'd need the precise dimensions. But if you ask me, it's Wishbone Prime," he said.

Pakistan claimed it had set off six nuclear weapons in the spring of 1998, he explained. The U.S. believed that three of the weapons were duds – what physicists called a "fizzle" – or possibly even nonexistent, claimed for reasons of prestige. Dr. Khan publicly boasted that the largest device measured 30 to 35 kilotons – significantly larger than the 13 kiloton bomb that destroyed Hiroshima. That was Wishbone

Prime. Seismic stations around the world had measured its blast at between 8 to 12 kilotons.

"Wishbone Prime is a real weapon," Zach explained. "The good news is that it's too large to fit in anything but a big tactical missile, such as the old Soviet FROG, which has a limited range. Just enough to reach major Indian cities – unless the wind happens to be blowing the wrong way."

"Oops," said Randell.

"The bad news is that it's not unique. The Chinese have tested an identical weapon at least three times. It's a basic, but very reliable gun-type design. We believe they gave the drawings to the Pakistanis, who in turn sold them, through Dr. Khan, on the black market. Any number of countries could have them by now."

"Remember when Colonel Qaddafi gave up his nuclear program in late 2003?" Randell said. He was so excited he could barely sit still, just like a kid. "That was when we really took the wraps off the Khan network. First, we intercepted the ship carrying centrifuges from Malaysia to Libya. Then we got the SCUD-Cs. And when we were sitting on the tarmac about the leave Tripoli just after New Year's, their guy gives us a present."

"Yeah, if he hadn't come to us, we never would have found it," Zach added. "It just shows you. No matter how intrusive the inspections, if they want to hide things, they will."

"We were delayed," Randell went on, picking up the story. "The plane had broken down and we were waiting for spare parts. Just when we're finally about to leave, three days late, Matouk Matouk comes out with this oversize document case. A little going away present, he said. It was the bomb design, annotated in English and Chinese. Wishbone Prime."

"So you think Dr. Khan sold the same bomb design to the Iranians?" Eva said.

"We don't know that as a fact," Randell said. "But if Libya could get it, with their limited nuclear program, the Iranians would be guilty of proliferation malpractice if they didn't. And so would the Saudis, for that matter."

Eva was stunned. Their information was sobering. It was exactly what she had feared the most. How could anyone be so arrogant as to believe that the Iranians did not have the technical skills to master technologies more than sixty years old? And yet, that seemed to be what Danny's bosses were saying.

She needed one more piece of information from the Z Division geeks.

"Look," she said. "Here are the dimensions, as best we've been able to estimate them from the photograph. I need to know from you the details of the physics package. Size, weight, isotopic breakdown, yield. And anything you know about the arming device and the PALs[1]."

Zach looked at her skeptically. "I thought that was your department, Doctor."

"It is," she said. "But you can never know too much. I like to double and triple check."

---

[1]The five declared nuclear powers have extensive security systems, known as Permissive Action Links, that require some form of double-key to enable the warhead to prevent accidental or terrorist use.

1215 hours, Thursday, June 14 – Washington, DC

Luther Powell was already seated at a corner table deep inside the restaurant by the time Brannigan arrived. Back to the wall, he could view the only entry and most of the vast indoor dining area. Just minutes from FBI headquarters, Jaleo was nevertheless an unusual watering hole for the Bureau. It was a bit too sophisticated – too much wine, too much unusual food, too much garlic, too *European* – for the pizza and coca-cola crowd. That's why they maintained a dozen tables outdoors beneath large parasols, despite the steaminess of summer in Washington. It was the type of place that attracted luncheon guests who could afford to dress casual, in a city where men were expected to wear dark suits and ties even during the dog days of summer.

Brannigan and Powell had gone through Quantico together, although they had come from dramatically different backgrounds. Brannigan was the lawyer; at least, the lawyer-to-be, having joined the Bureau after several years working for a DC law firm after college. Powell was also a late-comer to the FBI. But his first career had been with the U.S. Marines. He'd spent twelve months of his life killing insurgents in Fallujah, and never forgot how dishonestly the press had reported the U.S. victories in Iraq. It made him sometimes wish more journalists had taken the risk of reporting from behind enemy lines. But they never did. For those who survived, it might have changed their tune. They'd cut their gumshoes together at Hogan's Alley in Quantico, the FBI's replica of small town America, with its Laundromat, its Post Office, its soda fountain, and its hostage-takers holed up behind curtained windows.

"Brother Michael," Luther Powell said when he arrived. "It's been awhile."

"Hey, Luther. When you're down in the weeds, you don't often have time to hit the city lights."

When they had ordered and the waitress was beyond earshot, he leaned forward. "I need your help on something, Luther."

The black agent laughed. "I'd take a bullet for you, man. But no way I'm going to stand in between you and the wrath of a woman scorned. What did you do now? Mix up their birthdays?"

Brannigan laughed in spite of himself. During training at Quantico, they had often joked about their inability to understand the wants and needs of the young, lusty women they wound up dating. "This *is* about a woman. But not Morgan."

"That's even worse."

"No, really. I'm serious. This is Bureau business."

Luther's smile vanished. He shook his head slightly. "I'm listening," he said.

"I've just been ordered off a capital murder investigation by a female agent in the Baltimore field office who claims my prime suspect is off-limits because he's a CI in a counter-terrorism case."

"No shit."

"There wasn't nothing left standing when she stormed out. Hit us like a hurricane."

Luther shook his head in disgust. "That would be Agent Greary."

"So you know her?"

"I know about her. Hard not to, with the temper she's got. She claims to be running a whole network of sources. They've provided testimony to the grand jury in the Islamic charities case. It's true."

"Well her CI works for one of the charities," Brannigan said. "Sayeed Khan. He runs conferences and handles the website for Muslims for Free Enterprise. They claim to be a conservative group, from what I gather. Well connected to the White House."

Luther took to doodling on his napkin, distractedly, as if the subject had begun to bore him. Brannigan pressed on. "Can you help me out?"

"Look," Luther said finally. "You've walked into a hornet's nest. Muslims for Free Enterprise was founded by Hilbert Christensen. He's an old buddy of Major Sherman, the President's top political strategist. They've been placing Sayeed's friends in sensitive positions throughout this administration. Hilbert says the idea is to win the Muslim community to the Party."

"That's insane," Brannigan said. "Since September 11, all the mainstream Muslim groups have been highly critical of the administration. A number of them have counseled their members not to cooperate with law enforcement. Including groups run by Sayeed's friends."

"Don't I know," Luther said.

"I thought national security trumped politics."

"Welcome to Washington." Luther said. "If you want a friend, get a dog."

Brannigan leaned forward, rapping the table twice, quietly. "So what about Agent Greary. Can you help?"

The waitress brought their food, and Luther took a long sip from his iced tea as she laid out the different plates and explained what each was.

"No promises," he said finally. "I'll take a look. If it's on the up and up, I'll blow you off. If not – get your ass back in town for another lunch. I kind of like this. Octopus? Is that it?"

"Mine's squid," said Brannigan.

1230 hours, Friday, June 15 – Washington, DC

Paige had finished his chilled mocha long ago by the time Sayeed emerged from the magnificent glass foyer of 1776 K Street, in downtown Washington, DC. The Starbucks where Paige was watching gave him a direct line of sight to the main entrance across the street. Sayeed was carrying a small bag, and had left his suit jacket inside the building, as did many Washingtonians going out for a social lunch or to run noontime errands in the summer heat. He hesitated a few minutes out on the sidewalk, as if deciding what to do. Finally, he flagged a cab just as it approached, and jumped in. Paige took down the number and pressed the walkie-talkie button on the Nextel phone on the counter in front of him.

"He's heading your way, buddy boy. Capitol cab. Look for the number 4276 on the side door."

"Roger that," Kevin said." Then, after a minute, the phone chirped again. "Got him. They've turned right onto 18th street, heading toward the White House."

"10-4. I'm on my way," Paige said quietly.

He had parked around the corner on 21st street, to be in position to follow Sayeed if he crossed the street to head in the other direction. He started the powerful black Mercury and shot across K Street parallel to the target. In the lunchtime traffic, he knew Sayeed's cab wouldn't get too far. They figured they had the advantage because Sayeed had never seen either one of them, and probably didn't suspect he was being shadowed.

His phone chirped, and Kevin's voice came through immediately. "He just past the Old Executive Office Building, heading for the Mall."

"I'll join you at Constitution."

Brannigan had instructed them to back off if Sayeed went into the Old EOB, so Paige was relieved. They didn't need to have the president's top political advisor ripping them a new one – at least, not until they had something solid on Sayeed.

Sayeed paid off the cab at the far side of the White House, and began walking casually by the concession stands down on the Mall, as if he was just looking to buy lunch. The Mall was packed with tourists and with lunchtime strollers, enjoying the rare dry summer day. Paige watched from a distance as Kevin put on his ghetto walk and tailed him. With his basketball shoes, the long t-shirt hanging over his baggy jeans, and the comb stuck into his neatly-trimmed Afro, Kevin looked like he was out to meet a group of friends. When Sayeed stopped at a concession stand selling Tex-Mex, Kevin walked right past him and bought a hot dog at the next stand. He plunked himself down on a bench in the shade and tucked in with both hands.

Sayeed struck up a conversation with the concession stand owner, who bobbed his head back and forth as he listened. From the name of the stand, he was probably Hispanic; but he just as easily could have been a Middle Easterner of some sort. Both men were smiling. Sayeed began fiddling with his shoulder bag, pointing to something inside, and the man waved his hand, acquiescing, affable, friendly. Sayeed pulled out a small camera. From behind the stand, the concession stand owner emerged, along with another, younger man. Sayeed handed the younger man the camera, showed him how it worked, and posed with the owner in front of his truck. The younger man looked up uncertainly after taking a picture, so Sayeed waved his hand in a circle, for him to take another. He then took the camera and looked at the screen. He showed the pictures to the owner, who smiled.

When the two men went back inside the truck to return to work, Sayeed spun around and took a quick shot of the side of the truck, where the Capitol Police permit was posted, and another one of the license plate, then came back to the window to talk to them as they handed him his quesadilla. He paid, told them to keep the change, and waved good-bye enthusiastically. He had made friends.

Paige didn't glance up from his magazine when Sayeed came back his way, heading back toward the Washington Monument. He let him go past him another 50 feet or so, lost in the crowd, then he got up and slowly began to follow him. Sayeed found a bench in the shade and sat down at the far end from a

Hispanic woman, taking her baby out in a stroller. He began to eat. In another few minutes, he was joined by two young men of Middle Eastern origin, who began talking loudly, pushing each other playfully, until the woman left. Paige took out a camera with a 300mm telephoto lens from his shoulder bag and took head shots of both of them.

When the woman left they sat down, and Sayeed wiped his hands and took out his camera. Looking intently at the screen, he found what he wanted and held the camera over so they could see the picture. They nodded excitedly, pointing at something in the screen, and Sayeed appeared to agree. Sayeed pursed his lips, and gave a quick toss with his head, and the men quickly checked themselves and became less voluble.

Did he see me? Paige wondered. He turned and began walking off in the other direction, passing Kevin without a glance. His partner had finished eating and sat nodding his head to a walkman, apparently oblivious to everything around him.

2030 hours, Saturday, June 16 – Burtonsville, MD

"Danny, I'm worried," Eva said, after they had tucked Paul into bed and returned to the couch in their modest living room. On the coffee table was the report she had brought back from Livermore. She pushed it away from them with her big toe and took a sip of wine.

"What if that's it? What if the Iranians are hoping to bring a nuclear device into the United States?

You work right across the river from downtown. I don't want to bring up Paulie without a Dad."

"We'll get it in time," he said.

"I'm not so sure. It's not as easy to detect as you may think."

She had gone on hunts like this with the NEST – the Nuclear Emergency Support Team. During the 2004 Democratic Party convention in Boston, an intruder managed to penetrate the perimeter they had set up around the convention center, carrying some kind of radioactive device. She would never forget the look of astonishment that came over her team leader when the red box flashed above his computer screen. He nearly spilled his coffee as he swiveled back to his station inside the van and began pecking at the keyboard, hurriedly running a check on the sensor. That was when the fear gripped her belly. Ninety seconds later she watched, stunned, as a second sensor went off within the next ring, showing the yellow and black radiation symbol. Whoever was coming in knew exactly what they were doing, because he charted a zigzag course through all of the NEST defenses. They simply didn't have enough people to track the guy.

They rushed out of the van, cell phones glued to their ears, and headed into the crowded convention center, flashing badges, jumping turnstiles, dodging people as they ran up the escalator. But when they reached the detection point, he had moved off someplace else and it looked like he was heading right for the convention floor. By that point, they had gone to full alert. The Boston police shut down all points of entry and were told to stop anyone carrying a backpack. The Secret Service tightened their detail around the candidate, ready to knock him out if they had to in order to rush him from the arena. In the end, the target moved out across the perimeter to the far side of the convention center, into the press gallery and came to a halt. When they finally caught up to him, it turned out to be a journalist who had come out of the hospital three days earlier after receiving a tomography. To detect a potential blood clot, his doctors had injected him with a tiny, radioactive pellet, which normally he should have passed by then.

If he had been a terrorist, they all would have been dead. It just didn't work as in the movies.

"God is great," Danny was saying. "He has a plan."

She lay back against the cushions, staring up at the ceiling, the wine glass trailing in one hand. He leaned over and buried his face in the smooth olive skin of her neck, nudging at the hem of her pale silk nightgown with his nose. She gripped his head with both her hands and held him out in front of her. "I'm not sure I want *you* to be part of that plan," she said.

She had already lost him once before, or almost. It was during his second tour in Iraq, when he had been working with the Iranian-American woman. *Aryana.* What was it he had told her the name meant? Some flying Goddess, wasn't it? She had known from the far-away look that first time she came to visit him in Walter Reed. It wasn't just the morphine. He had stared at her, his new titanium shoulder wrapped in bandages, his lower arm in a cast, and seemed to just look through her. She had felt it immediately. He was looking at someone else; at *her.* Another woman had stepped into his soul. The knowledge of his infidelity came over her like a great fist tightening inside her chest. She felt crowded out, physically short of breath, as if the woman were competing for the very air she breathed.

She had said nothing that first time. Nor the second, or the third. Each time she came to visit him in the brightly-lit hospital room, he had fewer and fewer bandages. Each time, as the weeks stretched into months, her stomach grew until it stood out before her like a football. And then, finally, the mist departed from his eyes and she felt his soul return. She took his good hand and placed it on her belly and said to him quietly, *feel this life. He is your son.* And Danny, her big fearless Danny, began to cry.

I almost lost you, he said finally.

I know, she said.

Forgive me, baby. Forgive me.

As she felt the new life kick in her stomach, she knew she would forgive him, no matter what he had done. And she knew she would have spat at him and walked out just six months earlier. They began to pray together after that. And after he left the hospital she took him to Saint Jude's and, without a word, led him to the confessional. He balked.

I'll confess to you. But this is not my way. You know that.

You'll confess to him, she said forcefully. *If he can forgive you, I guess, so can I.*

But there was nothing carnal. Ever.

'*I did not have sex with that woman,*' she said mockingly.

Really! It's true.

It had better be, she insisted. There was no wiggle room in this one, no way, no how. *Now, in you go.*

She watched him kneel down, and heard the murmur of his voice. She heard the priest, and she knew that their life was about to begin again. She couldn't explain it, even to herself. What she could never have accepted just months earlier, all of a sudden became inconsequential. With his life in her belly, whatever he had done with Aryana seemed so – *lightweight.*

"Of course you do," he was saying, stroking her face. "You must have faith. It is God's will for us to combat evil, not just give in to it. Remember?"

He kissed the small gold cross she wore around her neck, then ran his fingertips lightly over the smooth silk of her nightgown. She opened her lips slightly, giving way to his caresses, and he kissed the skin beneath her ears and her chin, from one side to the other. Arching her back, she pulled him closer, slipping her fingers beneath the elastic of the brown silk boxer shorts he wore around the house, just for her. He drank in her rich perfume, mingled with fresh soap and her woman's scent, as he buried his nose into her flesh.

"You take me, baby. You take me wherever you want to," she whispered, raising her legs and entwining them around his back. "Just make sure you stay alive."

And if you even think of it again, I'll kill you.

1030 hours, Tuesday, June 19 – Bolling Air Force Base

Victoria Brandt, from the State Department's Bureau of Intelligence and Research, was having a field day at the sherpas weekly meeting. She had been warning her colleagues for weeks not to jump to interpret recent missile deployments and speeches by Communist Party leaders in China as signs of imminent military action against Taiwan. Until now, she had been fighting a losing battle, but just yesterday the PRC sent party boss Hu Jin Pen to Taiwan for high level political and economic talks. It was the first time ever that the mainland had made such a conciliatory overture to the Taiwanese. Victoria Brandt was a star.

"This ship you've been tracking," she said once the subject of the *East Wind III* came up, "is another example of the type of over-reaction some agencies have gotten accustomed to passing off as intelligence." She shot a deadly glance at Danny Wilkens, who had just finished his update on the ship's whereabouts. "So far, neither Mr. Wilkens nor anyone else has presented one shred of credible evidence that would justify us boarding that ship."

"We believe there's a strong possibility the *East Wind III* could be carrying a nuclear weapon," Danny said.

Victory Brandt tossed back her hair and rolled her eyes. "And that's based on what?"

"An evaluation by proliferation analysts at Livermore."

"I'd like to see that analysis, and who signed off on it," she said.

Nathanial Charles hadn't said a word until now, but he knew where she was headed and didn't want to let her go there. He liked Wilkens, and he liked his initiative, even if he was using his own wife.

141

"I don't know about the nuclear dimension. But there is news," Charles said, cutting in. "The Israelis have found who really owns the ship. It's not an Iranian front. It's the SARI group."

"You mean Saleh Ibrahim?" said Charles Haas, the CIA man. "He wouldn't get in bed with the Iranians if you turned down the sheets and tucked him in. Surely you know that Saleh Ibrahim is bin Laden's money man. Nate? Hello?"

"Of course," said Charles. "And he's the business partner of Prince Azzi."

"You got that right. The boy wonder. Son of the late and lamented King. There's no way Saleh Ibrahim or Azzi are going – "

"I have a document," Charles said, cutting him off. "It was obtained by the Israelis, apparently in the British Virgin Islands, where the company that owns the ship is registered."

He nodded to Richard Stapleton, who clicked a button on the computer keyboard recessed into the conference table in front of him, and the document appeared behind him in the big curved screen.

Charles Haas gave a short barking laugh. "Fresh from Motta Singer's document shop. Come on, Nate. You don't really expect us to fall for that, do you? Why are the Israelis so interested in this old tub, anyway? How'd they hear about it?"

"I didn't ask, and I doubt they would have answered if I had," he said. "Perhaps they had the same source?"

Haas was livid. They had gone down this road before and he was damned if he was going to go down it again.

"Look," he said, turning to Jason Steinberg, the deputy National Security advisor. "It wouldn't be the first time the Israelis have fabricated intelligence in order to drag us into some mess of their own making. Don't forget that the Prime Minister is still fending off a judicial inquiry into allegations of influence peddling, not to mention an independent commission for his botched handling of the Lebanon war. What better way to call off the dogs than to get us embroiled in boarding a ship he will claim was carrying weapons to Israel's enemies? Who knows? Maybe the Israelis have planted something on board. It's not as if we've got eyes on that tub on the high seas."

"Mr. Haas," Nate countered. "I think you forget. I used to do BVI front companies for breakfast. Cali cartel and all that. This is no cheap fabrication."

Danny's shoulder ached, as the feeling of helplessness and utter disbelief gripped him. How could they possibly fail to see what was going on? Of course the Iranians were going through cut-outs; indirection was the Persian way... But this was Washington. He needed to stay calm, play the game. That's all these people cared about, he realized. Not one of them – not even Haas – considered this as anything more than an exercise in political gamesmanship. If they won, raw bureaucratic power was theirs. If they smelled defeat, they would crawl back into their hole to keep their powder dry and fight another day. None of them were fitted with metallic body parts, to replace the pieces they had lost defending their country. Danny made a mental note of that fact.

"Mr. Charles is right," he said, rolling his shoulders slightly to stretch the muscles around the titanium joint. "My agency concurs that we are potentially facing a grave danger to U.S. national security.

Haas threw up his hands in exasperation. "We're supposed to believe this shit?"

"The Livermore analysis isn't definitive," Danny went on, ignoring him. "Our people know it needs further investigation. We were hoping the Committee would authorize Mr. Haas to send a team to take gamma radiation readings on the ship the next time it comes to port."

"Can't we do that from the air?" Stapleton asked.

"Only in the movies, sir. The readings we're worried about don't travel that far and dissipate quickly. You need to have a stationary target. The closer, the better."

"So where's this tub headed?" said Haas.

"We believe it'll dock in Maracaibo this Saturday. That's the 24th."

Haas hit the ceiling. "You want us to pack our bags and send troops to Venezuela? With Hugo-I-love-Fidel-Chavez in charge? You've got to be kidding! That is one extremely hostile environment, people. It's almost as hard a target as Iran."

Jason Steinberg wasn't pleased with what he was hearing, and he let his impatience show. "Listen, Mr. Haas. The Clandestine Service has been able to maintain a significant budget within the Intelligence Community so it can perform precisely this type of mission. If you're not up to the task, maybe there are other elements of the Community that are."

"I wasn't saying that," Haas backpedaled. "I'm just saying that that's a pretty short fuse. What is it, five days from now? We've got to identify operatives who are fluent Spanish speakers, arrange covers for them, outfit safe houses, you name it."

"Then you'd better get started," Steinberg said. "Gentlemen? Ms. Brandt?" He stood up, effectively bringing the meeting to an end.

Haas stomped out, casting him an unmistakable dark look, but Danny just shrugged it off. Danny had won, and he could hardly believe it. Maybe they would listen after all.

1745 hours, Wednesday, June 20 – Washington , DC

Sayeed left his office at 1776 K street at 5:45 PM. Normally he walked five minutes down K street to the Farrugut North metro station and took the Red train to Glenmont, then a Montgomery county Ride-on bus up Layhill Road to his parents' house on Bryant's Nursery Road. The journey took upwards of an hour, and Sayeed read most of the way. Today, however, he walked past the metro station and turned north onto Connecticut avenue, away from the White House. He was carrying a small, leather portfolio under an arm, in addition to his usual briefcase. After two blocks, he turned into a building with a carport and a doorman in purple livery.

Paige pressed the walkie-talkie button on his Nextel phone. "He's gone into the main entry of the Mayflower. Cover the 17th street exit."

"10-4," he heard.

The Mayflower was one of Washington's fancier hotels. Its main ballroom could accommodate 1,500 people, and frequently hosted political fund-raisers and major think tank events. The elegant interior promenade with its 30-foot vaulted ceilings, crystal chandeliers and gold plate, was more than 200 feet long, and led all the way from Connecticut avenue to the next block, 17th street. Paige clicked his phone again.

"Boss, do you have a second?"

"Sure, Paige. What's up?"

"Our friend has gone into the Mayflower. Can you run a check and see if they have some kind of event going on, you know, some kind of conference or a fund-raiser or something?"

"Stand by."

Movement on the street seemed ordinary enough. Rush-hour traffic heading north, to the Maryland suburbs; light traffic heading south, toward the White House. Most of the pedestrian traffic was headed downtown toward the Farrugut North metro station, the men carrying their suit jackets over their arms, the women in short sleeves. Three men in business suits emerged from a taxi and were ushered by the doorman into the hotel. But there was no perceptible flow of well-dressed guests into the hotel, as there would be if there were an event.

"Negative, Paige. Cover both entrances and stick around."

"Roger that. Over and out," he said.

Being a watcher was not nearly as exciting as Kevin had said when Brannigan first put them on the case. But then, just about anything was more exciting than Calverton, Maryland, where the main event was midnight traffic stops of drug couriers making the run from Miami to Baltimore on I-95, or the occasional call-in of suspicious activity. He found a Starbucks two blocks up Connecticut and settled in to wait.

It was nearly 7 PM when Sayeed finally emerged.

Sayeed walked slowly, apparently heading back to Farrugut North, gazing into shop windows as he went. He was carrying his briefcase, but no longer had the beige leather portfolio. He swayed slightly from side to side, as if he had been drinking.

Paige got his partner on the Nextel walkie-talkie. "Get down into the metro," he said. "Looks like he's going back home."

Paige decided to stay at his post at the Starbucks for awhile. There were two good-looking blondes at a nearby table, talking about their jobs at a law firm. You never know.

Ten minutes later, he did a double-take. Emerging onto the street in a rush was Agent Greary, and she was carrying the beige leather document case. "God-damn!" Paige couldn't help muttering as he watched her strut down toward the White House. The beige v-necked blouse seemed about to fall from her breasts with every bouncing step she took. He could see the cut of her underwear beneath the skin-tight trousers.

"You still there, boss?"

"10-2, Paige. What's up," Brannigan said.

"You'll never guess who our friend was meeting. Agent Greary."

Brannigan didn't reply, so Paige beeped him again. "Did you get that, boss?"

"I copy. Over and out."

2100 hours, Thursday, June 21 – Lavisan, Tehran

Senior officers in the Islamic Republic Guards Corps lived in a special district within the vast Lavisan military zone in north-eastern Tehran. Many of them worked in nearby military factories, including a once-secret site the regime razed to the ground in early 2004 when the International Atomic Energy Agency identified it as a suspect uranium enrichment site and demanded access. Others worked at the IRGC headquarters, on Pasdaran avenue. And others, such as Hajj Imad, never went into regular offices at all, but worked from home and occasionally from non-descript buildings, that housed ostensibly private companies with names such as Kalaye Electric Company, or Lavisan Watch-works, or Kala-Naft, or South Pars Gas Development.

One advantage to living in the compound was that it let them avoid the worst of the Tehran traffic, so thick that in the summer months a bluish-purple haze hung in the air, trapped by the surrounding mountains. Another was that officers such as Hajj Imad could send their children to elite schools within the compound, without a security risk. The schools were heavily religious, but also gave students a solid grounding in math, physics, and natural science.

Mohsen, Hajj Imad's oldest son, had just turned sixteen. And like teenagers everywhere, he was curious about the world outside the confines of family, his father's colleagues, their close-knit social cocoon.

"Baba, when are you going to get off the Internet," he complained, poking his head into his father's office on the 2nd floor of their spacious villa for the third time that evening.

"If it's so you can download more U2 or Kurt Cobain, never!" Hajj Imad replied.

"Kurt Cobain? That's so old."

Dressed in blue jeans and a t-shirt that said, *I Love New York*, Mohsen's physical presence made his father bristle. But Hajj Imad wasn't alone among senior regime officials who found that his spawn failed to embrace the Islamic Revolution with the same enthusiasm as his parents. It wasn't much of a consolation, but at least it avoided him embarrassment. All of their sons and daughters were in love with the West, and only went to mosque when they were forced to attend. They preferred MP3 players to prayers.

"Are you on that satellite website?" his son asked, drawing closer.

"Come and look," his father said. "The Americans are so stupid, they put everything on line, even the orbits of their spy satellites."

The website was run by amateur astronomers who collected satellite sighting from around the world and posted them through a members' only bulletin board. You could plug in the name of a particular satellite, and find out where it was at that moment, or where it would be tomorrow, or a week or two weeks later. You could plug in a country, and find what satellites they currently had flying. You could plug in a city, and see which satellites would be flying over it at any given time. For the astronomers, it was a game. Open secrets, they called this type of intelligence. For Hajj Imad, it was an extraordinary tool that would have been beyond the reach of his government if they had been forced to duplicate it. He logged on as "Skydreams," using a server operated by a secret IRGC cell in Canada, that identified him as a user from the Physics Department at the University of Carlton in Ottawa, and plugged in the coordinates for Maracaibo.

"Why do you hate America so much?" Mohsen asked. "What have the Americans ever done to you?"

His father dug his fingertips into the skin from his forehead to his temples, as if trying to locate the right words. He had a handsome face, clean-shaven – the result of many expensive operations. He liked to think he looked like the actor, Richard Gere. He took a deep breath before he answered.

"Because they are weak," he said finally. "The weak deserve to die. It's is God's will."

"So babies deserve to die?" Mohsen said.

"Of course not. You're being foolish, Mohsen."

"But they are weak, too," his son went on.

"The Americans hide behind others. They do not have the courage to wage their own wars. The first time, when I was young – not much older than you, Mohsen – was in Beirut. The Americans hid behind the

Lebanese. Their goal was to drive Islam from Lebanon. But we stopped them. How? By hitting them directly, while they only attacked through others. We knew that if we hit them, they would run."

All these years later, Hajj Imad still remembered the glory of that bright sunny day in April 1983, when his first real creation came to life. That's how he thought of his work. He was an artist! That first time, when they blew up the U.S. embassy on the corniche in Beirut, the driver of the truck that rammed through the front gate thought he would be having lunch with his family. He was no suicider. But Allah had a greater purpose for him, and Hajj Imad was the Eyes of Allah, and the Sword of Allah. Just as the man put on his brakes in front of the ground-floor cafeteria, Hajj Imad pushed the plunger on the remote control, sending him across the river of Kosar, where 72 virgins awaited him.

"When have you ever fought the Americans?" his son went on. There was sarcasm in his voice, mockery. "When did you ever risk your life? You only risked the lives of others."

"What do you know?" Hajj Imad hissed, trying to control his anger. "You never knew your uncle Badr. He lost a leg fighting the Jews. The Americans were after him. But instead of sending their own men after him, they had the Kuwaitis arrest him. They were too frightened to do it themselves."

"You just get other people to blow themselves up. The same thing, over and over again."

Hajj Imad exploded with rage. He whirled around, driving a fist into the desk so that the plastic in-box jumped into the air. "I NEVER do the same operation twice," he said. "I am an artist! If you remember nothing of your father before the Jews finally get me, remember this. I never do the same operation twice. But the Americans – they are always preparing to prevent the last attack. They never learn."

His computer chimed, and the information he had been waiting for now appeared on the screen. When it sank in, his rage vanished and a huge smile made wrinkles appear on his forehead and below his eyes.

"One day I'll tell you, Mohsen. One day. The Americans are so easy to anticipate, we can play them like a piano. You've just got to learn all the notes."

1230 hours, Friday, June 22 – Washington, DC

Washington, DC was built on a swamp, and on hot summer days Brannigan felt that its true nature emerged from beneath the asphalt like an old green toad bursting through a fine suit of clothes. It was so muggy his suit jacket was damp, even though he carried it over his arm. Going through the double glass doors into Jaleo made the sweat on the back of his neck turn chill. He found Luther Powell at the table at the back, a perfectly-starched white shirt and gold cufflinks his act of defiance to summer. Despite his elegance, he looked grim.

"We've got a problem," he said, as Brannigan glanced through the menu. "Have you ever heard of the SARI Group?"

Brannigan drew a blank. "Shoot."

"Big Saudi financier. Close to the royal family. Also close to Usama bin Laden. We made him a few months after 9/11. Found out he'd been funneling money to a bunch of charities across the river in Virginia, who maintained ties with bin Laden's folks in London and Peshawar. We put him on the watch list."

"So he can't come into the U.S.?"

"That's right. We detain him and then deport him if he tries. Well it turns out that Muslims for Free Enterprise is secretly funded by SARI through some of those charities."

"So Agent Greary *has* been working Sayeed as a CI?" Brannigan said.

"That's correct."

"But?"

"But that reporting did not come from Sayeed. In fact, Agent Greary never asked him the question. We got the information from SARI Foundation bank records, seized in Fairfax, Virginia. We also found a check for $50,000, dated June 1998, when MFE was first established, made out to the organization."

"Seed money."

"Yeah. We found another check for twenty grand made out to Hilbert Christensen directly, apparently a down payment for lobbying work. Mr. Ibrahim wanted him to make some contacts on behalf of his association of Islamic banks – the same group we later tied to UBL. Seems they wanted to meet a number of U.S. Congressmen, exchange views, that kind of thing. Hilbert agreed."

"Hey, it's not illegal, as long as you register."

"That's right. But Hilbert never applied to register as a foreign agent."

"You're not going to prosecute him for that, are you?"

"Probably not," Luther admitted. "Unless my Director wants to turn into crab cakes."

Luther looked at his watch and suggested they order.

"So what is Agent Greary getting from her star CI, for all the taxpayer money she's spending on him?" Brannigan said once they had finished with the waitress.

"What are you talking about?" Luther said, suspicious.

He let his sentence drift, until Brannigan pulled a manila envelope out of his briefcase and slid it across the table to his friend. It contained photos taken by Paige in front of the Mayflower Hotel.

"These were taken earlier this week," Brannigan said. "Look. This is a capital murder case. Maybe I can't pull Sayeed in yet. But that doesn't mean I can't keep tabs on him. Those are pretty expensive digs for a debriefing."

Luther sat back in the leather bench and looked up at the ceiling, pursing his lips. "I do not like where this is going," he said finally. "I really do not like where this is going. Brannigan, you're going to get my ass fired."

IV

MARACAIBO

1145 hours, Saturday, June 23 – Washington, DC

Paige and Kevin were down on the National Mall on Saturday morning, staking out the concession stand Sayeed had visited earlier. Luther Powell had agreed to throw on additional surveillance teams from his section, but it was their turn to take up the watcher's post on the Mall. They had been there since ten and it was nearly noon. To pass the time, they tossed a football back and forth. After catching a long, loping pass from Paige, Kevin called it quits and took a few long steps back to the bench where they had stowed their gear. He took a towel and wiped the sweat from his face and around his neck.

"Man, I am starving," he said when Paige joined him. "You want a dog?"

Instead of answering, Paige grabbed his arm and nodded toward their target. "We just got lucky," he said quietly.

Joining the line that had now formed at the concession stand were the two young men they had seen with Sayeed the week before.

"You go get that hot dog – or whatever," Paige said. "And turn on your wire."

Kevin ambled over to the line in front of the Tex-Mex place as Paige got out the camera with the long telephoto lens and adjusted the focus. He managed to get several clear head shots by the time Kevin's turn came. The two young men hung around the concession stand, talking quietly, appearing to just hang out. Kevin ambled past Paige toward the Capitol building, doing his ghetto walk.

Later, when they listened to the tape they realized the two were not speaking Arabic, but a South Asian tongue.

"What do you make of it?" Paige said. "Pakistanis? Indians? Bangladesh?"

"Beats me," Kevin said. "It sounds like they're chewing bubble gum to me."

That afternoon, a watch team from Luther's shop followed Sayeed to the United Airlines arrivals lounge at Dulles International Airport, where he waited for someone to emerge into the baggage claim. On the board was a direct flight from Los Angeles.

A clean-shaven man with stylishly-cut brown hair joined Sayeed, pulling a wheeled carry-on bag. He wore a tan linen sports coat, open shirt and white trousers. He kissed Sayeed on both cheeks, French-style, showing a set of perfect teeth. His boyish good looks caused a young woman waiting for her bags to turn and stare at him. He returned her gaze boldly, almost cynically, as if well-aware that he was attractive to women. Sayeed tried to take his bag but he insisted on pulling it himself. The new arrival also carried a slim leather document case.

When the watch team checked later with the airline, there were no passengers on the LA flight with South Asian or Arab names. Ten foreign passengers had joined the flight in Los Angeles; four arriving from Hong Kong, two from Sidney, Australia, two from Kuala Lumpur, Malaysia, and two from Tokyo. All the other passengers had presented U.S. driver's licenses when they boarded in Los Angeles.

Sayeed took his companion to the short-term lot, where he had left his father's Toyota Camry. Luther's watchers followed him at a distance onto the Capitol Beltway, then north onto Connecticut avenue past Kensington onto Georgia. Eventually he pulled into a set of low gingerbread buildings nestled beneath old-growth trees and an abundance of recently-bloomed azaleas. A sign said Bel Pre Manor garden apartments.

Sayeed drove around to the back and parked. He led his companion to a second floor unit overlooking the forest, took out a key, and let them in. The apartment was invisible from the street. The parking lot continued along the woods to a second exit perpendicular to Georgia avenue.

Shortly before 7 PM, the two men emerged and got into the Camry and drove out the Bel Pre road entrance and turned north onto New Hampshire avenue, staying just below the 50 mph speed limit. A few minutes later, they pulled into Manny's Gas and Oil, just across from Bryant's Nursery Road. Instead of driving up to the pumps, Sayeed picked his way around to the back service bay and parked. The two men went inside. Sayeed's companion was carrying the leather attaché case.

Two hours later, they emerged. Sayeed drove the man back to the Bel Pre Manor apartment, then went home.

That was one day.

On Monday morning, Sayeed didn't show up for work at 1776 K Street. Instead, he picked up his visitor at the Bel Pre Manor apartments, and loaded his wheeled carry-on bag into the trunk of the Camry. They drove out Bel Pre going west, then turned left onto Norbeck road heading toward Rockville town center, seat of the Montgomery county government. A short section of divided highway diverts around the town center then turns into Falls Road. After a strip mall, the Camry stopped at a low-lying group of warehouses with a sign, Mir Construction. Sayeed parked in front of a glass door leading into an office, and the two men disappeared inside.

An hour later, the watchers got lucky. Sayeed drove his guest back out to Dulles airport, where he boarded United Express flight 5483, departing at 2:41 PM to Toronto.

That evening, back at the office in Calverton, Brannigan received the passenger list from the airline and compared it with the one from the flight from Los Angeles on Friday.

And then, the stars came into alignment. Now they had a name, a face, and a passport number.

It just wasn't what they had expected.

0830 hours, Saturday, June 23 – Maracaibo, Venezuela

Carlos Pena knew in his gut that the swaggering American from agro-industry giant AST was the man he had been waiting for.

Although he was new to Maracaibo, the counter-intelligence officer from Cuba's Dirección General de Inteligencia (DGI) had been handling Americans for years. As a junior officer in Washington in the 1990s, he took over as case officer of an American leftist named Ana Belen Montes, and convinced her to remain at her job as a junior analyst with the Defense Intelligence Agency instead of defecting to Cuba to live in the worker's paradise. For nearly six years Pena ran Ana Montes, guiding her on how to win promotions, until she became the chief Cuba analyst at the Defense Intelligence Agency. He was long gone by the time she was unmasked by the FBI on September 21, 2001, but he knew that her greatest success was not what the Americans believed. It was not her access to classified documents, nor even her role in drafting a now-infamous 1998 National Intelligence Estimate declaring that Cuba was no longer a threat to the United States. Ana Montes had opened the door to a far more important agent sitting on the National Intelligence Council, an agent who was still in place. His recruitment was Carlos Pena's greatest accomplishment.

Carlos Pena had been thrilled when he learned his assignment in Maracaibo, and had spent the last four weeks getting up to speed on the port and its operations. On Tuesday, he received a flash message from the DGI's electronic intelligence center at Bejucal, just south of the gigantic Russian listening post at Lourdes, alerting him of a spike in encrypted burst transmissions between Langley and the CIA code room in the U.S. Consulate in Maracaibo. On Wednesday, he had briefed Edgar Sambrano, the Maracaibo harbor master, and Victor Mendoza, who headed the port authority, that an American team was on its way, and that they were to go along with the Americans' requests. But until now, he hadn't known what the Americans would look like, and he was impressed. The team leader, Beau Cassidy, was a walking diversion. If Pena had not been trained as a professional intelligence officer, he would almost believe that the 60-year old Cassidy was indeed the hapless U.S. business executive he pretended to be, rather than an experienced CIA operator.

They were still drinking coffee, and already Cassidy filled the room.

"Hell, I ain't been down here in twenty-five years," Cassidy was telling Victor Mendoza. "It was the oil business back then." He pronounced it "awl," a mouthful of Louisiana gumbo.

"As you can see, Señor Cassidy, we have developed significantly since then," the dapper Venezuelan businessman said. Silver hair, grey moustache; faint line of perspiration around the lips, Mendoza was on his guard.

"And you are not the only ones." Cassidy jerked a thumb over his shoulder to indicate Maria Salazar, the young woman from the U.S. Commercial Service in Maracaibo who had made the introductions. "Truly, I am stunned. And not only by what my eyes doth behold. I wasn't even hit up for a contribution to the

Presidential library! This is a new world, Señor Mendoza, when political appointees don't hit on us rich businessmen. Hallelujah!"

"Shall we ask Señor Sambrano to take you on that tour?" asked Mendoza. Although Sambrano was the harbor master, but didn't seem to speak English.

"By all means! My betters back in Decatur are looking for covered warehouse space, around 2500 square meters. You know, we've greatly expanded our local manufacturing capabilities, what with that new food processing plant in Caracas."

"I do, indeed, Señor Cassidy. Now, please. I have asked my chief financial officer, Cesar Fuenmayor, to accompany you. Señor Fuenmayor will be able to answer any questions you might have about the leasing arrangements."

"I am much obliged, Mr. Mendoza. Much obliged."

They all stood up, and Fuenmayor came over to shake hands, first with Cassidy, then with Michael Chen, whom Cassidy had introduced earlier as his accountant. The diminutive Chen, with his tortoise shell glasses, had not said a word the whole time. He smiled distractedly.

When Fuenmayor turned to Freddy Luque, Cassidy's assistant, he addressed him in Spanish. The black former U.S. Army Ranger sharpshooter just shrugged. "Sorry," he said. "Third generation. By the time I came around, my folks only spoke English at home."

Carlos Pena quietly observed the CIA team, carefully keeping his skepticism to himself. Luque's shoulders and biceps were so large that they nearly burst out of his suit. He towered over the rest of them, and was almost comic as he attempted to fasten the middle button of the sports jacket. Cassidy was clapping Mendoza on the back, fumbling with his briefcase, waving his arms, laughing, jovial, engaging. Pena gave a quick glance around and saw Mendoza's accountant pointing Chen in the direction of the toilet.

Well done, he thought.

On a side street beyond the main gate, David French was waiting for Chen's signal inside an unmarked white delivery van crammed with computer screens and communications gear. He had monitored the entire conversation until that point, and had gotten a visual of the Cuban DGI counter-intelligence operative from the miniature camera lodged in Chen's glasses. Carlos Pena showed up in their data base as the deputy cultural attaché in Washington, DC who had handled Ana Montes until January 2001, then returned to Cuba where he was promoted to director of the North America division. Given his lowly status while in Washington, this was a rather significant elevation. It all became clear once Montes was busted and began to talk. What was Pena doing here? he wondered.

A green light flashed on the central computer screen; they were connected. "Downloading: 1% of 680 MB. Downloading: 4% of 680 MB. Downloading 10% of 680 MB."

He heard Chen move into the bathroom, and drummed his fingers on the metal rim of the ledge that held the computers as the download continued. "Come on, come on!" he said. If the Cuban had made the team, they couldn't risk leaving the transmitter behind, even though Chen was supposed to have placed the tiny device in the jumble of computer wires so it could not be easily found. The download reached sixty percent, seventy percent, and he heard the toilet flush. Eighty percent, and Chen must have gone to the sink, because he heard water flowing for what seemed like an eternity. He drummed his fingers on the metal rim as the green bars on his screen inched toward the right, and Chen started whistling and drying his hands. "Go get it, Mike boy," he said out loud, though there was no way Chen could hear him.

It was hot and sticky when they got outside the small administrative building, but at least − Fuenmayor gestured expansively, taking in the port − it was not raining. "You want rain, you come back in October," he said.

"I think I'll be fly fishing in Montana," Cassidy said.

They piled into a waiting oversize van, its huge airconditoner wheezing against the heat. Fuenmayor sat up with the driver to guide them around. Cassidy let Freddy Luque squeeze into the back, where he had to sit sideways to accommodate his huge frame. Carlos Pena edged in next to him. "So Carlos," he said, making small talk. "What brings you to these parts?"

"No comprende, Señor. No ingles."

"Now you're kidding me. Not one word? Nada?"

Pena simply turned aside, looking beyond them to the gigantic grain silo along the dock. He wasn't going to give the North Americans anything for free.

The concrete pavers between the grey warehouses rippled in the late morning sun, at times almost appearing like a silver-edged lake. A ship was moored alongside the grain elevator, a giant metal tube sucking at its innards, scattering bits of dust from the seams into the hot, damp air. Maria Salazar leaned forward and spoke to Fuenmayor over the din of the machinery and the air conditioner. "We need to be close to the bulk cargo docks," she said in Spanish.

I'll bet you do, Carlos Pena thought.

"We have several warehouses available for leasing," Fuenmayor said. He was carrying a large, color-coded map that showed each building in the port.

"Well that's what we're here for. Let's go," Cassidy said.

A black sedan with an orange stripe and police lights was parked in front of the grain carrier, windows open, empty. Cassidy let out a sharp, barking laugh. "Ha! You got Crown Vics, just like the County Sheriff back home. I'm feeling real good about this, José. Real good."

"Not José, Señor," Fuenmayor said. "It's Cesar, if you wish."

"Hail, Caesar!" he grinned, slapping the Venezuelan on the shoulder good-naturedly.

Visibly embarrassed, Maria Salazar pulled her skirt below her knees, as if Cassidy's words had been as palpably offensive as a wayward hand or an unwelcome squeeze. "Señor Fuenmayor," she said. "We do apologize for bringing you out here on a Saturday. Our friends from Decatur weren't able to catch a flight before last night. We really do appreciate your efforts to accommodate us."

"Don't mention it," he said, visibly reddening. The attentions of a woman as beautiful as Maria Salazar were not to be taken lightly.

They pulled over in front of a large warehouse under construction, across from the deep-water dock. A huge bluish-grey crane, its turret like a naval gun, stood idle on rails that ran parallel to the water, its long arm pointing skyward.

"We were thinking of something near the two piers at the west end of the port," Maria said.

"Of course." He consulted the map. "We have just one facility available. I am afraid it may be too small for your needs."

"Yo, Caesar," Cassidy jumped in. "In my country, if you don't start small, most times you don't start. If it's ready now, we want it."

Carlos Pena pursed his lips in disgust. Fuenmayor was so easy to play the North Americans might think it was a set up. He hissed a few words at him in Spanish.

"Mr. Pena tells me that we may already have a client for that area. Although, between you and me – he exchanged a glance with Maria Salazar – I'm not sure why he would know that. He just handles security, not leasing."

Cassidy didn't seem to mind the heat once they got out and began tramping through the stifling air of the closed warehouse, but Fuenmayor and the Americans were sweating profusely. The corrugated metal walls still smelled of fresh paint. The large empty hangar had six loading docks at the back. A large sliding door gave directly onto the end of the loose cargo pier, which jutted out into the harbor perpendicular to the string piece where the container ships docked.

"We'll take it," Cassidy said, once they finished the walk-through. "When we get back to your office, I'll have my folks wire through the deposit."

2100 hours, Sunday, June 24 – Maracaibo

It was after dark on Sunday by the time the unmarked white van turned off of Calle 97 onto Calle Liberrador, a broad deserted avenue flanking the wharves. Cassidy kept far enough behind so he could still see the van's taillights. By the time he wheeled the big rented Mercury alongside the van in front of the warehouse, Michael Chen was already opening the large rolling door. He slowed, then drove inside. David French followed with the van and Chen closed the door behind them, making a great cavernous noise. Cassidy nodded to big Freddy Luque. "Let's see if he heard anything."

"I'm on it."

French clambered into the back and was scrolling through lines of time-stamped text when Freddy opened the double van doors. "Not a ping," he said. "If they'd zapped us, I would have picked it up. Either Carlos is asleep, or he's on to us already and didn't need to track us."

"I'm not even going to start speculating why he's here," Cassidy said, sticking his head into the van. "Look, if we get caught, we're legal. It's not much of a cover, but that's our play. Cost Uncle damn near ten grand to rent this place! Y'all know what you're supposed to do, so let's get to work."

The rear part of the van was packed with black tool kits. Michael Chen looked through them, found the one he wanted, and headed for the far end of the warehouse. At regular intervals, he placed small wireless devices against the warehouse walls to monitor noise around their perimeter. If anyone approached, a flashing red light would appear on one of the French's monitors inside the van. He could listen and tape anything the detectors picked up.

Freddy Luque hefted a much heavier tool bag and a small black suitcase and headed for the front and side walls facing the docks. Inside the suitcase was a 1200 W power percussion drill, packed in special foam to absorb sound. Fitting a $3/16^{th}$ inch drill into the chuck, he pierced a series of holes in the outer skin of the warehouse and installed special low-light sensors that passively captured retained heat and electronically generated images that French could enhance inside the van. He also installed the liquid-nitrogen encased germanium gamma-ray detector.

When all the equipment was in place, they settled down to wait.

The *East Wind III* pulled up to the pier at 11: 45 PM and tied onto the mooring boot. Once he finished docking maneuvers and cut the engines, the captain emerged from the wheelhouse and shouted orders to his men. They scurried along the gunwales, unhooking the thick tarpaulins covering the bulk cargo on deck. It took six men working together to roll back the heavy tarpaulins. When they had finished, six bug-eyed monsters stood in a row, turrets swiveled round so their 105mm canons all pointed toward the wheelhouse at the rear of the ship.

Minutes later, a thunderous rumble filled the docks as two trucks and a tractor trailer from the Venezuelan army pulled up onto the string piece, their green camouflage lit clearly in the sodium lights of the port. Armed soldiers jumped out, and ringed off the perimeter. Carlos Pena emerged from an SUV along with a pair of Venezuelan officers, dressed in jungle fatigues. One of the officers bounded up the gangplank to supervise the unloading operation on board the ship. The other went with Carlos to watch the mobile crane crawl into place on rails set parallel to the channel.

It was exactly 12:30 AM when they set to work. The electric servo motors whirred and the heavy chains clanked as the yellow arm of the crane bowed down over the ship like a long-necked water bird to catch its prey. The deckhands untwisted the giant hooks of the sling and secured them one by one to the hard points on the chassis of the first vehicle. The crane operator put tension on the line and the thick chains creaked, going taut. The Venezuelan officer tested the rigging by hand – a gesture about as effective as kicking the tires of a used car – and gave the thumbs up. The chains seemed to bend and twist as the giant vehicle fought against gravity and stopped, hovering just a foot above deck. When it had stabilized, the crane operator revved up his motor and the wheeled monster rose into the air, turning and descending onto the quai in a single graceful motion as if the 12 ton vehicle were nothing more than a toy.

One by one they hoisted the wheeled South African tanks onto dry ground, metal chains clanking, officers shouting, crane engine roaring. Ninety minutes later, the convoy of light wheeled tanks stretched out along the quai, ready to roll.

Just after 2 AM, Cassidy slapped David Chen on the back of the head, a little harder than he had intended. "Hot damn!" he said. "You make sure you've got images of that every way from Sunday."

As they watched, a long, oblong form emerged from the main cargo hold, caught in the sling of the yellow crane. For what seemed like an eternity, it just hung in the air, swaying slightly, almost fragile. Four men steadied the black metal carcass, guiding it upwards. It was clearly heavier than the tanks, and somewhat longer, but the men's heads were just visible over the top. Pena and a Venezuelan officer were shouting orders to the driver of the tractor-trailer as he backed and filled into position to receive it.

There could be no doubt what they were seeing. And it just hung there, an inviting target.

Finally, by 2:20 AM, the mini-submarine was loaded onto the truck, and a smaller object, similarly shaped, was hauled up out of the hold and loaded gingerly alongside it. Then the precious cargo was secured with metal cables and covered with a dark green tarpaulin. By 2:30 AM, the unloading was finished, and the chief Venezuelan officer ordered his men back into the trucks. Diesel engines roared to life, and one by one the bug-eyed armored vehicles popped on their lights, cutting through roiling clouds of bluish smoke. With the SUV leading, they drove out of the port.

As Cassidy followed them on the central screen in David Chen's console, he thought he caught a glimpse of Carlos Pena leaning out the window, his fist raised to him in a middle-finger salute. But it was too far away to be sure.

"Okay, boys," he called. "Let's pack it up."

With the time difference, it was early afternoon in Lavisan when Hajj Imad received a brief email on his Hotmail account. Anyone tracing the message would see an innocuous note from a server in Vancouver, British Columbia, to another server in Ontario. The message could have been sent by a father to his daughter back home.

> "Hi, Sweetie. Guess what? I picked up your favorite chocolates an hour ago. Love, D"

He checked the time stamp of the message and smiled. That meant 0215 local time. Right within the window.

0400 hours, Monday, June 25 – Maracaibo

Two hours later, Carlos Pena unlocked a rear door to the warehouse and a team of Venezuelan commandos, automatic weapons on the ready, quietly slipped inside. He gave them thirty seconds to take up position in the darkness, then followed them in, gripping his Makarov pistol in both hands. Hearing nothing, Pena found the master-switch behind the door, and flooded the place with light.

The warehouse was empty, just as it had been on Saturday when they first showed it to the North Americans.

He ordered his men to search the ground for anything they might have left behind. He knew they'd been here, but he needed to know for sure.

A few minutes later, one of the commandos gave a loud whistle, pointing to something on the ground near the sliding front door of the warehouse. "Tread marks," he called, when Pena came up. "Looks like a van."

He ordered the man to photograph the marks. He'd compare them later on to the marks they had found from the white van the North Americans had parked outside the port security office, thinking that no one had noticed them.

Another commando shouted from someplace outside, rapping the metal wall with his fist. As he got closer, Pena could see the wall tremble from the banging. Outside, in the pitch black of the night, the man had found it because of the pinprick of light, emanating from the lit warehouse. Pena never would have seen the tiny hole otherwise. He ran his finger over the smooth hole, then examined his skin for metal filings. But there was nothing. These North Americans were professionals. He smiled.

He took the talkie walkie from his belt and pressed the talk switch. "All clear," he said. The radio crackled. Then a voice answered. "We're underway."

Fifteen minutes later, the Venezuelan army tractor trailer truck drove back onto the string piece, headlights doused, and came to a halt alongside the *East Wind III*. Four men emerged from the rear door of the cab and began stripping off the canvas, exposing the mini-submarine exactly where they had tied it down earlier. Pena gave the thumbs-up to the captain, who then signaled a crewman standing at an oily console just beneath the wheelhouse. He threw a long lever, and the white articulated arm of the ship's crane rose from amidships and swiveled around until it hovered over the top of the trailer. The driver grabbed the dangling hook and slipped it through a thick metal ring to which four metal cables were attached. These in turn were hooked onto hard points on the mini-sub, two at the bow, two at the stern, each secured by one of the soldiers. The driver thrust out his arm, palm upwards, so the crane operator could see him. When all the points held, he swept his hand up and over his head and jumped out of the way as the mini-sub rose up and swung onto the ship. The crane operator lowered it back into the waiting container in the hold with a loud thump. They repeated the procedure with the smaller object.

In less than fifteen minutes, it was all over. Headlights still off, they drove away.

0830 hours, Tuesday, June 26 – Washington, DC

Luther Powell was pensive as he approached the office of Assistant Director Nathanial Charles on the top floor of the Washington field office, just off of Judiciary Square. He pulled the white cuffs of his starched shirt until the gold eagle cufflinks were just visible below the sleeve of his dark suit. It was an old habit, but it did nothing to allay his nervousness. He took a deep breath, and pushed open the door.

"Hey, Harriet," he said to the receptionist. "Is the boss in yet?"

"What just fell on your head?" She gave the younger man her mother hen look, but when she saw his whitened finger tips clutching the expandable folder, she relented. "He's waiting for you. He said to just go right in."

Nate Charles was seated behind a desk as large as an aircraft carrier. It was old style Washington, the type of desk upon which United States Senators conducted amorous investigations. A classified computer sat on an extension to one side, in an ugly grey metal case to shield it from electronic eavesdropping and electromagnetic pulse. The screen was blank except for a single word, *Restricted*.

"Thank-you for taking the time to see me, sir," Luther began.

"You're one of my best section chiefs, Luther. You know that."

The younger man's nervous formality put him on his guard. He let him talk.

"It's about a CI, sir. But not one of mine. It's not my case and I shouldn't be anywhere near it. But I am."

"Go on."

"You might have heard about the sister's murder. She was pulled out of the Patuxent river in Maryland a few weeks back. Regional office thinks the brother is a potential suspect. But he's being covered by the officer who's running him."

Nate Charles took a long hard look at the ex-Marine in his perfect suit and starched white shirt and just shook his head. "Luther, are you really determined to deep six a perfect career? I mean, are you going out of your way?"

"That's what I'm asking myself, sir. Until we found this."

He slid over the surveillance photographs from the Mayflower Hotel. "Special Agent Joanna Greary, Baltimore Field Office. She waved the regional office off of Sayeed because he was providing information in a counter-terrorism investigation. Only thing is, he wasn't."

"What do you mean?" Nate Charles said. He didn't like the sound of this one bit.

Luther sketched out Sayeed's employment at Muslims for Free Enterprise, and the money trail that led back to the SARI Group. "Brother Sayeed was right in the thick of it, but Agent Greary never asked him about SARI. Instead, it was some bullshit about an uncle bringing in cash from Pakistan."

Nate Charles had seen this before, and every time it happened, it saddened him. It happened everywhere, he reasoned. Not just government. The private sector was full of corruption stories, of company officers, even corporate presidents, who skimmed and cheated and lied. But this was the Bureau. His Bureau. And while he knew there had always been Special Agents on the take, he had always hoped it would never happen on his watch. And now it was.

"Luther, you're talking general counsel. Maybe OPR." The Office of Professional Responsibility was the FBI internal investigation unit that picked up on findings from the Office of General Counsel and conducted witch hunts that landed FBI agents in jail. No one wanted to be investigated by OPR.

"Sir, it gets worse. Since this *is* a capital murder investigation, the regional office carried out surveillance on Sayeed."

Nate Charles gave a quick, worried shake of his head. "No wiretaps, right? You're telling me they played this by the books. That's what I'm hearing from you."

"Yes, sir. Only external contacts, public places. No interiors. Nothing an ordinary individual couldn't observe with his own eyes, should they want to."

That was the law, and they both knew it. But Nate Charles was not relieved.

"OK. So what did you find?"

"Turns out, Agent Greary's CI keeps interesting company."

He slid forward photographs of the meetings down on the Washington mall, then photographs of the same individuals entering Mir Construction in Potomac, Maryland. Other photographs showed Sayeed with a vaguely South Asian-looking individual in the baggage claim area of Dulles International airport; entering a garden apartment complex in suburban Maryland; at Mir Construction; and again, leaving Dulles.

"We don't yet know the names of Sayeed's two companions from the Mall, or whether they are relevant to the case. But we were able to trace his visitor from Los Angeles. His name is Albert Creely. UK national, arrived from Sidney, Australia.

"A Brit?"

"We don't know yet for sure. Sayeed greeted him at the airport using the word *mohandes*. It's an honorific title in Farsi and Pashto. It means, engineer."

Nate Charles shook his head. "That doesn't give you probable cause. Not even for a FISA court." That was a special magistrate court that handled FBI requests for emergency wiretaps and physical surveillance under the Foreign Intelligence Surveillance Act They required evidence suggesting that the suspect was involved in a potential terrorist plot and could take weeks – even months – deliberating. That was one reason the FBI didn't like the FISA court, and had never objected when the White House set up an institutional bypass after 9/11 that allowed the National Security Agency to intercept international communications of terrorist suspects.

"Does Agent Greary wear a wire when she debriefs Sayeed?" Luther asked. He was fishing, and Nate could tell. But he was just as disturbed as Luther was.

"No, and that's a sore point with us," Nate confessed. "I've had someone talk to her supervisor about that."

"Sayeed *is* supposed to be a CI on potential terrorism cases…" Luther let it hang.

"That's correct."

"Well, as Assistant Director, don't you want to have an audio-visual record of his debriefings, so you can evaluate him yourself?"

"I would say so, yes," Nate said slowly. "But I'm going to run that one by the General Counsel's office. And Luther," he added, as the younger man slapped his thigh and got up. "That means, you don't move on this until I give you the green light. You got that?"

"Roger that, chief."

1020 hours, Tuesday, June 26 – Bolling Air Force Base

Roger Kaminski often compared his job to the kid who plugged the dyke with his finger. Despite budgets that were growing exponentially, and ever-increasing numbers of officers at the nation's land, air and sea borders, U.S. Customs and Border Protection was still playing catch up with the bad guys. Sure, things were better than the day after the 9/11 attacks. On September 12, he said in talks around the country, we woke up to land borders with Canada that were manned just half the day, where the sole security was orange cones in the middle of the road. So we fixed that. Now we've got secure gates, cameras, and other monitoring devices, and armed Border patrol officers manning them 24/7.

The problem wasn't what they were doing; it's what they weren't doing and couldn't do, without shutting down the nation's economy, he liked to say – at least, in private.

After 9/11, everyone was worried about a terrorist bringing a nuclear weapon into a United States port in a cargo container. Nine million containers entered the country every year, and only two percent of them were ever inspected. The president's opponents in Congress liked to scream about that. So Kaminski set up a series of new programs to extend the borders outwards, and installed high-tech scanners at partner ports overseas that could peer inside containers without ever opening their doors. That gave the intel guys more time to figure out what truly presented a risk and what didn't, so the containers they eventually devanned were taken apart for a reason.

But if intel couldn't identify a threat, or just simply couldn't agree, then his men and women couldn't mitigate it. They were just the goalies. If you had no offensive team capable of taking the battle to your opponent's home turf, and no defense to protect your own goal, then it was up to the goalie to do his best to save the day.

"What I'm hearing," he said to Charles Haas, who had just given the sherpas an update from the CIA team in Maracaibo, "is that this ship doesn't present a threat. The initial intel may have been in error, and on-site verification came up with nothing conclusive."

"That's correct," Haas said. He was content, and didn't mind letting the others know it.

"And the passive gamma-radiation detectors?" Danny Wilkens asked.

"Negative," Haas said.

"How long did they collect samples for? How far away from the target?"

"Close enough and long enough. What do I know?" Haas said. "My guys are pros. They know what they were supposed to do and they did it."

"It matters," Danny said. "Our stand-off detection technology leaves a lot to be desired."

"And you know this because?" said Victoria Brandt, the State Department's resident skeptic. She knew that Danny's wife had worked at one of the nation's nuclear labs. She thought she'd just rub his nose in it.

"Assuming we're dealing with HEU," Danny said, not rising to the bait. "Gamma ray signatures are extremely weak. At fifty meters, you can shield it with tin foil."

"And I'm telling you," Haas said, "that the readings were negative. Look, this was an arms shipment, okay? I'm not pissing on your source. He – or she – was onto something. But we're talking South African tanks and a two-bit mini-sub to Hugo Chavez. Nothing more."

Richard Stapleton assumed his most professorial expression, half-moon reading glasses riding low on a richly-appointed nose, glancing from a sheaf of papers to Kaminski.

"Mr. Kaminski. You were telling us about the Customs manifest, before we got sidetracked."

"Indeed. Under our Container Security Initiative, we now require shippers to file a cargo manifest 96 hours before they leave a foreign port bound for the United States. Used to be they'd file it 24 hours before arrival – or sometimes, not until they actually reached port. This gives us time to do our homework."

"And so what did you find?"

"Maracaibo is not what I'd call a friendly port, what with Hugo Chavez and our friend Fidel. Nevertheless, the shipper doesn't want his containers impounded when they reach New York harbor. So he files a manifest."

"And what would that manifest contain?" Stapleton asked.

"Well, for starters we're not talking a big ship. *East Wind III* is a coaster, built in Russia in the 1970s, used to haul tramp cargo on demand. You're talking 150 containers, maybe 200 max, and not all of them for U.S. importers. You've got six containers of Persian carpets. Now, just because it originates from a high-risk country, doesn't make it a high-risk shipment. We've seen the same importer in Jersey City handling the same quantity every four months or so for over a decade. Besides, if there were anything radioactive in any of them, we'd pick them up when they went through the portal monitors exiting the port."

"What else?" Stapleton asked.

"Pistachios – again, a trusted importer. Most of the rest is South African goods. Car parts, iron ore, scrap metal, and wine," Kaminski said.

Victoria Brandt burst out laughing. "And Danny thinks they're Islamic terrorists! I knew Usama was moving drugs, but somehow wine doesn't seem his thing."

"What if they transferred the weapon to a container that isn't bound for New York, one that will stay on the ship when it's in port?" Danny asked.

Charles Haas threw up his arms in exasperation. "You're just not listening, brainchild," he said. "We've got American eyes on that thing being lifted out of the hold and crated away by the Venezuelan army. It's gone – *gone!* - if it ever really existed in the first place. *And* we've got corroboration from Vega."

He examined the faces around the table one by one, letting that last revelation sink in; then returned to

Danny and shrugged. "Maybe you're not cleared for Vega."

Danny didn't flinch. "We still call it Lacrosse," he said coldly, referring to the series of billion dollar Synthetic Aperture Radar satellites first launched in 1998 as the CIA director's answer to not having live agents in difficult places. They could see even through clouds and at night, and produced gigantic photographs that were so detailed you could read the Venezuelan license plate numbers on the army trucks that had hauled away the mini-sub and the weapon. When he had seen the pictures he knew instantly something was not right. The Lacrosse satellite had at most a thirty minute window over Maracaibo. How often did you manage to catch the bad guys in the act? Actually *physically moving* something you cared deeply about? The odds were so small it screamed *maskirovka*, the type of strategic deception the Soviets had mastered during the Cold War, when they built fake missile silos and entire divisions of cardboard tanks, just to deceive the U.S. satellites they knew were passing overhead.

He turned back to Kaminski. He wasn't going to give up yet. "What do you make of the new owners of the boat? Saleh Ibrahim and the SARI group?" Danny asked.

"Not much, actually. We don't track owners, just operators – although the two usually tend to be the same. In this case, the operator hasn't changed. Some investment group in Dubai. They run a couple of super tankers, a dozen bulk carriers and a handful of tramps like the *East Wind III*."

"I rather like the uniformed military," Haas said, to no one in particular. "They blow things up, don't waste your time."

"Enough, gentlemen," said Jason Steinberg. "Major Wilkens is not wasting anybody's time. In an earlier administration, I'd tell you that whoever was wrong was going to get his budget cut by half. But not this president. He'd rather be wrong than have another ground zero."

As they were leaving the secure meeting room, Nate caught up to Danny in the hallway. The younger man's jaw was clenched. He acknowledged Nate with a nod, but kept walking.

"You know, son. You really got chewed up in there," Nate said, falling into step. Neither man looked at the other as they walked. "You're following your gut. And it's the right thing to do. But you've got to learn not to show your cards until you know for sure what you've got."

Danny stopped and turned to face him. "Director Charles. Thank-you. But I guess I just can't play games with this."

"Well, you better learn. Because we're all playing games, whether you like it or not. Every one of us, son. Even when we think we're doing the right thing. Especially when we think we're doing the right thing."

"What do you mean?" Danny asked.

"Look. If you're right about this and the Iranians are trying to bring an atomic bomb into this country, hundreds of thousands of people are going to die. Probably, some of us that were in that room. And so what good has it done you to be right, if you can't convince them to do something about it?'"

"You heard them in there," Danny said. "They didn't want any part of it."

"That's the Iraq thing, Danny. Nobody wants egg on his face this time around. But believe me, they were all listening. You've got a helluva reputation, son, for somebody who's not a political appointee. When they get back to their agencies, they're going to be scouring the files. Trust me on that. But they're not going to get in front of the intelligence."

They fell silent as they caught up to Victoria Brandt, who was waiting for the elevator. Together, they rode down the eight floors with a gaggle of uniformed officers. Victoria Brandt didn't even pretend to be polite. When they all got off on the main floor, she walked briskly to the main gate, showed her pass, and strode out through the glass doors. Danny and Nate hung back by the cafeteria entrance, watching her.

"'Pro-liferation doesn't mean pro-life,'" Nate said, mimicking her twangy Rockville, Illinois accent. "Having children is so un-pro-fessional.'"

Danny couldn't help but laugh. "You caught that, too?"

"How could I miss it?" Nate gave a good-natured laugh, breaking the tension. "How many kids do you have, son?"

"Just one," Danny said. "We're still praying for more."

"My two are grown by now, out of college. Yours must be in elementary school. Am I right?"

"Just about, yes, sir."

"Listen up, Danny. We are not having this conversation, you understand?"

"Uh – sure," he said.

Nate put an arm on the younger man's shoulder and gently guided him over to a table in the cafeteria by the large glass windows overlooking the woods.

"I'd like to share a few details of a case that's been troubling me. There may be no connection whatsoever to what you've been looking at. But then again, there may be."

"You mean, it's your gut speaking?" Danny smiled.

"That's right, son. And you didn't hear it from me."

THE 12TH

IMAM

1100 hours, Tuesday, June 26 –
Rockville, Maryland

Lieutenant Slotnik had never seen Rex Morgan so angry.

The white-haired police captain had been through the gang wars. He had examined dead bodies in strip mall parking lots, and delivered over-dosed teenagers from the back seats of Daddy's Mustang in the MacMansion developments that surrounded Avendale golf course. But the one thing he couldn't tolerate was political interference in his job.

"Do you know how many times I've had to put off the State's Attorney?" he said, pointing to the phone on his desk. "He wants to know why we don't have a suspect to bring before the grand jury. He wants to know why we haven't hauled in the boyfriend. He'd love nothing better than see a nice white boy rape and murder a brown-skinned princess. Why, he might even consider running for Governor!"

"Scooter didn't do it," Slotnik said. "We're pretty sure of that."

"What's Brannigan been up to?"

Slotnik looked for refuge down at the manila folder on her lap. "There have been complications with the Bureau," she said.

"Like what?"

"They've got an ongoing intelligence operation with the victim's older brother. Something to do with the Muslim charities case. Possible al Qaeda ties."

"Does he have an alibi?"

"The best," Slotnik said. "He was being debriefed by his FBI handler when we believe the murder took place."

Morgan got up and paced behind his desk in the glass-walled office. "It's time you hauled every single one of them down here for interrogation," he said finally. "One by one. And I don't care what the FBI says."

A uniformed officer caught Morgan's eye, and poked in his head when the detective nodded.

"Lieutenant Slotnik, ma'am," he said. "There's someone here to see you. Says he's the victim's older brother."

"Take him into the witness room. I'm on my way," Slotnik said.

When the officer had closed the door, Morgan leaned against the filing cabinet in the corner and exhaled deeply. "Maybe you just got your first break," he said.

"Let's see."

Slotnik involuntarily gave a little gasp when she opened the door to the witness room and saw who was sitting at the table. She set down her files and the micro-cassette recorder she'd brought with her. "They hadn't told me it was you," she said. "What brings you here, Fayez?"

"There's something I have to tell you, Detective Slotnik," the young man said. "But you've got to promise me, you won't tell him. You won't tell Sam."

"What do you have to tell me, Fayez?"

The young man with the pencil-thin moustache grabbed the cuticle of his right thumb with his teeth and began taking small bites. He looked up at her with his big deer eyes, trembling. This was a different person from the proud younger brother she had met during their first interview. The self-confidant insouciance of the recent college graduate had evaporated. Today, there was only guilt and fear.

"I think they raped her," he blurted out.

"Who's they?" she said coldly.

"Zia and Jamal and Hossein Gill. Sam's friends."

She scrutinized him carefully, and consciously counted to five before she responded. She knew she would have to be cautious, especially with the State's Attorney breathing down their necks.

"Okay. So what makes you think Sam's friends raped her?"

"I'm not sure," he said. "I didn't think about it at first. It's just something that she said. The next morning she wouldn't get out of bed. It was Saturday and she was supposed to play girl's field hockey, but she just lay in her bed, crying."

"Did you talk to her then?"

"She wouldn't let me into her room. But when Sayeed saw me trying to talk to her, he pushed me against the wall. He told me to stay away from her. She was just a whore."

Slotnik had stopped taking notes, to make him feel more comfortable. She gave a sigh – of comprehension, compassion. "What did she say, Fayez?" she said softly.

"She wouldn't talk for almost a week. Something like that. This was several months ago, just before she started going out with Scooter. And then one morning, before school, she said she was going to a party on Friday night with Scooter and a bunch of friends. I argued with her. I told her it wouldn't look right. But she just turned away and said almost dreamily, 'it doesn't matter anymore'."

"And that's when you suspected something?"

"Yes. That's when I remembered that she had gone to the mosque that Friday night with Sam and his friends before I found her the next morning in her bed, crying."

She would take his statement later, on tape. But for now she wanted to hear the full story, and to hear it fresh. She wanted his horror, his guilt, his contrition. She had to be mother, priest and cop rolled into one.

"Why do you think your brother would have allowed that to happen, Fayez?"

"Because he was furious that she wouldn't marry our cousin back in Peshawar. He said only a whore would refuse to obey the wishes of her family. I think he had his friends make her a whore."

"I don't understand. Why would he do that?"

"It's in Islam. Our mullahs teach that any Muslim girl who dies while still a virgin will go to paradise. So if a girl is to be executed for whatever reason, they rape her first to make sure she goes to hell."

Detective Slotnik found it difficult to believe what she had just heard. Not here. Not in America. She thought she had left all of that behind, just like Dr. Kumar in the morgue.

"So you're saying that Sam – Sayeed – had her raped and then executed her for not obeying the wishes of the family?"

But Fayez had gone as far as he could go. He just looked up at her, his large deer eyes helpless, drained of hope, faced with a power much greater than his own small life.

Detective Slotnik felt that power. It rolled off the boy and washed over her like a gigantic wave. It made her want to clutch for the sky, screaming for air.

For the first time she could remember, Maryjo Slotnik was afraid.

1400 hours, Tuesday, June 26 –Manny's Oil and Gas, Silver Spring, Maryland

Brannigan wheeled his unmarked Mercury Grand Marquis into the right-hand service bay of Manny's Oil and Gas on New Hampshire avenue, and got out before a surprised Manijeh Dal could reach the car. Slotnik was in uniform, and her service revolver knocked against the work bench as she joined them around the front of the car.

"Okay, Manny. Which one's Zia?" Brannigan said. "Zia Mirsaidi?"

If Manijeh Dal had had the slightest thought of playing games, Brannigan's tone cut him short. He nodded to a mechanic behind him, who was hunched over, fitting an oil drain onto a car on the lift.

"Mr. Mirsaidi? FBI," Brannigan said, flashing his badge. "We want to question you about the murder of Salima Khan."

The young mechanic gave a frantic look around him, his jet-black eyes darting with fear. Although the long black beard hid the expression around his mouth, everything else about him bespoke the terror of a cornered animal. For an instant, seeing the blond-haired woman in uniform on the far side of the car, he tensed his body, about to bolt. Then Slotnik emerged from behind the rear bumper, her two hands holding her sidearm in front of her, and his muscles went limp. He said nothing as Manny took his arm and led him inside to his air-conditioned back office. Brannigan pointed to a chair and Mirsaidi sat down, sullen, afraid, mute. He wiped his hands repeatedly on his clean coveralls.

"Where's the mosque you and Sayeed go to, Zia?" Brannigan said.

The young man said nothing.

"Where am I going to find Jamal Nashashibi?"

Still the young man kept quiet. He exchanged a furtive glance with Manijeh Dal, and Brannigan felt sure he saw a smirk form briefly behind the beard.

"I want a lawyer," he said finally.

"I think you're going to have plenty of time talking to lawyers, Zia. But for the time being, you're not being charged with anything."

"I'm not saying anything without a lawyer," he repeated.

"Suit yourself. But let me paint a little picture for you. How old are you, Zia?"

"Twenty-six," he said. He scowled as the words came out, and turned his head away, ashamed at having broken his silence.

"And how long have you been in this country?"

The young man didn't answer.

"Well, let me tell you something. If you're here with a green card, and we convict you of a felony – and that can be anything from second degree manslaughter to immigration fraud – then you're going to serve some serious time in a real bad place right here in America. Real bad men are going to f--k you in the showers. And that's just to warm up. If you survive that, and are still alive at the end of your time, you're going to be taken to an airplane, hand-cuffed to a federal agent, and deported back to Pakistan. And I swear to you, Zia, if I am still alive and I'm still in the FBI, I am going to be that federal agent. I don't care if it's the day before I retire. And that's thirty years from now, you little shit. Do I make myself clear?"

The young man said nothing.

"You still want to make that call? Go ahead," Brannigan said, tossing the phone onto the metal desk so the receiver fell loudly off the hook. "You've got sixty seconds."

Zia hesitated an instant, then pulled the phone into his lap, clicked for a fresh dial tone, and dialed a number from memory. He spoke quickly in Pashto, quietly at first. Then his eyes went wide and he shouted something into the mouthpiece. Then he smiled, and hung up.

"Alright, let's go," Brannigan said, getting up.

But Zia remained seated.

"I'm not going to tell you fifteen times. You're coming with us for questioning. And if you've got a lawyer and he wants to join you, Lieutenant Slotnik will give uncle Manny the address."

It was Manijeh Dal's turn to express surprise. He apparently didn't know that Brannigan had figured out the family relationship between him and Zia. "You'd better go," he told the young man quietly.

Lieutenant Slotnik escorted the mechanic to the back door of the Grand Marquis. When they were out of earshot, Manijeh Dal laid a hand on Brannigan's arm.

"Agent Brannigan," he said hesitantly. "This is a young man in trouble. Surely, he has committed immigration fraud. I don't hold that against him, because I know the world he escaped from. Have a little compassion, Agent Brannigan. Maybe he's done something wrong, but he's no murderer."

"We'll be in touch, Mr. Dal," Brannigan said.

He extracted the older man's fingers from the sleeve of his sports jacket and bid him good afternoon.

1530 hours, Tuesday, June 26 – Mayflower Hotel, Washington, DC

Luther Powell leaned across the concierge desk until he caught the eye of the man in the burgundy uniform with the gold braids in the back room. When the concierge came out, Luther gave him a visiting card. "Ask the day manager if he'd have a few minutes for me in his office," he said.

Without betraying the slightest emotion, the concierge looked at the card, then turned it over to see if there was a message. "I'll give it a try, sir," he said.

Luther propped an elbow on the desk, and leaned back to survey the main entryway that gave onto Connecticut avenue. A huge crystal chandelier hung way overhead, suspended from the vaulted ceiling. Across from him was a coffee shop with a half dozen tables outside in the public area, and more behind the glass partition inside. The vastness of the place gave the impression of a luxury mall. He half expected to hear a fake waterfall in the distance. Why in the world the taxpayer was funding a room in this palace just so an FBI agent could debrief a source was beyond him. He just took his joes out for coffee.

"Special Agent Powell?" The day manager brought him out of his reverie. "You wanted to see me?"

"Yes, sir."

"Please. Follow me."

He escorted Powell into his office off a corridor behind the concierge desk, and closed the door. "What can the Mayflower do for our country today?"

"One of our Special Agents will be conducting a debriefing here later this afternoon," Powell said. "I need to get in there ahead of time with my men to prep the room."

"You weren't planning anything intrusive, I hope? Nothing that would require us to – ah – make repairs after you're gone?"

"No, no!" Powell said, with a laugh. "Nothing spooky, really. We just need to make sure everything's in place. Special Agent Greary will handle the actual meeting, as before."

"I understand," the day manager said. "You'd like to keep this discrete, I'm assuming?"

"That's correct. She will handle payment on her corporate card, as usual. The informant will come in later. You never saw us. "

"Consider me just a fly on the wall, Mr. Powell."

"I'd rather not."

He laughed, shook the man's hand, then followed him back out to the lobby. He nodded to the two watchers who had taken up residence in the outdoor portion of the hotel café with their bulky briefcases. They joined him at the elevator.

Once the elevator door closed on them, he smiled and showed them the plastic key card.

"We're in," he said.

Joanna arrived well ahead of Sayeed, and ordered them a bottle of Chandon Reserve *blanc de noirs* on ice from room service. Sayeed, and the half-dozen other confidential informants to whom he had introduced her, drank alcohol with relish, contrary to the popular notion that Muslims shunned alcohol. What she didn't know was that they were engaging in a ancient tradition known as *taqqiyah*. Loosely translated, it meant: do whatever is necessary to deceive the infidel. When Mohammad Atta, the lead hijacker in the September 11 plot, visited the United States, he made a point of going to bars and strip joints, as did the other hijackers, to dispel any suspicion of their strict Islamic beliefs. An al Qaeda training manual, seized by British police one year after 9/11, spelled out these deceptions in black and white, but Agent Greary had never read it.

It was just after 6 PM when she heard his knock. She flicked her long blonde hair off her neck and checked herself in the big mirror over the desk before she opened the door. She had shed her beige linen jacket with the heat, and wore a white silk shirt with a broad collar, open just enough to expose the single pearl she wore on a gold chain from her sculpted neck. Just to make sure, she peered through the fisheye in the door and saw him standing there, nervously looking from side to side, fingering the handle of his small briefcase. Even nervous as he clearly was, his energy drove her nuts.

"I've been waiting for you," she said, welcoming him into the room. "You need a drink, young man. Washington can be tough, can't it?"

He turned on her, his eyes on fire. "This has nothing to do with Washington. You've got to help me."

"Slow down, buddy boy," she said. She poured him a glass of the sparkling wine and pushed him gently into the armchair across the small table from her.

"First, *hello*, we say. Maybe even, *what a pleasure to see you.* Try it on. You might find it fits."

But Sayeed pretended not to hear her, and held the champagne glass without sipping as if it were a cigarette and he had never learned to smoke.

"They've taken Zia in for questioning. He's absolutely terrified. They're making all kinds of threats. Jail, deportation. You name it. You promised to keep them off my back. You promised!"

"Just hold on," she said. She took a long sip of the wine and nodded at him to follow suit. Finally, he did. "There. That's better. Now, remind me who is Zia, and who pulled him in?"

"Zia's my cousin. He works for uncle Manny at the gas station. Some FBI type and a county police-woman came to get him. They said it was in connection with my sister's murder."

Special Agent Greary shook her head in disgust. "That f--king Brannigan," she said. "I told him to stay the f--k away from you and this whole case. Guy about my age, dark hair, well-built, around 6 foot – that him?"

"Who else could it be?" Sayeed said. "When he came to our house I told him it had to be that stupid football jock who was dating my sister. I bet he never even went to talk to him. Do you see what we're up against in this country? Always blame the Muslim first."

"Just relax," she said, getting up and walking behind his chair. "I'll take care of it."

She leaned over him, holding her champagne glass in one hand, toying with the buttons beneath the tie with the other, slipping her fingers through the slit in his shirt onto his hot bare skin.

"You've got to promise me this time you really will," he said.

"I promise," she said, running her tongue over his earlobe and down his cheek.

Still holding her champagne glass, she slipped her free hand in beneath the shirt to where it plunged into his trousers and she found what she was seeking. He closed his eyes and pulled her toward him roughly, spilling her champagne onto his neck. He laughed at the sudden chill as she climbed onto his lap, hiking up her short skirt, riding the proud sentinel of his youth.

2100 hours, Tuesday, June 26 – Somewhere over the Atlantic

Danny was glad he had remembered the sleeping tabs. This trip was going to be murder, but it was the only way he was going to convince the sherpas that they were at war.

Because that's what this was all about.

Once the Iranians handed back our hostages in Tehran after 444 days of captivity, most Americans were ready to call it quits. Game over. We lost, but so what? No one got hurt. Move on.

Only, that wasn't the way the Iranians looked at it. In their mind, they had won, because they had humiliated America. *America can do nothing,* Ayatollah Khomeini said.

"We just never got it," Danny said out loud.

"What's that, sir?"

Danny opened his eyes and saw his seat mate, Alex Moore, staring at him with interest, all of his 200 pounds of Scottish beef, his red hair, his hairy forearms on edge, waiting for his response. Moore was his security officer. He was a good man, if not too bright. Danny had made small talk with him over dinner, then he had taken the sleeping tab and started to doze off.

"Ayatollah Khomeini. Remember him?"

"That I do, sir. The old man with the white beard who started all this mess.

"Amen to that," Danny said. "We just never understood that he kept trying to kill us. And that his successors still have the same goal."

"That's what this is all about, isn't it, sir?"

"You bet, Alex. Now you get some sleep. We're going to have one hell of a rough ride ahead of us. It's field drill for the next two nights."

Eva had suspected something when he had packed his overnight bag and told her he'd be away for a few days. It happened often, to her as well. The best moments were always when they returned from whatever ridiculous meeting they had been attending. They ate with Paulie but got him to bed early because it was a very special night, and then Danny realized why Eva was simply the most wondrous creature God had placed on this earth. Loving her was like being at peace.

But today had been different. He couldn't tell her where he was going, but she had sensed something. *No, not something.* She had smelled *her.* Aryana.

Danny was glad Alex had been assigned to him for this trip. They knew each other vaguely, but no more. Alex didn't know Eva, had never met Eva, had no friendship with her or loyalty. And he was as red-blooded as they came. Surely he would understand immediately the moment he set eyes on Aryana that such a woman would be hard to resist.

What was he thinking! He wanted to slap himself awake. But somehow, no matter how he tried, he just sank deeper and deeper into Aryana's arms, even as he tried to talk himself back to sanity. As consciousness became a blur he knew that he had lost, and he felt her presence hovering over him, enveloping him like the wind.

1100 hours, Wednesday, June 27 – Silver Spring, MD

Brannigan and Slotnik found Hossein Battarjee in the small office off the prayer room of the Georgia Avenue mosque in Silver Spring. As imam to the small Muslim community in the Maryland suburbs north of Washington, DC, Hossein Battarjee presided over marriages, counseled families on schools, and collected zaqat (alms) for the mosque and for Muslim causes around the world. Since September 11, he had become a mouthpiece for the community, one of the "moderate" Muslim preachers invited to the White

House and the National Prayer breakfast. Hilbert Christiansen lobbied intensively on his behalf with presidential advisor Major Sherman, and made sure Battarjee got his picture taken with the president whenever he met with Muslim-American leaders.

Since interviewing Zia the night before, Brannigan spent several hours on the Internet with Paige to learn more about Battarjee and the Georgia Avenue mosque. For one thing, he learned that Battarjee had never actually condemned the 9/11 hijackers. His initial reaction, the day after the attacks, was that "no Muslim could have committed an act such as this." When it became apparent that Muslims on orders from Usama bin Laden had carried out the attacks, he said that Islam condemned all attacks against innocent civilians, whatever the ostensible reason. This gave rise to speculation that he tacitly condoned the attack on the Pentagon, headquarters of the U.S. military.

On September 13, Hilbert Christiansen's Muslims for Free Enterprise website posted a notice to American Muslims, urging them not to cooperate with the FBI, and gave them numbers of ACLU lawyers they could contact if they suffered harassment from U.S. authorities. Battarjee was one of the imams whose authority Christiansen and his Palestinian deputy, Khaled Nasser, cited in posting these instructions to the community. Two weeks later, Brannigan read, Muslims for Free Enterprise removed the notice, reportedly after Major Sherman learned about it and phoned Christiansen in a rage, using language a Marine drill sergeant would find crude.

The imam greeted them politely, standing up as his secretary ushered them into the book-lined study. With his trim goatee, speckled with grey, his neat but not overly elegant suit, his open collar and trim figure, he seemed humbly studious – except for the huge gold rings on the index and pinkie of his right hand. He asked them if they would like tea or coffee.

"Actually, if you have Arabic coffee, I wouldn't mind tasting that," Brannigan said.

"I am not an Arab, Mr. – "

"Brannigan," Brannigan said.

"Americans often think that all Muslims are Arabs. In fact, I come from Eritrea, although it is true that I have family living in Saudi Arabia and received my education there. Samiha, bring Mr. Brannigan a Turkish coffee, please. *Masbout.* And for the lady?"

"Nothing, thank-you," said Lt. Slotnik.

"Please," he said, spreading out his hands to indicate they should sit in the sofa.

"Mr. Battarjee," Brannigan said "I think you know why we are here. It's about Samila Khan."

"I have spoken to the family. A terrible tragedy," he said. For all the emotion he displayed he just as easily could have said, 'it's going to rain today.' "So have you arrested that young man?"

"Which one?" Brannigan asked.

"The football player. The family is very upset about him. Indeed, the whole community is."

The imam's secretary came back bringing coffee for Brannigan and Battarjee. As he stirred the small cup, Brannigan looked straight into Battarjee's eyes. "We don't arrest people because the community thinks they are guilty, Mr. Battarjee," he said. "We arrest people when we have evidence they have committed a crime."

Battarjee shrugged. "What more evidence do you want, Mr. Brannigan? In Islam, our law requires four witnesses to a crime. And you have more than that in this case. I should think that would suffice even for an American grand jury, no?"

"I've got to warn you, Mr. Battarjee. Withholding evidence from a grand jury, especially in a capital murder case, is itself a felony. If you know of four witnesses to this crime, you have a legal obligation, sir, to come forward and provide us with their names."

The imam laughed, unphased by Brannigan's tact. "I know what everyone knows. What everyone could see. This girl was not obeying her family. She was dating an American boy when her family had pledged her in marriage. This is forbidden in Islam. It was not a secret."

"In our law, Mr. Battarjee, what Samila Khan did was not a crime. What someone – or some group of individuals – did to her, was. My job and Lieutenant Slotnik's is to find those people. We think you can help."

The imam took a slow sip of coffee, thinking. Finally, he said: "I doubt I can be of much help, Mr. Brannigan. I've told you what I know."

"Actually, you haven't," Brannigan said. He opened the leather folder he carried with him and placed a 9x12 glossy photograph of Zia Mirsaidi on the coffee table in front of the imam. "What can you tell me about this man?"

"Zia something," Battarjee said. 'He comes to Friday prayers fairly regularly. He observes the fast. Sometimes he gives zakat, in cash, but my sense is that he does not have a lot of money to spare."

"Did you know that he works at Manijeh Dal's gas station?" Brannigan asked.

"No."

"Did you know that he got his green card from Maqsood Bajwa in Potomac?"

"I don't know a Maqsood Bajwa, so I couldn't know this."

"Did you know that he had a fake green card?"

"Mr. Brannigan, I am not in the habit of asking members of my community to decline their immigration status to me. It's a sensitive issue, in the best of times. Since 9/11, it's become an invitation to hysteria. A climate of McCarthyism has come over this country that some of us find extremely disturbing."

Brannigan exchanged an exasperated glance with Slotnik, but didn't take the bait. If there was any McCarthyism in the country it was in Congress, where powerful committee members took delight in summoning FBI officers to closed door sessions to berate them for investigating legitimate "religious" groups. Brannigan had heard plenty about that.

"What can you tell me about Jamal Nashashibi? Or Zulfiqar Ameen?"

"Do you know these men, Mr. Brannigan? Do you know anything about them?"

"That's why we are here. We were hoping you could enlighten us," he said. It was getting hard to remain polite, but he let it go.

"Jamal is Palestinian. He comes from a good family in Jerusalem. For centuries, they had lived near Nablus, to the north, until Zionist settlers uprooted his family's olive orchards and murdered his grandfather. Jamal came here as a young man with his parents."

"So you're saying you know him well."

"He's a good boy. He had a bit of trouble in high school, but then we straightened him out. He did two years at Montgomery College and now works for a builder in Rockville."

"Did you send him to Pakistan to attend an Islamic school, Mr. Battarjee?"

"I don't send anybody anywhere, Mr. Brannigan," he said. "Many people in our community go to Pakistan to study Islam, because our resources here are so limited. Look at this library! This is all that we have. Serious study of the law requires books, scholars, a knowledge of jurisprudence."

"Are you saying you are not aware that Jamal Nashashibi traveled to Pakistan in November 2002 and stayed there for fourteen months?"

"I'm not saying anything, Mr. Brannigan. But I would remind you that it is not a crime to travel to Pakistan."

"And Zulfiqar Ameen? Do you deny sending him to a madrassa in Pakistan, too?"

"Mr. Brannigan, please. Zulfiqar Ameen is Pakistani. His parents are from Lahore. The father's a trader, as I recall. I imagine he goes home for vacation just about every year, like tens of thousands of others."

"How about these two men? What can you tell me about them?"

He placed in front of the imam photographs Paige and Kevin had taken down on the National Mall of the two men Sayeed met over lunch.

"This one, I believe, is Azam – Azam Dariani. He's from Pindi, outside Islamabad. That's where most senior Pakistani officers live. His father's a general, I think."

"He comes to the mosque for Friday prayers?"

"He is a Muslim, Mr. Brannigan."

"I take that as a yes. Where would we find him?"

"Am I being subpoenaed for information, Mr. Brannigan? If so, I would like to call my lawyer. I'm sure I have Azam's address somewhere in our records, but I'm not sure I can give it to you."

"How 'bout his job. He works, doesn't he?"

"You might try the same builder in Rockville."

"Look, Mr. Battarjee. We can do this any way you like. If you want us to come back here with a subpoena and for you to pay good money to get a lawyer to accompany you down to police headquarters in Rockville, that's fine with me. Just say the word. Now, does this builder have a name?"

"Mohammad Mir. On Falls Road."

"The same place Jamal works?"

The imam shrugged. He took a sip of coffee, but didn't answer.

"What about the other one? Recognize him?"

"Am I the only person in our community you are interrogating, Mr. Brannigan?"

"If you think this is an interrogation, Mr. Battarjee, you're in for a real surprise. How about a name?"

"Faisul," he said finally, dropping the photograph back onto the coffee table with evident disgust. "Faisul Gohari. This is not right, Mr. Brannigan. You wouldn't ask a Catholic priest to reveal to you secrets from the confessional."

"I don't think I've asked you to reveal any information given to you in confidence – unless you are trying to use this mosque to run a vast immigration fraud operation, Mr. Battarjee."

The imam stood up abruptly. "You'll be hearing from me, Mr. Brannigan."

"Oh, I'm sure of that, Mr. Battarjee. In fact, I think we'll be seeing quite a bit of one another in the coming weeks."

Battarjee watched them leave from the window in his study, then picked up the phone and dialed a number.

Out in the car, Slotnik scratched a few notes on a notepad. "I'll see what we've got on Mohammad Mir."

"We've got three of them now working the same job. And they're all using the same immigration lawyer in Potomac. No wonder the distinguished imam is so worried. If he doesn't become a bit more cooperative, he's looking at RICO and maybe worse. And he knows it[2]."

---

[2] The racketeering statute known as RICO was used initially to prosecute mafia dons and later, drug kingpins. Under RICO, it is a crime to have knowledge of a criminal enterprise carried out by others.

1000 hours, Wednesday, June 27 – FBI Washington, DC field office

Nate Charles was expecting him this time. As soon as Harriet showed Luther Powell through the door, he nodded for Luther to shut it behind him. It wasn't the habit of Assistant Director Nathanial Charles to work with his door closed. His reputation for openness was legendary, as was his fairness. The open door was how he wanted his agents to treat their minds, he liked to say.

He chuckled when Luther joined him in the sofa in front of the 32 inch flat screen TV in a corner of the huge office. "I'll bet Harriet's got her ear glued to the door. She likes you, you know. She probably thinks I'm taking you out to the woodshed."

Luther tried to grin, but it didn't come out quite right. He took the DVD from the pocket of his suit jacket and handed it over. "Here it is," he said. "Agent Greary debriefing her star CI. In Technicolor. Rated X."

Nate gave a humph. "That's more than a wire, but I guess it's okay." He inserted the disk into the DVD player and sat back to watch.

"What's with the champagne?" he said, sitting up soon after the video began.

"Oh that's just for starters. It gets much better. Fasten your seat belt, sir."

Fifteen minutes into the sequence, FBI Special Agent Joanna Greary was riding Sayeed in the armchair of her hotel room in the Mayflower. Nate Charles paused the disk.

"Let me get this straight. From the time Sayeed comes in until now, she hasn't asked him a single question. Not a word about the uncle coming in from Pakistan. Nothing about al Qaeda. Nothing about the money trail."

"That's correct."

"It's all Sayeed asking her to obstruct another Special Agent's murder investigation, in exchange for sexual favors."

"Yes, sir."

"Is there more?"

He had picked up the telephone and was preparing to make a call.

"Unfortunately, yes. You might want to wait before calling the General Counsel."

Agent Greary gripped Sayeed and, as their rhythm subsided, covered his face with kisses.

"I don't need to witness the afterglow, Powell."

"You won't, sir," Luther said.

As they watched, Sayeed lifted her off his lap and got up, undiminished for all his effort. His eyes were glazed over with desire as he led her to the still-made bed, placing her knees on the floor, with her arms spread out over the coverlet. Nate Charles hit the fast-forward so they didn't hear the screams they could see her uttering – whether in pleasure or pain was unclear. After Sayeed collapsed on top of her, spent, they saw Agent Greary speak again.

"Okay, so what's this?" Nate said.

"This is what you want to hear, sir," Powell said.

She shook him off of her, turned back the coverlet and the blanket beneath, and sat down squarely on clean sheets.

"Okay, goat-f--ker," Agent Greary said. "Now tell me why I'm supposed to help you. When's this uncle of yours bringing the money in?"

"I already told you," Sayeed said. "It's this weekend. Sunday. He's coming from Lahore via Amsterdam, then he's going back out to Los Angeles."

"You got a flight number yet? Like a date, and a time?"

"Didn't I tell you I would?"

She poured them more champagne, handing him a glass. "Sure, you told me." Toying with him as he relaxed on the coverlet, she gave a raucous laugh. "But I like a man who stands and delivers."

Luther Powell reached for the remote and stopped the disk.

"This will break her career," Nate Charles mused. "As I see it, we have only two choices. Either we confront her directly, to see if she's willing to give us Sayeed. Or we go to the General Counsel and eventually, OPR."

"What if she gets one of those whistle-blower lawyers, and sues the Bureau for sexual harassment?"

"All depends what price she's willing to pay. I'd like to give her a more attractive solution. Allow her to redeem herself, so to speak, bring her guy in… All this is just talking out loud, of course. Don't you repeat it to anyone."

"You're assuming that this uncle of Sayeed's is for real.

"True."

"We haven't seen him anywhere. But Sayeed's guys are all over the place. We've got them casing out the airport, we've got them meeting down on the National Mall. We've got them traveling to southern Maryland. We've got them working at that construction firm in Potomac, and in a gas station on New Hampshire avenue. We don't have a clue what they're up to, and in the middle of it we've got a bent agent."

Nate Charles hit himself in the forehead. It suddenly dawned on him.

"Fourth of July," he said.

"What about it?"

"Didn't the President announce he was going to be here for the fireworks?"

"Yeah, now that you mention it."

"What if the plan is to blow something up during the fireworks, or assassinate the president?"

"At this point, we don't have the evidence to support that, sir. But we'll know about the uncle real soon."

1500 hours, Wednesday, June 27 – Mir Construction, Potomac, MD

It was 3 PM by the time Brannigan and Slotnik pulled up at the offices of Mir Construction on Falls Road, just south of Rockville town center in the greater Potomac area. A brand new Mercedes 320 and a half dozen older cars were parked outside. Through the glass door of the low-lying brick building they could see a female receptionist, and two doors. One appeared to lead into a warehouse area off to the side. The other led to Mohammad Mir's office. Both doors were closed.

Brannigan flipped open his badge and asked if they could see Mr. Mir.

"I believe he's gone for the day," the receptionist said. She wore a scarf to cover her hair.

"Then how come his Mercedes is still parked outside," Slotnik said.

"Oh. Perhaps he has come back. Let me check."

The receptionist dialed his extension, and when he answered, told him that the FBI was there to see him.

Mohammad Mir was short and officious. He wore a cheap suit and tie, and his white shirt hung partially out of his trousers. A window air-conditioner blasted the small office with cold air. He was sipping tea when they came into the cheap wood-paneled office. Brannigan introduced them and handed him a card.

"What can I do for you, Mr. Brannigan?" Mir asked.

"We're looking for three of your employees, Mr. Mir. Jamal Nashashibi, Azam Dariani and Faisul Gohari. Any idea where we might find them?"

Mir was nervous. He offered them a Marlboro, and when they declined, he lit a cigarette with a butane lighter and puffed at it hurriedly. "They're gone for the day, I'm afraid," he said.

"Gone where?" Brannigan asked.

"They were out on a job."

"Oh ka-ay." Brannigan spun his hand for more. "Whereabouts?"

"We've got a small development up near Olney, off Georgia avenue. Jamal is a bricklayer. Azam and Faisul are electricians. Here's the address, if you'd like to have a look. We're hoping to complete four one-family units by September."

"We'd like to have a look at their employment records, if you don't mind."

"You mean, their paychecks? You said you're FBI, not IRS. Anyway, the accountant's got all of that."

"Let's start with their employment application forms. That would be in your records, wouldn't it."

"I suppose so. Do you have a subpoena, Mr. Brannigan?"

"Mr. Mir," Brannigan said. He was losing patience now. "Are you aware that as an employer, you are required to know the identity of your employees and to provide that information to the government when requested? I am requesting that you provide us with that information. Is that clear enough for you?"

"Yes. Yes, of course. Please wait."

He phoned to the receptionist and said something in Pashto, then hung up the phone. "I've asked Suhaila to get the records from the files," he said.

When she brought in the thin manila folders for the three men, Brannigan made quick work of them. "Do none of them have green cards?" he asked, as he leafed through the papers.

"All three are legal, if that's what you mean, Mr. Brannigan," Mir said.

"So why don't you have copies of their green cards here?"

"Aren't they in the files? Suhaila?"

"If someone presents us with a valid driver's license and Social Security number, we don't ask them their immigration status," she said. "No area employers do."

"Under the Immigration Reform and Control Act, you are required to," Brannigan said. "Just a friendly reminder. In the meantime, I'd appreciate it if you would make us a copy of these files."

Mir shrugged his assent when Brannigan handed the folders backed to the receptionist. She went back to the front office to copy them.

"Oh, and Mr. Mir," Brannigan said, getting up. "We're probably going to subpoena those records formally, so make sure they don't disappear. That's called obstruction of justice."

Out in the car, Slotnik started leafing through the stapled pages in the envelope the receptionist had given them. "If we had taken my car, I could have run those driver's licenses right away," she said.

"So phone them in," Brannigan said. "I prefer discrete. At least, for now."

1610 hours, Wednesday, June 27 - Kensington Garden apartments, Wheaton, MD

The address that came back from the Department of Motor Vehicles for Azam Dariani, and Faisul Gohari was a small apartment in a run-down complex near the Wheaton mall, a few miles north of the Capital Beltway off of University boulevard. When they knocked on the door, they could hear scurrying inside. Brannigan whirled around, pulling his gun, when he caught movement behind the closed front window-shade.

"Mr. Dariani? Mr. Gohari? Open up. FBI," he shouted, rapping the door harder this time.

Lieutenant Slotnik had moved to the other side of the door, her weapon drawn as well, when finally they saw the front door open a crack and a scared-looking Hispanic man begin fiddling with the chain. When he opened the door fully they could see into the apartment, where a woman and a small child sat at a small round table, clothes and dirty dishes strewn about everywhere. They put away their revolvers. Brannigan showed the man his badge.

"We're looking for two men named Azam Dariani and Faisul Gohari," he said. "They listed this apartment as their residence. Do you know where they are?"

The man shrugged his shoulders, tucking his dirty white t-shirt over his large belly, and turned to his wife. She was the one who spoke English.

"We just moved in two months ago," she said. "Maybe they were here before us, but how can we know?"

Slotnik asked to see the man's driver's license. She took down their names in her notebook.

"Where's the super?" Brannigan asked.

The woman came out onto the stoop, pointed down the path and off to the right. "Down there. Mr. Wu."

"Okay. Thanks," he said. "Let's go."

Mr. Wu was clipping buds from a sorry-looking rose bush in front of his apartment with a pair of scissors, collecting them in his brand new garden gloves. He wiped the sweat from his forehead with the back of his hand. "Dariani? Gohari?" He struggled with the names. "You mean, Pakistani guys. Left two months ago," he said.

"Any idea where they went?" Lieutenant Slotnik said.

"Na. Why they tell me? People come, people go. They no tell me. I here so they pay the rent."

"And did they always pay the rent?" she asked.

"Sure. Never no problem with that. Cash always."

"So how long did they stay here?" Brannigan asked.

"Maybe year. Maybe 14 month. They all like that here. They come. They go."

"I don't imagine they left a forwarding address," Brannigan said. "You know, so they could get their mail?"

The super just laughed, rising up and down on his bent back, his milky eyes twinkling. "No, no mail," he said. "Just visitors."

"Visitors?"

"Sure. Always men." He laughed again.

"How about this man?" Brannigan asked, pulling a photograph of Sayeed Khan from the folder he was carrying.

"Oh sure. He come many times. He stay late, drink tea. Always talk."

"What about this one?"

He showed him a photograph of the Engineer, taken at the airport over the weekend. Mr. Wu shook his head.

"I no seen this one. No. I remember the face. This one never come here."

1640 hours, Wednesday, June 27 – Olney, Maryland

They found the small development near Olney with difficulty. There was no sign off Connecticut avenue indicating the site, and it was only when Brannigan noticed dried mud on a newly-paved road behind them that they doubled back from the Olney town center and found the place.

Just as Mir had said, four wooden frame houses were in various phases of construction. A cement mixer was turning at one site, as a few workers prepared to pour a foundation. Only one of the houses had a roof.

"Not much going on," Brannigan said. "Wonder if brother Mir is having problems with the bank?"

"It wouldn't be the first time," Slotnik said.

They walked up to the foundation crew as they waited for the cement. Brannigan showed his badge and said they were looking for Dariani and Gohari. The foreman was a heavy-set South Asian man with a black moustache. "Why you want them, Mr. G-man," he said.

"And to whom would I have the honor of speaking?" Brannigan asked.

"I'm the foreman here. I work for Mr. Mir."

"So I gather. And would you have a name? Let's see some ID."

Grumbling, he pulled a fat wallet from the back pocket of his jeans, and handed over a Maryland driver's license. Brannigan read, as Slotnik wrote:

"Hossein Gill. That's G-I-L-L. Born July 22, 1980. Address: 14000 George Avenue, Unit 216, Silver Spring, MD."

"Isn't that Bel Pre Manor?" Slotnik asked.

"Well, Mr. Gill?" said Brannigan.

"And what if it is?" he said.

"How long have you been in this country?" Brannigan asked.

"I was born here, copper. And I know my rights. Satisfied?"

"So where are Dariani and Gohari?"

"They work over there." He pointed to the house with the roof. "They're electricians. But you won't find them there now."

"And why's that?" Brannigan said. "It's not even five o'clock."

"Beats me. Something came up. They left over an hour ago."

"Where do they call home?"

Hossein Gill blew out air in contempt. "How do you expect me to know? It's none of my business."

"We'll see about that, Mr. Gill," Brannigan said.

He and Slotnik went over to the house where the two electricians had been working and walked through it. It had what appeared to be two master bedroom suites, at opposite sides of the house, each with two smaller bedrooms, a small living/dining area and a separate kitchen. "I thought these were one-family houses?" Brannigan said.

"All depends on how you conceive of family," Slotnik said.

They found the electricians' gear abandoned on the second floor. They hadn't even bothered to put away their tools.

"Looks like our friendly imam gave someone a call," Brannigan said.

"Let's run the Socials and see if some other address comes up."

Brannigan caught her arm as she turned to leave. "Wait."

Something had caught his eye. He stooped down to one of the toolboxes the electricians had been using, then pulled out a pair of latex gloves and a baggie from his pocket. "Well, what do you know."

"What are those?" Slotnik asked, as he held up a coiled bunch of thin plastic strips.

"Cable ties." He straightened them in his gloved hands to their full length, then let them collapse again into black coils he tucked into the baggie. They were clearly long enough to fit around a person's wrists.

A couple of cheap kitchen chairs were set around a cardboard box the workmen had been using as a table. Two plastic cups, still half-full of tea, sat on the box, along with a coke-can they had been using as an ashtray.

"Let's see if the Lab can't get some prints off those cups. And maybe some DNA from the cigarette butts."

He bagged the plastic cups and extracted cigarette butts from the coke can with tweezers.

"Wonder when our friends are coming back?" Slotnik said.

"We don't have the manpower to stake this place out. I say we lean on Mr. Mir."

1800 hours, Wednesday, June 27 – Dubai International Airport

Danny watched his security man, Alex Moore, hand his official passport to the Dubai immigration official, who quickly flipped through the visa section before putting it into a scanner.

"Official business, Mr. Moore?" he asked politely.

"Oh yah," Alex said good-naturedly. "Got to check up on all them young sailors on R&R. We got some rowdy ones, you know."

"Have a pleasant stay in Dubai, Mr. Moore," he said, handing back his passport after a red light flashed on the scanner.

Danny went through a different line, and was using a tourist passport in his own name. He was impressed at the silent efficiency of the Customs officer, a woman of indeterminate age wearing a black robe and a yellow head scarf. After scanning his passport, the woman stamped in a visa, no questions asked. He hadn't even needed to use his carefully-concocted story to explain why he was planning to stay in the city-state for less than nine hours.

Signs were still up for the Dubai Open golf tournament, which had been held in March. Billboards enticed visitors to try out their snow skills at Ski Dubai, an indoor ski resort in the desert at Mall of the Emirates, and advertised new villas available at The World. "Own a piece of England," one banner said. "Buy America!" said another. The whole place had a Disneyworld quality to it. Everything seemed focused on money and pleasure.

Danny caught up with Alex beyond the Customs barrier. He was talking with a young woman with long dark blond hair tied up in a pony tail she had stuffed into a cap. She was wearing cammo trousers and a long-sleeved khaki shirt despite the heat.

"Danny? Lieutenant Sellers," Alex said.

"So this is the 'old buddy' you were telling me about?" Danny laughed as he held out his hand. "Alex didn't quite prepare me for you," he admitted.

"Michelle," she said. "Come on. We don't have much time. I'll get you briefed up to speed in the car."

Lt. Sellers would have been quite attractive if she only got rid of the baseball cap and let her hair down. There was an energy, curtness and muscularity to her that emphasized competence, but beneath it was a liveliness no amount of military clothing could suppress. Danny wondered exactly how Alex had gotten to know her, then quickly put that thought from his mind.

She took them to a huge GMC Yukon SUV, dark blue with tinted windows. From the way the doors closed, Danny suspected it was armored.

"I thought this was supposed to be a peaceful place," he said, banging the armor plate. "No bombings, no shootings, no crime."

"It is," Sellers said. "Except if you happen to be doing something the Ruler fears will disturb the tranquility of his desert paradise."

"That would be us," Danny said with a laugh.

"Does the Sheikh still have the live video feed from the airport immigration lines piped into his office?" Alex asked.

"Roger that," Sellers said. "He even gets his flaks to brag about it to the press. If he sees any back-up in the immigration lines, he phones the head of Customs and gets him to lay on more officers."

"I'll bet," said Danny.

"There are other advantages, of course," Sellers said. "So we have to take it for granted that he knows you're here. That still doesn't explain the MOIS teams."

"What MOIS teams?" Alex asked.

"Three of them, sir. Action teams. We tracked them coming in separately over the past three days. I don't know how they knew you were coming, but I'm betting that they did."

Somewhere, there had been a leak. But who? Danny had kept this trip completely under wraps. Only his division chief knew what he was planning to do. But of course, others knew as well, because there had been a mass of paperwork to get cleared. Somewhere in that chain of command – a secretary? An accountant? A travel clerk? He doubted it was Aryana's organization. She had gotten here two days ago, and traveled daily to her small office in Jebel Ali, using her computer software business as cover. If Aryana had been made, they would have taken her out by now. Unless it was

Rahimi… Could the Rev. Guards Colonel be a dangle? But then why would they have given him the pictures of the *East Wind III?* Surely the Iranians would not jeopardize their strategic plans just to roll up an exile intelligence operation and kill a few American military types? *Hell, they are killing enough of us in Iraq.*

"When we get onto the Makhtoum Expressway," Sellers went on, "Alex is going to reach beneath his seat and pull out the packages I've been told to give you. They're standard-issue 9 mm Beretta M9s, two clips each. You'll return them when we rendezvous tonight at the downtown Sheraton before your flight, hopefully without having used them. "

"Change of plans?" Alex said.

"That's correct, sir. You are to take a circuitous route to your rendezvous point. As far as we can tell, the hotel being used by Miss Pourmanesh is clean. You want it to stay that way."

When she swung onto the Expressway and picked up speed, Alex reached beneath his seat and pulled out the weapons. He broke down the first pistol to make sure there was no chambered round, then rammed in the magazine until it clicked. Then he withdrew the magazine and handed the pistol and two magazines to Danny. "No shoulder holster," he said. "Blackwater style."

Danny knew all too well what he meant. He had crossed paths with the former spec-ops guys who hired on as private security guards with Blackwater in Iraq. They always carried their sidearms tucked beneath the belt of their jeans in the small of the back. Only the Arabs slipped the weapons in the front of their trousers – daring God, perhaps, to blow their manhood off.

"I'm going to drop you across from a shopping mall," Sellers said. "Walk into the mall, turn right and go to the end. There will be an exit on the left-hand side that gives onto Dubai Creek – that's the inner harbor, where the local freighters dock. Wander around for a bit. Get a feel for the street. Then you'll want to proceed up the Creek toward the gold souk and take the water bus to Bur Dubai, the other side of the Creek. If you're clean by then, take a taxi to the hotel, which is back here in Deira.

They had reached the city center by now, and Lt. Sellers pointed to the shopping mall on the other side of the street. "There it is," she said. "Also in the package is a map of the city and photographs of the MOIS teams. We'll be watching the hotel from afar, but we won't be able to help you get there. Get out here and cross over."

As they shouldered their bags out on the sidewalk, she rolled down the window and leaned toward them. "Good luck, gentlemen."

The shopping mall was starting to fill up as evening approached. Alex stopped in front of a clothing store advertising cut-rate Italian suits and carefully used the window to scan the crowd behind them. Satisfied, he led them deeper into the air-conditioned indoor mall, then directed Danny into one of the stores. They spent a good ten minutes flipping through designer suits on the racks, Danny with his back to the front window, flipping through the pictures one by one, while Alex faced him from deeper in the store, scanning the mall. Finally, Alex nodded for them to leave. "So far, so good," he said.

They found the exit to Dubai Creek, and as soon as they opened the glass doors, a blast of hot, humid air engulfed them. The sky was overcast and leaden. Somewhere the sun was getting ready to go down, after having baked the earth and sucked every bit of moisture out of the rocks.

They threaded their way through traffic to the quayside. It was packed with trucks, small freighters and traditional Trucial Coast dhows, now powered by motors, not sails. Paletted cargo lay under bright orange tarpaulins to shield it from the sun. A pair of Somali longshoremen sat in the shade of a heap of burlap bags, drinking tea, swatting flies. The breeze off the Creek smelled of salt water and rotting fish.

Across the street, facing the Creek, was a brand-new high-rise office complex. A large neon sign proudly announced, "The Twin Towers."

"Friendly place," Alex said, nodding toward the sign. "What kind of country would actually find The Twin Towers appealing after 9/11?

Suddenly, walking straight toward them across a small square came an Iranian with a trim beard, carrying a briefcase. Neither man paused, or exchanged glances with the man, who was somehow too well-built for the grey business suit he wore. In unmistakable regime fashion, he had buttoned his white shirt up to the thin collar, but wore no tie. No one else in the Middle East dressed that way. He vaguely resembled one of the MOIS men in the photographs Sellers had given them, but Danny wasn't sure.

As they moved further up the Creek, Danny pointed to the office buildings across the street. "He could have been coming from the bank. I'd forgotten that the Iranians have built new bank offices here."

They passed the shimmering glass office front of the Bank Sepah, the Revolutionary Guards bank; the Bank Melli, the National Iranian bank; and the housing bank, the Bank Tejarat. Another dozen Iranians came in and out of the banks, in groups of twos and threes. "Let's hit the gold souk," Alex said. "I don't like this." It was hard to tell if any of the Iranians going in and out of the banks were among the men in the photographs. There were simply too many of them.

Unlike the indoor shopping mall, the gold souk was a traditional market, with tiny stalls heaped with gold chains and gaudy jewelry. They wandered through the narrow crowded streets, out of the sun, where clusters of women in black robes were shopping. After ten minutes, Alex declared them clean, and they headed back to the Creek to catch the water bus.

It was crowded on the dockside. Dozens of sweat-stained south Asian laborers waited for the low ferry to back into the loading area. It was more like a floating cattle pen than a ship; a kind of small, motorized barge. The laborers jumped across the gunwales before it had finished docking. The ferry was already packed by the time the driver, who stood in the center of the boat at the controls, had finished maneuvering. When his conductor determined they had taken on enough customers, he simply reversed his engines and started to pull out, without ever coming to a halt. "This sure ain't New York City," Alex said.

The next ferry was already chugging toward them from the other side of the Creek as the first one left. This time, Alex and Danny maneuvered their way among the laborers and women carrying large bags of shopping, and jumped with them onto the ferry before it left. "Looks good," Alex said, once they got under way.

The ride across the Creek took less than five minutes, and they went through the same procedure to disembark, leaping out with the crowds onto one side of the small dock as incoming passengers leapt onto the boat from the other side.

A row of taxis was waiting on the next street. "Let's give it a try," Alex said. "We're as good as we'll ever be."

2130 hours, Wednesday, June 27 – Dubai

Colonel Rahimi was nervous when Danny finally arrived in the hotel suite. Danny had learned enough Farsi from Aryana to understand his discontent. Why was he late? Why had he come alone? Was he going to offer Rahimi and his family asylum? They were in danger. They had risked everything. Was this American going to deliver? Was this all that the United State Government had to offer? One man? So far away from home?

And there was more.

What about security? How had the American come to Dubai? Had he used his real name? VEVAK would have picked that up immediately. And everyone knows – at least in Iran – that the Dubai leader's chief of intelligence was an Iranian government agent. He speaks fluent Farsi! And has business in Iran. If this

American used his real name coming into the Dubai airport, it's all over.

Danny watched Rahimi intently as Aryana translated bits and pieces of his tirade. He nodded his head in sympathy as Rahimi spoke, giving the impression that he understood all that was being said before Aryana translated it. He wanted Rahimi to feel comfortable. He wanted him to feel wanted. Because Danny wanted Rahimi; he wanted him desperately. Preferably, he wanted him alive.

"Tell him we have a solution for him and for his family," Danny said. "But there are things that I need to know."

Aryana translated. The Iranian Revolutionary Guards Colonel was not amused.

"He wants to know things? After all I have gone through?"

"Tell him that I need the cell phone," Danny said. "The one that he used to take the pictures at the naval base at Bandar-e Lengeh."

Rahimi threw the phone on the coffee table, with a curse. "Here it is. And so what? I erased everything long ago. You want a dead cell phone, it's yours. But when are you going to make good on your promises?"

Danny reached into his shoulder bag, and pulled out a legal-size white envelope.

"Colonel Rahimi," he said, turning to Aryana to translate for him word for word. "I want you to know, first of all, that my government appreciates everything you have done up to now. We appreciate your courage, and we understand the risks you have undergone. "

Aryana translated. Rahimi fell silent. Danny knew he now had Rahimi's attention.

"I am prepared to offer you and your family political asylum in the United States. I have brought these papers with me for you to take to the United States consulate here in Dubai tomorrow morning."

He handed the Iranian the envelope, which contained a series of neatly typed letters on official stationary of the Defense Intelligence Agency, the Department of State, and the Department of Homeland Security. "When the American consular officer see these papers, he will give you and your wife and your daughter visas for the United States. It has already been approved."

Rahimi took out the papers. Danny was sure he understood little of what the letters said, but the gold-embossed official seals were unmistakable, and Rahimi looked at each one carefully, rubbing the ridges and valleys in the paper between his fingers.

"When you arrive in the United States, I will meet you at the airport and take care that you get settled. I have never doubted you," Danny said. "But my people tell me that we need your cell phone to validate the information you have already given us. We can examine it technically, even if you have erased the pictures, to find enough traces to satisfy our people that they were there."

Rahimi nodded after Aryana translated that part. "I understand. But there is more," the Iranian said. "They are very excited in Tehran. They believe they are about to vanquish America. I don't know what this weapon is that they talk about. But they believe they have some weapon that will bring America to her knees. Hajj Imad was there. They treated him like a shah. There are things I will only tell the head man in your country."

At 11:30 PM, Danny's phone rang. It was a special cell phone he had set up ahead of time so Alex could communicate with him from the lobby of the hotel, where he had taken position to cover their exit.

"Bad news, boss. This place is crawling with MOIS types. The guys in the pictures. Don't know how we missed them earlier. But the gang's all here and we're in the shits."

As Danny communicated the news to Aryana, he realized he was proud of her. He was thrilled by her professionalism, by her sang-froid. Was that love?

"There's only one way you're getting out of here," she said. "You need to flood this place with U.S. soldiers, or whoever is around and in uniform. Flood the place, do you hear?"

"You're not talking about them taking the place by storm, I hope?"

She rolled her eyes. "*No-oo.* I'm talking about a party. Loud and rowdy and dowsed with booze."

"A diversion."

"If you wish. Just flood this place and make sure you get all of us out of here while the *etelaat* types are scratching their Korans."

Now I know why I've always loved you, Danny thought.

"I forgot to tell you," he said. "I've also got papers for you. You've been reactivated, clearances and all. Take those when you take him to the Consulate tomorrow."

But Rahimi wasn't going to the Consulate tomorrow.

He had heard the dreaded word: *etelaat*. And he went completely berserk.

"What have I done!" he moaned, tearing his hair. "The *etelaat* has found me, because I trusted this stupid American. And now they are going to kill us all. I don't care about myself. But why should Mahnaz and Claudia have to die?"

Danny did a double-take. *Claudia?* But then he remembered that Rahimi had briefly been posted to Italy after the 1980-1988 war with Iraq, and that is where his wife gave birth to their only child.

"Tell the Colonel to calm down," Danny said. "We may have a few VEVAK types down in the lobby, but they don't know that the Colonel and his family are here. If anything, they are looking for me."

Rahimi slammed his fist down on the coffee table, so hard that their coffee cups jumped. "You must take us with you - tonight, when you leave. If those documents are real, they will be real whenever we use them. And if they are not real, then I will know that you have lied to me."

Danny thought for a moment, then realized that Rahimi had a point. All the clearances were there. The only thing he hadn't thought of was the logistics of getting Rahimi and his family from Dubai to the United States.

Normally Alex, his security officer, would handle the arrangements. But he was occupied downstairs. So Danny rummaged through Alex's shoulder bag until he found the secure phone they used to communicate with headquarters. He briefly explained the situation and gave the duty officer Rahimi's name, and that of his wife and daughter. "I don't care how much you have to pay for them or what strings you have to pull. I want them on that plane with us tonight, period. And I don't want any questions when we get to the airport. We could have company."

He put a hand over the phone and gave Rahimi a grim smile. "Tell your wife and daughter to pack their bags and be ready to leave in an hour."

0030 hours, Thursday, June 28 – Dubai

It didn't take Lt. Sellers more than an hour to muster the troops.

On any given evening, there were thousands of American servicemen on board ships at Port Rashid, where Bur Dubai meets the Persian Gulf, or in bars and nightclubs around town. They came to Dubai under special arrangement with the Ruler. For the Americans, Dubai meant R&R, a good time with easy women from the Philippines after months in the sandbox, nerves on edge, each moment possibly their last. For Dubai's Ruler, the Americans were an insurance policy. If ever the Iranians or the fundamentalists got too close, he wanted them to understand that he would call in his chits with the Americans.

There must have been thirty of them by the time Alex phoned Danny the next time. The first group had come quietly and taken up position in the hotel bar, where they had a good view of the lobby and the MOIS teams. The second group joined them, but by now there were not enough bar stools, and they began spilling out of the bar into the lobby itself, drinks in hand. By the time the third and the fourth group arrived, it was 1:00 AM and the party was in full swing out in the lobby. A pair of drunken female Marines, linked arm in arm, went over to a group of MOIS men, seated in lounge chairs around a small coffee table. Without the slightest introduction, they sat themselves down.

"Hey there, handsome," one of the women said lewdly. "Buy us a drink?"

"Come on, big man," said the other. "Show us what you're made of."

The MOIS men, in their grey suits and white collars, bolted in fright, and after whispering among themselves, headed for the door.

Five minutes later, the women scared off the second team, who were milling around the hotel elevators.

"Brilliant idea, calling out the female sailors," Alex said to Sellers, as they watched the scene together from just inside the bar.

"They don't have a clue what this is all about, but they love it," she said. "Why do you think they joined the Marines? To f—k the enemy!"

Once the female Marines had chased all three MOIS teams from inside the hotel, their colleagues moved outside to expand the perimeter. Drinks in hand, they occupied the main entrance of the hotel. Couples of drunken sailors, men and women, strayed into the parking area to make out. When the way was cleared, and their SUVs accessible, Sellers whistled and

Alex, who was still inside the hotel, phoned to Danny to bring them down.

Rahimi had brought a Bedouin cloak, just in case. Danny had him shave his short beard, then told him to get make-up from his wife to darken the white skin. He wanted the two women in full hijab, head to toe. To the hotel staff and to anyone seeing them arrive at the airport or checking in, he wanted Rahimi to look like another Arab prince with his two wives.

It took the colonel another fifteen minutes to get ready, and Alex phoned again for them to get going. Danny was nervous about the time. It was already past one-thirty, and their plane left at five minutes past three AM. But when Rahimi finally returned with the two women, each of whom was carrying a small hard-cover valise no larger than a carry-on, his heart softened. The women were petrified, and were carrying all their worldly possessions. If he knew his Iranians, they would have jewelry, cash money, birth certificates, wedding papers, and photographs of the girl when she was young. From their comfortable existence in Iran, they were about to become refugees. The fear and uncertainty of their new stature was writ large all over their terrified faces.

The two women said nothing to Danny and stared down at their hands.

Danny turned to Aryana. "Tell them we have to hurry. Everything's clear. Alex has taken care of the bill."

Down in the lobby, the sailors were still partying, and the hotel staff were giving them a wide berth. The night manager had retreated to the back office. The coffee shop waiter had disappeared. The

Filipino bar tender and waitress stayed inside the bar, clearly ready to flee the minute the bottles and chairs started flying.

Out front, five SUVs were waiting, engines idling. The sailors and Marines now clearly had formed a perimeter, and while none of them had their weapons drawn, they all carried sidearms and were prepared to use them.

Danny rushed Rahimi into the second car. He wanted Alex up front with Lt. Sellers, and Rahimi and his two "wives" in the middle seat. He had Aryana squeeze next to them. He stowed their scant luggage in the jump seat and climbed in, facing backwards. "Let's get moving!" he called to Sellers.

She called the lead car on a talkie-walkie. "Let's roll," she said.

The lead car moved out and they followed, close on its tail. As soon as they had cleared the parking lot, the sailors and Marines fell back from the street and jumped into the remaining three SUVs, and in less than two minutes were soon behind them, speeding out along the still-busy boulevards to the clock tower, where the Makhtoum highway joined the airport road.

They were still fifteen minutes from the airport when the trouble began.

Although they were doing around 75 mph, no one had paid much attention when the first silver BMV passed them. Danny saw the car approach and realized in a flash that Alex had instructed the other drivers to stay in single file, so not to attract attention. When the second BMW sped by, Danny realized they should have been spread out, occupying all three lanes. It was too late for that now.

"Alex, watch your port side," Danny called out. "Aryana, tell our friends to get their heads down. How much armor you got on this thing, Sellers?"

"Actually, sir," their escort said. "It's just single-plate. Probably stop an AK, but that's about it."

"And the windows?"

Before she could reply, Danny knew the answer.

The two BMWs had dropped back, and the passenger in the rear vehicle had opened his window and took aim at the rear window, straight at Danny's face. The bullet impacted the glass, but did not shatter it. For a split second, Danny saw the glass around the bullet turn red, as the heat from the slug melted the area around it. His heart must have stopped as the bullet hit, as he realized he was about to die, and then, just as instantaneously, that he wasn't. A spider web of cracks radiated outward from the spot.

Praise the Lord, he whispered. Then his mind kicked back into action and he ducked. "It's not going to take many of those," he shouted.

Sellers shouted into the talkie-walkie. "Mackie, you copy me?"

"Yes, ma'am," came the reply.

"We're taking fire from the rear. I'm going to brake hard and fall behind you. I want you to swing out into the far left lane and see if you guys can get a shot at these clowns."

"Roger that."

The next instant, Danny was thrown against the rear seat as they braked hard. He lifted his head just in time to see two more bullets slam into the side window where Rahimi was seated, shattering the glass, and then he heard the roar of the engine of Mackie's Yukon as he sped past them in pursuit. He pulled out the Beretta and leaned an arm over the seat so Rahimi would understand to stay down, covering his wife. Then he flicked off the safety and took aim at the passenger in the second BMW and squeezed off two rounds.

He missed. But he got the man's attention. Another three rounds slammed through the broken window in rapid succession, knocking out the far window of their car.

Just then the BMW swerved as its rear tire exploded. Sellers turned the wheel hard to avoid the careening Iranian car. In seconds, the BMW fell off behind them, hit a retaining wall, and burst into flames.

"Yo, Marines!" Mackie hooted over the talkie-walkie.

"Yeah, good shooting," Sellers said. "But we still got that other one up ahead."

Just then, bullets hit the windshield, as the second BMW hit its brakes hard and came back into range. Sellers swung into the far left lane, and Alex put down his window and took aim. But before he could get off a shot, Sellers slammed on the brakes again, nearly knocking the Beretta out of his hands.

"How 'bout a little warning before you do that?" he said.

"Sorry. We're dropping back."

The other Yukons roared past, blocking all three lanes of the highway now, and the driver of the BMW took off. It was a fast car, and he must have had it floored. In an instant he was gone, with two Yukons on his tail.

"Mackie, Charles, stay with us," Sellers called into the talkie-walkie. "We're almost at the airport turnoff. Let the other two cars chase him out into the desert We need another fifteen minutes and we're clear."

Danny leaned forward to check on the others. Rahimi's dishdash was covered with broken bits of glass, which fell off him with a fresh crash when he sat up, pulling his wife up with him. Claudia was whimpering quietly, her shoulders shaking. "Everyone alright?" he asked.

Aryana gave the terrified girl a hug.

"*Hamichi dorost mishavad,*" she said in Persian. "It's going to be alright. Soon you're going to be free."

0900 hours, Thursday, June 28 – FBI field office, Washington, DC

Nate Charles was pensive when Harriet showed Special Agent Greary into his office. She was wearing the same tan linen jacket she had on yesterday, but instead of the short skirt she wore trousers and a bright blue shirt, buttoned demurely to her neck. He stood up behind his desk and indicated that she should sit across from him in the dark wooden chair with the black leather trim that was reserved for official meetings. He fingered the DVD case distractedly, knocking it against his blotter, then he walked over to the door and shut it quietly. When he turned around, he realized from her slightly startled, almost amused smirk, that she was wondering whether he was intending to make a pass at her.

"This is about Sayeed, Agent Greary," he said. "I read your report."

"Thank-you, sir. It looks like we're finally closing in on his uncle."

"That's not what I meant."

He rapped the jewel case against the palm of his hand, as if in emphasis, then turned to face her. "What's that you call him? 'Goat something'?"

She shook her head slowly. "What are you talking about?"

"Mr. Stand-and-Deliver. Sit down!" he said harshly, when she tried to get up in protest.

"You didn't…"

Her eyes clouded over in scarcely-suppressed rage.

"We probably should have done it from the start. It would have saved you some embarrassment."

"Embarrassment, in this city? You do what you've got to do."

"No, Agent Greary. You play by the book and do what you're supposed to do. Or else you're shark-bait. This is a firing offense. And if you don't know that, I'm going to ask for your badge right now."

"You don't have the authority," she said.

"Try me. And I'll have copies of this with the General Counsel and OPR within ten minutes."

He walked back to his desk and sat down, tossing the jewel case onto a stack of paper in disgust.

"You're going to answer a few questions, Agent Greary. And how this case goes is going to depend on your answers. Do you understand me?"

"Yes, sir," she said. It was finally beginning to sink in.

"Why didn't you mention this business about Zia in your report?"

"I didn't think it was relevant, sir. CI's will ask you all kinds of things. It's how you manipulate them. You string them along, give them something here and there."

"You didn't report his request that you get Special Agent Brannigan to back off his investigation, either."

"Not directly, sir. But I did tell Agent Brannigan."

"Oh, I'm well aware of that," Charles said. "You were way out of line."

"I felt the prize was more important, sir. If we could entrap a top al Qaeda courier bringing money into this country—"

"That's not for you to judge, Agent Greary. That's why you have a supervisor."

"I was reporting directly to you, sir."

"I know.

He opened the case file in front of him and leafed through if for a few moments in silence. She crossed her legs; uncrossed them: she tried to look away.

"When you first reported about the uncle."

"Yes?"

"That was just a few days after the murder of Sayeed's sister."

"That's correct."

"Didn't you find it odd that he wanted you to get Brannigan to back off his investigation? I mean, this is his own sister we're talking about. If he's anything like normal, I would think he would want the FBI on the job."

"You don't understand the mentality, sir. There is widespread paranoia within the Muslim-American community about us, about law enforcement in general. They don't trust us."

"Still. Didn't you find his attitude suspicious?"

"There was a clear suspect, sir. And Brannigan didn't seem to want to pursue him."

"I don't think you're read into Agent Brannigan's case file, Agent Greary. Again, you're making judgments that are way above your pay grade."

"Isn't that what we're supposed to do, sir? Think for ourselves?"

"No, it's not, Agent Greary. Not when you don't have access to all the information."

"I apologize then, sir."

Nate snorted. That was an apology made out of horse manure.

"I don't think you get it, Agent Greary. I'm not interested in getting an apology out of you. I am interested in finding out what this Sayeed is really up to. The way I see it, you've been protecting him all along. Was it just the sex, Agent Greary? Or was there something else?"

"I don't understand."

"Do I have to get OPR to pull your bank records to see if he's been paying you off?"

"No, sir. I mean, you can, but you won't find anything."

Nate just shook his head. "Has it ever occurred to you that he might be playing you on the uncle story?"

"He'd better not be, sir."

"Why do you say that?"

"If my instincts are that wrong, then I really don't deserve to wear this badge."

"Well, I'm willing to put them to the test, Agent Greary. One last time. And in the meantime, we're going to put some serious surveillance on brother Sayeed. So be prepared when he comes whining to you."

He took the DVD out of the jewel case and placed it into the manila folder with Sayeed's case file, then slipped it into his top desk drawer. "If your instincts are good, this stays here," he said.

After she left, Nate Charles picked up the phone and dialed a Virginia number.

"Major Wilkens," Danny said. He was in London, changing planes on the return leg to Washington from Dubai. Rahimi, his wife, daughter, and Aryana were with him in the British Air business travelers lounge. That was thanks to Rahimi's tickets, not Danny's.

"Nate Charles here. Has that friend of yours gotten into town yet?" he asked.

"No, sir. Tomorrow morning on the red eye, if all goes well."

He exchanged a thankful glance with Aryana, as he thought about taking her and Rahimi to meet Nate Charles in Washington. It had taken Rahimi's wife and daughter hours to calm down on the plane. Now the two of them had fallen asleep, exhausted.

"Keep me posted, son. Use my cell phone."

"Will do."

1600 hours, Thursday, June 28 – Calverton, MD

Brannigan was surprised when Luther Powell showed up at the FBI regional office in Calverton, MD late in the afternoon. He welcomed his former classmate into his small private office and closed the door.

"Couldn't wait until tomorrow," Powell said with a grin. They had been planning another Friday lunch at Jaleo. "I've got results."

"You mean, the latent prints?"

"Straight from the lab. Director Charles has taken an interest in your case. He asked me to keep on top of things, grease the skids."

"I'm honored, I guess," Brannigan said.

"So am I," Powell said quietly. "You were right not to back down. She won't be hassling you any more."

"Agent Greary?"

"The one and only. Now look at this."

He took a piece of paper out from an envelope and shot it over to Brannigan's desk. He caught it before it slid off the desk and turned it around.

"That's odd," Brannigan said. "They're both legal."

"On paper, at least. Both of them were granted Legal Permanent Resident status two years ago. The same lawyer in Potomac processed their applications. They came in under a Department of Labor program that allowed a U.S. employer to sponsor their entry to the United States."

"And that employer was Mohammad Mir."

"You've got it. The green cards let them get in and out of the United States, without difficulty. To be legal, however, they've got to actually work for Mir Construction full time, as their application states." He handed Brannigan another sheaf of documents. "We tracked their employment records and withholding taxes, and they're only working intermittently."

"So is it enough to constitute visa fraud?"

"Legal counsel thinks so."

"I am impressed," Brannigan said. "Help is on the way."

Powell smiled. "Mr. Mir has sponsored 126 Pakistani, Bangladeshi, and Afghan citizens to work at various firms he has incorporated in Maryland and Virginia, all of it in the last three years. We haven't finished running traces on all of them, but you can bet most of them aren't doing much work. And he appears to have sold some of those immigration slots. It's called 'substitution.' It's legal if the buyer – the new immigrant – meets all the employment criteria. It's not if the employment application is a sham."

"I'm glad I don't do immigration law," Brannigan said.

"So are most of us. It's a rat trap. Oh, and one more thing."

He handed Brannigan a set of photographs. One showed Samira Khan's wrists, as they found her at the crime scene. The other showed the cable ties Brannigan found at the construction site.

"They're a match," Powell said. "And even better. Remember those fibers you found on the inside of the head scarf of the deceased?"

"Yeah. Vaguely," Brannigan said.

"Well, the lab found a match there, too. Pulled from our collection. They came from a 2001 Honda Accord."

The FBI had the most extensive data base in the world of automotive carpet fibers, as well as paint samples from every single make, model and color of car manufactured or imported into the United States since 1916. Law enforcement officials from around the country sent forensic evidence to Quantico for the FBI lab technicians to examine.

"Zia's car," Brannigan said. "You've sent a copy of the report to the State's Attorney?"

Powell nodded.

"That should get us arrest warrants," Brannigan said. "Now we have to find them. Something tells me we're going to have to get lucky."

1730 hours, Thursday, June 28 – Union Station, Washington, DC

Agent Greary was finishing her first glass of white wine above the main hall of Union Station when Sayeed cautiously made his way up the cotillion stairs to the bar. Perched high above the commuters who strode purposefully across the ornate hall, she could survey everyone who came into the station from the two main street entrances, but because of the angle no one could see her from down below.

"This isn't discreet," he said, without even greeting her. "Why'd you call me at work?"

"Well, hello to you, too," she said. "Sit down."

"No, really. Someone could have recognized your voice."

"On your cell phone?"

He draped his suit jacket over the back of a nearby chair and placed a brown expandable folder, crammed with documents, on the small marble gueridon. To anyone casually watching them, they looked like any pair of Capitol Hill staffers, engaged in a mating ritual. She waved to the waiter to bring a glass of white wine for Sayeed.

"I'll have a coffee," he said. "Expresso."

"Leave the wine," she told the waiter.

Despite the immensity of the space all around them, the small booth along the marble balustrade felt isolated and intimate. Their voices were tiny compared to the roar from down below. She let him stew until the coffee came.

"I've been real accommodating with you, you little prick," she said once the waiter had gone. "Tell me about Zia. Why did Brannigan pick him up? What are you hiding? Who are these people, Sam?"

"I told you. Zia's family. You said you'd protect him."

"I can protect him if he's being unfairly harassed. I can't protect him if he was involved in a murder."

"What are you talking about?"

"You know very well what I'm talking about. What do you know about your sister's murder you're not telling me?"

"They got to you, didn't they?"

"They know about us, Sam."

She thought he was going to be sick. He turned visibly pale, and gripped his head in his hands, then banged his head quietly against the marble table.

"That's not cute, Sam. Cut the games."

"But you promised this was our secret."

"Yeah, well. Some promises are beyond my powers to keep."

She took a long sip of wine and contemplated her lover. Director Charles had been right about one thing: wearing the wire made her feel more self-confident in confronting him.

"What about Khaled Nasser, is he involved?"

"Involved in what?"

"With your uncle, the money plot."

"No, no, of course not. He's just my boss."

"He and Hilbert Christiansen."

"Yes, of course."

"You had better be right about this uncle. My guys are going to do the fully Monty, and they want you there to identify him."

"No way."

"We'll put you behind glass, he'll never see you. But we want positive identification. From you."

"If he ever finds out, he'll have me killed," Sayeed said.

Agent Greary swished her wine, relishing his discomfort.

"Is that what they do back home, Sam? What they do to girls who don't obey?"

"What have you been reading? These are lies."

"Are they, Sam?"

She watched him disappear toward the Metro, and contemplated having another glass of wine before she took the Marc train up to Camden station in Baltimore. She was going to miss the vigor of his youthful body. But there would be others. She wondered for a moment if his dismay at being discovered was a put-on, then dismissed it. Muslim men, she thought. Getting them to undress the first time was a feat. Getting them to keep their clothes on after that was a joke.

He was well out of sight when he pressed the walkie-talkie of his Nextel phone. The familiar voice responded instantly in English. Although he was on the other side of the American continent - in Calgary, Alberta, in fact - he sounded right next door. He was going to be busy on Sunday, Sayeed said, so they were going to have to make other plans.

"Please give my regrets to Albert."

2030 hours, Thursday, June 28 –
Burtonsville, MD

Eva and Paul were on all fours when he got home, intent on a pair of flashing red and blue gyroscopes as they battled each other on the coffee table. The trick was to keep them on the table, to see whose spinner could knock the other one onto the floor. Eva was batting after hers, trying to keep it in play by swatting the air, and their son was jumping with excitement. Glenn Gould was mid-way through Mozart's *Goldenberg Variations*, the wizardry of his ten fingers sounding like fifty as they romped across the piano. With the music and their concentration, they didn't notice him at first when he turned his key in the lock and quietly cracked open the door.

Danny stood silently watching his wife and his son, and a flood of desire mixed with relief came over him. He knew every curve of her buttocks, every muscle in the back of her thighs and in her abdomen, and the absolute perfection of God's creation made his blood surge with joy. He wanted to come up to her silently, without her noticing, and whisper something silly in her ear. She would turn her head slightly, beckoning ever so slightly for him to approach. That's when he would place a long soft kiss on her neck, and she would arch herself to his touch, like strings on a cello being tuned.

Moments of their life together washed over him, like wild arpeggios running up and down the piano. He caught her eyes from the far side of the conference room in the Green zone in Baghdad, and her bold look was a dare he knew he would take. Back in Washington, on the rooftop bar above the Old Ebbitt Grill, he could read the wave of disgust on her face as vulgar young lawyers referred to sexual acts in ugly ways. He wanted to wrap her in his arms, to shield her eyes from their vileness and seal her ears with words of truth and rush her away. The world they shared was a special place, where they could be vulnerable and unafraid. *You have been bought at a price,* Danny thought. *You are not your own; you have been bought at a price.* God had put them on this earth to join them forever. What he had joined, no man or woman could undo. How foolish he almost had been to sacrifice the temple of her flesh for a moment's vulgar pleasure!

"Well, hello, Mr. Man," he said finally.

"Quiet, Daddy – I'm going to win!" Paul said.

So much for no one noticing him come in. "I brought you a present from London. Want to see?"

That got the boy from the game instantly. He jumped up and ran over to Danny and tried to grab the bag from his shoulder. Danny grabbed him in mid-air and swung the boy up onto his hips. Eva joined them and he wrapped her in his other arm, pulling her close so the side of his head knocked gently against her forehead, the quiet acknowledge of soldier and wife, still alive after perils unspoken.

"You don't know how glad I am to be here," he said quietly.

"Why don't you tell me then?"

"There's nothing I wouldn't do for you."

"Including self-control?"

"Yes. Including self-control."

"What's the present!" Paul shouted, pawing at his shoulder bag.

"Do you know what they drive in London?" he said, setting the boy down.

"Cars!"

"And also buses."

He pulled out a red, double-decker London bus in a stiff cardboard case and handed it to his son. "And in the summertime, you can ride up top in the open air," he said.

Eva slipped her arms around his waist and pressed against him gently, unmoving, as if by pressing her body against his she could read the experiences he had lived through in her absence over the past 48 hours. He stroked her hair lightly with both hands and finally she came up for air and gave him a quick kiss.

"She's here, isn't she?"

Danny nodded, always amazed at how no thought could remain secret from her, no matter how deeply buried. "You're going to meet her."

"Whatever for?"

"Because I need help from both of you."

1100 hours, Friday, June 29 – Tehran University

The three men sat in Hajj Imad's spacious study in Lavisan, watching the Supreme Leader deliver Friday prayers at Tehran University. Known familiarly as the "imam," or "Agha," the Leader claimed to be the representative on earth of the Mahdi, the savior figure of Shia Islam who would reappear in the last days and reign for seven years in justice and peace.

Parvaresh nervously clicked his prayer beads as the Leader began. Mullah Hashemi, his secret patron, smiled like a Chesire cat, resting his hands with their four large rings on top of his belly. Unlike most senior clerics in Iran, Mullah Hashemi wore no beard, just a thin, wispy moustache. It was one of the privileges of power he relished. Years ago, as a young seminary student in the Islamic underground, he had let his beard grow as a sign of loyalty to the exiled Khomeini. His wife turned him out of the bedroom and pledged not to touch him again until he shaved. Ever since, he had remained clean-shaven. And married. And extraordinarily rich.

"In the Name of Allah, the Compassionate, the Merciful," Agha began.

"I express my congratulations on this great feast to the entire Muslim Ummah and all Islamic nations and governments. To our dear and honorable nation and government officials, I say 'good fortune awaits you.' To the venerable guests and diplomatic representatives of Islamic countries who are present at this gathering, I say 'welcome.'

"The Feast of Mab'ath is a feast for all human kind, not only for Muslims. The anniversary of the appointment of the Prophet (Peace Be Upon Him) as the messenger of Allah is a feast for all humanity...."

Hajj Imad turned down the sound and a servant brought them tea. "Is it two sermons today, or just one?"

"Just one," Mullah Hashemi said. "First, he will talk about the appointment of the Prophet and the beginning of his mission. He will announce the Mahdi at the end."

Hajj Imad turned to Parvaresh, who was flicking his prayer beads back and forth. "Are you sure about the satellite feed?"

"Of course. We've been doing it for years," the intelligence man said. "It reaches all of North America, including Canada."

"Calgary," Mullah Hashemi said. "One of my sons is there now. We have a small hotel complex."

Hajj Imad smiled. "You are too modest. You own half of the city."

Mullah Hashemi gave a great laugh, so his hands rose up and down on his belly. "You exaggerate," he said. "But it is true that I had to recalibrate my investments to limit my exposure in America after Congress passed those laws to seize our assets."

"Their day is coming," said Hajj Imad.

"God willing," said Mullah Hashemi. "There is nothing we might desire from America or Europe that we can't get today from Russia or China. As America falls, so they will rise. And we will rise with them."

The Leader was sketching out his vision of the state of Islam in the world, thanks to the enlightened leadership of the Islamic Republic.

"The arrogant powers are the enemies of the Islamic awakening of Muslim nations, and the reason is quite clear. The reason is that Islam is opposed to the submission of Muslims to domination, to the dependence of Muslims on outside powers. Islam is opposed to scientific and technological backwardness, which has been imposed on Islamic countries for many years. Why should the Muslims be the only ones not to have nuclear technology?

"The intense enmity of Global Arrogance toward Islam is revealed by their hostile cultural, political and military acts against the Muslims. Dear Iranian nation: can we imagine a world without America, without Israel? Truly, I tell you that this is possible! It is possible today. It is possible when the Mahdi reveals himself."

A voice in the crowd cried out, "*Allah-o Akbar*," and a great roar filled the packed outdoor seating area as the crowd responded.

Sitting just behind the Supreme Leader, who was cloaked in his customary long dark robes and black turban, was the Iranian president. He looked boyish behind the white-bearded Leader. Wearing a beige windbreaker, a starched shirt open at the neck, he listened modestly, his head slightly bowed, as the Leader began to preach about the 12th Imam.

"My dear brothers and sisters," the Leader continued. "When Imam Mahdi left us so many years ago, it was with a promise that he would return.

"I am here today to announce wondrous happenings, answered prayers.

"But first, let me tell you of a vision I had recently. Our dear president had gone to the capitol of Global Arrogance, New York, to address the United Nations. As I watched him here in Tehran, I saw a light fill the room when he uttered his first words, 'In the name of God.' At first, I thought it was just a trick. Maybe they wanted to blind him? But then I saw that the light surrounded our dear president, protecting him, not blinding him, and that everyone in that great hall,

all the leaders of the world, could see it. For 27 or 28 minutes, they could not even blink! They looked puzzled, as if a hand was holding them down and making them sit. No one got up from that hall for as long as our dear president spoke. Not one single person.

"This is when I knew that our dear Iranian nation will be blessed to welcome the Imam Mahdi's return," he said.

The crowd again erupted with chants of *Allah-o Akbar*, and the Leader, beaming, drew back, gently pulling the boy president to the lectern.

"In the n-n-name of God, the Merciful, the Compassionate," the president began, almost in a whisper.

In front of the television, Mullah Hashemi gave a chuckle. "He's even got the stutter down. Isn't he perfect?"

"Isn't that one of the attributes of the Mahdi?" Parvaresh asked. He wasn't a religious man, but he was always careful to express the proper deference. Mullah Hashemi just blinked and smiled, mysterious.

The young president began with a story. He told the crowd how, during the first weeks of his presidency, he had signed a pact with the Hidden Imam. "I just did this myself," he said. "I did not tell anybody. It was a private thing. Just between me and the Imam, May God Hasten His Reappearance."

To his surprise a few days later, when he was meeting his Cabinet, one of his ministers stood up and declared that they all should declare their allegiance to the Hidden Imam, just as they had done to the new president. "At first, the others were astonished," the president said. "They asked, 'how should we do such a thing?' I said, 'You know how it has always been done.' And I drew up a contract, right then and there, in front of them."

The crowd gave an audible gasp, and the camera panned to the front rows as bearded clerics turned to each other with expressions of wonder.

"Every member of the cabinet came to the head of the table, without being asked, to sign the contract," the president said. "And then, one of them said, 'how should we get word of this great deed to the Hidden Imam? We do not know where he is?' Again, I replied: 'You know how it has always been done.' And so we took the contract and went out of Tehran to the Well of Jamkaran, where tradition tells us the Mahdi is waiting, and dropped it down the well. As we were leaving, a wealthy man from the bazaar came up to us and offered 70 billion rials so we could feed the needy pilgrims at Jamkaran mosque. We thanked the Mahdi's blessing for this man."

Strengthened by these experiences, the president said, he traveled to New York. "My advisors were telling me, 'be humble. Do not anger the Americans.' But I replied, 'If the Mahdi wants me to become a martyr, then I am ready. The Americans, they can do nothing!'"

It was a phrase used repeatedly by Ayatollah Khomeini during the early days of the revolution, when Islamic "youths" held American diplomats hostage at the U.S. embassy in Tehran. It was instantly familiar and called up a Pavlovian response in the crowd, which erupted with chants of "Death to America."

When the chanting had subsided, he went on with his story. "And so I told them in New York,

'Global arrogance can do nothing. Islam will bring a new world into being, a world of justice.'

"I told them, 'Why is it that permanent membership on the Security Council is accepted for some, but not for others? Why is it that over fifty Islamic countries encompassing more than 1.2 billion people do not have a permanent seat in the Security Council?' And to this, the great men in that hall had no answer. They just sat there, drinking in the words and the wonder of your glorious Islamic message, suspended in the light so they could not blink. They could do nothing as the message of our blessed Islamic Republic reached them."

As he was saying these words, light appeared in a halo around him, seemingly from out of nowhere. It burned with increasing intensity, bright white, like a collar of shimmering diamond. He stood without speaking, beaming at the crowd, for what seemed like several minutes as the light burned around him like a diamond on fire. Finally, a lone male voice in the crowd broke the spell:

Man: "The Brightness of his Eyes…"

Crowd: *"Imam Mahdi!"*

Man: "The Brightness of his Eyes…"

Crowd: *"Imam Mahdi!"*

Man: "Let them Burn like Fire…"

Crowd: *"Death to America!"*

Man: "Let them Burn like Fire…"

Crowd: *"Death to America!"*

Man: "Let them Burn like Fire…"

Crowd: *"Death to America!"*

With the light still encircling him, the bearded young president, his eyes now aflame, put out his hand to hush the crowd. "I have just one word for you," he said. "*Shaitan der artash!* We must throw Satan in the fire, the purifying fire that the Mahdi will bring. *Shaitan der artash!*"

The crowd picked up the chant, "*Shaitan der artash! Shaitan der artash! Shaitan der artash!*"

Hajj Imad turned off the television and turned to Mullah Hashemi. "Do you know why we will succeed?" he said. "It's because the Americans are looking in the wrong place."

Parvaresh added: "They're looking at their seaports. They believe they have a hole in their container-screening procedures. They have spent billions of dollars trying to plug it up."

"Why would we play into their strength?" Hajj Imad said. A great smile broke out on his beautiful, boyish face, and his great pot belly shook with boyish laughter.

Mullah Hashemi became pensive, and plucked a set of jade worry beads from a pocket in his clerical robe. "Even if we fail," he mused.

"We will not fail, Excellency," Parvaresh said.

Mullah Hashemi clucked his tongue, silencing him. "Even if we fail, we will have achieved our objective. Who will trust America in the future to guarantee their security, when they can't even guarantee their own? If some tiny group like these Arabs can do such a thing, think what a great power could do to them?

"In twenty years from now," he went on, lost in his dream of a glorious future, "perhaps someone will remember America as a once-great power. China will be the dominant force from Europe to Asia. Mexico will control the northern hemisphere. And America?"

He clucked his tongue again, this time in contempt. "They will be making bicycles from recycled plastic. And young Iranis will be riding them."

VI

KOUROSH

1325 hours, Friday, June 29 – FBI Headquarters, Washington, DC

Hilbert Christiansen arrived ten minutes late, and they were all waiting in awkward silence by the time he blew into the secure conference room on the 7th floor of FBI headquarters in downtown Washington, DC, with Khaled Nasser in tow.

At Christiansen's request, FBI Director Louis Adams had convoked Special Agent Brannigan and Nate Charles, Assistant Director for Counter-Terrorism. Also present was David Farahani, one of Hilbert's protégés, an Iranian-American whose father was a major donor to the president's party. As Executive Assistant Director for Criminal Investigations, he outranked Charles. To his right, Director Adams had seated the head of the Office of Professional Responsibility, Eleni Venture. Her presence was a chilling addition. As the FBI's internal cops, OPR had the power to break an Agent's career. She was attached to a yellow legal pad and had already written the date, time and attendees of the meeting at top.

"Mr. Director, this is outrageous," Hilbert began, without any introduction. As a confidant of top presidential advisor Major Sherman and a frequent television guest he expected everyone to know who he was.

"I appreciate you taking time from your busy schedule to come over here, Hilbert," Director Adams said. It was important to show familiarity, since that was what Christiansen wanted. "We all know how important your support of the president has been."

"Well this investigation is undermining everything the president stands for," Hilbert said. "Years of work to bring the Muslim community into the Party are being sabotaged, all because of one flat-footed FBI agent who doesn't get with the program."

He was stabbing his finger at Brannigan, who sat across the conference table, watching Christiansen's performance noncommittally.

Hilbert Christiansen was a short, stout man with a reddish-blond beard, who looked and behaved more like an ageing Trotskyite than the conservative political activist he pretended to be. He was positively sputtering, and he had hardly begun. And yet, Director Adams was taking him totally seriously.

"Singling out a Muslim as a suspect in the murder of his own sister is racist, it's bigoted, and it has no business here in America. If the president ever learned of what's been going on over here, I guarantee you heads would start to roll."

Director Adams could absorb anger and criticism like a sponge, without ever seeming to be affected. "I can assure you, Hilbert, that the president follows what we do here in the Bureau with great interest. I personally take part in the daily brief every morning, so I'm not just saying that."

But Hilbert Christiansen was firing on all cylinders. "This is a political attack by racists and bigots. Sayeed works for Muslims for Free Enterprise. There are some people who don't get it. They spread bizarre lies that we get a million dollars a year from various places. But nobody has ever come to me to say that, or that I am a bad person. Never."

"Nobody is accusing you of anything, Hilbert," the Director said.

"Racists tried to attack Khaled. They published a phony letter, that he had danced in the streets on 9/11. The whackos finally pulled it from their websites and apologized. These bigots are spreading things that aren't true. They would never do it to another ethnic group. We know who they are, and it's got to stop. There are four or five anti-Muslim activists in the United States, who admit that their goal is to keep Muslims out of the political process. This type of behavior has no place in this administration. Period."

Seeing an opening, David Farahani consulted some notes he had brought with him. "There is a suspect in the case, Mr. Director. His name is Scott Glazer. He was the boyfriend of the deceased girl. But Mr. Brannigan apparently didn't find him worthy of further investigation. He interviewed him once, down at Ocean City during beach week, and has never questioned him since."

The words "beach week" were said with infinite disdain, as if they embodied the den of sin and iniquity that filled the mind of most parents of new high school graduates.

Director Adams turned to Brannigan. "Is that so?"

"Yes, sir," Brannigan said.

"And you never pursued this further?"

"We continue to pursue this actively, Mr. Director. But the Glazer kid was a dead end. The boy had broken up with the deceased several weeks before her death, and was already at the beach on the night she was killed."

"David?" the Director said.

"I don't see that Agent Brannigan has run that down, sir. He's taken a witness and potential murder suspect at his word."

"That's just what I mean," said Hilbert. "The word of a Muslim is worth nothing. But the word of a white boy is instantly credible. We know bigots are putting these lies forward. It's got to stop! This kind of investigation creates an anti-Muslim atmosphere that is intolerable! It affects the whole community! When Agent Brannigan interviewed the family, he purposefully isolated the father in a bedroom with a female officer. That's an outrage!"

"Plus, sir," Brannigan added quietly, "we have established that the girl was already pregnant when she got to know the Glazer boy. We think we've got a DNA match. But it isn't him."

Hilbert's fist was still in the air, poised to slam down on the table, when Brannigan spoke. When he understood the words, a brief sigh escaped his lips. He shot a quick glance to Khaled, then closed his mouth. Director Adams looked round the table. "Does anyone else have something to say?"

Nate Charles looked away, studiously avoiding Brannigan's eyes. David Farahani shrugged. They all were secretly waiting to see how Eleni Venture would respond. She laid down her pen and crossed her hands, and gave the Director a slight dismissive shrug of the shoulders.

"Very well, then. We certainly appreciate your input, Hilbert. And I guarantee you that this office is extremely sensitive to the concerns of the Muslim community. Don't hesitate if something comes up in the future to contact me."

As they got off the elevator and walked down the corridor to Nate's office, Brannigan tapped his boss's shoulder with a brown envelope.

"Thank-you, sir, for getting me those DNA results back from Quantico in time."

Nate just smiled, stopping in the doorway to Harriet's reception area. "Wouldn't have done you much good tomorrow, now would it?"

"No, sir."

1430 hours, Friday, June 29 – Calverton, MD

Lieutenant Slotnik's car wasn't going anywhere.

When Brannigan pulled up behind her, he saw the problem immediately. At least a dozen protesters were blocking the driveway to the small parking lot in front of the FBI field office in the Calverton strip mall.

Another half-dozen or so had gathered in front of the building carrying picket signs and bullhorns. Leading them was the imam from the Georgia Avenue mosque, Hossein Battarjee.

Brannigan got out and, carrying his sports coat over a shoulder, tapped on the window of Slotnik's squad car. It was hot, muggy and overcast, but the protesters didn't seem to care.

With Brannigan now in view, they began chanting. "Bigots! Racists! FBI Respect Our Rights!"

Slotnik rolled down her window and gave him a grim smile.

"They been at it for long?" Brannigan asked.

"The first ones must have gotten here just before I arrived," she said. "They kept pouring in once they'd managed to block the entry."

"How about we have a chat with the friendly imam?"

Battarjee was waiting for them, and when Brannigan and Slotnik approached, he had them chanting full tilt.

"Bigots! Racists! FBI Respect Our Rights!"

For so few people, they were making quite a racket. Brannigan spied Paige at the window upstairs and gave him a smile and a wave.

"Well, well. Look who we have here," Brannigan said. "Would you be blocking entry to federal property, Mr. Battarjee?"

Instead of answering, Battarjee turned to his troops like an orchestra conductor, speeding up the beat of the chant.

"Bigots! Racists! FBI Respect Our Rights!"

Most of them were teenagers, Brannigan saw. The girls all wore head scarves and long dresses; the boys were dressed in the traditional shalwar chamiz, their wispy adolescent moustaches twisted into ugly snarls, their eyes wide and glazed over with hate. A few older women also filled out the crowd, not one of them under 200 pounds. At the edge of the crowd, Brannigan spied a youngster with a digital video camera, filming his encounter with the imam. Great Americans, all of them, he was sure. They could have been in Peshawar!

"Just fortuitous timing, Mr. Battarjee?" Brannigan said. "Or did someone give you a phone call about forty-five minutes ago? How about Khaled Nasser? Name erased from your memory already, Mr. Battarjee?"

Battarjee had broken out into a sweat by now from his crowd conducting efforts. "You are harassing me, Agent Brannigan," he shouted, taking the bullhorn away from his mouth. "We are on a public right of way. You can't interfere with our right to peaceably assemble."

He turned back to the protestors, and ginned up the chant again. Brannigan turned to Slotnik as if to say, have at him.

"Let's see your permit, Mr. Battarjee," she said, moving closer, one hand keeping her service revolver steady as it bounced against her hips. She tried to back him toward the door of the building, crowding him with her wide shoulders, elbows out, but the imam wouldn't budge.

"Back off from me!" he shouted. "I have a lawyer present! If you so much as touch me, I'll sue you for assault and battery!"

"I think that just might make my day, Mr. Battarjee," she said. She pulled at the microphone attached to her belt and clicked on the switch. "Hello, dispatch. This is Lieutenant Maryjo Slotnik. I've got a 407 in front of the FBI field office in Calverton. Repeat. I've got a 407 and a possible 415. Requesting backup, over."

"10-1. 10-1, Lieutenant. A bit noisy around you." the dispatcher came back. "How many of them do you got?"

"Around two dozen or so. We'll need a wagon."

"10-39. That unit is en route to your position."

"10-4. Slotnik out."

Turning to Battarjee, who had been shouting along with the crowd while she was on the radio, she pointed a finger at his face.

"We don't mind taking all of you down to the station, Mr. Battarjee," she said. "Without a permit, this is called Unlawful Assembly."

The imam fumbled in the pocket of his dusty suit jacket, and pulled out a neatly folded piece of paper. He flipped it open in the air with one hand, while conducting the crowd to continue chanting with the other.

"Here is your bloody permit, police lady. We are legal!"

Slotnik made to take the permit to examine it, but Battarjee pulled it away from her. "Look only, police lady! You think I am nuts?"

A man in a business suit who was not chanting along with the crowd whispered into the imam's ear.

"Okay. My lawyer says you can examine it. But I want it back. And I've got witnesses if you try to destroy it!"

The spittle was forming at the sides of Battarjee's mouth and his forehead was now soaked with sweat. Brannigan was enjoying the imam's discomfort. But at the same time, he was troubled. The permit was on official stationary from the Montgomery County Executive's office of Public permitting, and mentioned the date, place and time of the protest. As long as Battarjee's tiny mob remained on public property, there was nothing they could do to get them to leave. How in the devil had they gotten a permit so quickly after Khaled Hassan's call? Or was someone else in the FBI director's office coordinating with them?

"Dispatch, this is Slotnik again. 10-22. Repeat. 10-22. The situation is under control. These clowns have a permit. No further assistance needed, over."

"10-4, Lieutenant. Have a nice day! Dispatch out."

"Yeah, thanks," she replied, stowing the radio back on her belt.

Brannigan put his hand on Slotnik's elbow, firmly moving her with him toward the building through the crowd.

"Bigots! Racists! FBI Respect Our Rights!" they shouted directly into his ears.

And then, all at once, the chanting stopped. The imam walked up to them as they were about to go inside, alone, carefully waving to the protestors to stay back on the public sidewalk.

"I've got news for you, Brannigan," he said. "Every time you come out of this office, I'm going to have somebody on your tail with a video camera. And every time you go to harass a member of our community, I'm going to make sure there is a lawyer present. We're not going to let you get away with this! We have our rights and you can't take them away just because you're Mr. FBI."

Brannigan let the door fall closed in the imam's face, happy to seal out the heat and the noise. They took the elevator upstairs, where Paige and Kevin were waiting for them in the office.

"Life gets complicated," he said, jerking a thumb toward the window and the protesters below. He explained the imam's threats.

"We're finally ready to move on this case, so when we go for the arrests, I want everything done by the book. No mistakes, no omissions. Got it?"

Kevin and Paige exchanged a puzzled look. They were aware of the carpet fibers from Zia's car that the lab had identified on the deceased girl's clothes. "Arrests?" Paige said. "We got probable cause on anyone but the mechanic?"

Brannigan pulled the brown envelope from the inside pocket of his sports jacket.

"You bet," he said. "This is going to the State's Attorney this afternoon. Remember those cigarette butts we picked up at the construction site? The DNA results have come in and we've got a match. One of those two men raped Salima Khan."

1630 hours, Friday, June 29 – Jefferson Hotel, Washington, DC

Nate Charles was waiting for them when Danny and Aryana arrived. He had selected a corner table in the bar at the Jefferson Hotel, relatively crowded despite the early hour because it was Friday afternoon. Groups of young people in once rigorous business attire filled many of the tables, happily drinking, laughing, chatting each other up. Mostly lawyers, Danny guessed. Charles had been right to choose the Jefferson, he realized. None of these folks could care less about an older black man meeting a handsome, younger couple. They'd had enough business for one week. Now it was party time.

"Glad to see you, son," Charles said, getting up. "You must be Miss Pourmanesh." He took Aryana's hand warmly in both of his.

"I'm honored to meet you, Director Charles," Aryana said quietly.

"You don't know how glad we are to be here, sir," Danny said. "It was rough sledding there for awhile in Dubai."

"Dubai, was it? That was quick."

"Long story, sir."

Danny gave him a brief run down. He had gone to Dubai initially just to debrief Aryana's source, but changed plans when the MOIS action teams closed in.

"That's what I don't understand, sir. Somewhere, there had to have been a leak. I don't see how else they could have known I was there."

"What about the joe? He's Rev. Guards intelligence, right? Maybe he was playing you, leading you into a trap?"

"I don't think so, sir. He's just too damn scared. And the secrets he is betraying are too valuable for a dangle."

Nate Charles pondered this for a moment. "What are we talking about here?"

"Hajj Imad, sir."

"Hajj Imad?" Charles leaned forward and chewed the name between his teeth, looking around at the nearby tables to see if any of the Friday afternoon revelers had heard.

"Yes, sir. He personally supervised the loading operation that our guy photographed, and organized the deception at Maracaibo."

"What deception at Maracaibo?" Charles asked, suspicious.

"He's just told me bits and pieces of it," Aryana said.

"He says he will only talk to the 'head man'," Danny added.

"Cute," Charles said. "I'd say he's not in much of a position to be bargaining now."

Danny could see Charles struggling between the bureaucrat in him and the tiger team analyst. He knew the drill well. The bureaucrat would insist on procedures and protocol. They'd have to put Rahimi on the box, to determine if he was trustworthy. But that could be a treacherous enterprise. How many Iranian agents had ever passed a polygraph? But every single one of the CIA's Cuban agents had passed the box with flying colors. And every single one of them, no exceptions, had turned out to be DGI assets. The difference was that the Cubans trained their operatives to deceive the box. The Iranians simply took it as an insult.

"You know we're going to have to put him on the box," Charles said.

"I know," Danny said. "But before we do that, perhaps you'd like to do a little meet and greet. Just a friendly visit, stop by to see how he's doing, that kind of thing."

Danny didn't understand why Aryana shot him a sharp, warning glance, but whatever it was, he ignored her.

"Where have you put them?"

"Safe place, sir. Out by the National Arboretum."

"Are they there now?"

"You bet."

1730 hours, Friday, June 29 – Days Inn, Washington, DC

The only advantage of the Days Inn out on New York avenue, NE, was its distance from downtown Washington, DC. That kept it discrete, far from chance encounters with the press. Even though the Washington Times had its editorial offices less than a half-mile up the road, no journalist would ever conceive of an important person taking lodgings at the Day's Inn. The 1950s bungalow style motel looked as if it had never been renovated since it was built. Even the flower beds out front were untended. The only attraction of the

Day's Inn was its price, which is why it was regularly full of citizen-activists, the Mr. Smith-Comes-To-Washington types who wandered the corridors of Capitol Hill, in hopes of rubbing shoulders with the powerful and dressing them down to size. It wasn't even on a metro line. Taxis came rarely and only on call.

"I told Rahimi to send his wife and daughter out for a walk in the National Arboretum," Danny said as they drove up in Director Charles's black Mercury Marquis.

But the Iranian was still too spooked from their escape from Dubai to venture outside, let alone allow his wife and his daughter to do so. When they knocked on the door to his small suite, they could see him surveying them through the fisheye before he unhooked the chain, slid back the security latch, and opened the deadbolt.

He backed away from the door to allow them come in, then he closed it quickly behind them.

"Who's this?" he asked Aryana in Persian, indicating Nate Charles.

"Director Nathanial Charles of the FBI," she said. "That is the American domestic *etelaat*," she added in Persian.

"Surely this black monkey is not the head man," Rahimi said.

"No. But he opens the door to the head man," Aryana said.

Rahimi clucked his tongue, his scorn evident.

"What's going on here," Charles said, when Rahimi wouldn't touch his outstretched hand.

Just then, Rahimi's wife and daughter came in from the bedroom. Seeing Nate Charles, looking rumpled in his inexpensive suit and loosened tie, Claudia broke out in a laugh, then covered her mouth with a hand, embarrassed.

"He says he will only talk to the head man," Aryana said quickly, trying to head them back onto safe territory. But Charles had understood the insult all too well. It brought back ancient feelings of dark resentment and rage he thought he would never know again.

"Is there something about me they find objectionable?" he said quietly, turning to Aryana. "Perhaps you should remind them that they are no longer in Iran. If they regret having come to America, we can arrange for them to get back to their homeland."

Danny had never seen Nate Charles so angry. It was not anger for show. He was not shouting and waving his arms. It was anger from the depths of indignation; his voice went low and cold and deadly deliberate.

"You must excuse them," Aryana said. "The only black men they have seen in Persia are the Somali immigrants who clean their houses. On Persian New Year, we have an impish character, a trickster, who dresses in black face, like you used to have here in the 1920s. This is what is going through his mind."

"Not a beautiful mind," Charles snorted.

"We didn't bring him here because we liked him," Danny said.

Aryana tried to explain to Rahimi how important it was to speak to Charles, that he had come on a courtesy call, and that he could facilitate their resettlement in America and help cut corners so Rahimi could meet the head man quickly. But the damage had already been done.

Charles was ready to go.

"Tell him we'll have him picked up at 2000 hours tonight," he told Aryana. "This gentlemen is going to spend the evening on the box."

2030 hours, Friday, June 29 – Bristol Hotel, Washington, DC

The old Bristol Hotel on Pennsylvania avenue near the bridge to Georgetown had been used by generations of CIA polygraphers to test foreign operatives visiting Washington. The CIA men were so familiar with the establishment and the establishment with them that they no longer even stopped at the front desk for a key.

Dr. Phil and his assistant were already set up in the third floor room by the time Aryana arrived with Colonel Rahimi. Even through the closed door, they all could hear the distant rhythms of the jazz band playing downstairs at the bar. When the CIA man approached him with the electrodes, Rahimi clearly would have preferred to be down at that bar, even if they did serve alcohol, which was *haram*.

"What is this?" he said, when Aryana told him that the man operating the machine wanted him to unbutton the top two buttons of his shirt. He pointed to the electrode the white-robed Dr. Phil was holding delicately between thumb and forefinger. "Are they planning to torture me? Is that what America does to people who help it?"

"Rahimi-jan," she said, using the respectful form of greeting. "I have already told you. This is a machine the Americans use to determine if you are telling the truth."

"They haven't even spoken to me and they think I am lying?" he said.

"This is standard procedure. They use it on their own people. They have done it with me as well."

Dr. Phil smiled unctuously as he positioned electrodes on Rahimi's chest, two on his neck, and one delicately at the tip of the pinkie on each hand. "That's it," he said soothingly to Aryana. "A little coaching is not out of order. Never done this before, have we?" he addressed Rahimi. "I see. English a bit spotty. In that case, Miss Pourmanesh, please explain to the gentlemen how we operate. First, we will agree on a set of questions, which Mr. Black will write down. Then I will ask them, one by one, and he will give a yes or no answer. Is that clear? Mr. Black will be my backup and will keep score, if you will.

"If it's Friday, it must be Persian, right?" he kept chattering away. "Remind me, please. The yes and no answers in Persian, my dear?"

"That would be *baleh*, yes, and *nah*, no," she said.

Rahimi sat sullenly in the strait-backed kitchen chair, wired to the box, as Dr. Phil juiced up the machine and checked his readings.

"OK, now do we have that, sir? All I want is *baleh*, or *nah*. Got it?"

Rahimi said nothing, clearly unhappy.

"Let's just run a few control questions, just to get started. Are you ready?" Dr. Phil said cheerily. "Please translate, my dear. Is your name Abd al-Rahman Rahimi Golpour?"

When she had translated, Rahimi exploded. "What is this? Do they not even know my name? Why are they wasting my time like this?"

"No, no, no," Dr. Phil said in a singsong. "That would not be a correct answer. It's *baleh*, or *nah*, remember? Now let's try that again. Again, my dear. Is your name Abd al-Rahman Rahimi Golpour?"

"*Baleh*," he said finally.

"Are you from Iran?"

"*Baleh*."

"Are you lying to me now?"

Rahimi exploded. "What right does he have to ask me such things? This is an insult!"

Aryana tried to explain to him how the procedure worked, but it was no use and Dr. Phil could tell. "Alright now, boys and girls. That was off the charts. Let's take a little break." He took the electrodes off Rahimi, smiling. "You will now emphasize to our friend that he is supposed to answer only yes or no, or else we will be here until tomorrow morning. Got it?"

"He finds it insulting," Aryana said.

"Well, my dear. So he may. Tell him it's a bit like taking an enema. Not something one chooses to do for pleasure, but from time to time, a necessity."

Aryana tried to explain to Rahimi, but the Rev. Guards intelligence officer was implacable, sullen, and angry. "Why should I talk to these people?" he said.

"What authority do they have? I am not going to give them my information!"

"No one is talking about you giving them your information," Aryana said, soothingly. "This is just a formality. But you have to go through it."

"If the Americans want to check whether I am lying, let them check the information," he said. "They will see that I am telling them the truth."

As Aryana was trying to get him to understand, she heard Mr. Black joking with Dr. Phil in the next room.

"How can you tell an Iranian is lying?" Mr. Black was saying. "I bet you can't guess!"

"Oh come now, my dear. You underestimate me. I've been doing this for years. It's when his lips are moving."

Aryana exploded, and without thinking, she slapped Dr. Phil fully across the face.

"You stupid, racist fag," she said. "When was the last time you risked your life to help people from a country that was not your own?"

Stunned, Dr. Phil nursed his red cheek, and then began to pack up his machine, glancing up from time to time to make sure Aryana got no closer.

When he had finished, he turned to Mr. Black. "I think I'll report back to mother," he said. "Are you coming, Mr. Black? This session is over."

0100 hours, Saturday, June 30 – Burtonsville, MD

Danny was sound asleep when the cell phone at his bedside table vibrated. Although he was still exhausted from the Dubai trip, his instincts kicked in and he was wide awake in a flash. He found the phone from the glow, and saw that it was Aryana. He silenced the call but said nothing for an instant, watching his wife sleep, curled toward him on her side, breathing slowly and deeply in another world. For an instant, he saw her face in the concentration of child birth, her eyes wild, her nostrils flared in a surge of pride as her last push thrust their son into the world. And then he saw the same dark hair, falling over his face. Only it wasn't her hair, it was Aryana's.

"Hold one," he whispered, as he rolled out of bed. Grabbing his bathrobe from the chair where he had flung it earlier, he slipped his good arm through and held the other side close to his body with his stiff arm, holding the phone. Twisting the doorknob slowly, he made his way into the carpeted hallway and into the living room, where he turned on a light by the sofa.

"Trouble?" he said, finally.

"Yes," Aryana said. "Our man is spooked. Seems the night porter is from his home country. Spoke to his wife in their language."

"Well, what did he say?"

"I don't know exactly, but the wife was terrified. Whatever he said was enough to make her believe that they had found them."

"Where are you now?"

"I'm on my way back there," she said.

Eva came up from behind the sofa and placed her hands on his shoulders, gently massaging the muscles he had built up so carefully around the titanium joint. *Of course,* she had felt his absence. How could he ever have thought otherwise?

"You can't go there alone," Danny told Aryana. "Tell our guy to keep his phone close and to pack their bags. Call him when you reach the Arboretum. If the situation's stable, I want to you go up to the Washington Times exit and make the U-turn. Wait for me at the end of the service road before the motel. It's going to take me forty minutes or so. But keep me posted if there is any change."

When he got off the phone he quickly explained the situation to Eva, then went down to the basement to his gun cabinet. Because of Paul, he didn't want to leave firearms around the house, so he had invested in a proper, locked cabinet shortly after their son had been born. He had two M-4 assault rifles, which he fired during the weekends at the Andrews Air Force base rod and gun club, and a half dozen hand guns of varying calibers. He liked the Bulgarian-built Makarov because of its unusual lines. He was just checking the action, to make sure it was clean, when Eva came down the stairs in jeans and a tight, black tee-shirt.

"What are you doing?" he said.

"I just phoned my sister. She's got a key. She can come stay here with Paul. If you've got trouble, you're going to need an extra hand."

Danny just shook his head in amazed admiration. "You are really something. Every day, I find some new reason to thank God I could convince you to marry me. It was the only smart thing I've ever done."

He passed her the Makarov, found the silencer and ammo, and took a standard-issue Beretta 9mm for himself.

"You'd better take one for her," Eva said.

Her. There was no malice. Just matter of fact. Danny pulled out another Beretta, some more ammo and silencers, then turned and embraced his wife. She was still warm from sleep, but the muscles of her neck and her shoulders and at the small of her back were hard and taut.

"Can you fit this stuff into two bags while I go up to get dressed?" he said finally.

"Anything you want, baby," she said. "You know that."

While they were en route in Eva's Ford Explorer, Danny phoned Nate Charles. After apologizing profusely for waking him up, he explained the situation.

"It looks like we've got an MOIS team at the motel," Danny said. "I think they're just trying to show our friend that they can get him anywhere. Still, I don't like it and want to move him."

"I've got agents out of our regional office in Calverton. Need back-up?"

"I'm not anticipating that," Danny said. "I think this is just a display of force by MOIS."

He could hear Charles swearing under his breath at the other end of the phone. "What is it, sir?"

"This isn't your problem, son. Well, actually. It is your problem. I'm asking myself, why am I hearing about an MOIS cell now? Why hasn't my Iran team pulled them in before this? Why isn't the FBI doing its job?"

He glanced at Eva, who was driving at high speed down Interstate 95, her senses alert to the road and to every car on it.

"Maybe, sir, it's the same thing we hit in Dubai."

"What do you mean?"

"Not everyone we think is on our side, is really on it."

"God forbid."

0140 hours, Saturday, June 30 – Day's Inn, Washington, DC

They met up with Aryana on the service road by the Washington Times printing plant. It was a dismal industrial area, that had been passed over by several generations of urban planners. After the ugly loading bays for the newspaper, there was a gravel parking lot, closed in by a chain-link fence, where a half-dozen wrecks seemed to have permanently taken up abode. Aryana was waiting in her rented Chevrolet Malibu on the shoulder where the service road rejoined New York avenue heading into Washington, DC.

"Turn off your lights," Danny said to Eva, as they came up alongside the parked car. This was going to be interesting, he thought. Until now, he had pushed to the back of his mind the fact that the two women of his life would now be meeting for the first time face to face.

"He's barricaded himself and his wife and daughter inside the room," Aryana said, after rolling down her window. She was full of anticipation, until she caught sight of Eva. Then a dark, querulous look clouded her eyes.

Danny and Eva got out of the Explorer. Eva handled Aryana the gun bag and watched as she opened it and tentatively took out the 9mm revolver.

"You *do* know how to use it?" Eva said.

She had donned a black baseball cap from the *USS Normandy*, CG-60, and with her black tee-shirt and tight jeans, Eva looked dangerous, professional and lethal.

Aryana handled the weapon briefly as if it were a foreign object, then cocked it expertly to make sure it held no chambered round and rammed in a magazine. "Of course. It's one of the things the Army taught us in Iraq." But there was something too feminine in her gesture. Danny thought he saw the flicker of a brief smile twist Eva's lips.

All three of them screwed on the silencers, checked their weapons, and found pockets for extra ammunition.

"Aryana," Danny said.

It was time to give orders.

"You're the only one who can evaluate how serious a threat this potential MOIS guy is. I need you to go into the lobby and engage him in conversation. I'm assuming this guy is a lone ranger, and that our Colonel is just spooked because he's hearing Farsi. But if he's not alone, or if you think there may be other MOIS types deployed elsewhere in the motel, I want you to use the walkie-talkie function on the cell phone in your pocket and let me know immediately. Unless we hear from you in the next five minutes, Eva and I are going to drive around to the back, lights off, and extract the Colonel and his family. Is that clear?"

"Clear," Aryana said.

"Then mark my time. "

They synchronized their watches, and then she was gone.

Danny watched her drive down toward the motel, headlights lit, then pull up into the semi-circle driveway beneath the reception canopy and get out. Suddenly it dawned on him, and he hit himself in the forehead.

"I can't believe I've done this," he said.

"What's the matter?" Eva said.

"Look at her. A single woman, almost two o'clock in the morning, heading into the reception area of a flea bag motel in a rotten area of town."

"She'll be fine," Eva said. She touched his arm reassuringly, then gave him a quick kiss.

"Besides," she added. "She's armed."

"Yeah. I guess if it's good enough to handle MOIS types, it's good enough for your average DC rapist or mugger."

He checked the time. First, on the dashboard. Then on his watch. Then on the dashboard again, and then on his watch. Only three minutes had gone by.

"*Relax*," Eva said. "She's better than you want to make me believe that you think."

"I guess you're right."

Five minutes went by, and they had heard nothing.

"Good to go," Danny said, slapping his wife's thigh in his relief. "Take a right down there and head around the back."

The motel was built around a series of courtyards. The two connecting rooms where Rahimi and his family were staying gave directly onto the rear parking lot, and were not visible from the reception area. Danny and Eva ran up the stairs to the outdoor corridor, weapons drawn, and knocked on the Colonel's door.

"*Chee ast?*" Rahimi said in Farsi when he saw Eva. "Who's this?"

"*Khanoom-e man,*" Danny said. "My wife."

The Iranian looked over his shoulder at his own wife, deeper in the darkened room, her dark head scarf drawn so her pale face stood out white in the moonlight, making her look frail and vulnerable. He looked at Danny with grudging admiration and grunted.

Danny waved for them to hurry. "Let's go!" he said, grabbing one of the bags that was standing just inside the door.

Just then, his cell phone chirped and his heart leaped. Had they set off too fast?

"What is it?" Eva said. Her worry was visible.

"Don't know. Now we're exposed. Let's get them into the car and get out of here."

Eva ran back to help Claudia, taking her bag and rushing her along. Danny ran ahead, in a half crouch, carrying one of the bags in one hand, his berretta in the other.

"Get in! Get in!" he hissed at Rahimi and the women when they reached the car.

"What's the story?" Eva asked.

"Just drive. We'll find out soon enough," he said.

"You're not going to leave her, are you?"

"She'll be fine."

Eva had her hand on the steering wheel and was about to turn the key in the ignition when she stopped dead. "Call her. Now," she ordered.

"No," Danny said firmly. "She'll call when she is able."

"What if she's in trouble?"

"She's armed, don't forget."

"Yeah, and so are we. I'm driving around to the front," Eva said.

Before he could say a word, she fired up the engine and roared out of the parking lot, spinning around the corner onto the main driveway to the front entrance. Danny paged Aryana twice, but received no response. Her rented Malibu was still out front.

"There!" Eva hissed, pointing toward the door.

Aryana burst out, a look of terror on her face, and in the next instant Danny's heart stopped beating. He saw the orange flash of the muzzle and an instant later the loud *craaack!* of the pistol shot, like a truck backfire echoing dryly from the street. He saw Aryana stumble, and then he saw his wife fly out of her seat, weapon drawn, running somewhere behind the car. "Get down!" he shouted to Rahimi and his wife, batting the air with his hand. They understood immediately and dove for the floor of the backseat.

Danny's side of the car was facing the reception area of the motel, but Eva had stopped at enough of an angle that he could crack open his door, slip to the ground, and combat crawl to the shelter of Aryana's Malibu without the attackers having a clear shot. Eva was already there, and she was breathing heavily.

"There are two of them," she said. "They've hit Aryana, but can't find her."

"There she is!" Danny said, pointing to a miserable hedge of disease-ridden azaleas. She had fallen on their side of the hedge, and was waving a hand at them to go after her attackers, but the two men at the entry to the motel couldn't see her.

"Aim for their legs," Danny said.

They fired almost simultaneously, the bullets spitting out from their silenced pistols hitting true to the mark, bringing the two men down, screaming in pain on the pavement.

Danny ran up to them carefully and kicked their weapons away. The man that Eva hit had stopped moving and gone silent. For an instant, Danny thought he was dead, but then he saw that the bullet had missed the chest by several inches.

"I aimed for his shoulder," said Eva, coming up to him "Eye for an eye. Tooth for a tooth. My man's shoulder for his."

Danny just looked at her — the Makarov with its long silencer hanging from one hand, her USS Normandy black hat at an angle, a long strand of hair hanging down below her chin — and shook his head in appreciation.

"Remind me not to get you angry when you're armed," he said.

0205 hours, Saturday, June 30 – Days Inn, Washington, DC

Danny phoned Nate as soon as he searched Aryana's attackers to make sure they had no other weapons, and explained what had happened.

"Good thing this happened on federal territory," Nate said dryly. "That way I don't have to ask the president to suspend posse comitatus."

"Sorry about that," Danny said. "It wasn't in the plans, but they fired first."

"I'll let our forensics guys know they're looking at a C/I case and not just your average DC armed robbery. That ought to keep the DC cops at bay until you can get out of there with your guy."

"I appreciate that."

Now they had to figure out where to take him. Danny had wanted to bring Rahimi and his family to the Marriot at White Flint to keep him away from downtown. But now it was clear they were going to need round-the-clock armed protection.

"I'll have my guys phone the Mayflower and book a suite," Nate said. "He's on my nickel now, son."

Eva got a bottle of water from her car and a roll of paper towels, and gently rolled Aryana onto her good side to check her wound.

"You're lucky they can't shoot," Eva said, after she had wiped off some of the blood with a wet paper towel. The bullet had grazed the flesh beneath Aryana's left shoulder, but had not penetrated. "They were aiming to kill you. Hasn't anybody ever taught you what to say when you meet an armed man alone at night in Washington, DC?"

"No," she grunted. Her whole body was tensed from the pain.

"Sir," Eva said.

She started to laugh but the pain in her ribs made her want to cry. "Now I know why Danny married you and not me," she said finally.

"Oh?" Eva said, cocking an eyebrow. "Why's that?"

"Your bedside manners."

An ambulance arrived a few minutes later, and a pair of paramedics jumped out with a stretcher and rushed to where Danny was crouched over the two Iranians. Eva called out to them.

"Treat her first. She's the victim."

And then the unmarked Crown Vics began to arrive. First was the head of the Iran unit at the FBI Washington, DC field office, Dave Fielding. Still rubbing his eyes from sleep and from the balling out he had received from Nate Charles, Fielding hadn't managed to tuck in his shirt completely before leaving home, and his expansive stomach peeped out. "Whose got my clients?" he asked the paramedics, as they were lifting Aryana into the back of the ambulance.

Luther Powell came next, with a forensics team. They began putting up yellow tape, drawing circles around the spot where Aryana was first hit, where she fell, and bagged the spent shell casings and the shooter's weapon.

And then came Michael Brannigan.

Danny didn't notice him at first. He had gone back to the car to reassure Rahimi that he would soon drive them to a new hotel and that no one was going to be asking them questions about the shooting. Brannigan came up from behind and slapped him on the back. He was wincing from the sudden pain when he turned around and saw him.

"Brannigan!" he said

"What, you getting creaky in your old age?"

"Just my titanium joint, that's all."

"Oh, Jeez. Sorry. So that's why Nate Charles absolutely wanted me down here at two-thirty on a Saturday morning. I take it the shoulder wasn't Afghanistan. Iraq?"

"Second deployment," Danny said.

"And still keeping other folks out of harm's way?"

"Not always successfully."

"Yeah, I can see that."

Neither would think much of their brief encounter. It was the type of thing that happened in Washington when you worked for the government. People you had known in other circumstances had a way of popping up unexpectedly.

Brannigan gave Danny a card, and scribbled Danny's numbers on the back of one of his own. A thoughtless gesture, almost automatic. But it would save thousands of lives.

VII

THE ENGINEER

1130 hours, Saturday, June 30 –
Manny's Gas and Oil, Silver Spring, MD

Manijeh Dal was standing at a computer, looking up parts for a customer, when Brannigan and Slotnik arrived shortly before lunch on Saturday. Lieutenant Slotnik leaned her elbows on the customer side of the walk-in window that separated the convenience store from the garage and stared at him.

"What you working on, Mr. Dal?" she said finally, when he refused to acknowledge her. "That wouldn't be a 2001 Honda Accord, now would it?"

He squinted through his reading glasses and continued scrolling down the parts list on the screen. Without looking at her, he said, "Since when is the Montgomery County police interested in the make of cars I service?"

"We are, when it belongs to Zia Mirsaidi, Mr. Dal," she said. "By the way. Where is Zia this morning?"

Two men burst in through the glass front door. Brannigan recognized the well-dressed "lawyer" from the Georgia Avenue mosque. He thought he had noticed a car following them from Calverton, but hadn't paid it much attention. It had taken him several hours to fall asleep after the two am shooting. He was so groggy it felt like his head was stuffed with cotton.

"We told you we'd be following you, Mr. FBI man," the lawyer said. "Is he harassing you, sir?" he said, addressing Manny Dal.

That woke Brannigan up. He rolled his eyes. "Hey. You know these jokers, Manny?"

Dal peered at the two men over his reading glasses and shook his head.

"Then why don't you tell them to get lost," Brannigan said.

"They've got as much right to be here as you do, sir," Dal said, going back to his computer screen. He tapped the Enter key and the order form printed out. "Now. What can I do for you?" he said, turning toward them for the first time.

"We're here for your nephew," Slotnik said. "Where is he, Mr. Dal?"

"Who is this?" the lawyer said. "Why do you want to see him?"

That got Brannigan riled. "Gentlemen," he said. "I know that you are aware that I am a federal law enforcement official, and that my colleague here is a Montgomery County police woman. We are here on official business. Now. If you would like us to take you in for impeding the action of law enforcement officials, I'd be more than happy to oblige. Is that what we're after this morning?"

"We're just here to observe, Mr. FBI man. You can't keep us from that."

"No, I can't," Brannigan acknowledged, "as long as you stay out of the way."

"He's around back," Dal said. "You can go through here."

He turned the knob and the counter swung toward them. Dal led them into a small waiting room and opened a door at the far side that led into the rear garage area. Brannigan pulled the door behind him, but before the latch clicked the lawyer had caught it and held it open. He had half a mind to yank it shut and lock it, but relented.

Filling most of the rear garage was a huge Ford 350, with a concession stand box cab fitted onto the pickup bed. A silver sun-protector had been spread out on the inside of the windshield of the pickup, which was facing the glass garage door. No one was immediately in view.

"I didn't know you did conversions now, Mr. Dal?" Brannigan said. "Thinking of a new line of business?"

"Just one of my customers," he said. "Zia, come out. It's the police," he said.

He rapped on the side of the concession stand, which was completely shuttered. The door in the rear opened a crack, and Brannigan saw the young man's black beard and black eyes glare at him, and something silver like stainless steel shine behind him. He stepped down quickly and closed the door before they could see inside.

"Zia Mirsaidi?" said Lt. Slotnik. "You are under arrest in connection with the rape and murder of Salima Khan. You have the right to remain silent. You have the right to an attorney. You have – "

"I'm an attorney, Zia," the lawyer from the mosque said. "Don't say anything! Don't admit anything! Don't talk to them without me right next to you!"

Brannigan sighed and turned to the man. "Thank-you," he said with exaggerated politeness.

"I don't know any Salima Khan!" Zia blurted out, as Brannigan worked his arms around to his back to handcuff him.

"And any false statements you make could be used against you in a court of law," Lt. Slotnik went on.

"Don't *say* anything!" the lawyer repeated. Brannigan wondered if the lawyer knew that Zia and Salima were in fact first cousins.

"I'd take that advice, Zia," Brannigan said. "Uncle Manny's told us all about you and Salima. Haven't you, Mr. Dal?"

"You know that's not true, Zia," he said quickly. "Where are you taking the young man?"

"For the time being, he'll be at the county jail in Rockville, off Seven Locks road. You can call to get visiting hours. It's right before the police substation."

"How convenient," Dal said.

Slotnik patted Zia down and stopped at his left trouser pocket. "Those your car keys?" she said.

He glared at her sullenly.

"Mr. Dal, would you oblige us, please? I don't want him kicking me," she added, as he continued to squirm.

"Stop right there, Lieutenant!" the lawyer said. "Illegal search and seizure."

He tried to approach, but Brannigan got in his way and just stood there. "No, it's not," he said deliberately. "We're impounding it. Mr. Dal?"

"Here they are, Lieutenant," Dal said, handing Slotnik the keys. "The car's parked out front with the others."

"Thank-you. I've already called for a tow truck."

1700 hours, Sunday, July 1 – Calverton, MD

This time Brannigan noticed the silver Nissan Altima before he started his car.

"The watchers are here again," he said to Paige. "How about we blue light 'em?"

Paige got the police light out of the glove compartment and placed it on the dashboard of Brannigan's unmarked Mercury Marquis. He turned it on once they reached I-95 heading south toward the Capitol Beltway. The light was shielded so it wouldn't blind the driver and that only cars in front of them or on the side could see it flashing.

"They keeping up with us?" Paige asked.

"You bet," said Brannigan. "Call them in."

They found a State Trooper cruising a few miles ahead of them who agreed to pull over and wait for them to arrive. Once they reached the Capitol Beltway, Brannigan increased his speed. By the time he saw the trooper parked on the shoulder, they were doing 85 mph, and the Nissan Altima was keeping close on their tail.

"I think I'm going to enjoy this," Brannigan said.

He flashed his lights at the trooper, who saluted with two fingers to the side of his hat in reply.

"Oops. They just saw him," Brannigan said.

The driver of the Nissan frantically put on his brakes, but it was too late. The trooper popped his lights and pulled out after him.

"That ought to hold them," Brannigan said. "I didn't think we needed to have them join us at the airport. Call it cooperation among federal and local law enforcement."

"What they wouldn't do for a tax," Paige laughed.

A half-dozen unmarked FBI vehicles had arrived ahead of them, and were parked in a row at the curb of the main terminal at Dulles airport. Brannigan parked behind them and they headed up the ramp to the international arrivals area. On the board, a KLM flight from Amsterdam was showing in Customs, while a Pakistan International Airlines flight from Lahore had just landed. Brannigan went to the small door to the right of the double doors where the passengers exited, and pressed the buzzer. An armed Customs and Border Protection officer opened the door and, after checking Brannigan and Paige's ID, waved them through. He took them up a short flight of stairs and punched in a four-digit code into the cipher lock. "All the others are already here," he said. He left them to return downstairs to the interrogation booth.

"Agent Greary," Brannigan said, greeting his colleague with a wry smile. "What a pleasure to be working together."

She was dressed solemnly in a dark blue pants suit, a white shirt buttoned up to her neck, and black half boots with two inch heels. "Hey, Brannigan," she said. "And you must be?"

"Paige," he said, extending a hand.

"Gentlemen, you're just in time," a uniformed CBP officer greeted them. "I'm officer James Middleton, and I'll be coordinating with our people on the floor when our suspect arrives."

Sayeed was seated in front, next to Luther Powell, who was coordinating the FBI team. There was an empty seat next to him, which Brannigan assumed had been occupied by Agent Greary before they arrived. He decided to take it.

"Hello, Sayeed," he said. "Agent Powell has explained the drill to you? You know what to do?"

The young man did not look comfortable. "Yeah," he said.

Through the long, narrow observation window, with its one-way glass, they had a clear view of the entire baggage claim area. Arriving passengers, brought in on people movers from the mid-field terminal, were split into two main lines for immigration control. Non-U.S. citizens used the lanes closest to them, while U.S. citizens went through at the far side. Once passengers were processed, they walked along a glassed-in corridor on the other side of the immigration coral, then turned right past the interrogation booth and entered the open baggage claim area. Baggage from the KLM flight was exiting at carousel number four at the far end of the baggage claim area. The PIA flight soon came onto the board. Customs had arranged for it to be routed to carrousel one, directly in front of the secret observation window.

"We've got him," Middleton said after a bit. He swiveled around from the computer terminal to where Brannigan, Sayeed and Powell were sitting. "He's at Lane 24, for U.S. citizens and green card holders," he said, pointing to the far end of the Immigration coral.

"Can you see him, Sayeed?" Brannigan asked.

"It's too far away."

"Well keep looking. I want you to point him out when he starts walking down the corridor after clearing immigration. You got that?"

"Yeah."

After a moment, he pointed to a middle-aged, clean-shaven man in a pale green safari suit, carrying what appeared to be an expensive leather brief case. "Okay, there he is."

"Do we know how many bags he checked?" Brannigan asked.

"Yes, sir," said Middleton. "That would be two. We've got Sergeant down on the floor standing by."

"Sergeant?" Paige said.

"Over there," he pointed. "The black Lab."

A female dog-handler, dressed in dark blue, was chatting with an agricultural inspector at the table at the far end of the baggage claim area. Sergeant was turning around in circles, mouth open, eager to work, coming back expectantly to the pocket where she kept the dog treats.

"I don't get it," Paige said.

"You will," said Middleton, "if our friend's information is correct."

Sayeed pointed again as his uncle entered the baggage claim area. He paused in front of the board to search for his flight, then found a spot right next to the baggage handlers where the bags came sliding down the ramp onto the carrousel.

Middleton called the dog-handler on her black talkie-walkie. "Your subject is the middle-aged oriental gentlemen in the light green safari suit, standing by the Sky Caps at carrousel 4," he said. "One of his bags just came out."

They watched as Sergeant eagerly went to work, nostrils flaring, his huge, hard tail banging back and forth. She led him to a bag, he lowered his head briefly, then he pranced on to the next. When he got to Sayeed's uncle's bag, he sniffed, then sat down next to it and she patted him and gave him a treat.

"Sir, I've got a potential violation on the floor by carousel 4," they heard the woman signal the chief inspector. Suddenly, three burly, armed CBP officers swooped toward her from different parts of the hall.

"He's not bringing in drugs, is he?" Paige said.

"No way," Middleton said. "Sergeant has been specially trained to smell currency ink. You'd be surprised how many people are moving money these days."

Brannigan decided to congratulate Joanna Greary, who was standing by herself at the back of the observation booth. "Looks like you were right. We got our courier. Good work, Agent Greary."

Instead of answering, she just shook her head in disgust.

Yeah, it's been real pleasant working with you, too, Brannigan thought.

"Alright," Powell said. "Let's get Sayeed out of here. He's done his part. "

"You won't let him see me!" Sayeed said, panicky.

"No. That's precisely why we want to get you out of here now, before we question your uncle."

As they got back out to the curb where the cars were parked, they passed a handsome-looking man with a blonde moustache, waiting in the taxi line. He was carrying a leather document case under an arm, and had a wheeled carry-on bag. He looked up, as did everyone in the taxi line when the federal agents began to get into the unmarked police cars. If they had known to look, they might have noticed a slight smirk on his face when he saw Sayeed studiously avoiding his gaze.

The name on the California driver's license he had used to board the flight from Los Angeles to Dulles said Richard Halstead. He had left the Albert Creely passport, credit cards, and driver's license in Calgary, Alberta the night before.

Now Abd al-Latif al-Haq al-Libi was an American. And he had come to Washington, DC to murder 500,000 of his fellow citizens.

The Engineer had arrived.

2200 hours, Sunday, July 1 – Silver Spring, Maryland

By the time Sayeed joined him at the safe house at Bel Pre Manor Garden apartments, al-Libi had examined his tools for the sixth time. He had laid everything out on a red cotton table cloth on the Formica eating table, ready to pack into the tool bag. There was a metric ratchet set and a half-dozen box wrenches; a pair of vise grips; a battery-powered soldering iron, solder, needle-nosed pliers, wire and wire cutters, a box of wire nuts, a sets of electrical screw drivers, carpenter's screwdrivers, and two cheap quartz wrist watches. It was not much, really; and most of it he had asked Sayeed to purchase just in case they encountered an unforeseen problem with the timing mechanism.

There was also a hammer and a small crowbar, in case the salt water had damaged the outer casing, two fresh Nextel cell phones, and a sterno lamp.

The most critical item was the half-sheet of paper al-Libi had sewn into the lining of the carry-on bag. It bore no header or explanation, just eight groups of four numerals each, split into two equal rows. The first row began with the numbers 5437, and the second began with 4147. In the highly-unlikely event that al-Libi was compromised and the paper discovered, the codes appeared to be nothing more than MasterCard and Visa card account numbers. Even an innocent traveler might want to keep a copy of his credit card numbers in a safe place, in case the cards got stolen.

When Sayeed told him about Zia's arrest, the Engineer exploded.

"You stupid, stupid fool!" he said. "There were to be zero contingencies. None!"

"Look, it's not serious," Sayeed explained. "He knows nothing. His only role was to work on the truck and buy cell phones. He's expendable."

"He knows about the truck?"

"Yes, of course. He worked in my uncle's garage."

The Engineer pondered this a moment, pulling at the skin next to his mouth where his moustache used to be. He should have remembered that. He could not allow his anger to master him!

"You said that bitch was protecting you."

"I think they got to her," Sayeed said.

"What does she know?"

"Nothing."

"She leads them to you," he said, almost to himself. "This is not, not, not good."

For ten years, the Engineer had been training for this moment. His Iranian handlers had been extraordinarily cautious. In all the missions they had sent him on, they had never asked him to carry anything compromising. They were testing his nerves, testing his reflexes, testing his ability to live out the legend they had carefully constructed for him. Once, arriving at Heathrow airport in London, British immigration questioned the visa in his Pakistani passport. In that exercise, he was posing as an exporter from Lahore who was selling oriental canned goods. Who was his partner in Britain? they had asked him. Why did he have a tourist visa, and not a business visa? His answers had all been carefully scripted in advance, but he knew it wasn't the answers that counted so much as his manner in presenting them. That was the lesson that Hajj Imad had hammered home with him during the training again and again. *Use that smile,* he said. *Always be friendly, be polite, be charming. These stupid infidels think that the only people who want to kill them are bearded, snarling fanatics.* The Engineer passed with flying colors.

But this young man had been sloppy, and sloppiness was not something he tolerated. He asked Sayeed a dozen questions about Joanna Greary, where she lived, where she worked, how she got back and forth, her schedule, what bars she frequented on Federal Hill in Baltimore, how late she usually stayed out. Then he asked him how many people were in the Baltimore cell.

"We don't need to kill her," Sayeed said, panicky.

"I want back-up plans. No contingencies. Remember?"

He ordered Sayeed to call his contact in the Baltimore cell. "Tell him to send someone down to Washington, DC tonight to purchase another handgun from his gang contact, just in case. I want a weapon with no history, that they can't trace. These drug dealers are very good."

Next, he asked about Zia's arrest. He could tell from Sayeed's answers that the young man was hiding something from him.

"We have lawyers," Sayeed said.

"Who's we?"

"From the mosque."

A hot vise of panic gripped the Engineer in the gut. "What do they know?"

"Nothing – I'm telling you," Sayeed insisted.

"What are the charges?"

"I don't know. The lawyers are trying to find out."

"That is not possible in this country. There have to be charges. He cannot be arrested without charges. Why are you not telling me what I need to know?"

He grabbed Sayeed with both hands as he said this and slammed him against the wall of the living room.

"Okay, okay, it's accessory to murder. He helped kill the girl."

The Engineer let go of him and collapsed into a chair at the small eating table and grabbed his head in disbelief. This was going seriously wrong. He had to know everything, at once.

When Sayeed finally blurted out the story, he slapped him hard with the back of his hand.

"This is not honor. This is stupidity," he said, getting up and pacing nervously.

"But you don't understand," Sayeed wailed. "I thought she was going to go to the police on us. And we were careful. I had Azam and Faizul take her after a party. They slipped her a sleeping pill then they pushed her off a bridge in a deserted area into a river. There were no witnesses, no fingerprints, no nothing. The police still don't have a clue."

The Engineer paced. He pondered. He turned over all the pieces that Sayeed had just given him, searching for thread leading back to them. In the end,

Sayeed just might be right. But if so, it was just blind luck. And luck was one element he had banned from his calculations.

"Do Azam and Faizul know about the truck?" he asked finally.

"They bought the pick-up for the construction company, but they know nothing about the modifications," Sayeed said quickly. "I kept everything separate, like you told me."

"Allah willing, things will still go as planned," he said.

The Engineer got up and packed the tools carefully into the reinforced canvas bag. "Come, it is time," he said, clapping the younger man on the shoulder. "We are in Allah's hands now."

When they got out to Sayeed's car, he took a deep breath, exhaling profoundly, first from the abdomen, then from the lungs, emptying his body of the tension that had built up.

"If you had wanted to kill her for dishonoring your family, you could have sent her down to the fireworks," he said finally.

0005 hours, Monday, July 2 – Manny's Gas and Oil, Silver Spring, MD

Hossein Gill, the cement foreman from the Olney construction project, and Jamal Nashishibi, the Palestinian carpenter from Nablus, met them just after midnight in the parking lot of Manny's Gas and Oil. It was pitch dark, with only a crescent moon in the sky. Without a word of greeting, the four men walked around to the rear of the building. The security lights from inside cast faint yellowish squares onto the oil-darkened cement in front of the glass garage bay doors.

Sayeed pulled out a ring of keys and opened the access door. Up on the lift was a Ford F-350 long-bed pick-up. Sayeed went over to the far wall and pulled a large, greasy lever and the lift hissed and the truck came down to the floor. He unlocked the rear access door to the box cab that had been fitted onto the pickup bed, so the Engineer could see inside.

Stepping up into the concession stand, he closed the door behind him. Inside, he set his tool bag in a corner, then examined the walls by the interior lights. They had used quarter-inch steel plate, as he had instructed, since it was lighter weight and more common than lead sheeting. Then they had coated the entire interior of the cabin − floors, ceilings, and walls - with heavy duty aluminum foil they had purchased in 3 foot wide rolls, two at a time, at local super markets. The cabin space was approximately eighteen feet long, eight feet wide, and six feet high. Before they had installed the steel plate and aluminum shielding they had stripped out all the food preparation equipment, cupboards, and counters, then reinstalled about half of them in their normal places. In a cleared space at the back wall, they had fitted the electric winch with its twisted iron cable and grappling hook, according to his drawings. He checked the controls to make sure they worked, unwinding the cable several feet. The twisted metal strands were slightly oily to the touch. That was good.

He felt beneath the winch assembly until he found the recessed ring tab. He pulled, and the bottom panel dropped down beneath the winch. He had designed the winch cabinet just slightly larger than necessary for the cable, although the extra volume would go unnoticed to the untrained eye. He reached up underneath and found the Velcro strips and undid them, and carefully caught the two canvas bags before they fell to the floor. He checked the .38 Smith & Wesson revolvers, released the cylinders, checked the ammo, then carefully replaced them and closed up the panel. They were lousy American police weapons, but they were readily available. For their purposes, they were enough. In one corner was a stack of brand new beach towels– reds and blues and dark browns.

Satisfied, he came back out and ordered Sayeed to open the garage door. On the side panels of the box cab, they had stenciled in red paint, "Maria's Tex-Mex." In smaller letters below was a menu and price list: chicken quesadillas, cheese burritos, veggie and meat tacos, and hot dogs.

Those stupid Americans and their hot dogs, he thought.

There would be a lot of them when he was through. With crisps.

0130 hours, Monday, July 2 – Hay's Landing, Scotland, MD

Sayeed had described the place to him many times in great detail, but he was in utter awe of it when they arrived. It was perfect. No, it was better than perfect. At the bottom of the curve in Hay's Beach Road, an unmarked dirt path led nearly a half-mile through abandoned tobacco fields to the water. There were no houses in sight all the way through the fields. The land was flat, empty, and dark.

"This is good," he said, tapping the young man on the shoulder from behind.

Sayeed nodded, acknowledging the special relationship he had to the Engineer. He had told the others few details of the operation they would be conducting, and they had asked few questions. All had pledged *bayat* – loyalty – to Usama bin Laden and his Egyptian deputy, Ayman al-Zawahiri – during their training at the camps in Pakistan and knew not to ask questions. They all understood that they were to live exemplary lives in the United States, blending in, not betraying outward signs of Muslim zeal, until the day the leader of their cell appeared with orders from the emir.

Sayeed had called them more than a year ago, one by one, using the secret names they were given when they pledged *bayat*. He had told each one of them what to do. He had provided the money to purchase the cell phones, to purchase the truck, and the equipment. They knew they were to obey him without question, and that their actions had one goal, and that nothing could come before it. Their goal was to inflict maximum damage on the United States and the Jews who ran it. That was the cause that drove them, and for which they were prepared to sacrifice their lives.

He drove slowly down the rutted dirt road, lights out, until the dunes and the tall sea grass began and they could see the ink-black water stretch out in front of them. There was nothing on the horizon, not even the light from a cargo ship or a sailboat. The Engineer could distinguish the faint green blur of a buoy in the distance, marking the entrance to the Chesapeake Bay.

"Look!" Sayeed said, pointing.

"There's someone here," said Hossein Gill from the front passenger's seat.

The Engineer watched the blurred forms in the front seat of the parked pick-up truck slowly separate as they pulled up, then join together again. He motioned to Jamal, who was sitting next to him in the back seat to slide down out of sight.

"Kill the engine," he whispered. "Light cigarettes. Hang your arms out the windows. Look sleepy. Listen closely."

"I can take them out," Hossein said eagerly. "Come on. I know you hid the revolvers back there."

"Keep your voice down," the Engineer hissed, bringing his hand up from behind and clamping two fingers on Hossein's windpipe. "If they don't leave in ten minutes, you'll have your chance."

He checked his watch. It was just 0134 hours. They had plenty of time. If the pick-up truck lovers were so stupid to continue their ridiculous display in full view of an audience, they deserved to die. Otherwise, they were not a threat. The chance that they would report the presence of a pair of Hispanic workers, having a smoke after a late-night shift, was nil, since it would raise questions about what they were doing at the Landing themselves.

By 0140, the lovers gave up and left.

They waited another five minutes, then the Engineer gave the sign for them all to get out. Now they owned the place.

He surveyed the area, comparing every detail to the mental image he had created from the descriptions he had received from Sayeed, looking for anything out of place. The boat landing itself was wide enough for two large cars, and had a concrete ramp leading down into the water where the boaters could launch. The tall grass on either side hid the landing from view of the houses that fronted the Bay beyond the abandoned tobacco fields. He doubted anyone would be coming through the fields, where the red earth showing through the sprawling tobacco plants was cracked and heavily-rutted. The whole place smelled of rotting vegetation, dead fish, and motor oil.

He climbed up into the rear of the vehicle and released the canvas bags from their hiding place beneath the winch. The night was cool for summer, but sticky damp, and he had to wipe sweat from his palms before he set to work. He opened the first bag and spun the cylinder of the long-barreled revolver. He loaded six blunt-nose Special .38 rounds, then clicked it shut. Repeating the procedure with the second gun, he took off the safety, chambered a round, and took aim at the green buoy out on the water. Satisfied, he flicked the safety back on and tucked the long-barreled revolver into his jeans.

"Jamal," he said, when he came back outside. "Set your phone to vibrate. I want you two hundred meters up the road. If someone comes, signal us first. Use this only if you have no other way of keeping them away."

He handed him the other revolver, and a handful of extra bullets.

"What about me?" Hossein Gill asked.

"I'm going to need both your arms," he said. "Let's get the dollies in place."

Sayeed and Hossein Gill folded open the rear doors of the concession stand, dropped the ramp, and rolled down the two dollies they had purchased from a piano mover.

The Engineer checked his watch again. It was just 2 AM. They were due to signal him in another fifteen minutes.

So now they waited.

At exactly 0214 hours, the Engineer's Nextel cell phone chirped. A low voice said, "Richard, this is Josh. Are you there?"

The Iranian on the other end spoke in barely accented English. He had practiced the words hundreds of times, until he could pronounce them properly.

"Hi, Josh. I can't wait to see you."

"Me, too," the voice said.

The Engineer lit the sterno lamp he had brought in his tool bag, waved it three times in front of him, then handed it to Hossein to hold up.

The cell phone chirped again. "Five minutes."

The Engineer just nodded, but didn't reply. He turned to Sayeed. "Let's get on the boots," he said.

Sayeed rummaged in the storage locker behind the back seat and brought out three pair of hip boots. The big ones, size twelve, were for Hossein. He handed Sayeed the sterno lamp while he put them on.

They heard the vessel before they actually saw it approach. A rippling sound in the water, a slight whirring of an electric motor; noises that clearly didn't belong to the night, but which fit no object any of them had ever encountered before. "*Allah!*" Hossein muttered under his breath, to allay his fear. "*Allah!*" he wailed. He stepped back from the water, afraid to get too close. The smell of dead fish was overpowering.

"Keep quiet," the Engineer said. "You'll see."

Finally, small waves reached shore and lapped up against the landing slip. The Engineer waded into the water, carrying the two stainless steel hooks attached to the winch line. "Let it out slowly," he called back to Sayeed.

Then they saw the dark form of the hatch, sticking up above the inky black water, and then the head of a man sticking up above it.

"*Jelotair,*" the Engineer said if Farsi. "Closer. *Penj meter bishtair* - five meters more."

They could see the dark outline of the mini-submarine now, the flat deck rising several feet above the water, and long dark objects attached to either side, giving it a complicated, decidedly unseaworthy shape. It didn't look like any vessel any of them had ever seen before, but some kind of giant robot with ray gun arms.

The captain of the sub maneuvered until he brought the ship parallel to the shore. The Engineer waded out until he was nearly chest-deep in the water, filling his boots and drenching his clothes with the warm, muddy waters of the Bay. Finally he reached the cylindrical object closest to shore and lifted himself partway up on it so his head wouldn't go underwater, then set the stainless steel hooks one by one into the rings set in its surface. The man in the hatch watched him impassively. They had practiced this maneuver many times before, and both of them exactly what to do.

The Engineer spun his hand slowly for Sayeed operate the winch to pull the line taut, then abruptly gave a downwards chop for him to stop. He pushed off from the sub and waded back toward shore, pulling himself forward along the tow line. Still in water up to his hips, he began a slow, circling motion with his hand again. This time, the electric motor whined loudly, straining with the weight, as it gradually pulled the mini-submarine and the long object closer to shore.

"That's enough! Bring the dollies," the Engineer hissed, when the object reached him.

Hossein brought up the piano mover's dollies and the Engineer helped him fit them at either end of the fat cylinder, cinching them to the underbelly with broad canvas straps. Although he was several inches taller than the Engineer, Hossein was sputtering and flailing his hands in the water, trying to finish as quickly as possible. It was clear he didn't like being in the water.

"Stand back," the Engineer called.

"*Baleh*. Ready," he called to the man in the hatch.

He ducked his head below and then reappeared. "*Amadeh – bash – sherough!*" he called. "Ready, set, go!"

Suddenly, the bolts securing the cylinders on either side of the mini-submarine exploded with a loud, low report, echoing out to sea, as the cylinders on either side dropped into the water and sent waves up over the tops of their boots, violently tossing the mini-sub from side to side. The man in the hatch braced himself but stayed in place, rocking with the ship.

Once the ripples died down, the Engineer waded out to where the cylinder closest to them had dropped, following the winch lines with his hands beneath the water. Satisfied, he circled his hand for Sayeed to set the winch in motion and walked back with it, step by step, as the electric motor strained to haul the heavy cylinder on the dollies through the last bit of sand and onto the cement of the boat slip. He had Sayeed back off the winch line and released one of the hooks, then he and Hossein muscled the long object around in the water until the end of it faced the open end of the truck. He reattached the hook to the other side of the cylinder, and Sayeed slowly began pulling it up the ramp. Meanwhile, the submarine had used a tiny docking motor to maneuver around the sunken ballast tank.

By the time they got the cylinder up into the truck, it was gone.

Crouching beneath the stainless steel countertop, the Engineer took two of the beach towels from the stack in the corner and wiped down the top of the cylinder until he was satisfied no water could seep in. Then he got out the ratchet wrench, fitted it with a 19mm socket, and removed the eight bolts securing the waterproof top panel one by one.

Inside was a numeric keypad, and a small display that showed three sets of four zeros, flashing red. He found the slip of paper with the codes from his tool bag. Discarding the first group – the Visa card sequence – he entered the twelve digits of the arming code. The display then shifted to the next page. He checked his watch: it was precisely 0253 hours, Monday, July 2. He entered that as the current time, then entered the end time: 2204 hours, Wednesday, July 4. Then, after discarding the MasterCard sequence, he entered the final three groups of four numerals, the confirmation code.

The display flashed three times, signifying that the arming code had been verified and accepted. Then the display shifted to the final page.

He watched it for fully thirty seconds, mesmerized, until the knowledge that they were going to succeed filled him with great joy. He praised Allah seven times beneath his breath, then carefully replaced the top panel.

It was the last time the Engineer would glimpse at the timer in this life.

It read: 67 hours, 10 minutes, 58 seconds.

1000 hours, Monday, July 2 – Washington, DC

If Danny could read the mind of FBI Director Louis Adams, it wasn't because he was clairvoyant.

It was clear Director Adams wasn't impressed by Rahimi's theatrics. *You say he's a Colonel?* he asked Danny at one point, while Aryana was translating back and forth. *How many Colonels are there in the Revolutionary Guards Corps – as many as in our army? How many of our Colonels have ever met the president?* Danny didn't take it as a slight, nor had that really been Adams' intent. It was merely a statement of fact. Was this Iranian incapable of smelling the raw power of the vast corner office overlooking the United States Capitol and the National Mall? Did he not understand that Louis Adams had the power to reward men and deprive others of their freedom? That on his orders alone, Rahimi and his family could live happily ever after under assumed names in the United States, or become like Kleenex, used once and tossed into the garbage?

"Tell him that's fine," Director Adams said to Aryana. "If he's not willing to speak to me, perhaps he'd like me to arrange a meeting with the director of the CIA? Translate that, Miss – uh"

"Pourmanesh, sir," she said.

"--word for word."

Rahimi brightened at the mention of the CIA. Clearly, it was more familiar to him than the FBI.

"And tell him that I will recommend to the director of the CIA that he send the Colonel back into Iran as an American agent. Word for word, Miss Pourmanesh."

"Yes, sir."

Director Adams relished watching Colonel Rahimi turn green as Aryana translated his words. With seeming nonchalance, he turned again to Danny. "I take it you haven't been able to talk sense to him."

"No, sir," he said. "He's very worried about his security, and the safety of his family."

"I understand. And I appreciate the fact that you have risked your life to protect him. Both of you," he added, indicating Aryana, who was in the midst of a heated exchange with the Colonel. "But I'm not going to sit here and negotiate with some Mohammad you've brought in from the souk. This is his chance. If he doesn't take it, he's not going to get another."

Danny felt as if he were swimming up through molasses, struggling to reach the surface, but that it was just out of reach. He uttered a silent prayer, asking God to give him the words he needed to convince this man.

"With all due respect, sir. It's we who are not going to have another chance if what I think he knows turns out to be true."

"Director Charles? Has he spoken to you?"

Nate snorted and gave the Iranian a skeptical look. "I don't think I fit his profile of rich and famous."

They were all surprised when Rahimi spoke to them next in English. "I am telling that I know," he said. "But please, my English. Kourosh to translate me."

Then Danny realized what had happened. Rahimi was looking at a picture that showed the President of the United States draping the Medal of Freedom around Louis Adams's neck. While he couldn't possibly know the significance of the medal, it was clear from the photograph that Adams was not just a subordinate of the president, but was close to him, because the president's eyes were moist with tears. "You tell big man," he said, pointing toward the picture.

Adams saw it, too, and gave him a deep nod, full of meaning. "Yes, I will tell the big man if what you tell me has such importance," he said.

Rahimi appeared to be satisfied and launched into his story, speaking slowly, without gestures, his hands crossed in his lap. Aryana stopped him from time to time, getting him to explain certain details, asking him questions, before she turned back to them with the gist. She moved carefully, still in pain from the bullet wound in her back. The restraint was not like her. Danny ground his teeth in sympathy when he saw her grimace in pain.

"He has two things to tell you," she said. "The first involves some kind of deception in Maracaibo, something he thinks you should know about. The second involves Hajj Imad. He is in charge of bringing the weapon into the United States."

"Hajj Imad?" director Adams said. "*The* Hajj Imad?"

"Yes," she said simply. "He knows him like a brother."

How many Rev. Guards colonels could say they knew Iran's top terrorist like a brother? Danny wanted to say. But he bit his tongue.

"Tell him we're very interested in what he has to say," Adams said curtly.

Even Danny was stunned when Rahimi explained what the Iranians had done at Maracaibo. As Aryana talked back and forth with the Colonel, Danny filled in the gaps of the CIA surveillance operation with Director Adams. The satellite deception was the easiest part of it to understand. While Rahimi couldn't know the capabilities of the Lacrosse, it was true that civilian satellite-watchers had managed to track their orbit with precision, he explained. For Hajj Imad to log-on to one of these websites using a Canadian Internet Service Provider and exploit that information shouldn't be a great surprise. The Iranians had long showed themselves to be software geniuses. After all, they had invented the game of chess.

"We let ourselves be fooled by our own technology," Danny concluded.

"You're being charitable," Director Adams said. "Goddamn CIA was fooled by their own concept of what they thought was going on. They saw only what they wanted to see and then got out of Dodge. That asshole Haas ought to be shot. Reloading that ship was obvious. Are we just too dumb to conceive of this?"

"For the Iranians, this is war," Danny said.

"And we're the ones caught in the fog of it," Adams said.

Director Adams wanted to know everything about the Lacrosse, and if the satellite had picked up anything that would corroborate the Colonel's story from its next pass over Maracaibo. How about the truck convoy? Had they seen the same trucks back at the dock? Surely they must have compared the license plates?

"No, sir," Danny said. "If the Colonel's story is true, they timed the unloading of the ship to coincide with the flight envelope of the bird, and made sure they were out of the envelope when they came back to reload the mini-sub."

But Rahimi wasn't finished. He understood now that the Americans were listening and that he was the star. "*Shaitan der artash,*" he said, explaining the phrase and how he had heard it to Aryana.

"It means, 'Satan in the flames'," she said. "It's the code-word Hajj Imad has devised for this operation. It was used originally by Ayatollah Khomeini. Everyone in Iran knows what it means. It was his image for the final battle with America. He believed it was the destiny of the Islamic Republic."

"Only now, they have the capabilities to wage it," Director Adams said. "If Hajj Imad is in charge of this operation, as the Colonel says, then we're in trouble. This man is not just a pathological killer. He's a highly skilled planner, who has demonstrated his ability to recruit and manipulate large networks of non-Iranian assets. For his ground team, we could be talking about anybody. Nathaniel? You're thoughts are welcome," he said, turning to Nate Charles.

Danny watched his new mentor gather his thoughts, weighing what he felt against what he felt he could say. For an instant, he thought Nate was going to blow them out of the water, as he took another look at Colonel Rahimi, appraising him with a scowl. *We all know he didn't pass the box,* Danny thought. *Come on, Nate! You can do better than that!*

"The threat does not all hinge on the word of this man," he said finally. "We have enough corroboration from other sources to warrant asking Customs to intercept that ship before it gets anywhere near a U.S. port. In the meantime, DHS is going to want to raise the threat level to Orange."

"On what grounds?" Adams asked.

"Fourth of July."

As they emerged from the underground parking lot of the FBI headquarters building, Danny drove Rahimi and Aryana down by the National Mall, so the Iranian colonel could get his first glimpse of the White House. As they reached 14th street, workmen were finishing the installation of rows of bleachers along Constitution Avenue. Huge canvas tents were being set up on the White House grounds, in preparation for the 4th of July fireworks and the president's open house that night.

"The big house," Rahimi said in English, pointing to the presidential mansion. "*Inja hadaf ast,*" he added in Farsi. "That is the target

Inside the concession stand of Maria's Tex-Mex, somewhere in Maryland, a red counter set inside a long metal canister read: 59 hours:17 minutes: 48 seconds.

1300 hours, Monday, July 2 – Port Elizabeth, NJ

The rotor blades of the black and gold U.S. Customs Blackhawk helicopter were still thumping when Danny and Nate Charles jumped down from their canvas seats onto the asphalt dock area at Port Elizabeth, New Jersey. As far as they could see were stacks of shipping containers, bright blues and reds and oranges and yellows, all in neat rows on the asphalt. Towering just beyond them, a line of gigantic, light grey unloading cranes stood over the string piece, hauling containers on long overhead rails from a container ship to tractor trailers lined up in lanes on the blacktop below. The most stunning thing about the port area was how clean it was, Danny thought. There wasn't a piece of paper or a smudge of oil anywhere in sight.

Chief Morris Haggarty was waiting for them by an unmarked Jeep Grand Cherokee. He was the chief inspector from U.S. Customs and Border Protection, in charge of the Newark/Port Elizabeth/New York port facilities.

"They stood right over there," he said after he greeted them, pointing to a hole in the skyline of lower Manhattan. "I'll never forget watching the second aircraft hit the south tower. The other one was already in flames by the time I got out here, but I saw the second plane hit. That's what we're doing here," he said, crossing himself instinctively. "We're trying to keep September 11th from ever happening again.

Everyday I look at that skyline, that's what I'm thinking."

"Amen to that," Danny said.

Haggarty had enlisted in the U.S. Army on November 5, 1979 – the day after Iranian "students" seized the U.S. embassy in Tehran – and retired as a Staff Sergeant twenty years later. His long years of service and his talent for training young men and women helped him land a supervisory position at U.S. Customs after just two years on the job, even if these days he had to tuck in a sizeable paunch getting into his blue uniform.

"Are you gentlemen familiar with the Midnight Express?" he said, when they arrived at the Customs dock area, discretely tucked into the back of the Elizabeth Channel.

Danny and Nate exchanged shrugs.

"I take that as a no," Chief Haggarty said. "This is Officer Jermak. He's going to be our captain today. And this is Officer Washington. They've each got ten years of Coast Guard service under their belt, before they came to the bright side to drive these boats. So if you think you're about to take a drink, don't blame it on them."

The boat drivers were dressed in dark blue combat uniforms, black waterproof boots, and silver reflective Ray bans. They wore grey headsets with thick ear protectors. Boom microphones covered their mouths so they could communicate with each other while at sea.

"Welcome aboard, sir," Jermak said, without leaving the controls of the low-slung Go-Fast boat. He had slipped down the microphone and gave them a businesslike nod. The four 225 horse-power Mercury outboard engines made the thirty-nine foot boat throb even at idle.

"You'll want these," said Officer Washington, handing the three of them life vests with large stainless steel belaying clips and cables they could attach to various hard points on the boat. On the thick, padded straps of the life vests, U.S. Customs was written in bright yellow capital letters.

Jermak showed them the map of the harbor area. Once they exited Newark Bay they would enter the Anchorage channel and then the Narrows, the neck of water separating Staten Island from Brooklyn that led into Lower New York Bay and ultimately out over open water to Ambrose Point. That was where the Sandy Hook Pilots' boat was scheduled to rendezvous with the *East Wind III* in approximately 30 minutes.

"How fast can you make on open water?" Danny asked, once they got underway.

"Upwards of 50 knots, sir. We're the fastest thing on the water."

Danny would soon realize there was nothing cocky or even boastful about that statement. It was just a fact.

Ten minutes later, they reached Constable Hook and could see the Anchorage channel off Staten Island open out ahead, where a dozen large ships waited, idling in the water, for orders to approach New York harbor.

Jermak turned to them and pointed to the stainless steel rail just behind the controls.

"You're going to want to stay up close to the bulkhead and clamp on," he said. "Sometimes the waves can get a bit rough."

Once he made sure that Danny and Nate and Chief Haggarty had secured themselves to the rail, Jermak throttled up and the boat took off, accelerating from 15 knots to well over 50 knots in a matter of seconds. It was a calm day, and they seemed to skim effortlessly above the still water, the wind blowing their hair flat against their heads. Jermak dipped his head to see between the struts of the open canopy for traffic, then he swung the wheel hard left. Almost instantaneously, the boat canted up onto its side at a 45-degree angle and they headed around the bow of a large container ship. Seconds later, he spun the wheel three furious turns to the right, and the boat pitched just as far in the other direction, like a Lamborghini on skids. They sped past the ship, then hit the Anchorage channel and the water got rougher, crashing over the bow and soaking Danny and Nate and Chief Haggarty in the face and chest. Jermak spun the wheel round and they headed southward along the Staten Island coast.

"The pilot boats leave from over there," Jermak shouted, pointing off their starboard bow to the Edgewater street docks on Staten Island. "We'll be rendezvousing with *P/B New Jersey* and the rest of our guys out at Ambrose Point, seventeen miles out."

"What's our ETA?" Chief Haggarty shouted.

The Midnight Express driver looked down at a computer screen that calculated his speed and time to destination. "1345, sir. Right on schedule. Fifteen minutes from now."

Seen from wave top level at more than 60 miles an hour on a warm July afternoon with the sun reflecting off windshield wipers and car mirrors up above, the Verrazano Narrows Bridge seemed miraculous, indestructible, eternal. But as they sped beneath it, Danny realized it was nothing of the sort, and that if they failed, that magnificent man-made creation and much of lower Manhattan would soon be turned into a gigantic fireball.

Somewhere in Maryland, a red counter set inside a long metal canister read: 55 hours: 51 minutes: 12 seconds.

1345 hours, Monday, July 2 – Ambrose Point, Atlantic Ocean

Danny knew they were coming up on Ambrose Point pilot station when Officer Washington took a pair of high-powered binoculars from a waterproof cupboard to scan the horizon. Jermak turned to them and shouted, "Hold on!" Without slowing down, he swung the wheel hard left and they headed northward into the Nantucket traffic lane, then a minute later, swung back to the east and then circled down to the south. Shortly, they could see the giant Ambrose light tower, built up on stilts, flash in the distance. This was the area in the North Atlantic where the pilot boats met up with commercial vessels entering New York harbor.

A few minutes later, they saw the *P/B New Jersey* on station, making its slow pass back and forth near the light tower. While it was dwarfed by the giant container ships that regularly came into New York, its white wheelhouse and twin smokestacks rose some fifty feet above the waves. The *P/B New Jersey* served as a floating office and lounge for the Sandy Hook pilots as they waited to join inbound ships. The tiny motor launch they used to board the commercial ships hung alongside, squat and solid, like a miniature tug. Hovering behind it were two more Midnight Express boats, low and menacing, even smaller than the motor launch. Each was packed with a half-dozen black-uniformed commandos.

"What's the plan?" Nate shouted to Chief Haggerty.

"When they're busy pulling the pilot on board from the motor launch, our guys come up from the stern on the other side and board her."

Nate looked down at the black waters of the North Atlantic and scowled. "You ever done this before, son?" he asked Danny.

"No, sir."

Haggarty looked beyond them toward the intercept point. "Seas are calm, two foot swells. It shouldn't take more than about two minutes for our guys to get on board, another two minutes or so for them to secure the ship. They'll radio us when it's time. You can watch through these."

He handed Nate another pair of binoculars. In front of them, Jermak was talking into the boom microphone to someone on the radio.

They watched the motor launch with its squat white wheelhouse and giant red letters "PILOT," break away from the mother ship. It headed out across the horizon to meet the *East Wind III*, next in line in the Barnegat to Ambrose traffic lane. From where they were, they could see the ship in the distance, dazzling in the early afternoon sun; beyond it, they could see the

Manhattan skyline, faint grey blocks on the horizon. As the motor launch approached the ship on the leeward side, the two Midnight Express boats moved off slowly, so close to the waves they became nearly invisible to the naked eye. Jermak prowled behind them at a distance, the huge Mercury engines idling behind them. Through the binoculars, they could see someone on the deck of the *East Wind III* toss the Jacob's ladder over the side for the pilot as the motor launch approached.

"On a calm day like today, they usually catch it on the first toss," Chief Haggarty said. "But something tells me they're going to have problems today. Keep 'em occupied."

Danny and Nate watched, mesmerized, as the harbor pilot on the deck of the tiny motor launch made an effort to catch the swinging rope ladder with its wooden rungs, but missed as the launch caught a wave and bobbed away like a cork from the cargo ship whose black metal sides, even fully loaded, rose a good thirty feet straight up. On the third toss, he grabbed the ladder part way up and swung himself up onto it, climbing rapidly before the motor launch crushed him against the side of the *East Wind III*. Up above him, a half dozen crew members had gathered near the wheelhouse to help swing him on board.

That was when the commandos of the Customs and Border Protection Air and Marine branch struck.

The two Midnight Express boats had been approaching the weather side of the ship steadily but silently. Now, seeming to stand on the sea itself, four men fired grappling hooks, pulling the ropes through gear on their belts until they went taught, then seemed to rise up the side of the ship as if on some kind of hand-operated elevator. The instant the first four disappeared over the gunwale, the next four men came forward, fired their grappling hooks, and rose up the side, and then the final four, until all twelve commandos were on board. Danny and Nate watched the whole boarding operation through binoculars.

Three minutes later, the engines on the *East Wind III* suddenly went dead.

"Show time," Chief Haggarty said.

Jermak turned around at virtually the same time and shouted, "Hang on!"

He throttled up to full power and the Midnight Express boat rose above the waves and seemed to leap forward. It took them less than a minute to come up along the leeward side of the *East Wind III,* where the Jacob's ladder now hung motionless against the side. Up above, one of the Customs ninjas waved his arm for them to board.

Chief Haggarty climbed part way up, then stopped, visibly winded. Without looking around, he shouted: "Alright, Washington, quit laughing. I used to do this all the time when I was your age."

Once he reached the top, Danny followed, and then Nate, with Haggarty talking them up the side of the ship. "Don't look down," he called when Nate stopped to catch his breath.

Two of the Customs ninjas were standing guard over the first mate and the dozen or so crewmen he had assembled on deck. Two more Customs men were with Captain Mahmoud in the wheelhouse, going over the ship's manifest and other documents they could find. The rest of them had fanned out across the ship, banging on the sides of containers with the butt ends of sleek black Mag lights, to see if any of them rang empty.

"Over here!" one of them called shortly.

Chief Haggarty, Nate and Danny ran down to join him, as did two more of the black-uniformed special ops men.

"The seals looks intact," Danny said.

Chief Haggarty gave a quick barking laugh. "Oh, yeah! Got ten grand, and we can fix that. Some of these guys don't even bother with the seals. They just drill out the bolts holding the locks, and leave the seals intact. Gotten so they don't mean anything any longer."

He nodded to one of the ninjas, who took a cold chisel and compact hammer from his belt and removed the Customs seal with a single blow.

"Bettinelli, Reyes – get over here," Haggarty said. "We need readings from in there – now!"

One of the men, Reyes, took off his backpack and got out a handheld gamma-ray spectrometer. These 10 pound, battery-powered units, introduced after 9/11, used a sodium iodide sensor to detect the presence of radioactive emissions from nuclear sources. Also known as a radio-isotope identification device (RIID), the unit converted the gamma rays into visible light and then into an electronic signal, which it digitized and compared to a stored library of nuclides to determine which isotope was producing the radiation. The device then wrote the atomic map of the offending substance on a memory chip so it could be downloaded and transmitted via the SIPRNet, the government's Secret Internet Protocol Router NetWork, to one of several national laboratories for further analysis.

Reyes entered the dark, empty container, holding the detector out at shoulder height. The device began beeping almost immediately.

"So what you got?" Chief Haggarty asked.

When Reyes re-emerged, he looked puzzled. He adjusted a few dials, but the RIID still couldn't identify whatever isotope it had detected. "Not sure, sir. Let me take another sample," he said.

But the second sampling from inside the dark container was just as illusive.

"Is there enough data so we can send it to the labs?" Chief Haggarty asked.

"I think so," Reyes said, checking the small display. "Whatever it is, it's just too faint to be identified with these algorithms."

Two ninjas emerged from below decks, pushing a crew member whose hands they had secured behind his back with cable ties. The man struggled against the two black-suited CBP officers who held his arms, but said nothing. He was scared and dirty, and wore a grimy yellow sweatshirt. It was the mate who had tried to jump ship in Capetown.

"Where's the submarine?" Danny asked.

The man turned his head to the side and said nothing.

"We know it was on this ship. Now, where is it?" Danny repeated.

Chief Haggarty moved toward the uncooperative mate, his imposing stomach preceding him, his burly forearms unsheathed, and grabbed him by the shoulders and slammed him against the container with a thud. "We need some cooperation here," he said, smiling. "Now answer the man!"

"I know nothing," the frightened crewman said, looking about frantically for the Captain or other members of the crew. Then he hissed: "They'll kill me if they see me talking to you."

"You'll come with us," Haggarty said. "Betinelli! Call the Coast Guard and get them to send over a skeleton crew for this tub. We're taking these men into custody."

Somewhere in Maryland, a red counter set inside a long metal canister read: 54 hours: 45 minutes: 22 seconds.

1800 hours, Monday, July 2 – Bolling AF Base

Principal assistant deputy national intelligence director Richard Stapleton looked grave, his thick jowls and rippling neck furrowed like a freshly-ploughed field, as the other members of the sherpas committee and their aides drifted in. On the large, curved screen behind him was displayed a gigantic navigation chart of the Eastern seaboard from Charleston, South Carolina to New York, showing literally hundreds of coves and inlets where a mini-submarine could dock without ever being seen. Before him, a document with red borders, stamped Top Secret/NO FORN, contained the results from Lawrence Livermore National Laboratory of the samples taken by CBP Officer Reyes with his GR-135 Radio Isotope Detection device on board the *East Wind III*. Without any doubt, they showed the presence of HEU – uranium enriched to weapons grade.

The room was far more packed than usual, and the atmosphere was tense. Lower-level aides filled strait-backed chairs in a double row behind their principals around the long oval conference table.

"Gentlemen, ladies," Stapleton began. A hushed silence came over the room as papers stopped shuffling and folders closed. "We have a bomb."

Turning to the navigation chart that filled the huge display behind him, Stapleton gave them a quick run down of where the submarine could have off-loaded the weapon, circling with his laser pointer the Chesapeake Bay, the Potomac River basin, the Delaware Bay, the New Jersey coastline and then New York harbor, increasingly animated, increasingly frustrated, increasingly desperate. It physically took his breath away, and by time he reached New York he was almost gasping.

"The truth is, we don't have a clue where they brought the weapon in," he said. "And we have very little time to find out. The enemy has scored one against our goal-line defense. The Director of National Intelligence brought the president up to date on the situation two hours ago."

That piece of information unleashed tongues all around the room. Aides leaned forward to their bosses, and bosses conferred amongst themselves, all of them in various stages of shock and awe, wondering who was going to be made to take the blame. Major Danny Wilkens watched the jitters seize the room, but said nothing as his boss, the deputy director of the Defense Intelligence Agency, conferred with assistant FBI director Nathaniel Charles.

"As for targets, they could be going for Richmond, Washington, Baltimore, Philadelphia, Newark, or New York City. Take your pick," Stapleton said.

There were a whole bunch of people from Homeland Security and the Pentagon Danny had never seen before. One of the uniformed types sitting at the table spoke up.

"We have a carrier battle group currently on patrol in the Persian Gulf. That's 22 surface ships, 72 combat aircraft, and one Ohio-class SSBN, retrofitted to carry 150 conventional submarine-launched cruise missiles," the officer said. By the anchor and the single star, Danny took him to be a Rear Admiral.

Stapleton cut him off immediately. "Admiral, we have no actionable intelligence linking this directly to Iran – at least, nothing we can talk about in public. Major Wilkens and Assistant Director Charles can fill you in on our sources. For now at least, this is not about retaliation, let alone deterrence. This is about detection."

"*And* prevention," said Jason Steinberg, cutting in. "The president specifically authorized me two hours ago to work with this committee to devise and implement a plan to interdict this weapon by whatever means we deem appropriate. All the resources of the United States government are at our disposal, people. That means, I expect total cooperation from each and every one of you and from your agencies. Is that clear?"

A murmur of assent quickly rose from all quarters of the room, although Danny thought he saw Charles Haas exchange a worried glance with Victoria

Brandt, then hurriedly look down at the red-lined folder on the workspace in front of him.

"We're going to have to prioritize, Jason," said Roger Kaminski quietly. His "goalies" had missed the weapon, and he took that personally, although in truth they never had a chance.

"What do you mean?" Steinberg said.

"We simply don't have enough detection gear to cover the entire eastern seaboard," he said bluntly.

Kaminski explained that $2 billion had bought several hundred Radiation Portal Monitors since 9/11. These were large stationary devices that looked like toll booths, and were now installed at virtually every major seaport in the United States. Tractor trailers hauling cargo containers were required to pass through them when entering or leaving the port, to determine if they were carrying radioactive materials. But the portal monitors were useless against cargo that was still on board ships and couldn't be moved, even in an emergency like this.

Steinberg couldn't believe what he was hearing, and he didn't attempt to hide his frustration. "We have spent billions of dollars to upgrade port security!" he said. "You're telling me we don't have any portable radiation detectors?"

"We have mobile VACIS – perhaps forty of them," Kaminski said.

The Vehicle and Cargo Inspection machines were mobile gamma ray imaging systems that could be driven to impromptu inspection points. They looked like telephone installation trucks equipped with a long, articulated arm that beamed a passive signal through the target to a sensor located on the other side. Under normal usage, containers selected at random were driven through the U-shaped VACIS arm on tractor trailers as soon as they were offloaded from incoming ships. They not only detected radiation sources, but gave operators a visual image of the contents of the container without ever opening it. In principle, they could be deployed anywhere within hours.

"If we chose, we could position them on bridges and tunnels to screen all traffic coming into Lower Manhattan for the 4th of July fireworks – if, of course, we felt confidant that New York was the target," Kaminski said. "I have absolute confidence the VACIS would pick up a bomb hidden inside any kind of vehicle, even if it was shielded. But to get any reasonable coverage, we'd have to bring in just about every unit we've got from Miami to Boston," he added. "That would leave other cities vulnerable to attack."

"What about those hand-held devices they used on board the ship?" Steinberg asked. "What about NEST, for crying out loud!"

"The RIIDs only work at close quarters," Kaminski said. "We'd have to actually stop traffic and send officers walking down the line to take readings. You're talking about creating mass panic."

"As soon as the president announces we've stepped up the Security Advisory Threat level to Code Red, there will be panic enough," Steinberg said.

The eerie hush came over the room again as distractions and idle whispers melted away and division chiefs and assistant secretaries wondered which one of them was going to lose their job.

"When will he make the announcement?" Stapleton asked quietly.

"In a nationally-televised address tonight at 8 PM."

After he had measured the impact of that bombshell to his satisfaction, Jason Steinberg slapped his hand on the table. "So what about NEST? Who's here from DoE?"

"I am," said Eva. She was sitting in the second row, behind Roger Kaminski. "Dr Eva Romera, from Lawrence Livermore National Laboratory. Do you want the truth, Mr. Steinberg? Or do you want the Hollywood version?"

Steinberg rolled his eyes unconvincingly, and Danny suppressed a laugh. Eva could stop them dead when she wanted, and he loved her for it.

"I'll take that to mean you want the truth. At full bore, we can mobilize a half dozen helicopters, a dozen ground units, and perhaps sixty qualified technicians."

"So can you detect the damn thing from the air?"

"The labs are working on that," she said. "But at present, no. The helicopters are for transport."

"God save us," Steinberg said quietly.

"What we can do is establish safe zones, set up perimeters, monitor anything going in. But we can only do that once we get a clear idea where you think they are going to strike. We need hard intelligence to go on."

From the sudden riot in the room, it was clear that she had touched a raw nerve. Principals turned to consult their aids, heads were shaking, chairs knocked against desks, papers shuffled. Everyone seemed to be talking at once. The air was thick with recrimination.

Jason Steinberg rapped the table in front of him with the classified binder. "People! Somebody please tell me this isn't just a crap shoot!"

He gave a dismissive wave at the huge navigation chart up on the display, and tossed the binder angrily onto the table. "I can tell you this: there is no way the president is going to order the evacuation of every city on the eastern seaboard!"

Stapleton cleared his large throat, and took control of the room. If nothing else, Danny thought, his years in the bureaucracy had given him the ability to instantly size up the equities of a dozen different agencies and the egos of their representatives, to know when to lay his cards on the table.

"Director Charles? I believe you have fresh information."

Danny silently prayed as Nathaniel Charles coughed twice, adjusted his reading glasses, and looked through a sheaf of papers in front of him. Come on, Nate: it's time for the full armor of God, he thought. *For our struggle is not against flesh and blood, but against the rulers, against the authorities, against the powers of this dark world....*

"I do," Charles said finally.

He found the paper he was looking for, and scanned it quickly before speaking. "We've got the crew in custody and one them is talking. We're trying to work with him, but it's been slow going because he's scared."

The crew member had confirmed early on that they had offloaded the mini-sub at some point during the night. Now they were trying to get him to be more specific. "The only thing he's clear about at this point is that they never left the commercial shipping lanes, and that the launch went without a hitch. They slowed down for something like ten minutes, but that was it. It was before the last shift, between 10 PM and midnight. By our calculations, that places it somewhere off the coast of Virginia or Maryland."

Stapleton rapped the table to silence the commotion this information provoked. "That eliminates New York and Charleston," he said.

"Not necessarily," said Victoria Brandt. "Is there any technical reason why they couldn't just travel up the Atlantic coast in this mini-sub?"

"Admiral?" Stapleton asked.

The Vice-admiral who was ready to launch cruise missiles on Iran shrugged. "I wouldn't sit in one of those tin cans for more than ten minutes."

The laughter his comment provoked was a welcome relief.

"Al Qaeda has always wanted to attack New York again," Victoria Brandt added, undeterred.

Danny scrawled two words in capitol letters on his yellow legal pad, tore off the page, and handed it to his director, who was sitting with Nate Charles in front of him at the table. When he saw it, Nate turned and gave Danny a look he would never forget. If he was wrong, this was going to be Nate's execution, it said.

"Our source, the Iranian colonel, tells us the target is the White House," Nate said finally. "He called it, 'the Big House.' He told us that the information came from his cousin, who is a senior official in MOIS in Tehran," he added.

That was too much for Charles Haas. "So we're going to evacuate Washington, DC because of chatter picked up from the cousin of some raghead who can't pass a polygraph? Come on, people. This is not serious!"

When Stapleton had called the room to order again, he turned to Nate and asked simply. "Do we know the identity of the cousin?"

"We do," Nate said. "It's Ali Akbar Parvaresh, head of Section 43. The man who runs Hajj Imad."

Even Haas was impressed, Danny thought. And so they decided to focus all their efforts on one city: Washington, DC

Less than fifteen miles away from where they sat, a red counter set inside a long metal canister read: 50 hours: 51 minutes: 08 seconds.

VIII

EVA

0800 hours, Tuesday, July 3 – Bel Pre Manor apartments, Silver Spring, MD

The President's prime time speech was all over the morning papers. The *Washington Times* ran large verbatim quotes, without commentary, then cited an unnamed administration official who provided on background a more detailed account of the extraordinary government mobilization the president had ordered. "Terror Threat Crosses Red Line," their headline read. It included a box on practical steps FEMA recommended every family should take in the event of emergency. The two main points were deciding on an out-of-state phone number family members could call to coordinate their whereabouts if the local phone system was out, and an emergency assembly point away from the home.

The *Washington Post* account was more nuanced. Its front page news story was accompanied by an above-the-fold analysis that got Richard Halstead's attention. "Advisors Divided Over Terror Response," the headline read. Beneath it was a subhead: "New York Seen As Likely Target."

The article cited an unnamed presidential advisor as saying that the President had made a "questionable" call when he ordered roadblocks on all main thoroughfares leading into Washington, DC while pulling assets out of other cities considered to be likely targets. "Intelligence is always a murky business," the unnamed source told the Washington Post reporter. "But in this instance, it was murkier than usual. Basing your evaluation of a terrorist threat on chatter from the third cousin of Mohammad the taxi driver is no slam dunk."

The article went on to describe the workings of a portable radiation monitor known as the RIID, and pointed out that the President had ordered Customs and Border Security to relocate all forty-two of its mobile VACIS machines to the nation's capital, where they would begin operating this morning.

It also revealed that the President's decision to raise the terror alert to red for the first time since the color-coded system was introduced in 2002 was based on a "questionable linkage" between al Qaeda and Iran. "We know that such ties do not exist," said Khaled Nasser, a respected analyst with Muslims for Free Enterprise. "The Iranians are Shia Muslims, whereas bin Laden and most al Qaeda operatives are wahhabis, and wahhabis eat Shias for breakfast. I mean, they hate each other worse than Irish Catholics hate Irish Protestants."

When the Engineer had read the article for the third time, he turned to Sayeed, who had brought him the papers and was getting ready to drive downtown to work. "This Khaled Nasser," he said. "You know him well?"

"He's my boss," Sayeed said.

"That is not what I asked you," he insisted.

"No. We hardly talk," Sayeed said.

The Engineer appeared satisfied with his response, and said nothing as he looked through the article yet one more time.

"Where is the nearest public library?" he asked Sayeed finally. "I need to get on the Internet."

A few miles away, the red counter inside read: 37 hours: 45 minutes: 06 seconds.

0900 hours, Tuesday, July 3 – FBI Regional office, Calverton, MD

Maryjo Slotnik was prepared for the protestors, but not for the rain. It opened up just minutes before she arrived at the strip mall in Calverton where Brannigan's office was located, and slammed the roof of her squad car with such suddenness she thought hail stones were hitting her. It was only about twenty feet between the parking area and the dry area beneath the overhang of the building, but she had no umbrella and her poncho was in the trunk. That didn't seem to bother the protestors, who burst into their chant the moment she pulled up, wet, angry, and very loud.

"Bigots! Racists! FBI Respect Our Rights!" they chanted.

A young white man in shirtsleeves ran to shelter beneath the overhang just as the rain began – a reporter, she surmised. A photographer was with him.

341

She couldn't see his face because he had brought his camera with a long telephoto lens into position, covering his face, aiming at her. She figured she'd give the rain another two minutes. Most of the times in summer it came in bursts, so a little patience helped you avoid the worst of it.

When it hadn't let up after five minutes, she decided to make a run for it. She was going to look just great when the pictures hit tomorrow's papers, she thought. Her thick tan shirt soaked up the water and stuck to her skin like paper mache, and her blond hair fell down in sodden waves from beneath her hat.

"Bigots! Racists! FBI Respect Our Rights!" they chanted, blocking her way into the building.

She hit the first row of demonstrators full force, head down, neck tensed, and flew into the building. Sensing her seriousness, they blew apart at the last minute and let her pass.

As she was waiting for the elevator, the reporter came up. "Are you planning any further arrests?" the young man said, moving so he could face her as he gripped his notebook tightly, pen in hand. She could see him reading her name tag and writing down her badge number, all the while he looked straight at her.

"First name's Maryjo," she said. "That's M-A-R-Y-J-O, one word. And if we make any arrests, we'll be calling you."

Upstairs, Brannigan and Paige were immersed in a computerized map of the Maryland suburbs, cut into grids, and didn't look up when the receptionist let her in. She just stood there for a minute, dripping, humiliated. Finally the receptionist came over and dropped a few paper towels at her feet to soak up the water.

Detective Slotnik pulled two official papers from her breast pocket and waved them in front of Brannigan's face. "I realize I'm no Bo Derek," she said. "But what's it take to get your attention?"

Brannigan looked up vacantly. "You get the arrest warrants?" he said, noticing the papers.

"Well, yeah," she said. "What's got you?"

"We've been pulled off the case," he said simply.

"Excuse me?"

"Something's come up," Brannigan said. "Didn't you see the papers? Watch TV? Listen to Rush?"

He nodded to a pile of newspapers on the desk next to them, and went back to the computer screen with Paige. Annoyed with herself for not having read the papers, she glanced furtively at the headlines and realized that the one time in her life she had gone to bed at 8 PM, absolutely exhausted from chasing the State's Attorney all day long for the arrest warrants, something monumental had occurred.

"Rush's not on until noon," she said. "But anyway, no. Guilty as charged."

Paige had isolated the major roads leading into Washington, DC, then plotted choke points where any vehicle would have to pass in order to make it to the National Mall. Just on the Maryland side of the District, they would need twenty, perhaps twenty-two of the VACIS machines if they were to screen all vehicles large enough to carry the bomb. It was easier to monitor traffic coming in from Virginia, because of the water border formed by the Potomac river. Everything came across on eight bridges. But funneling traffic on them through the VACIS machines was going to be a bear.

"Ever find the two electricians?" Brannigan asked distractedly, as he and Paige tried to figure out the best place to monitor traffic on New Hampshire avenue.

"Gone to ground," she said. "I was hoping you could help."

"You know, Slotnik – Maryjo. Sorry," he said, shaking his head. "We're into this thing feet first. I'd love to help. But somehow, finding that girl's murderers has become a bit less urgent than stopping the bad guys from bringing a bomb into the White House for the fireworks. Haven't you been briefed?"

She just shrugged. "Are you kidding?

Suddenly it hit him. "Wait a second. You've got – what is it? – 1100 officers in patrol cars, capable of doing traffic stops, and DHS hasn't yet brought you in the loop? This is going to make the response to Hurricane Katrina look like a model of government efficiency."

"Don't blame it all on DHS," she said. "The County Exec has got us filling the coffers by chasing dog walkers who don't use a leash."

Never before had the utter irrelevance of her job hit her quite so blatantly right in the face. For the past few weeks, working alongside Brannigan and the FBI, she had been re-invigorated. She had a purpose. She was doing something important, working side by side with a man whose reputation in law enforcement walked before him wherever he went. Brannigan was her link – not just to the FBI, but to the vital world of national security. In pursuing this girl's murderers, Maryjo Slotnik had felt she was pursuing those who wanted to destroy America. They were the same thugs who had murdered her father all those years ago in Serbia. They had the same ideology. In Kosovo they who smuggled drugs to buy guns and explosives to blow up churches. Here, they murdered girls who refused to marry old goats in a cave. They would just as easily bring a bomb into the White House as kill a minor Serbian official.

"They're wrong to take you off the case," she said.

"It's all hands on deck," Brannigan said.

But what if the deck were one and the same? Would Brannigan understand that? Would anyone at the FBI understand who had not been raised side by side with Muslims? Certainly the State's Attorney and the commissars running Montgomery County, Maryland didn't have a clue. She had even been warned by Rex Morgan not to lay a hand on the Muslim protestors, lest the County Exec's office file a complaint with the Equal Opportunity Commission.

"You're missing the point, Brannigan," she said. "I'll bet if we find this girl's murderers, they will lead us sooner or later to your bomb."

Brannigan didn't seem to hear, as he and Paige examined the maps they had printed out. She started to leave.

When still he didn't respond, she turned from the door.

"That's it?" she said.

"That's what?" Brannigan gave her a smile at last. "Go get 'em tiger. Sooner would be better."

The counter read: 36 hours: 28 minutes: 52 seconds.

1800 hours, Tuesday, July 3 – Washington, DC

In a normal year, Washington, DC emptied shortly after noon on July 3rd as government employees took advantage of Congressional recess and the general inattention that swept over offices on the eve of the national holiday, to get a few hours head start on the traffic to the beaches.

But the president's dramatic national address struck the stubborn core of resiliency lodged deep within the American character that emerges when Americans are challenged to show weakness or capitulate in the face of danger.

Rather than flee Washington, DC with the elevated terrorist threat the president announced, Washingtonians choose to stay at home.

Instead of avoiding the National Mall and its celebrated fireworks display, families from suburban Maryland and Virginia packed minivans and pick-up trucks with bedding and coolers and headed back into the city after work, preferring to sleep outside in the company of perfect strangers than to die in the cowardly comfort of their own beds.

Not everyone did these things, of course. Many of them fled. But the traffic was much heavier going into the District than leaving it.

By 6:30 PM, the day's thunderstorms had cleared, but the air was still heavy, hot, and smelling of ozone. Brannigan and Paige were patrolling the northern entries into the District in a UH-60 Blackhawk from Charlie company, 12th Aviation Battalion, flying out of Fort Belvoir. Brannigan couldn't believe the traffic – or the patience of what appeared to be an unending stream of families willing to brave the roadblocks and the heat in their determination to reach the nation's capitol for the night. Cars were backed up for more than five miles on the Baltimore-Washington Parkway, from the Route 50 merger all the way to the Capitol Beltway. Just beyond the merger, Customs and Border Protection had positioned one of their VACIS units. DC Capital police performed an initial triage, waving passenger cars into the left-hand lane so they could creep past the inspection area without stopping. Larger vehicles merged into the right-hand lane, where enlisted men and women from the Military District of Washington examined the drivers' ID. Roughly one in ten vehicles was then selected to pass through the VACIS, which had been set up in the middle lane. As the traffic crept forward, uniformed Customs officers walked up and down the middle lane and the shoulders, taking readings from their portable radiation monitors as the larger vehicles passed.

A group of boys, none of them older than twelve, ran up and down the median with a long-haired mutt, tossing a ball and forth. When they heard the helicopter overhead they all stopped and looked upward. Some of them jumped, as if they could reach up and touch the chopper; others waved. LtC Thomas Crozier, their pilot, waved his heavy gloved hand in return, the early evening sun glinting off the reflective surface of his goggles. Crozier was Charlie company commander.

"I can't believe somebody hasn't pulled a gun," Brannigan said.

"It's the uniforms," Crozier shouted, thumping his insignia. "Same thing after 9/11. People find it scary. And reassuring."

Crozier radioed to the team on the ground to clear the way, and they quickly stopped traffic in the left lanes so he could put the chopper down in the median. No sooner had they touched ground than Eva ran up to them, clutching her black baseball cap in the downwash from the rotors, and slung a large backpack into the chopper. She grabbed the arm of the loadmaster who was leaning out of the open bay doors and hoisted herself aboard. Once she was safely inside, the loadmaster gave Crozier the thumbs up and the helicopter bucked, breaking its loose bonds with the earth, and they were airborne once again.

"How's it going?" Brannigan asked, coming back to join her as she unpacked her gear in the cargo area of the chopper.

"Nothing yet," Eva said.

She wore black trousers with large pockets, a tight-fitting grey t-shirt and black combat boots, and Brannigan could see the sweat glistening on her forehead and her bare forearms. She worked quickly and expertly, extracting several electronic devices from heavily padded compartments inside the backpack, and plugging them into a black box with an antenna on top of it. Finally, she reached into the bottom of the backpack and extracted a laptop computer that looked like it was made out of armor plate and connected it to the communications array.

"I bet you grow special muscles just to handle that thing," he said.

"No kidding," Eva said.

Once she fired up the computer, she called up a satellite image of the northern approaches of Washington, DC. On top of it, she overlaid a schematic grid showing the main traffic arteries and the location of the VACIS machines and other NEST radiation detection sensors.

"We have full interoperability with DHS," she said. "All of the data from the VACIS and the handheld RIIDs streams into our system and gets integrated into it. But they don't see the big picture. That's our job. We've got a whole bunch of other sensors that we've deployed around the National Mall, the White House, and along all the main approach streets. That's the ultimate perimeter we've got to protect."

"Let's hope you're right," Brannigan said.

They flew to similar VACIS triage zones on New Hampshire avenue, 16th street, North Capital street, and Georgia avenue, inspecting them from the air since there were too many trees to land easily without shutting down traffic entirely. Washington was in utter chaos, Brannigan thought; and yet, people were calm, disciplined, even good-humored. In most areas where traffic had come to a standstill, parade marshals had set up first-aid stations on folding tables stacked with bottles of water, which people could take as they needed. They had even set up garbage cans lined with plastic bags!

When all the gears of government finally engaged and were pulling in the same direction it was an impressive sight, Brannigan thought. He couldn't remember seeing anything like it outside of a war zone.

Well beyond the NEST perimeter, the counter read: 26 hours: 15 minutes: 02 seconds.

0508 hours, Wednesday, July 4 – Aspen Hill shopping mall, Wheaton, MD

Jose Hernandez and his 14-year old son Michael had gotten up at 4 AM to make preparations for the big day. After a quick breakfast, Jose checked the truck; made sure they had enough propane in the tanks to keep the stove going all day long, and made a list of supplies they needed to pick up from the super market before heading downtown to the National Mall.

At 4:45 AM, they pulled into the parking lot of the Giant at Aspen Hill. By 5:02, Jose had paid cash for the eighteen pounds of fresh guacamole he had ordered the day before, forty pounds of frozen quesadillas, and other supplies. By 5:04, they were back on Connecticut avenue, heading south along the overgrown median. Jose put on a cassette of Vicente Fernandez, hoping to chase the sleep from his brain. 'El Rey' had hardly gotten started when his son turned off the music. "Dad, it's five in the morning!" he moaned. "Can't you let me sleep?"

Jose sighed, and acquiesced. He would never speak English without an accent as his son could do; and his son would never really appreciate the crisp brass and snapping drums of the mariachi bands.

The clock on his dashboard radio showed 5:07 AM when he caught sight of the blinking red lights at the Veirs Mill intersection in the distance and slowed the truck. There wasn't really any need to stop at this time of the morning, but you never knew when the police would be around. He didn't need another ticket, especially not today. Fourth of July was just about the biggest take of the entire year, even bigger than Labor Day. And this year promised to be even better, with the huge crowds expected at the fireworks.

It was 5:08 AM when he felt the jolt from behind and instinctively slammed on his brakes, even though they were hardly moving.

"*Estupido!*" he shouted, raising his fist to the rear-view mirror. "Do you have no eyes?"

He saw a man get out of the driver's side of the light-colored sedan behind him and pointed to the glove compartment with a sigh. "Get out the insurance papers," he told his son.

Neither of them was paying attention when both front doors of the Ford F-350 opened at once and two men yanked Jose and Michael Hernandez out of their seats by the hair and threw them onto the asphalt. The last thing Jose Hernandez saw before the copper garrote cinched tight around his neck was a piece of dirt lodged beneath the big toenail of someone wearing sandals. His son Michael had been knocked unconscious when he fell and saw nothing before he died. Because of his hair, his attacker didn't notice the deep gash the fall had caused at the back of his head.

One of the two attackers ran to the back of the pick-up truck and opened the door into the box cab. The other began to drag Jose Hernandez by the feet to the rear of the truck. Together, they lifted him, threw him inside, and went back to get the boy. The first man ran back, climbed up into the driver's seat of the truck, and threw it in gear. The second followed him in the light-colored sedan. The entire incident took less than 45 seconds. They didn't pass another car until they reached University Boulevard in Kensington.

A few streets later, they turned left onto Plyer's Mill Road, also blinking at the early morning hour, and presented a magnetic card into a reader that opened the gate of Kensington Self-Storage. They drove past the first row of storage lockers to a rear area with rows of garages on either side of the narrow street. They found number 16 and the driver of Maria's Tex-Mex got out, unlocked the garage doors and drove the truck inside. Once he had turned off the engine, he rummaged inside the glove compartment until he found the registration and the insurance papers, which he took with him.

By the time he had locked the F-350 and the two men had secured the garage doors behind them, the counter read: 16 hours: 45 minutes: 32 seconds.

1400 hours, Wednesday, July 4 – Kensington, MD

66-year old Chien Chih Lu, the manager of the Kensington Self-Storage facility, loved everything about the 4th of July parade. He loved the floats, he loved the fire engines, he loved the sirens and the marching bands. He even loved the politicians he had never seen before, waving from open convertibles. He didn't even mind the heat. And like the local Mayor, he watched the sky earnestly in hopes the afternoon thundershowers didn't spoil the fun.

He didn't mind the fact that Connecticut Avenue, the main thoroughfare bisecting the town, was closed from 9 AM until 1 PM to accommodate the parade, barring access to the Self-Storage. Like many town residents, being able to walk on the sidewalks, even through the thick holiday crowds, was for Chien Chih Lu a welcome relief to the fast-paced rush hour traffic that divided the town in two. As far as he was concerned, they could hold parades on 4th of July, Labor Day, and any other day Americans wanted to commemorate. He was more than happy to trudge up and down the holding area outside the Self-Storage facility with his shopping cart full of bottled water, emblazed with the corporate logo, which his bosses had him distribute free of charge to the Fire and Rescue Squads, the Kensington Players, the Peewee roller-skates, the local Montessori school, and whatever rolling antiques presented themselves for applause. After all, it was a public service and brought them good publicity.

There was only one thing Chien Chih Lu didn't like. That was having to clean up after the screaming children of the lawyer and IT work-at-home mothers. If you ever encountered them at the local Safeway or at the park or at the tennis courts, those highly-competitive working moms never let their offspring out of their sight. But the minute they engaged in conversation with their peers during the 4th of July parade, some social gene kicked in and they suddenly focused intently on themselves, becoming utterly oblivious to their progeny. Papers were tossed with abandon from baby strollers, ice-cream cones dropped onto the pavement, and Coca-cola bottles deposited full to the brim on the curbside without a care. No Mom ever came to pick them up after the parade. That became Chien Chih Lu's job.

By 2 PM, he had collected a full 40 quart garbage bag full of kiddy litter, and Chien Chih Lu was wondering whether his ancestors' culinary practice of eating live monkey brains could not be transferred in place and species to somehow allow the murderous ingestion of offending children.

At least, that's what he was thinking when he came upon the viscous puddle on the pavement in front of garage number 16.

Chocolate ice cream, was it? Milk-shake? Or was it raspberry? Dark cherry? Whatever it was, the sun had cured it into a hardened mess he would not be able to scrub away easily. Chien Chih Lu was thinking he would have to call his grandson to bring a gardener's spade to scoop it up when he noticed the flies.

That's when he realized it was not ice cream. And it had seeped out onto the pavement from inside Garage number 16, *his* Garage number 16.

"Oh my God, Oh my God," he muttered, dropping the black plastic garbage bag full of kiddy refuse and scurrying back toward the tiny cubicle he used as an office. "Oh my God."

He was trembling by the time he found the phone, seized with memories from his childhood back in China when the Communists had burst into his neighborhood in Guangdong and murdered every male over the age of 18, drenching the cobbled street with blood. When he and his mother had finally come out of hiding there were so many flies they could hardly see the bodies of the dead. The flies left red footprints when they landed on their arms, faint reminders of their own loved ones.

"9-11?" he said, his voice trembling, swatting the air of flying horror. "You must come."

The counter read: 7 hours: 54 minutes: 11 seconds.

1415 hours, Wednesday, July 4ᵗʰ - Taft bridge, Washington, DC

The Engineer had died his hair that morning, bringing it back to his "natural" color, which was jet black. He had been careful to die his eyebrows and the hair on the backs of his fingers as well, erasing every vestige of his identity as California resident, Richard Halstead.

Now he was José Hernandez, landed immigrant of long-standing, resident of Wheaton, Maryland and owner of Maria's Tex-Mex.

He had been coached to learn just enough Spanish to make small talk in the event a white officer addressed him in his "native" tongue. But if he encountered a Hispanic officer, which his handlers considered would be unlikely in Washington, DC, he was to speak English. That was his pride, as a U.S. resident. It was an insult to be addressed in Spanish.

They had been stuck in traffic for well over an hour, as the DC Police performed the triage on Connecticut avenue. They were sending passenger vehicles off to the right onto 24ᵗʰ street, across Calvert street and down the hill to Rock Creek Parkway. Larger vans and commercial vehicles crept forward along

Connecticut. The Engineer handed his driver's license to the policeman, then called to Hossein Gill to get out their DC concession stand license. He pronounced his name "Hosaine," as if it were a variant on his own name, José.

"Big day for you guys," the officer said, handing back the Engineer's driver's license. He glanced summarily at the DC concession stand license in its plastic sheet, and handed it back.

"Yeah, we stocked up," the Engineer said.

"Hey, you wouldn't have a cold Sprite there, would you?" the officer asked. The midday sun was shining almost directly in his eyes and he was sweating. If he had looked carefully inside the cab, he might have caught the look of panic that came over Hossein Gill.

"The coolers are all in back," the Engineer replied casually. "I can go back and get you one, if you like."

"Nah, I don't want to put you out. You guys've got enough to do. Have a good one!"

A block further down the giant white arm of the VACIS machine was stretched over the line of vehicles in the center lane. The Customs officer took the small green card the DC police officer had placed under their windshield wiper, and waved them over to the right. They inched past the inspection area and onto the Taft Bridge, crossing into the downtown area. Home free.

After the curve at the end of the bridge, the Engineer turned left onto Wyoming avenue, jogged down on 18th street to California, then drove into the back streets in the Adams Morgan district. This part of Washington, DC was full of Ethiopian and other "ethnic" restaurants and cafes. He drove on slowly until he found the Augustana Lutheran church and the side street where the two "electricians" were waiting. They had taken the metro downtown from Wheaton, and climbed into the rear compartment of the cab.

"Time to head down to the Mall," the Engineer said.

Inside the concession stand, the counter read: 7 hours: 04 minutes: 32 seconds.

1504 hours, Wednesday, July 4 – Kensington Self-Storage, Kensington, MD

As the old saying goes, if you want to rob a bank, wait until the President comes to town.

Although fire and rescue trucks from four separate stations had paraded through Kensington streets that morning, none could be summoned to respond to Chien Chih Lu's 9-11 call for over fifty minutes. The streets had just reopened, but the trucks still had to extricate themselves from the holding area down near the Town Hall, where a moon bounce and street vendors had taken over streets packed with townspeople. When the firemen finally arrived, Chien Chih Lu was sitting on the doorstep of his tiny office, trembling.

"You could have walked across the street," he said.

The volunteer fireman and the paramedic who accompanied him didn't think that was funny.

"Why don't you just show us where you found the blood," the fireman said.

He had turned off the siren of the Rescue squad ambulance, but the blue and red lights were still flashing. On any normal day, it would have attracted a small crowd of on-lookers, but not on 4th of July, after the parade. He was carrying a long-handled axe and was around 35, blond, and red in the face from spending most of the day out in the sun.

Chien Chih Lu took them to the door of Garage number 16. "In there," he said.

He unlocked the door with his master key, but he stood back to let them work. They swung back the doors to expose the Ford F-350 with the concession cab. Although the trapped heat radiated out at them, in the darkness the blood had not yet fully congealed. A large pool had formed beneath the truck and trickled beneath the door to where Chien Chih Lu had seen it earlier.

"Wait a second. I know these guys," the paramedic said.

He was younger than the fireman, black, with a trim beard, and was dressed in a dark blue jumpsuit.

"I see this truck almost every day parked outside where I live."

The fireman tried the back doors of the concession stand and found them unlocked. On the floor inside were Jose Hernandez and his son, Michael.

"These your friends?"

"Lord, have mercy," the paramedic sighed.

A half hour later the police arrived and cordoned off the area with yellow crime scene tape. Twenty minutes after that, Detective Slotnik drove up and got out her notebook.

Even with the heightened terror alert, she was the only police detective on duty in the area that afternoon. That's what always happened, she thought, wiping the sweat off her forehead as she followed the crime scene tape to the garage. The married ones took off at Christmas and holidays, and she always got stuck with the double shifts.

They had kept the bodies in place until she arrived. Putting on latex gloves, she examined them quickly but professionally, lifting the head of the boy so she could see the wound to his scalp.

"The assailants must not have seen this," she said. Turning to the paramedic, she asked how long he thought they had been dead.

"Judging from the consistency of the blood still inside the truck, I'd say more than six hours, but less than twelve."

She walked the clock back in her mind and realized that it had to be earlier because of the parade. Had Jose Hernandez failed to make a payoff? She knew the allocation of concession stand licenses in the District was tightly regulated. But even if kickbacks were involved, how much could it really amount to, a few thousand dollars at most? Was someone really prepared to kill – and to kill with such professionalism – over such a small amount of money? It was hard to believe.

She took down the license number of the truck; and noted the Washington, DC concession stand license, but something was out of place. This was the second time in just a matter of weeks she had been sent to investigate a homicide that just didn't fit with the normal pattern of gang killings, break-ins, and dumb burglaries. This was no Vietnamese soda clerk pulling a rifle from beneath the counter in a 7-11 to defend himself against some punk with a Saturday night special. These people had been strangled to death; no, not strangled: garroted.

As she drove back to her office to file a preliminary report with Major Crimes, Detective Maryjo Slotnik couldn't help but thinking that somehow these murders were related to the honor killing she had been investigating. But there was no rational connection, no real similarity in the evidence. It was just a feeling, and it nagged at her.

It was just after 5 PM by the time she reached the police sub-station on Randolph Road in Wheaton. It took her another fifteen minutes to write her report, and it was only after she had reread her own account for the third time that it hit her.

The counter read: 4 hours: 45 minutes: 00 seconds.

1805 hours, Wednesday, July 4 – Manny's Gas and Oil, Silver Spring, MD

When she reached Manny's Gas and Oil on New Hampshire avenue, it was around 5:45 PM and the gas station was closed. After three tries, she finally reached the owner on his cell phone and asked him to come to his place of business.

"I'm so sorry, Detective," he said. "I'm out with my family for the fourth of July. We're in Olney for dinner before the fireworks."

"Mr. Dal," she said forcefully. "I recommend that you find a way of getting down here as soon as you can. If you're not here in fifteen minutes, I guarantee you I will have a warrant from the State's Attorney office and will be inside your office, whether you like it or not."

He arrived at just a few minutes past 6 PM in a white BMW 700 series sedan, wearing a slate grey Italian suit, a blue Egyptian cotton dress shirt with a starched white collar, expensive moccasins, and the stub of a cigar. She had never seen him dressed in anything but his work coveralls and betrayed her surprise. He looked like some Middle Eastern playboy, not a middle aged grease monkey.

He puffed on the cigar repeatedly as he unlocked the door to the convenience store, and kept on puffing despite her evident distaste at having the smoke blown her way. "Detective," he said, relishing her discomfort. "You are on my property, on a public holiday, when my place of business is officially closed. If you don't like my cigar, I suggest you move upwind."

Once they had gone inside to his office, he went around behind the service counter and fired up the computer and she felt more in command. He had returned to the familiar ground of their previous encounters. She could almost feel Brannigan next to her.

"I need the service records on this vehicle," she said, sliding over to him a sheet of paper with the license number of the Ford F-350 used by Maria's Tex-Mex.

If he recognized the number, he showed no sign of it. Taking his reading glasses from the vest pocket of his suit, he looked down at the paper, frowning as if the writing were only partly legible, then turned back to the screen and entered the wrong number in the search box.

"I'm sorry, Detective," he said, peering at her over the tops of his glasses. "We have nothing on record for this vehicle."

"Look again," Slotnik said.

She could see it clearly now, up on the lift, at the periphery of their attention as she and Brannigan came to arrest Zia Mirsaidi. Why hadn't it registered before? But she knew the answer to that. There was no reason for her to have connected the truck to anything of importance. Fill your mind with useless clutter and you got lost. Keep it focused, and you would find what you needed later on, just as her mother always found the missing sock under the bed.

He came up dry again, but by this time Detective Slotnik's attention had turned elsewhere. She had turned her head sideways and was scanning the labels on the binders in the grimy bookcase behind him.

"Let me see your receipts for the past ten days," she said. "No, that one, Mr., Dal," she insisted, pointing, when he tried to hand her the wrong book.

It only took her a few minutes before she found what she was looking for. She set the service binder on the counter and turned it toward him with a satisfied air. "That one, Mr. Dal. Don't tell me you purge your system every week?"

"No. No, of course not," he said quickly. "There must be some mistake with the license number, that's all."

He returned to the computer screen and this time managed to find the service records.

"So what would like to know, Detective?"

She had him print out all the service records for the Ford F-350 pick-up, the heavy-duty shocks, the new coil springs, the plumbing and the propane connections for the concession box cab.

"Will that be all" he said.

She was leafing through the pages, comparing them to the hard copies in the book to make sure she had missed nothing. All showed the name of the client as Jose Hernandez.

"I hope Mr. Hernandez paid you," she said.

"Why, has he gone bankrupt?"

"Yeah, you might say that. We just found him dead along with his son."

Dal didn't show any reaction to the news. It was as if he was simply made of wax.

"One more thing," she said finally.

She reached into the breast pocket of her uniform and pulled out a 5x7 photograph and laid it on the counter. "Do you recognize these men?"

Manijeh Dal was very good, but even he could not disguise the panic that seized him for an instant when he set eyes on the photograph of the two electricians, standing in front of Maria's Tex-Mex down on the National Mall. It was the photograph taken by Brannigan's watchers several weeks earlier when they had been tailing Sayeed.

"I'm not sure, really," Dal said finally, pushing the photograph away. "Maybe I've seen them at the mosque? Maybe they are friends of my nephews? I couldn't tell you, exactly."

She was going to really enjoy calling Michael Brannigan with the news. She'd found the one sock. Now they had two murders, and circumstantial evidence suggesting clear links between them.

It was time to go searching for the pair.

Inside the concession stand, the counter read: 3 hours: 34 minutes: 12 seconds.

1900 hours, Wednesday, July 4 – National Mall, Washington, DC

For Marty Bloch, 4th of July was just a routine free-lance assignment. She had agreed to do a two page spread for the Washington *City Paper*, a free weekly that paid its skeleton staff from abundant advertising revenues. By a reporter's standards, it wasn't much of an assignment; but Marty Bloch was no ordinary photo-journalist. She didn't think in terms of assignments, and free-lance fees, and audience. She thought about the subjects she was shooting. Each one had a story and she knew that if she opened herself up and allowed herself to listen, it would wash over her and guide her to just that instant when she could capture it. Marty Bloch actually talked to the people she was shooting, and once she got them to start telling their stories, the camera did its work on its own. Each and every one of them had come here for a reason, braving the terror alert. American flags were everywhere.

Although Marty Bloch was decidedly overweight, no one looking at her would call her fat. Tall, athletic, with piercing green eyes and flaming red hair, most of her excess pounds had settled around her hips, which were partially covered in the reporter's safari jacket she wore despite the heat, its many pockets bulging with notebooks and film and batteries and junk. When she approached someone those eyes lit up, her thin lips spread into a tremendous smile, whose warmth somehow convinced them in an instant it was real. Marty Bloch *cared.*

As she looked at the families who had flocked to the National Mall to watch the fireworks, she could let herself be deluded into thinking it was an ordinary scene: mothers taking sliced ham and deviled eggs out of coolers, fathers spreading blankets, children running and squealing and complaining and pushing. But Marty Bloch kept thinking how mysterious were the ways of God, bringing all these perfect strangers together, possibly to die – and for what? Sometimes He rewarded the unrepentant, the corrupt, the selfish, the miscreant, showering them with tremendous riches and joy; and sometimes He ripped the guts out of His faithful. For what reason? That's what she had always wondered. But she trusted God to have His purpose, no matter how brutal and uncaring and unfair it might seem.

It had been nearly ten years since her brother had been murdered by terrorists who burst into their small Gaza home and pumped six bullets into his head as they made him kneel in front of his wife and children if he wanted to save them. Marty had grieved; she had spent months with her nieces and nephews in Israel, trying to be a surrogate parent but knowing that nothing could ever compensate for their father's death. Even now, as the oldest boy himself had begun his military service in Israel, she could not help but believe that God had somehow taken her brother for a reason. Marty Bloch had devoted her life to trying to pierce that mystery. That, perhaps, was God's design for her. She felt her camera, if used properly, could be a lens to Divine intent, seeing through the cloak of the ordinary to the hidden life beneath.

By seven PM, she had been on the Mall for three hours and was hungry. Why did she find herself buying a chicken quesadilla at Maria's Tex-Mex? She didn't particularly like Mexican food, but it was the only concession stand with no line. Once she paid for the food, sat down and unwrapped it, she understood why. It was disgusting.

"Do you mind heating this?" she said, smiling to the young, dark-complexioned man inside the stand.

"Can't," he said.

"Can't?" She bit her tongue. Not, "sorry, we've run out of gas, " or "sorry, the microwave is broken."

"Can't," he repeated to her querulous look.

Odd, she thought. Her next gesture was automatic; it was ingrained, not conscious. She brought the camera up from her neck and focused on the young man inside the concession stand and snapped two pictures. He freaked out.

"You can't do that!" he shouted. "Stop that! Get away from here! Faisul!" he called to someone else inside.

She heard the tell-tale chirp of a Nextel phone, and a minute later, someone else came to the window and handed her a cold Coke.

"I'm sorry, miss," he said. "We've been having problems with the microwave and don't know what to do. We asked the owner to come down and fix it, but he's stuck in traffic. Please, let us give you your money back. And take this. On the house."

"No, you keep the money," she said. "Looks like you're going to need it."

She took the Coke and sat down, storing the incident away.

But an hour later, she couldn't stop thinking about it. She continued to stroll through the blankets, talking, shooting portraits, and every fifteen minutes or so she doubled around within range of her 400 mm telephoto lens, shooting Maria's Tex-Mex and the people around it. Hardly anyone bothered to patronize the stand, and the two men rarely showed themselves at the window.

At 8:15 PM, she found a white-helmeted patrolman from the Capital Police in a patrol car on Independence avenue, two blocks away. He was young, black, well-built. Ex-military, she thought.

"Officer, I think you might want to take a look at that concession stand over there." She went to explain her encounter, how no one was patronizing the stand, and how odd that was on the 4th of July.

"Did they assault you, Miss?" he asked.

"No, that's not what—"

"Did they threaten you?"

"No."

"Unless they do, they've got a perfect right to be here. Now move along."

Maybe she was just over-reacting, she thought.

Inside the concession stand, the counter read: 1 hour: 48 minutes: 02 seconds.

2030 hours, Wednesday, July 4 – 16th and Independence, Washington, DC

Eva Romera was troubled. She ran through the data again and again, but still she came up with nothing. She turned to her colleague, Dr. Lowell McClosky.

"I'm open to ideas, Lowell. Now's not the time to be holding back.

"If I had anything for you, Dr. Romera, it's a long time I would have given it to you."

They had been closeted off in the NEST van below the White House, monitoring every sensor plugged into their powerful mainframe computers for the past two hours, but so far every reading they had gotten was negative.

"What if Danny's information is wrong?" Eva wondered.

"He's not wrong," said Brannigan. "You know that. You've just got to work the data harder."

Eva had done everything she could think of. She had examined the data from individual VACIS machines over the past twelve hours. She had compared the radiation readings to what the Customs officers had picked up on their hand-held monitors, the RIIDs. She had lowered the alarm threshold of the NEST sensors placed every one hundred meters around the White House. Either they showed no radiation targets at all, or the entire White House flashed yellow. In her book, that meant they had nothing.

"I think it's a false alarm," she said. "Lowell, how about you?"

Unlike Eva, Lowell McClosky was not a product of the national nuclear weapons labs. He was a Department of Energy physicist, whose job was to work on new technology capable of identifying radiological targets − dirty bombs − from the underlying nuclear clutter.

"How about we reconfigure the sensor grid?" he said.

"How?" she asked.

"By creating non-linear detection grids. Rhomboids and triangles, random patterns."

"You mean, move the sensors."

"Yes. But not systematically. Move some, leave others where they are. Fuzzy logic, that's the key."

"You got an idea?"

"Yeah. How about Sympathy for the Devil?"

"What do you mean?"

McClosky showed her. He had the Rolling Stones hit from his college years on his MP3 player. He'd have the NEST sensors display sequentially, and every time Mick Jagger screamed, he'd reprogram the sensor then displayed by whatever number came to mind.

"Kind of like musical chairs," Eva said.

"Musical bomb."

He was entranced. He actually liked the idea, and she didn't appreciate that one bit.

"Whatever. But move them, randomly - that's what you mean."

"We've tried everything else," he shrugged.

Inside the concession stand, the counter read: 1 hour: 18 minutes: 30 seconds.

2115 hours, Wednesday, July 4 – 12th and Independence, Washington, DC

Night was slowly coming over Washington, DC when Marty Bloch saw the huge motorcycle with its telltale license plates. She was hot, and her feet ached, but she was always happy to see the Chaplain. How many people knew that the huge man with the motorcycle helmet and the handlebar moustaches was Chaplain Duncan O'Garrity of the Capitol Police corps? Even fewer would ever guess that the MSGR on his license plates was not a misspelling of MANAGER, but stood for his clerical rank, Monsignor. She had done a photo feature of him two years earlier, and had remained friends with him ever since.

She waved when she saw him approach, and he immediately pulled up to the curb, swung down the kickstand, and turned off the 1200 cc motor. He lifted the visor on his helmet and smiled.

"Do you know what we say to children on Passover?" she said. No introduction, no small talk. That was just the way she was. After spending three weeks with her doing the profile, the Monsignor had gotten used to it.

"No," he said. "But I'm sure you're going to tell me."

"We say, 'Why is this night unlike any other night?' For some reason, I've got that phrase running through my mind."

O'Garrity chuckled, gesturing toward the White House. "Leaving the Almighty out of it, you wouldn't be far wrong. The President is going to address the Nation from the south lawn at 10 PM, then the fireworks begin at 10:02. With a red alert going, every cop from here till Baltimore is going to jump when the first rocket goes off."

She told him then about her intuition, and about the cop who had brushed her off. Something was not right about the men in that concession stand. "It's supposed to be a Tex-Mex joint," she said, "but trust me, these guys were not Hispanics. They weren't Arabs, either. They were speaking something else. My guess is, Pashto or Dari or something like that."

Unlike the cop earlier, the Chaplain took Marty Bloch and her intuition seriously. He had gotten to know her well, and knew that the big red head was no Madame Moonbeam. She wasn't the type who saw a terrorist lurking around every dark corner. If she thought something was out of place, it was worth investigating.

So with Marty leading the way, he started his big motorcycle and drove up onto the sidewalk, following alongside her, slowly making their way through the crowds.

It was 9:40 PM by the time they reached Maria's Tex-Mex.

"There's nobody here," the Chaplain said.

She couldn't believe it. They had been there just half an hour ago, but now the serving window was closed and the cab of the truck was empty and the doors were locked. Even the two guys she had been sure were hanging around the stand on purpose, watching from a distance, were gone. The Monsignor pounded on the rear door to the concession stand. He waited thirty seconds, then radioed for back-up.

"This is Monsignor O'Garrity," he said. "I've got a 11-54 on Independence avenue along the Mall, east side of 14th street," he said. "Requesting Hazmat." 11-54 was the code for a suspicious vehicle.

Inside the van the counter read: 00 hours: 24 minutes: 03 seconds.

2146 hours, Wednesday, July 4th – 16th and Independence, Washington, DC

Eva turned to Lowell McClosky inside the NEST van. "Do you see that?" she said.

"Amplify."

The possible target showed within their perimeter as a faint yellow glow against a green background, but it faded in and out of sight.

"I'm not getting a hard reading," she said. "It could be something, but the signature is too weak."

"Let's throw on some more sensors," McClosky said. "And the hand-helds."

The fireworks were scheduled to start in just over fifteen minutes, and Brannigan was getting claustrophobic inside the van.

"I could do with some fresh air," he offered.

"Take one of these," McClosky said, taking a portable radiation detector from a charger along the wall.

He showed him how the simple unit worked, then logged it onto the system so they could upload its transmissions automatically as soon as Brannigan took readings.

No sooner had Brannigan gotten outside the vehicle than his cell phone beeped, receiving a message. Someone had been trying to call him, but the shielding of the NEST van had broken the signal. Calling his voice mail, he heard the familiar voice of Detective Slotnik.

"I think I've got our break," she said when Brannigan finally reached her. She was home by then, having dinner in front of the TV.

"What's that?" he asked.

"There was another murder early this morning. I think it was the two electricians who killed Sayeed's sister. They killed a Hispanic man and his son and ditched their bodies in the back of a concession stand and left it in a self-storage garage in Kensington."

She told him what she had found out, and the work done on the truck at Uncle Manny's garage, but Brannigan's mind was wandering. Just two blocks ahead, toward the Capitol building, police lights were flashing and a crowd was gathering, even denser than where he was. He jogged toward the scene as they spoke, stumbling over blankets, avoiding legs and coolers and children and dogs, but the best he could manage was a hurried walk. He lost the connection and called her back once he had made his way through the crowd.

"What'd you say was the name of that concession stand?"

"Maria's Tex-Mex."

"I'm coming up on it right now on the Mall. It looks like it's been abandoned."

"That's impossible," Slotnik said. "We've impounded it."

"Well, I'm standing right in front of it."

Inside, less than twenty feet away, the counter read: 00 hours: 09 minutes: 55 seconds.

2202 hours, Wednesday, July 4 – Medical Center metro, Bethesda, MD

They had arrived in pairs, in separate cars. First, the Engineer and Sayeed; then, five minutes later, the two electricians. Although no one else was sitting on the platform at the Medical Center metro center, they made no sign to each other and sat at opposite ends of the station. The Medical Center station was one of the most deeply-buried stations in the entire Washington, DC area, a natural bomb shelter. That's why the Engineer had chosen it as their rendezvous point. Once the bomb went off and blew out the electrical grid, they would feel their way down the metro tunnel using the emergency lighting system, until the tunnel emerged above ground a half-mile later near the Capital Beltway.

Finally, at 10:02 PM, just as a new train was pulling in, the Engineer got up and, with Sayeed in tow, merged with the stragglers who had decided to come home at the last minute to watch the fireworks on TV. Once the passengers had wandered out, they joined the two "electricians" on the concrete bench. He checked his watch with a look of exaltation.

"In just one minute," he said, "all that we have worked so hard to achieve will come to pass. Al-LAH akbar," he murmured, almost under his breath. Then, as he watched the seconds tick down to zero, he held his arms out, palms up in supplication to the god that he worshipped, and began to chant: "Al-LAH akbar, Al-LAH akbar, Al-LAH akbar," and the others joined him.

When the second hand reached twelve he closed his eyes and fell silent, a radiant smile on his face.

2206 hours, Wednesday, July 4 – Above the U.S. Capitol

Danny was hovering above the U.S. Capitol building in the NEST Blackhawk helicopter when the alert came through the system. Ahead of them the fireworks had just begun, and they were glorious. Rising up on invisible stalks, the rockets spread red and green and blue glitter across the sky, like bits of confetti from a celestial firebird. Strapped across from the open door of the chopper, Danny felt for an instant as if he could scoop them up in his hand. But his attention was quickly drawn to the flashing yellow and black radiation icon on the computer screen of the NEST scientist sitting next to the pilot. He pointed to something up ahead, the pilot radioed forward, and the chopper shifted course and picked up speed. Danny realized in an instant they were heading toward the White House and then it hit him: *Eva*....

They flew so low over the crowds gathered on the Mall, Danny could see women grabbing for their hair and paper plates and towels as the downwash from the rotors sucked at them. Up ahead, through the open door, he saw mounted policemen pushing the crowds back, and others, on foot, moving police line barricades to create an open space for them to land.

Danny jumped out and ran to where Brannigan was standing with the hand-held radiation monitor, about thirty feet from the row of concession stands at the edge of the mall. The police were setting up giant spotlights up on poles, illuminating the area, and a bear of a man with great moustaches was sitting on 1200 cc Harley. Next to him was a female photographer, calmly observing the scene. From time to time she brought a large black camera up to her face, took a few quick shots, and brought it down.

"They found the bomb inside the truck," Brannigan said. "I couldn't get a reading until they got the rear door off."

Eva came jogging toward them, carrying an enormous NEST backpack. She saw Danny, and their eyes met briefly, and his every instinct told him to seize her in his arms and run as fast as they could, but he knew just as soon as that thought crossed his mind how silly it was. There was no escaping this. If they were to be delivered, it wasn't mere human strength that would save them.

"Pray for you," he mouthed to her.

2208 hours, Wednesday, July 4 – Inside Maria's Tex Mex

The police spotlights illuminated the interior of the truck like a million diamonds, reflecting off the crinkled aluminum foil on the ceiling, the floor, and the walls. No wonder they hadn't picked up anything with the monitors, she realized. Weapons-grade uranium gave off such feeble gamma ray emissions that even unshielded it was difficult to detect. With three layers of tin foil covering every surface of the truck's interior, and the metal plates she found beneath them, the device was invisible. Not even Brannigan's hand-held sensor had picked up any reading until the police ripped the back door off the van. *Smart.*

She set her backpack on the floor and got to work. As she crawled on hands and knees along the casing, she knocked into an electric cable and froze. She followed it upwards slowly, then realized that it was merely the microwave. *False alarm.*

Wrapping her arms around the casing, she realized that the device probably was much smaller than they had estimated from the photographs. The casing itself was roughly forty inches in diameter. As she ran her hands along the sides, she felt the hard points and the taut cables attached to them and followed them to the winch along the back wall. *Not exactly high-tech, but adequate,* she thought.

Like a sapper who worked with mines on the battlefield, she had always been taught to work first with her hands, and she ran them all along the skin of the device, reaching around both sides to feel the underbelly. That was how she discovered the cover plate near the front end of the casing and realized that the recessed bolts were not more hard points or part of the structure, but an access panel.

She found a ratchet wrench set inside the backpack and fitted sockets one by one until she found a match. Her black tee-shirt was now dripping with sweat, and she wiped her hands on a rag she kept inside the backpack. How much time did they have? What if the panel were booby-trapped? They had never encountered a live bomb from the Khan network before. She understood the design; the physics of the gun-type weapon was so simple that three high school seniors had been able to design a workable version in the late 1960s. But as she began to slowly turn the socket wrench, she realized she didn't have a clue what type of security measures they used…

The 4th of July display continued to burst overhead, in ever-expanding ripples of fire. But the crowd beyond the police line and the NEST-team Black Hawk was no longer looking skyward: they were all trying to get a look at what was going on inside the truck where Eva was working.

That was when Danny noticed O'Garrity's brass nameplate.

"Father O'Garrity?" he said. "Would that be Monsignor?" he asked, pointing to the MSGR license plate on the giant Harley.

"That it would, son."

"I'm not Catholic, father," Danny said. He let his gaze drift out to the crowd, which, in total silence, had begun as a mass to move beyond the police line toward them, awestruck, wondering, afraid. "Most of them probably aren't either. But Eva is. Perhaps you would think to say a prayer?"

The Chaplain sighed. Marty Bloch caught the sigh on camera, and caught his eyes closing as he kissed the tip of his thumb before he completed crossing himself. He took off his helmet. Then he loosened his tie and unbuttoned the top button of his police uniform, so the clerical collar showed through. When they saw it, a handful of people in the crowd fell to their knees. O'Garrity motioned to them, embarrassed, palms up, as if he were telling the Congregation to stand. And yet they remained kneeling.

"Father of us all, Lord of the Universe," he began. For such a big man, his voice seemed small, hesitant, almost broken. Marty Bloch got that too, down on her knees, framing his outstretched hands and his face against the exploding sky.

"You who are all powerful. You the all-knowing. We commend ourselves into your hands, O Lord, and ask that you guide those of your servant, Eva. Give her the strength and the wisdom to combat the Evil One. Show us your plan. We trust in your goodness, O Lord. We ask for your grace. We deliver ourselves into your hands and stand in awe of your might. Amen."

O'Garrity knew it wasn't much of a prayer. But it was all that he could muster. He crossed himself, and seeing Danny next to him do the same, he whispered. "God have mercy on us all."

At ten minutes past ten, Eva removed the last bolt on the access plate. Holding her breath, dripping with sweat, she gripped it with all ten fingers and gingerly began to pry it loose from the rubber seal holding it in place. She closed her eyes, concentrating on her fingertips, gently rocking the metal panel back and forth, trying to feel if there was any obstruction. Just one wire, one spring, and they would all die.

It came free with a familiar gasp as air rushed past the seal into the device. *Breathe.*

Looking inside, she had two surprises. First, the counter had gone black. It was dead, or had gone on some kind of stealth mode.

Second, the writing in small white letters on the back plate of the access panel was in Cyrillic.

Could it be a Russian weapon and not a Khan device after all? If so, it would have a much greater yield. A Khan device would obliterate the White House, the U.S. Capitol and the tens of thousands of people who had flocked to the National Mall for the fireworks, but the radius of the firestorm would not extend beyond two kilometers. If the Iranians had acquired a Russian weapon, however, it would be an implosion device, several times more powerful. But the Russians didn't use this type of jury-rigged initiator…

As her mind raced across all that she knew about Russian weapons and their initiators and PALs, another, sickening thought came over her. If the counter was dark because of a malfunction, the bomb could be live. Perhaps a connector had come loose while they were transporting it? Or a battery had come unseated when the police ripped off the back door? If so, the slightest movement could cause it to reconnect. That's when it hit her that she didn't have a clue how much time they had left. What if the malfunction had occurred with just seconds to go, or there was a secondary timing device embedded in the high-explosive casing? Every gesture she made could be her last, and she would never know.

Outside, the fireworks continued with loud, booming explosions, but that wasn't what made her almost jump: it was a sudden jostling, as if someone was getting into the cab of the truck.

"Get away from the truck!" she shouted. "DON'T – TOUCH – THE TRUCK!"

As she was shouting, she noticed the photographer she had passed on her way in. Unlike the others who were trying to catch a glimpse of the bomb, the woman was seeking her. Eva felt her eyes penetrate her own and hold her. It was an odd look; almost comforting. And in that instant, before Eva even thought to look away, the woman brought the camera up to her face and clicked.

2212 hours, Wednesday, July 4 – Medical Center metro, Bethesda, MD

The lights on the platform began to blink, the sign that another train was approaching the station.

The Engineer was furious. "Impossible!" he was saying, pacing back and forth as the headlights of the train appeared in the tunnel. "There is nothing they could have done to stop it! Nothing!"

The train was approaching the station. He made up his mind.

"Sayeed! What time do you have?"

"10:12," the other replied.

"Since the trains are still running, we will use them. You two ride to the terminus. That is Grosvenor. Take a taxi back to retrieve your car. Then you must disappear. Sayeed, come with me."

When Sayeed and the Engineer finally reached the surface it was 10:14 PM and it was dark. Faintly, in the distance, they could hear the fireworks.

2214 hours, Wednesday, July 4 – Inside Maria's Tex-Mex

Danny came up to the rear door of the box cab, but was careful not to touch anything.

"How are you doing?" he asked quietly.

"I could use some water," she said. "And a fresh towel. And radio back to Lowell to print out the schematic for the TRN-N-6 series initiator. This is not Wishbone Prime. Most of the casing is just air, for ballast. The actual device inside is smaller, but more powerful."

Parts of the bomb casing were packed with foam to hold the device in place and to increase buoyancy. The counter with the high-voltage initiator was at the front end of the delivery cylinder. As she felt beneath it, she followed the connectors to where they entered hard foam covering what she assumed was the physics package, centered in the middle of the watertight casing. A typical implosion device would have a spherical core the size of a large grapefruit, surrounded by high-explosive lenses and beryllium plates. The entire mass would be slightly larger than a soccer ball and weigh just over 100 kilograms, 225 pounds. But unless she started hacking away at the foam, she couldn't know for sure.

Danny returned a minute later and handed up to her the water and a towel, which he'd begged from one of the families. She mouthed him a kiss and took a long drink, letting the rest of the water run down her t-shirt.

Rummaging through her backpack, she found a low intensity neutron counter. She plunged the small, cylindrical emitter into the foam at the bottom of the nuclear device, and the saucer-shaped sensor into the foam at top. By the time Lowell joined them a few minutes later, she was getting a reading that showed the presence of 30 kilograms of uranium enriched to 91.2%. If properly boosted, it was enough to wipe out the entire city of Washington, DC.

"I just can't believe this," Lowell was saying as he came up to them. "You mean to tell me-"

Eva could tell that he was simply going to climb into the truck. 'Lowell, stop right there! Don't move!"

"What'd I step on?" he said, turning to Danny gingerly, one foot still in the air.

"Loose connector," she explained quickly. "They've jury-rigged the timing device. My guess is it has nowhere near the robustness of the Russian ones. We've got to remove or disable the entire initiator. If something knocks into it and the thing reconnects—"

"Oh yah. Messy," Lowell agreed. "Washington, good-bye!"

He scoured the printed sheets, flipping through page after page, then returning to something he had seen earlier. Because he had used the commercial inkjet printer they had in the van, they couldn't print the schematic on a single page.

"If I read this right," he said. "There ought to be a 72-pin gold-plated connector at the rear of the counter."

"72- pin?" Danny said. "Not 68, or 90 or 140?"

Lowell didn't hear him or had tuned him out. Eva felt beneath the dead counter, but couldn't find any connector.

"Look again," she said. "The counter is recessed into some kind of mounting assembly."

"No problemo," Lowell said. "You ought to find four hex screws in the corners. They hold it in place."

"There's no anti-tamper mechanism?"

"What do I know? You're the one who's got her hands on it."

"Thanks."

Eva unscrewed the first hex screw three turns, then stopped.

"What's the matter?" Danny asked, worried. Then he heard her breathing change; short, shallow breaths. Lowell gave him a disgusted look and rolled his eyes.

He couldn't see it, and she didn't say anything. But her action had caused the red lights of the counter to flicker.

"I'm going to bring them all out three turns, and if I don't feel any pressure, I'll take them out," Eva called, without taking her eyes off her work.

"That's a plan," Lowell said.

In another minute, she had all four screws on the floor and inserted a flat-bladed screwdriver beneath the lip of the counter, which had gone dead again. She pried it up ever so slightly, then worked her way all the way around it, as if she were opening a paint can. When she prized it up a half inch, she grabbed it with both hands and slipped it out gently, careful not to knock against anything.

Once again, it started to flicker, and she caught her breath.

This time, Danny saw it. "What's happening? What's going on?" he said sharply.

"You need to concentrate," Lowell said. "Dr. Romera! Do you hear me? Coming out of the back of that thing, you're going to find a flat cable with that connector."

"I'm going to call Army Demolitions," Danny said.

"There's no time!" Eva said. "I've almost got it.

Still on her knees, she inched forward and stuck out her stomach to cradle the counter assembly against the bomb casing so she could free up both hands to reach behind it. Her face was a mask of concentration and Danny turned away. Just in case she looked toward him, he didn't want to distract her.

"Got it!" she said finally. "Here goes."

They could hear her grunting as she tried to work the connector apart, careful not to hit anything, restraining herself at the same time she exerted force to pry apart the thin plastic casing. Lowell cocked his eye, curious, when she seemed to fall forward, resting her head on the bomb.

"Did you get it?" he asked.

Without a word, she stood up, took a step toward them, holding the counter assembly out to them with both hands like an offering. That photo of Eva Romera-Wilkens emerging from the concession stand, her hair drenched in sweat, with the bomb casting a shadow that almost engulfed her, would win Marty Bloch a Phillips prize later that year.

0015 hours, Thursday, July 5 – Bel Pre Manor apartments, Silver Spring, MD

Special Agent Joanna Greary had received the all-points bulletin like thousands of other law enforcement officers in the Washington, DC area. But unlike most of them, she not only knew immediately what to do and where to go, but she had a personal motive for her actions.

She left her station on Columbia road in Adams Morgan, not far from the Taft bridge, and raced up 16th street, blue lights flashing, until she reached Georgia avenue. She popped on her siren all the way through downtown Silver Spring, passed the Beltway, then turned off her flashers and the siren until she reached the Bel Pre Manor apartments, where she knew Sayeed would be waiting. Despite her disgrace, the FBI hadn't cut her access to the Bureau's Automated Case System database.

The apartment was dark when she arrived, but she could smell him. He was there, hiding out behind the closed Venetian blinds, and she knew it.

"Open up, Sayeed!" she said, rapping the hollow door. "Sayeed, it's me. Joanna!" she hissed.

She saw someone peek through the blinds, then release the door, letting it fall open an inch so she would have to open it herself. She drew her .357 Magnum and went in.

Sayeed was standing just inside, leaning against the kitchen counter. She eased the door shut behind her. Then she hit him full force in the jaw with the butt end of the revolver. The force of the blow sent him sprawling to the floor.

"You stupid, lying little prick," she said, kicking him in the groin. That sent him rolling away from her on the floor. "You thought you could get away with tossing us that uncle of yours." She kicked him again. "He's a dead parrot. And that's what you're going to be. An ex-parrot."

Sayeed brought his knees up to his chest, rolling onto his side, trying to protect himself. She kicked him again, this time in the kidneys in the small of the back.

"You thought we'd fall for that crap about him being some kind of al Qaeda courier."

"But he was bringing money!" Sayeed moaned "You found it!"

"Sure, he was bringing money. But it was to build a Sufi mosque. A *Sufi* mosque, butt boy. The kind al Qaeda blows up."

She kicked him in the jaw, causing him to reach up to his face reflexively, then brought the two-inch heel of her boots square into his groin, stomping him with such force she hoped it would eliminate what was left of his manhood forever.

0100 hours, Thursday, July 5 – Wheaton, MD

Azam Dariana and Faisul Gohari – the two "electricians" – did not succeed in eluding law enforcement much longer than had Sayeed. Detective Slotnik arrested them at 1 AM as they were trying to leave the small apartment they shared near the Wheaton metro station. Each was carrying a small gym bag with a few clothes, a fresh Costa Rican passport, and $12,000 in cash.

Thanks to the photographs taken on the Mall by Marty Bloch, a separate all-points bulletin was put out for the Engineer that for the first time joined a face to every known alias he had used during the *Shaitan der artash* operation.

Despite this critical intelligence, he was never found.

0130 hours, Thursday, July 5 – Hay's Landing, Maryland

The commander of the Hoot-class mini-submarine switched off the power to the electro-magnetic plate in the upper port side of his hull ribbing shortly before 11 PM, and carefully separated himself from the wreckage of the *San Marcos*, where he had been hiding for the past three days. He'd brought his ship up to snorkel level after dark each night, so they wouldn't have to divert battery power to their Swedish-built air-independent propulsion system, resubmerging before dawn. It was a perfect place to elude detection. The watermen who plied Tangier Sound and the mouth of the Chesapeake Bay south of Smith Island rarely approached the wreck, the former USS *Texas*, scuttled by the Navy as a target ship in March 1911. And if the US Coast Guard or the Navy flew a P-3 Orion overhead, the tiny mini-sub would appear on its Magnetic Anomaly Detector as an integral part of the long iron hulk of the *San Marcos* wreck. A massive ship for its time, the *San Marcos* had been targeted repeatedly by the big 12 inch guns of U.S. navy battleships *Tallahassee, New Hampshire*, and *Virginia*, and, in later years, by U.S. Navy F-4 fighter pilots who fired rockets into the iron wreck. Despite the pounding, the remains of the *San Marcos* were still visible above the waves from nearby Cod Harbor on a clear day, a faithful reminder of the solidity of former times.

At 1:15 AM, the commander surfaced in the channel off Point Lookout, Maryland. Just minutes later, the familiar voice of the Engineer came over his Nextel phone.

"Hello Josh, this is Richard. Do you think you could take me home?"

Fifteen minutes later, Hossein Gill drove slowly, lights extinguished, down the dirt road to Hay's Landing, outside of Scotland, Maryland. Although it was a holiday, the pick-up lovers were long gone and they were alone.

"You have done well, my brother," the Engineer said once he had turned off the engine. "You will drink of the river Kosar."

Before the other man could respond, the Engineer grabbed his hair from behind and pulled him against the head rest. As he opened his mouth in astonishment, the Engineer fired one bullet through the top of his mouth into his brain. Then he carefully wiped the Smith & Wesson .38 with a handkerchief and wrapped the fingers of Hossein Gill's right hand around it.

"Welcome to heaven," he said.

Four hours later, the mini-sub rendez-vous'd out in the commercial shipping lanes with the bulk cargo carrier *Burmese Express,* en route from Boston to Maracaibo.

1500 hours, Thursday, July 5 – The White House

"Thank-you, Mr. President," FBI Director Louis Adams began, as the assembled press corps buzzed with anticipation.

Now it was his turn to lie. He didn't understand why the President had decided to say anything at all about this latest near-miss. After all, it wasn't the first time that terrorists, with the backing of a sovereign state, had attempted to carry out a massive attack on U.S. soil. He could still remember working as U.S. Attorney in Oklahoma City in 1995, when the senior FBI agent in charge of the Murrah Building bombing told him they had been ordered to drop their investigation of Terry Nichols' trips to the Philippines, where he had met with Iraqi intelligence officer Ramzi Youssef. Why? Orders from Washington.

Better to say nothing than to lie, Louis Adams felt.

"As the president indicated, we have apprehended three of the terrorists involved in yesterday's failed attempt to detonate a truck bomb on the National Mall," he began. "Another was found dead in Southern Maryland, an apparent suicide. Preliminary investigations have established that all four were trained in al Qaeda camps in Pakistan."

"What about the weapon?" one reporter shouted.

"Why was NEST deployed?" shouted another.

"If it was al Qaeda, who provided the bomb?" a third shouted.

"Were there others involved?"

"Yes. We are pursuing a number of leads as I speak," he said. It was an old trick the press people had taught him years ago. Choose the question you want to answer and ignore the rest. "You will understand that I cannot say anything more about this at present," he added gravely.

"Mr. Director." The loud-mouthed correspondent for a national television network stood up, nodding to his camera crew to make sure they got his question on air. "How do you account for the reports that surfaced on Tuesday in the *Washington Post*, citing senior U.S. intelligence officials, that New York may have been the intended target, not Washington, DC?"

Louis Adams paused, then in perfect deadpan, he replied. "Don't believe everything you read in the papers, Charlie."

The president chuckled at that, although the reporters groaned.

"But seriously, I can tell you that we have the weapon in our possession, and we believe it was the only one involved in this attack. As the president stated earlier, this is a case where outstanding intelligence and excellent cooperation among the various agencies of our government succeeded in preventing a terrorist attack that could have inflicted massive casualties.

"My message is very simple, Charlie: the system worked."

EPILOGUE

0200 hours, Sunday, July 22 – Tehran, Iran

Mullah Hashemi had the smile of a Cheshire cat. With his white turban, his beardless face, the elegant silk robes that rippled across his copious belly whenever he laughed – which was often – Mullah Hashemi reassured his visitors of his good humor, his good intentions, his moderation. He had worked hard to cultivate that image of basic goodness, but those who knew him well understood that it was all for show. Mullah Hashemi had personally ordered the assassination of 204 dissidents living outside Iran. These were individuals named in intelligence files as threats to the survival of the Islamic Republic of Iran. He had issued blanket approvals for the murder of tens of thousands of others – students, teachers, Kurds and other minorities, arrested in various sweeps inside the country.

For more than a quarter century, his smile and bonhomie had endeared him to Western reporters. Prime among them was Cynthia Wronge. She had come from Washington to Tehran a few days earlier at Mullah Hashemi's personal invitation, to conduct her 36th exclusive interview with the Iranian leader. She had asked him tough questions, as he always invited her to do. "You may ask me anything, my dear," he had told her all those years ago at their first encounter, when he had been nothing more than a satchel-carrier for Ayatollah Khomeini during the exile in France. That didn't mean he intended to answer her, of course. But he made what she printed his business. And he wanted her to know that he would judge her on what made it into her newspaper, and that her access – the golden key to Washington reporters – depended on it.

"It is always a pleasure, your Eminence," Wronge said, offering him her hand in the elegant parlor as she took her leave. It was a gesture the hard-line ayatollahs abhorred, but Mullah Hashemi willingly took her hand and held it as he escorted her past his next visitor. She once had told him she was stunned at the softness of his skin. He must be a man who had never touched dirt in his life.

Once she was safely out the door, he chuckled and welcomed Ali Akbar Parvaresh into his private study.

"Do you think that was wise?" the intelligence officer said.

"What, you think she would recognize you?"

He gave the man who had coordinated *Shaitan der artesh* the Cheshire Cat smile, challenging him, just daring him, to make his case. It was hard to counter, so Parvaresh gave it up.

Mullah Hashemi called for tea. Once they were served, he placed a sugar cube in his mouth, then sucked tea between his teeth to make it dissolve. It was a bad habit that had turned his bottom teeth black.

"We have answers," Parvaresh said simply, once Mullah Hashemi had devoured his third sugar cube.

"What about the cousin?" he asked.

This was a sore point with Parvaresh, and his discomfort must have showed. He had endured two extremely unpleasant days at Evin Prison over the presence on his security detail of a cousin of the defector, Rahimi.

"We have taken care of him," he said.

"Taken care?"

"Removed. He will pose no more threat."

Mullah Hashemi grunted, bringing his tea cup to his chin, but not drinking.

"This morning, I received a communication from one of our agents in Washington," Paravaresh said. "He has read the internal report from their nuclear department."

"You mean the Americans figured out what happened, even if we didn't?" Mullah Hashemi said.

"Yes, your Eminence," Parvaresh said, staring down at his hands.

After a long silence, Hashemi shrugged. "Well?"

"The battery went dead, your Eminence."

"Excuse me?"

"Inside the timing device, there is a small battery. This is separate from the capacitor that sends the charge to the detonator. This battery is just a common, low-voltage disk, similar to what you might put in a watch, but bigger. When the Americans ran their diagnostics on the device, they discovered that it had gone dead – probably from the high heat it endured in the container during transit."

The look Mullah Hashemi gave him at this news sent a chill down his spine. "Your experts did not foresee this?" he asked coldly.

"No, your Eminence. Apparently it failed just seven minutes before the device was set to go off."

Ali Akbar Parvaresh lived and died at least three times in the few seconds it took for Mullah Hashemi to absorb that information. But finally, the cleric smiled.

"Then we will do better next time, *inch'Allah,*" he said.

"Inch'allah," the intelligence chief repeated, relieved. God Willing.

"People from many nations will pass by this city and will ask one another, 'Why has the Lord done such a thing to this great city?' And the answer will be: 'Because they have forsaken the covenant of the Lord their God and have worshipped and served other gods.'"

Jeremiah 22:8-9.

ACKNOWLEDGEMENTS

AND

A PRAYER

Thanks to Steve Bryen who steered me away from my initial scenario, against which the United States has no conceivable defense, to this more detectable version, which allowed me to highlight the inefficiencies and absurdities of the United States government.

Thanks to my wife, Christina, and to my brother, William A. Timmerman, who regularly critiqued passages and ideas.

Thanks to David Justman, Janet Ellen Levy, Dave Bossie, Brandon Hogan, Siamak Tash, and Jerry Molen, for their encouragement and for holding out hope that Hollywood's greed might yet overcome the politically-correct virus that prevents stories depicting the reality of radical Islam – including as it has spread to segments of the American Muslim community - from reaching large U.S. audiences.

Thanks to Diana and Simon, the last of our five children still young enough to live at home, who rarely objected to the life-style cuts (and painting those shutters!) that writing a full-length novel without a publisher's advance required.

Thanks to Mel Berger, my agent at William Morris Agency, for all his efforts to keep us solvent while I was writing this book.

Thanks to all my Iranian friends, living and dead (some of them, assassinated by regime agents), for opening a window onto their native land and the perversities of Khomeini's peculiar brand of Islam.

Thanks to the many unnamed heroes in the FBI, U.S. Customs and Border Patrol, Immigration and Customs Enforcement, the Department of Energy, the Defense Intelligence Agency, the National Security Council, the White House, Treasury, CIA, the U.S. Navy, the Coast Guard, and elsewhere who shared their knowledge, experience, and fears.

Thanks to my editors at Newsmax.com – Christopher Ruddy, David Patten, Cable Neuhouse, Ken Williams and the gang – who gave me the opportunity to learn more about America's defenders and to ride that Lamborghini on skids pictured on the back cover of this book, while pretending to work.

Thanks to my former editor at Insight, Paul Rodriguez, for sharing his experiences with NEST at the 2004 Democratic National Convention.

And praise to Jesus Messiah, without whose grace my life would have ended as a mere footnote to the 1982 war in Lebanon. To you I owe everything, Lord. Let readers judge whether Your spirit flows through the sinews of this tale.

Printed in the United States
85617LV00001B/73-258/A